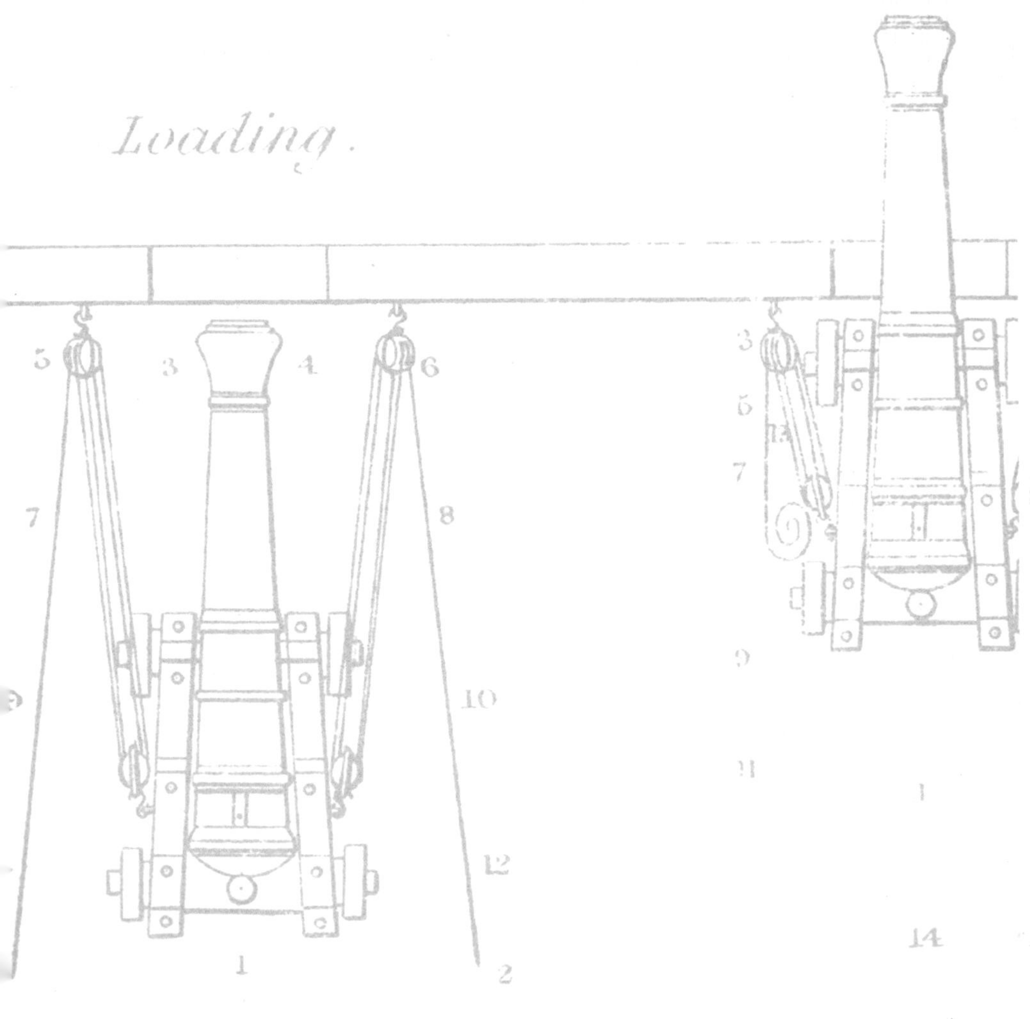
Training
Loading.
5
3
4
6
7
8
9
10
12
1
2
14
3
5
7
9
11
1
14

PORT ROYAL

PETER SMALLEY

PORT ROYAL

A Sea Story

C

Century · London

Published by Century in 2006

1 3 5 7 9 10 8 6 4 2

This novel is a work of fiction. Names and characters are the product of the author's imagination and any resemblance to actual persons, living or dead, is entirely coincidental

First published in the United Kingdom in 2006 by Century
The Random House Group Limited
20 Vauxhall Bridge Road, London, SW1V 2SA

Australia (Pty) Limited
, Milsons Point, Sydney
Vales 2061, Australia

New Zealand Limited
l Road, Glenfield
10, New Zealand

ouse (Pty) Limited
Boundary Road & Carse O'Gowrie,
2198, South Africa

The Random House Group Limited Reg. No. 954009
www.randomhouse.co.uk

A CIP catalogue record for this book is available from the British Library

Papers used by Random House are natural, recyclable products made from wood grown in sustainable forests. The manufacturing processes conform to the environmental regulations of the country of origin

ISBN 1 8441 3687 6

Typeset by SX Composing DTP, Rayleigh, Essex
Printed and bound in Great Britain by
Clays Ltd, St Ives plc

For Clytie

Necessity is the plea for every infringement
of human freedom. It is the argument of tyrants;
it is the creed of slaves.

William Pitt
(Pitt the Younger – November 18th 1783)

PART ONE: THE NEW COMMISSION

The moment of waking in the morning is for some few men always bright, confident and glad. For others it is a dour thing, the breaking into easeful darkness of unwelcome and unwelcoming light, the factual light of consciousness and the burdensome world. So it was for Captain William Rennie RN. He had determined to wake early, rouse himself, splash water from ewer into basin, sluice his face and neck, sit down at his desk by the window, take in the long view across rooftops and cobbled streets to the sea beyond, dip quill pen in ink, and begin to write the most important letter of his life. Instead he farted, scratched his head, yawned biliously, and stumbled from his bed to the commode behind the screen in the corner.

Presently, in his nightshirt, he sat at the desk, fiddled irritably with inkwell and pen, dropped the quill on the floor, stared disconsolate at the street below through the grimy window pane, yawned again, and rang the bell.

'Tea,' to the attending maid. 'By all or any means, tea. Jump now.' And then, regretting his peremptory tone: 'That is, that is, if you please.'

'Are you poorly, sir?'

'What?' He looked at her. Was she attempting to mock? Was there a knowing sneer in her tone? He saw only her plump concerned pink face, her head turned a little to one side under her white cap, and was ashamed.

'You do not want no breakfast, sir?'

'No no. I will take nothing but tea. I am perfectly well.'

The maid brought him a quart pot of tea, and he drank it, gratefully drank it, and was restored. The leaden light of the day, as he threw open the window, was lifted into sharp clear freshness. The dulled sea beyond the Hard in the middle distance was transformed into silver. Birdsong lilted above, the familiar sound of hooves and wheels drifted up from the street, his heart rose and his frown disappeared.

'Well well, I am whole after all.' He sniffed in a breath, drank off the last of the tea, pushed aside the tray, sat down and began to write his letter.

It took him the better part of an hour. When he had finished he rang the bell again, sealed the letter with wax, and gave it to the maid, with a handful of coins.

'This must go by the mail-coach to London. The noon coach, you apprehend me?'

'Yes, sir.'

'I have added sixpence.'

'Thank you, sir.'

He reached and took up his purse, and put a further coin into her hand. 'And a further shilling for your, your, your very kind and efficient work, in attending to me.'

'Oh, thank you, sir.' Her pink face became pinker, and she bobbed.

'Yes, hm, very good.'

He was not at his ease with servants, he reflected as the girl retreated down the narrow stair. He must endeavour to be more at his ease with them, else why had he wrote his letter?

This important letter, like so many such letters, was about money. It was, he thought, a moderate communication, well reasoned, well couched, and sincere. It contained, he must acknowledge, certain phrases that could only be called succinct. Not terse, certainly not that, but concise and direct. In short, Captain Rennie felt himself ill-used in the matter of monies due to him from his previous commission. The Admiralty had been at fault in this; they had employed tactics, and language, unworthy of Their Lordships. Accordingly, his letter was certainly one of complaint; but a letter not at all bitter, or little-minded, only close-argued.

He said as much to Captain Langton, when they met by chance in the street. He had recently renewed his acquaintance with Captain Langton—now of the *Tamar* sixty-four—after several years; they had met first at Port Royal after the Battle of the Saints in '82, had become friends then, and had now happily renewed the friendship upon discovering themselves at Portsmouth together. They were much of an age, though nothing like in appearance, or manner. Rennie was spare, and looked older than his years; Langton was tall, well made, with a confident air and a ready smile. They had in common that they were sea officers, had seen action in a great battle and had survived undamaged, and held new commissions. And now Rennie spoke of his letter, in a general way spoke of it, but did not reveal its content (they had bumped into each other late in the morning, Langton returning from the Port Admiral's Office, Rennie from the dockyard, and were now in a tailor's shop).

'Aye, that is the expression,' said Rennie. 'In dealing with Their Lordships you must always write a close-argued letter, which they must consider. Acknowledge, and consider. Don't you think so?'

'Eh?' Captain Langton, over his shoulder. He saw his reflection in the glass, and was not displeased.

'No, I do not see how they could ignore it,' said Rennie, standing at the window.

Captain Langton now glanced over his shoulder. 'Is it about your commission? I thought you had *got* the commission, dear fellow.'

'Oh, yes. Yes, I have got it. But I was vexed, you know, at first, and altogether unsure that I should accept it.'

Captain Langton twisted a little one way, peering in the glass, then twisted the other way. 'Tolerable,' he said, frowning. 'Hm, yes, not at all bad.' Then: 'You was *unsure*?'

And now he turned right round and looked at Rennie. 'A new commission, and you was *unsure*?'

'Oh, well, at *first*. I have accepted it, *now*, in course. Only there is one or two things that do not sit right with me, and I was obliged to write and say so, close-argued. Hey? You see?'

'No.' A smile, shaking his head, turning back to the glass.

'Well well, I had a plan about investing some capital, you know, in the West Indies. I could have bought into a syndicate there, and doubled my capital in a year or two. However—however, it was not . . . I was obliged to throw over the scheme.'

'Ahh.' Captain Langton nodded briefly, understanding nothing his friend was saying. And now he nodded to the tailor, who stood waiting.

'Yes,' continued Rennie at the window, 'it was an estate in Barbados, a syndicate. I heard of an opportunity there, and I would not have had to lift a finger beyond putting up the capital, only sit at home in England and wait.'

'Ahh.' Again over his shoulder, a half-comprehending sound.

'However, due to the . . . the circumstances, I lost heart, d'y'see. In any case, waiting ain't my preference in anything. To wait is a waste of time, intolerable to a sea officer.' A sniff.

'Yes, yes, I do see that. But what, pray, has Barbados to do with your letter to the Admiralty?'

'Nothing, nothing.' Rennie shook his head. 'I mentioned it only in passing, you know. I have got the commission.'

'I am glad. Bracewell? Step over to this side, will you?'

'Yes, sir?'

'Now, d'y'see the lace at the cuff? The left-hand cuff?'

'I do, sir.'

'I am not quite sure of the look.'

'Do you mean the lace fabric of your shirt, sir, or the gold lace?'

'Naturally, the gold lace.' Impatiently.

'I do not see any fault, sir.'

'You do not think it too bright?'

'I do not, sir. Gold lace is bright by its nature.'

'Hm, well. Not too bright, you think, Bracewell?'

'The coat is well fitted, I should say, sir. It sits very handsome across the shoulders, and hangs very well behind. As to the lace, the gold lace, it is only what is regulated to an officer of your rank, sir, and is no brighter, nor less, than lace always is, I assure you. When it is new.'

'Very good. Very good. Then I am satisfied.' He shrugged himself free of his new coat, stood tall a moment before the glass, and adjusted his stock. 'Please to have it sent round to my rooms, will you, at the Marine Hotel?'

'You do not wear it now, sir?'

'Wear it now? Good heaven, no. Or, wait. What d'y'think, Rennie?'

'You are right.' Turning from the window, a sniff. 'An officer don't refuse a new commission just because there is a dispute about the last.'

'Eh?'

'If he is not a bloody fool he accepts it, and does his duty. Well well, I am damned hungry. What d'y'say to dinner?'

'By all means, let us dine as soon as you like. But what is your opinion of the coat?'

'Of what?'

'Should I wear it, a new dress coat?'

'What on earth is the use in a coat, without you wear it? Is not that why you have had it made?'

'Thank you, Bracewell, I will like to wear the coat after all.'

And the two sea officers went out into the street.

Beyond, across the narrow entrance to the harbour, a freshening breeze ruffled brailed canvas on moored ships, and drove a hoy heeling towards Gosport, dipping and glinting on the swell.

A horseman, well mounted, rode past the castle ruins, past the low, narrow cottage rows and the low square tower of the Norman church, and came to a bend in the road from which a drive turned down into a pleasant recess and a glimpsing house. He reined in, and rode down there.

Birch Cottage at Winterborne Keep in Dorset had been vacated by its previous occupants, the Misses Ibbetson, and now lay empty upon its modest plot of ground under the lee of the hill. Their cousin Lieutenant James Hayter RN had come there to look at his new house; not quite to take possession, but to look at what would soon be his, a few weeks hence, when he was to be married. What he saw as he dismounted on the paved forecourt dismayed him. Jackdaws rose cawing from the chimneys, and twigs scattered down the slate of the roof and fell from the iron guttering. Inner shutters at two of the lower windows hung loose. The fanlight was dusty, and paint had begun to bubble and flake at the bottom of the door. The brass knocker was tarnished. A green stain spread down above the architrave. Roof moss had fallen on flagstones, and weeds grew in the cracks between. Over the house to the west stood a great white filling cloud, and the chimneys seemed to sail there, the whole house to sail on the sky.

'A house cannot sail, y'fool,' said James aloud. 'In least, it cannot be permitted to sail in this damned deplorable condition.'

His horse snorted and rolled its eye as a fox dashed across the forecourt and fled down the slope into the trees.

'The impudent villain,' said James. 'Not you, old fellow, not you.' Taking the bridle and leading the horse to the rear.

In twenty minutes he had inspected his property, what would soon be his property, and his first impression had been wholly and disagreeably confirmed. There was not a stick of furniture in the house; nothing remained there to make it civilised; there was not a rug, a curtain, a chair nor a cushion anywhere within. A dank smell of neglect hung in the air on the stairs. On the walls of the upper rooms fanning stains of damp had appeared. Yellow whorls of damp stained the ceilings there, and plaster had fallen in what would soon be his bedroom.

'Our bedroom,' he corrected himself as he came out into the stable yard. 'Hell and fire, Jaunter, hell and fire. What will my bride think of me, bringing her to this? We must refit. Repair and refit, right quick.'

He swung up into the saddle. What had Fanny been thinking of, to allow the house to fall into such a ramshackle condition? Had she no regard for her cousin, that she could allow him to spend his wedding night in a ruin? Very grimly he turned Jaunter's head, dug in his heels, cantered up the drive—scattering gravel and moss—and began the long ride back to Melton.

'I must see Fanny,' he said to his mother, at Melton House. 'I must go to East Lane Cottage, and speak to her.'

Lady Hayter put down her flower basket. 'I hope not in that tone, James.'

'It has been quite deliberate.'

'What has? What do you mean?'

'How long is it since you was at Birch Cottage, Mother?'

'I don't know that I have been there in a twelvemonth——'

'Then you can have no idea of its present appearance.'

'Appearance? Dear James, please do not walk up and down so vigorous. What is the matter?'

James paused at the fireplace, and kicked a fire-iron with his boot. Turning to his mother: 'I must go and see Fanny, and have it out with her. Not that it will do any good.'

'Then why see her, if it will not?' Mildly. 'What on earth can Fanny have done, to vex you so? Do you mean that she has had the temerity to remove her own furniture? Is that all she has done?'

'Hm, more than that. Or rather, a great deal less.'

And with that vexed contradiction he left his mother, and rode towards East Lane Cottage. When he was in the lane between Melton Abbas and the road to Blandford, he reflected at last that it would serve no purpose to berate his cousin. In truth the condition of Birch Cottage could not be described as her fault. His cousins' very modest fortune, inherited from their late mother, was just adequate for their domestic needs, but nothing more.

'No,' he said to himself, reining in, 'I must tax my father with the condition of Birch Cottage.'

His father Sir Charles had assumed ownership of Birch Cottage in return for settling the debts left by the girls' late father, at a time when these debts had necessitated the sale of the home farm, and had threatened to deprive them of their home. The arrangement had been that when James took a wife the house would come to him, and the girls would remove to East Lane Cottage at Melton.

'He should have kept it up, not poor Fanny and the girls,' he muttered to himself as he turned back. 'Why the devil has he not done it?'

By the time he had returned to Melton House he had thought it all through, and was altogether of the opinion that he had better say nothing reproving to his father about the poor condition of Birch Cottage, under the circumstances, excepting to ask if the estate carpenter might not accompany him there on the morrow.

'You wish to take Hodge down there with you?' Sir Charles pushed the decanter. He and James were alone after their dinner, neither of James's brothers being at home.

'Only to make an estimate of repair, you know. I do not mean to steal him entire.'

'Is there much needed in the way of repair?' His father raised his eyebrows. 'Fanny has said nothing to me about dilapidation, or repair.'

'Well, it is prudent to know anything that may need doing,

before we take up residence, Catherine and I. Don't you think so, sir?'

'Indeed, indeed, very wise in you.' Sir Charles drank off half his glass, and stared at the fire a moment. The light of the flames flickered on the ceiling, and a log crackled in the brief silence. Then: 'Was you intent upon Hodge himself carrying out the work—if any work is needed?'

'Well, I—that is, I had rather hoped that he might, yes, sir.'

'Ah. Ah. And should this work, whatever it may be, should it occupy him for more than say a day or two, or three, what had you in mind, then? If he was detained there, away from his proper work at Melton?'

'What had I in mind?'

'As to cost.' Sir Charles turned from the fire and looked at his son. 'I pay him to work here. If he is detained there, what then?'

'Well, sir. Well. I cannot—I cannot accurately *know* such cost, until Hodge has made his estimate.'

'Hm. Hm. Was you not my son, and a gentleman, I should take that as a very slippery reply.'

'I am sorry that you should think me slippery, sir.' With some asperity. 'It is really a very little thing, after all. If you do not wish me to take Hodge to Birch Cottage, then in course I shall not take him there. The work can be managed by some local man, I don't doubt.'

'No, no, James, do not get on your high horse. Y'may take Hodge, by all means. I can spare him a day or two, certainly.' He drank the last of his port. 'We had better join your mother, else she will think we have drunk too deep, and gone to sleep.' They rose from their chairs. At the door his father turned to James, and said: 'But what is your own estimate—in the rough?'

'Mine? Of the repairs, d'y'mean?'

'Come, James, you are an officer in His Majesty's service, with experience of dockyards, and the like. You have seen repairs carried through, and know their cost, certainly.'

'In ships, sir. Birch Cottage is not a ship.'

'And I must not call you slippery, hey, by God? Ha-ha. Very well,' opening the door wide, 'you may take Hodge, and Windle, and Baines. They may work there a full week, and we will say no more of cost.'

'Thank you, sir.'

'Why did not Fanny tell me that the place was falling down, I wonder? The female sex is very adept in talking about nothing at all, but when it comes to serious business they fall mute. Hey?'

James thought it wiser to make no reply as they walked through together.

Daily, Captain Rennie expected a reply to his letter; none came. Daily, or some times twice a day, he was at the dockyard. By now the marine sentries at the gate knew him, among the many sea officers who came and went on business, and the gatekeeper did not ask him his purpose as he came in. He knew his way to the Commissioner's House, but did not seek him out. The present Commissioner, Captain Harcourt—a retired sea officer—did not wish greatly to influence matters, but preferred the workings of the yard to be managed altogether by the yard officers. Accordingly Rennie had sought the Master Shipwright, Mr Rundle, by means of his obliging rodentish clerk, Tite.

'Bide with me, sir. Bear with me, eh? Mr Rundle is about, today, you see my meaning? Not about in this building, but about in the yard isself.' Removing extraordinary quantities of wax from his ear with a little copper loop, and darting away like a squirrel, with Rennie in pursuit.

A few days ago Rennie had seen the Master Attendant, Mr Tipping. Tipping was a florid man, rather grand under his over-powdered wig, which scattered loose grains on the shoulders of his coat as he shook his great head, nodded, was sage, &c. But grandeur did not prevent agility of mind in the allocation of moorings.

'She must be moored, your frigate. She must have her numbered mooring, so the sheer hulk may come to her,' consulting a document, 'in-in-in-in—yes, in a fortnight. We are agreed?'

Rennie would have preferred to see his ship refloated and moored in a few days, a week at most, but in his heart he knew it could not be. The copper of His Majesty's *Expedient* frigate had been severely damaged in her late first commission. Timbers had been damaged, worm had got in, and timbers had rotted. All of her copper had been examined, condemned, and prised off sheet by sheet in the dry dock as she lay naked of her masts and rigging, shored up amid the echoing crack and clatter of mallets, the rasp of saws, the stink of dung and hot tar, and the saline clinging green reek of the sea, closed in the great basin outside. Refitting could not even begin until the work of repair and re-coppering was completed, and the ship refloated.

A day or two after his interview with Mr Tipping, Rennie said approvingly to Mr Rundle: 'Your artificers here at Portsmouth are in every way more congenial than those fellows at Deptford. Your people get on with their work, and do it with a will.'

'Ah, well, Deptford. Hah! You know my meaning? Hah! to Deptford.' Rolling up a document. 'This here is a proper dockyard, Captain Rennie. Portsmouth is *the* dockyard.'

'Aye, I suppose so. Even over Chatham.'

'I will say nothing against Chatham, nor Plymouth, neither. Chatham is the natural home of ships such as yours, frigates. But whatever ships you may bring to us here to repair, or ask us to build, will serve His Majesty well. Woolwich I know little about, so will say little, or nothing. But Deptford, sir—*hah*!'

Now, as Rennie returned to his lodgings and climbed the narrow stair, he thought of his new commission. He had got the commission weeks since, with his instructions—instructions that were, admittedly, deficient in detail:

> Whereas we have reappointed you Captain of His Majesty's *Frigate Expedient*, now at Portsmouth, and intend that you shall command her during the present proposed voyage to Port Royal at Jamaica, in the West Indies, and there Undertake such Duties as may be conveyed to you prior to your Departure from Portsmouth, at a fitting date; and whereas we have ordered the said *Frigate* to be repaired & refitted at Portsmouth for Foreign Service . . .

&c., &c.

There was not a word of explication, or expansion, as to the purpose of the cruise to the West Indies. Surely, had Their Lordships wished him merely to join the fleet there, they would have made that plain? They had not. The content and substance of his duties was entirely a mystery. The Port Admiral, by whom Rennie had been invited to dine, could make no response to Rennie's discreet inquiry. He knew nothing about it, he said. Rennie must wait.

'Christ's blood,' he had sighed afterward to Captain Langton, a fellow guest, 'I am to wait, and wait, and wait. Waiting gives me a headache.'

'Will I tell you what I think has given you the headache, instead?' As they made their way to their lodgings, in darkness.

'Eh?'

'Claret.'

'Claret!'

'And port.'

'Can you be right? No no, I tell you it is all this damned waiting.—Langton? Where the devil have you gone to?'

Splashing on a wall, nearby. Footsteps, and Langton's dark shape loomed, the facings of his dress coat white in the dim light.

'Claret, and port,' he said. 'What has flowed in at one place must flow out again at t'other, hey?'

Rennie, reflecting on that evening of headache, smiled as he reached the top of the stair. Langton was a good fellow. His ship, also refitting, would be ready when it was ready, as he frequently and sensibly said. Rennie pushed open his door, and heard the heavy step and panting breath of the maid behind and below.

'Sir, oh sir. Captain Rennie.'

'What is it?' Turning.

'There is a gentleman has been asking for you, sir. He has give me this message, in writing. He was most partic'lar I must give it to you myself, sir.' She handed him a folded paper, sealed with wax. Rennie fumbled, found a coin, took the paper in return, nodded his thanks, and went in. It must be a message from his old friend Admiral Bailey, thought Rennie. The admiral had lately written to him from Deal, where he lived, saying that he would before long be at Portsmouth, where he would visit his elderly and ailing sister at Kingshill. Would Rennie, the admiral had asked, would Rennie dine with him, soon upon his arrival? Rennie had replied that he would, gladly. And now here was the admiral's message in his hand. He broke the seal, and his heart jumped—not with joy, but a flood of bitter emotion, dark and bitter, tasting in his throat. The message read, in a swift, precise hand, in black ink:

> I will like you to meet me at the Marine Hotel at seven o'clock, in the private parlour. Pray ask for Mr Scott, and you will be brought to me. Say nothing of this appt to anyone.
>
> R.G.

'R.G.' The initials, stark and black at the bottom of the page, could only be those of Sir Robert Greer.

Rennie sank into the chair by the bed, let the message fall to the floor, and took up his new commission. He reread it, and allowed his thoughts to grow dark. It was a flaw in him, he knew it, that he could and would always see ill when events, circumstances, the world, were neither ill, nor otherwise. Why could he never wait and see how the wind blew, and how he might harness it, instead of imagining always a lee shore, booming with malignant surf over fatal rocks? Alas, he never could. It was not his good fortune to have been born an optimist. He saw his commission, lying in his hand, not as a document of hope and opportunity, but—in light of this visit from a man he despised and feared—as a document blighted. Had not the signs been there from the beginning, the fatal signs? The trouble about the money? He sighed deep, and allowed his thoughts to drift disconsolately to more general things.

Yes, he had secured Hayter again as his first, when that officer might well have been given his own command. And he thought that he could be sure of young Makepeace again as his second. But as to the other Expedients, they were scattered to the four winds. Storey and Tangible, Adgett and Trent, came with the ship, in course, as her standing officers. The cook, Stamp, had died at Valparaiso.

'And I did not and do not regret his death,' murmured Rennie. 'He was loyal, he did his best, but by God he made wretched dull pies.' Another sigh. 'Dull pies, very dull.'

He lifted his head, and caught sight of his reflection in the looking glass across the room. 'Good God, who is that hangdog fellow?' he said aloud. 'Now that is a, *is* a dull fellow! A damned down-at-mouth, defeated mope, for Christ's sake!—Make your back straight, sir! Face the world square! And be damned to Sir Robert Bloody Greer!'

'I am seeking a Mr Scott.'

Rennie was led up the broad stair, to the left along a passage into a further passage, and to a door which opened on a quiet, blue-curtained room with a dining table and four places set. A crackling fire in the grate, gleaming irons, and flames mirrored in wineglasses did not lend the room warmth or cordiality; instead reflected flickerings upon the ceiling and walls made the room oddly comfortless, or so it seemed to Rennie. Except for himself the room was empty.

'Where is Mr Scott?' Turning to the maidservant. Either she did not hear his question or chose to ignore it. She disappeared, closing the door with a quiet click.

'Well, I'm damned.' Half under his breath. The room was not warm, but it was stuffy, as if it had not been aired in a month. Rennie sniffed, strode to the curtains, and flung them wide apart—and was disconcerted by the bare brick wall that confronted him. An irritable sigh, and he drew the curtains closed and went to the fire. There was not at the fire a deep, grateful chair, nor was there anywhere—upon a table or a cabinet—a bell to summon aid. He wished for aid, for sustenance, liquid sustenance. What must he do, in this damned place, to attract——

'Captain Rennie.'

And there in the room was his host. Rennie was so startled that he made no immediate reply. How had Sir Robert come in? There had been no squeak of handle or hinge as the door was opened, no step upon the floor. The door was in fact still closed, now, as Sir Robert came to the fire. He was dressed not in his habitual black but in a coat of dingy brown, dusty-looking breeches and stockings, plain unbuckled shoes and a wig wiry and unpowdered.

'You see before you Mr Scott,' he said. His appearance was very dull, very plain, but his voice—deep, modulated, powerful—was entirely the same.

'Ah. Hm. Good evening, Sir Robert.'

'I will come to my point at once.' Pulling a chair from the table and sitting near the fire.

Rennie too began to pull a chair from the table, the feet squeaking harshly on the floorboards.

'No no, there is not time for you to sit down.'

'Not time, Sir Robert?' His hand on the back of the chair. 'Do not we dine?'

'I do, you do not. In least, not here.'

'I see.' Rennie pushed the chair back in its place. He would not make a snappish reply, he would not lose his temper, and demean himself. He would not give the fellow that satisfaction. He stood with his hands clasped behind his back, firmly clasped, his feet set apart. Now let the fellow do his worst.

'How may I be of service to you, Sir Robert?'

'You have done yourself great harm in London, Captain Rennie.' Sir Robert took up an iron, and pushed a log in the grate.

'Great harm? I do not know——'

Sir Robert held up the iron and banged it once against the grate. His black gaze, turned briefly upon Rennie, was very severe.

'You have wrote a letter so immoderate, so intemperate, that you have risked everything.'

'You mean—you cannot mean—my letter to Their Lordships?'

'I do mean that letter.'

'Well, Sir Robert, with respect—I think it is a matter between myself and the Admiralty, a private matter, a naval matter——'

'You was warned never to speak of the matter at all. Mr Soames came from the Admiralty to Portsmouth upon your return, and warned you, in behalf of Their Lordships and myself. Did he not?'

'Indeed, Sir Robert, I did see the Third Secretary. However——'

'You was warned by him personal, and by letters he gave into your hand. Yes?'

'Well, when you put it in such terms, Sir Robert, you make it sound as if I had no right to pursue my claim, my legitimate claim——'

'There can be no claim, Captain Rennie, legitimate nor otherwise. No claim, sir, upon a matter so close to the nation's interest as this. Your duty is to *be quiet*, to say no more about it.'

Rennie found himself shocked, and very angry. He drew a furious breath, then turned away, not trusting himself. He stepped down the room, and bit down upon his fury, bit down until it was bitten off. He tasted blood in his mouth. Behind him, Sir Robert calmly continued:

'We both of us serve the King, sir, and the nation. Neither of us is a fool. Nor are we blackguards. You agree?'

Rennie turned. 'I would hope not indeed, sir.'

'Indeed. Let me be plain, then, in iteration. You must withdraw your complaint forthwith. You must let the matter rest, entire and absolute, in the nation's interest, and your own. Will you give me that assurance?'

And now Rennie was calm in his turn. He went back to the fire, pulled a chair from the table and quietly sat down opposite Sir Robert.

'Sir Robert, if you please, I will like to lay before you certain facts. Will you hear me out, now?'

Sir Robert's black gaze held Rennie's a moment. He said nothing, then gave the merest nod.

'Thank you. Since you have seen my letter, sir, you know its content and purpose, and I think you must concede—or in least admit of the possibility—that I have been wronged. I was awarded by the Admiralty Court a fraction of what was rightfully mine, from *Expedient*'s first commission. At very great cost to my officers and people we recovered specie to the value of 750,000 pound, and brought it safely home. Moneys that was thought absolutely lost, returned to the nation. We was awarded one per cent of its value. One per cent! As if we had been a merchant ship, bringing merchants' jewels home from the East as cargo. Do you know what my share of that is, sir, at one quarter? It is 1,875 pound. Was I to invest the whole of that, the whole of it would not bring me an hundred a year. Well, sir, that is not just. That is not right. Under the circumstances I reckon we should have got five per cent. I should have got above 9,000 as my share. Good heaven, Sir Robert, you must see—I *cannot* drop my claim.'

Sir Robert had sat impassive through all this, and now he said impassively:

'You was operating under secret instruction, Captain Rennie. Implicit in such instruction was the requirement that you must ever maintain secrecy—before, during, and after the fact. It is not *I* that must see anything at all, therefore, but *you—you*, sir.'

'But I have maintained secrecy. I have kept my mouth shut, in the outside world. But inside, so to say, inside the Royal Navy—well, Sir Robert, I find that I am unable to withdraw.' Meeting that black gaze.

'To press your claim can be nothing but folly.' Quietly, almost softly, shaking his head. 'It will result, I fear, as darkness follows the day—in your court martial.'

'On what charge?' Astonished.

'Something may be found, Captain Rennie.' With quiet menace. 'Something may be brought out—from who knows what corner of your activity?—that might very probably bring an end to your best prospects. You apprehend me?'

'You threaten me, sir?'

'And now it is time for my guests to arrive. Kindly see yourself to the door, will you?' Sir Robert did not stand up, nor offer his hand, but turned to the fire and crossed his ankles in dismissal.

James Hayter was again at Winterborne, inspecting the work in progress on his house. His father's carpenter Tobias Hodge had undertaken the work, with two other craftsmen from the estate, and now it was nearly completed. The roof was sound; a dozen slate tiles had been replaced and pinned, and the guttering swept free of rotting leaves and twigs. Shutters had been taken down, the hinges repaired, and the shutters painted and rehung. Paint had been liberally and carefully applied to window frames, the great door, &c. Crumbling and damp plaster had been torn from ceilings, fires lit in the upper rooms to dry them out, and new plaster mixed and applied. Everything that was crumbling or sagging or shoddy had been stripped out and made good, and the whole had been accomplished in little more than a week, with materials brought from Melton.

James rewarded the men handsomely. His father had not asked him to pay for anything, Hodge and his helpers were employed by the estate, but James considered it his duty to reward them, not with broad approving smiles and flattering words, but with gold.

'There is no need of it, sir,' said Hodge, removing his leather apron, and gathering his tools. 'We was happy to do this little service for you.'

'Oh, but I think there is need,' said James. 'It is more than a service, Tobias Hodge. You have transformed the house, so that now it is fit to live in, you have done it right quick, too, and I will like to show my gratitude.' And he gave him the coins.

'Well, sir, that is very kind. I am glad we have brought the old place into a handsome condition for your bride, sir, and may you both find much joy here.'

James was touched, and he shook Hodge warmly by the hand. 'Had you ever thought of going to sea, I wonder?'

'Going to sea? I fear I had not, no, sir.'

'The navy always needs good men, you know. Not only right seamen, but skilled men such as yourself. Ships are built of wood, after all.'

'I do know that, sir, yes. I am aware of that. But I could never leave Melton. Melton is my home, and your father has been very fair with me, always very fair, in wages, cottage, and everything. It would not be fair to him, like, would it, for me to bugger off?'

'No no, you are right, in course you are right. He would never forgive me, neither. Forget I said anything, will you?' And he rode away up the drive for the last time as a single man.

As the work had proceeded Catherine had been much in his thoughts. His bride-to-be was not staying—as had once, at first, months since, been proposed—with his cousins the Misses Ibbetson. To move into Birch Cottage as a spinster, then remove to East Lane Cottage, then return to Birch Cottage as a bride, seemed to all concerned rather to be tempting fate. Instead she had gone to her own distant cousins at Warminster. Catherine had lived—until she was orphaned by the death of her father the Reverend Dr Armitage—at St John's Rectory at Shaftesbury. Since his death she had been a governess at Wells, then upon James's return from HMS *Expedient*'s first commission she had removed to Warminster, until they could be married. She would bring not quite fifty pounds a year. James's share of the money allowed to *Expedient*'s officers and people by the Admiralty Court was very small, a few hundred pounds, which would soon be swallowed up. When that was gone he was certain only of his pay as a lieutenant RN, and Catherine's equally modest income. He had been given leave to remain away from *Expedient* during her repairing and refitting at Portsmouth, in order that he might put his house and affairs in order, and get married. He had—like Rennie—got his new commission, and was aware of their destination on foreign service: Port Royal at Jamaica. Other than that bare fact he knew very little, and had not permitted the business of the ship to enter his thoughts at all these last weeks. He thought constantly of Cathy, but did not go frequently to Warminster.

'It is not quite seemly to be seen at her side,' his mother had said.

'Not seemly? What on earth can you mean, Mother?'

'I mean that when you face a lifetime together, what is a few weeks?'

'Good heaven, it is seven days at a time, week after week, apart. Is it not natural to wish to be by her side?'

'Yes, it is natural enough'—a sigh—'I suppose it is natural enough.'

'And what can you mean by "face a lifetime together" as if it was like to facing the gallows? Good heaven.'

And then he saw what was behind his mother's absurd pronouncement: she wished not to lose her youngest son, her favourite son, and in consequence he went out of his way to be kind to her, and bowed to her wish. He and Cathy wrote letters—very fond letters—and waited.

'You are not much at Warminster, eh?' said his father.

'No, sir. I find there is so much to attend to at Winterborne that there is not enough time to go to Warminster as well.'

'Ah. Ah.—And what does Catherine say to this?'

'To what?'

'In my day it would have looked like neglect.'

'I assure you, it is nothing of the kind.'

'However, however, it is you that is engaged to be married, sir, to a very beautiful girl, and I am standing on the side. It ain't my business that you leave her alone, sighing. That is your affair.'

James and Catherine were married at the church of St John at Shaftesbury, because Catherine wished it. It had been her late father's church, the place of worship she had known all her life, and therefore had fond associations and the virtue of familiarity. Thus as she went down the aisle upon the arm of Mr Henry Armitage, her elderly cousin from Warminster, who gave her away *in loco parentis*, she was in no way nervous of her conduct, nor over-awed by the solemnity of the occasion. James was solemn, his heart full, as he stood beside his brother Charles, and waited. James had invited Captain

Rennie, but Rennie had been unable to attend. He had again been summoned, at Portsmouth, on official business.

A boat was waiting at the Hard, a launch with double-banked oars, the boat's crew very smart, very correct, with ribbons in their hats, and on their blue jackets, and a junior lieutenant in command. In usual a midshipman would have brought such a boat in to the Hard, but on this occasion the young lieutenant had been despatched out of respect for Sir Robert Greer. It was all at Sir Robert's instigation. He had conceived a plan of conveying certain information to Captain Rennie—not upon the shore, but aboard one of His Majesty's ships of the line, at sea. Sir Robert had persuaded himself that this would allow him to interview Rennie in the greater privacy of a ship, far from the prying eyes and cupped ears of the shore, on a matter of great importance, but in truth—had Sir Robert been honest with himself—he wished to give himself airs. He wished to be deferred to, obeyed, and treated just as if he were a senior sea officer in his own ship—an admiral, or in least a commodore. Naturally he had said nothing of this to Rennie, or anyone; it was his private whim, dressed up as something else.

The junior lieutenant welcomed them aboard, Captain Rennie in his dress coat, and Sir Robert Greer in black coat and cape, and a black hat worn athwart his head, naval fashion. The wind was a little brisk. To Rennie this was nothing, but he saw that Sir Robert peered at the white caps offshore, and was hesitant in making his way into the stern sheets.

It had all begun when Sir Robert had sent Rennie a further message, requiring him to attend upon him at a coffee house in the High. An awkward exchange had then taken place.

'You are acquainted, I believe, with one Captain Langton RN?'

'I am, yes. Langton, the *Tamar* sixty-four, presently refitting.'

'Who resides at the Marine Hotel, does he not?' A black, penetrating glance.

'That is so, yes.' Sir Robert had not offered him refreshment, a glass of wine, although wine was available. Rennie felt the need of wine; there was something in Sir Robert's voice he did not like.

'Yes. I have had occasion to exchange a few words of conversation with Captain Langton, when I learned of your acquaintance, during which he let something slip.'

'Let something slip, Sir Robert?' Politely.

'It was merely inadvertent in him, I think, when he allowed that you and he had discussed your letter to Their Lordships.'

Rennie felt an intimate part of him shrivel. Good God, it was true. He had talked to Langton about the letter, casually talked of it, one sea officer to another.

'Well well, I may have done, a little. It was not——'

'You gave me your assurance, at our last meeting, that you had discussed your claim with no one else. Did you not?'

'Well, I—I said "outside". That I had discussed it with no person "outside". And I——'

'How is this Captain Langton not "outside", pray? He is outside *Expedient*, he is outside our private discussions, he is altogether *outside*, sir. As I think you know.'

'He is not outside the Royal Navy, Sir Robert.' Stiffly.

'Pish pish, Captain Rennie, do not play with words like an avoiding child. Not with me.—How much have you told him?'

'Captain Langton knows nothing of the matter, in large. I may have mentioned my letter in passing, but he knows no detail of it, no exact detail at all.' Stung.

'He had better not. He had better not. For both your sakes.' Grimly.

And now in the boat Rennie noticed with guilty pleasure

that Sir Robert was not quite himself. They were being rowed out to a moored ship, moored far out at Spithead, HMS *Zealous* seventy-four. The swell was choppy, and spray flew back from cutwater and oar. Sir Robert in his black cloak and hat endeavoured to be resolute and officerlike as the boat proceeded, but his pale face grew paler, his grip on the thwart more clutching, and as the boat dipped heavily deep and rose again, and stinging salt water sprayed across him, he blinked, and blinked, in something like quiet desperation, already regretting this decision to conduct his business afloat. By sheer effort of will he held on until the boat came in under *Zealous*'s lee, and the pitching ceased.

Captain Holland greeted them as they were piped aboard. Everything was very formal and correct. Ropes for the side-ladder, ship's boys in attendance, marines formed up. Like Rennie, Captain Holland was in dress coat. He ushered them aft to the great cabin. Sir Robert, greatly relieved to be out of the boat, attempted to lift himself and lighten his mood by making a joke:

'I wonder, d'you call your hands "Zealots"? Hey, Captain Holland?'

Captain Arthur Holland RN was a square-chinned, square-bodied, plain-speaking officer of the old school, perfectly prepared to be polite, and gentlemanlike, but he did not much care for political men—however high—and he could not countenance such a wretched joke, so he said:

'I fear I do not, Sir Robert.'

'Ah. Ah.'

Captain Holland was at pains to be hospitable, however. He did not much like his ship being invaded, at short notice, on instruction from the Port Admiral, who had himself been instructed. But he was determined to be dutiful. He did not know Sir Robert. Neither did he know Captain Rennie. Judging by his appearance Rennie was an upright, honourable fellow, a good sea officer caught up in God knew what political intrigue and nonsense. If so, he deserved sympathy.

Holland offered them Madeira. Rennie accepted readily, but Sir Robert:

'Madeira, hm.—Have you anything—anything a little stronger, perhaps?'

'Stronger, Sir Robert? Do you mean gin?'

'No no, not gin.' A grimace. 'I meant—brandy.'

Sir Robert was given brandy, and a very faint tinge of colour appeared in his chalky face. Revived, he said: 'And now, Captain Holland, if you please, I will like the use of your rooms for a short while.'

'My rooms? D'y'mean the great cabin?'

'Indeed, the cabin, this cabin.'

'You wish to dine alone?' Puzzled, now. 'I had thought you was——'

'Dine, Captain Holland?' Sharply. 'There is no question of dining. I do not wish to dine. I am here on official business. Just go upstairs until we are finished here, will you?'

'Ah. Hm. Just as you wish, Sir Robert.' Very correct. 'I am at your disposal, I am your servant.' He bowed, then: 'You wished, I think, Sir Robert, to be shown how a ship is worked?'

'The Port Admiral suggested it, indeed. I will like to see over the ship, look at its "workings", so to say, in due course. Indeed.' A dismissive nod.

Captain Holland again made a leg, stiffly made a leg, and managed a stiff little smile.

When they were alone Sir Robert said to Rennie: 'Captain Holland lives very well aboard his ship, don't he? Very civilised.' Glancing about the quarters. 'I had always heard that life at sea was confining, and cramping, and anything but comfortable. I see no confirmation of that view, here.'

Captain Holland's cabin was unusually well appointed. Clearly he was a man of means, and liked to have about him, if not luxury exact, then as near to it as made no matter. There were silk hangings, a stove, handsome bookshelves, a long gleaming table and fine chairs, two desks, &c., &c.

Swords hung in scabbards on brackets. A pistol case lay open on the larger desk. Sir Robert peered at the case. In it were a pair of silver-mounted pocket pistols by Twigg of London.

'These are very fine,' he murmured in his deep voice. 'Hm, I had no idea you naval men lived quite so well.'

'We do not all live so well as this, Sir Robert.'

'Do you not? Do you not?' He glanced at Rennie, as if in mild surprise. 'Is that why you have pressed your spurious claim?'

Rennie did not reply. He drank off his Madeira by way of stopping his tongue.

'Very well, to business.' Robert drew from his coat a packet of documents, which included a chart, and sat down at one end of the long table, motioning Rennie to join him. Only the movement of the brandy in the decanter, the gentle canting of the liquid on the lift, reminded Sir Robert that he was not on dry land. Rennie sat down.

'You are to go to Port Royal, Captain Rennie, when your ship is ready.'

'Those are my instructions, yes.'

'You are there to make a charting survey of the Jamaica coast, the southern coast.'

'A charting survey?' Rennie was dismayed, and disappointed. Good heaven, a ship sloop or a brig could be employed for such an untaxing task. Nor could he believe that ships already there, either at the Leeward Islands, or Port Royal itself, would be unable to make such a survey as a matter of routine—if indeed it was needful at all. He said none of these things to Sir Robert, but instead:

'Very well.' Suppressing a sigh.

'Your purpose is to make such a survey as if you was an enemy ship. You are to look for suitable landing places, away from Port Royal and the Old Harbour, where an invading force might land, secretly land, proceed overland to Spanish Town and take it, then spread out into the island and take the great plantations by stealth. Such a force might then be able to take Port Royal, and Fort Charles, from the landward side, and the squadron in the harbour, also. Such an assault would be very calamitous. By finding out its probable route, we may know how to prevent its success.'

Rennie sat puzzling a moment, unsure what to say in reply. He regarded the plan as absurd, but felt that he could not say so without offence.

'Well, Sir Robert,'—at last—'I know Port Royal, I have been at Jamaica, and so far as I am aware there is no passage to or from it, from the Atlantick Ocean, that could be made entirely by stealth.'

'You mean, by ships of war?'

'I do. How else might a landing force come there? Sir Robert, we maintain a fleet at the Leeward Islands, which undertakes regular patrols. There is a further squadron at Port Royal. Great numbers of merchant ships, English merchant ships, come and go, from Africa on the Middle Passage, and to England on the homeward leg. I do not see how this "force" could push through all these ships without arousing great suspicion and alarum. And who will send such a force, anyway? We are not at war. Who are they? Pirates?'

'They are not.'

'Then I do not——'

Sir Robert held up a hand. 'You will allow me to say two things. First, even when England is not at war, it is the duty of her servants to be vigilant. Second, in keeping vigilant, in maintaining vigilance in the peace—there is much that is not straightforward.'

'In other words, Sir Robert, you know something that I do not.'

Sir Robert was about to reply when both men became aware, by sudden little jolts, and swinging sunlight through the stern gallery window, that the ship was moving. Her timbers creaked and groaned. Calls sounded on deck, and there was the thudding rush of feet, and muffled shouts.

'What has happened?' Sir Robert stood up, and was at once

thrown off balance as the ship lurched. He clutched at the table and his glass fell to the decking and smashed.

'By God, the ship is sinking!'

'No no, I think not.' Rennie rose and braced himself. 'She is coming to the wind.'

'What! What!' There was real alarm in Sir Robert's black eyes, and in his voice. The faint, brandy-brought colour vanished from his cheeks.

'Aye,' said Rennie, 'yards are bracing, sheets hauling. It is being managed right well.'

Again the ship lurched, and began to heel. A drum-roll sounded, dinning and rattling through the ship.

'I gave no instruction!' Sir Robert tottered three or four steps, and came up against the large desk, which he gripped with white-knuckled hands. 'The ship must remain still!'

'I think Captain Holland has decided to show you how *Zealous* may be worked as a fighting ship, Sir Robert.'

'What? Fighting?'

'We shall know presently whether or no he has decided to clear for action.'

'*Action?*' Outraged, aghast.

Rennie turned his head, listening. There came the crashing and clattering of bulkheads being struck. The door of the cabin banged open, and a midshipman appeared, with carpenter's crew, wielding mallets, bustling purposefully in the background.

'Captain Holland's compliments, sir, and will you join him on the quarterdeck. We are beating to quarters.'

Rennie stood at the rail with Captain Holland as the ship ran down to St Helen's Road, close-hauled into a southerly wind.

'It was a little extravagant of me to cut and clear,' he said. 'Eh, Captain Rennie?'

'It is not for me to make adverse comment, sir, when I am your guest.' Glancing aloft, then forrard. 'She points up handsome, Captain Holland.'

'She does. I am proud of her. Pride is a sin, but I am proud of *Zealous*, and my people.' He peered at the companion. 'But where is Sir Robert, I wonder? Does he not join us on deck? I have done this for his benefit, you know, so that he might see the ship at her fighting best.'

'He is in your quarter gallery, I believe.'

'Ah. Caught short, hey? I hope that he is in the leeward gallery, for his sake. Defecate leeward is the soundest principle. Always defecate to leeward.'

'Just so. However'—bracing himself as the ship's head dipped and her cutwater smashed a wave into bright fragments—'however, I do not think Sir Robert uses your quarter gallery for quite that purpose.'

'Eh? You do not mean the poor fellow is spewing there, I hope?'

'I fear so.'

'Oh, dear. What a very great pity.—*Mr Hamble!*'

'Sir?' The lieutenant, attending.

'Stand by to fire!' To Rennie: 'I let go my cable to show Sir Robert how it is done, how a ship of the line may go into action at a moment's notice.'

'And done excellent well, if I may be permitted to say so.'

'We are a fighting ship, and we must be ready to fight at any time. Anything may happen at sea, after all. You agree?'

'Indeed, just so, Captain Holland. I do agree, most certainly.' And Rennie allowed himself to smile as he braced himself for the broadside of guns.

* * *

The gunner Mr Storey was anxious. There had been such great trouble with the ship's guns on her first commission, and with the new powder, that he had never been quite confident of *Expedient*'s right and duty to call herself a fighting ship.

He had met Rennie in the dockyard, having come from his

temporary lodgings in the town, where he was housed while *Expedient* was still in dry dock.

'I have been wishing and meaning to ask you, sir, these past many days—what is to be our pattern?'

'Armstrong.' Rennie glanced at his gunner, nodded, then returned his gaze to *Expedient*, peering down critically over the shorings at her half-coppered bottom timbers.

'Thank God, thank God.' Mr Storey removed his hat, and mopped his face with a kerchief. He paused. 'And powder?'

'Standard, Mr Storey. Standard coarse.'

'Whhh. I am mightily relieved. The eighteen-pound Armstrong is a heavy gun, but a good sound one, sound and strong. I have never known one burst.'

'We are to have twenty-six Armstrongs, and the same thirty-two-pound carronades for our upperwork, only more of them. Two a side on the forecastle, and four a side on the quarterdeck, a dozen in whole.'

'Very good, excellent.'

'We might get some chasers into her, and in course we can mount swivels, a dozen one-pounders. It will mean a heavier ship, with the Armstrongs, and the greater weight of powder we shall need.'

'For my part a great burden has been lifted from me, sir, heavier ship or no.'

'I am glad, Mr Storey. We shall only know how she handles, heavier, when Mr Loftus has trimmed her.'

'Is Mr Loftus to rejoin the ship? I had heard, well I had heard that he——'

'You had heard what, Mr Storey?'

'I must not speak out of turn.'

'Heard *what*?'

'Well, that there had been some little trouble with a young person. It ain't my business.'

'By "young person" you mean a young woman, I am in no doubt.'

'I don't know the particulars. But, yes, a young lady.'

'What, he was engaged to her?'

'Aye, so the story goes. And she ran off, at the last moment, taking——'

'Ah. Now I have you, now I am with you. She stole his money, and ran away. Yes?'

'Yes.'

'Just so. But that needn't prevent him from rejoining the ship, certainly. It is hard luck, but Loftus is a sensible man, very able and level-headed, and once he has got over his loss, well.'

'It was not just the loss of his money, I think.'

They were walking now towards the dockyard gate. Rennie made a note in pencil on a list. 'Surely she did not steal his clothes as well?' He laughed briefly at his own joke, and put the list away in his coat.

'No, sir, not his clothing. Something more.'

'His horse, then, eh? Poor Loftus.'

'None of those things. None of those things. I will bid you good day, sir. I must go to the gun wharf, directly.'

Rennie's good humour did not last. His first, Lieutenant Hayter, whom he sorely needed in getting the ship ready for the sea, was on his honeymoon, and would not come to Portsmouth until another ten days. And there had been trouble about the *Zealous*, and Captain Holland's little venture. The Port Admiral had said nothing, but the admiral commanding the Channel Fleet, Vice-Admiral Hollister, had sent for Holland—and for Rennie.

Rennie knew that Sir Robert Greer must be behind this summons, that that gentleman had taken his little humiliation at sea very ill, and had contrived his revenge from his very considerable position of influence.

Captain Holland came in his launch to pick Rennie up at the Hard at noon, and the two officers were rowed out to the flag, His Majesty's ship *Vanquish* one hundred.

'Your friend Greer is a very weighty fellow,' said Holland grimly in the boat.

'He is not my friend, I assure you. Anything but.'

'He is certainly not mine, neither.'

'He had something to do with my first commission, and I knew him then. It is my misfortune that he evidently wishes to instruct me in my second commission, the fellow.'

'Is that why you came to *Zealous*? He brought you out to *Zealous* for that purpose?'

'I never quite found that out, you know. We was interrupted by events.' Half the truth.

'To whom is he attached?' Holland, after a moment or two, pulling his boat cloak up round his shoulders. 'Is he an official at the Admiralty, or is his connection political?'

'I have never been able to discover that, neither. But his connections are high.'

'He looks political. I should have known better, I expect, but I thought he would accept it in good part, as a—well, as a jest.'

'The run down to St Helen's Road?'

'Aye. It made him lose his rations, but what is that, at sea? It has happened to us all.'

'Just so, indeed.' Nodding.

'I am in a little difficulty about that anchor, though,' admitted Holland. 'In course, I said I would make it good out of my own purse, but the dockyard officers have made the devil of a rumpus about it. Losing best bowers ain't popular with them, I fear.'

'Does the admiral know about it?'

'Hollister? I expect that he does. Greer will have discovered, made it his business to discover, everything that is detrimental to me, to get athwart my hawse and be vengeful.'

'Then we must have a stratagem, Captain Holland.' Ducking as spray whipped across them.

'Eh?'

'Before we come under *Vanquish*'s lee, we must agree a plan.'

'Plan? What plan?'

'Well well, now—you had thought that Sir Robert's principal purpose in coming aboard your ship was to see her handled as a man of war, see her go about, exercise her guns, and so on.'

'I *could* argue that, I expect, but——'

'Accordingly, you made your best effort to show him how it is done. Slipped at a moment's notice, brought her to the wind, cleared for action and ran out your guns. You was, you thought, seamanlike and efficient, and you hoped that your guest would heartily approve.'

'Hm. Hm.' Doubtfully, rubbing his chin. 'You think so?'

'Good heaven, it was not your fault, was it, that Sir Robert was took ill below?'

'Puking ain't a thing we can any of us predict. But what am I to say about that damned bower, hey? An anchor cannot be talked away, glib and easy, just like that.'

'Sir Robert rated one anchor, in least, did he not? Such a high fellow as that? When he was to observe the Royal Navy at its fighting best?'

'Hm.' Captain Holland wiped spray from his cheek. 'Well . . .'

'This must be our stratagem, else we shall both be driven in upon a lee shore. I do not intend to allow myself be wrecked by such a fellow as Sir Robert Greer.'

'Aye, well said. Very good, I am with you.'

'Boat your oars!' called the midshipman as the coxswain at the tiller guided them in alongside the great wall of wood that was *Vanquish*, and they rode there a moment, rising and falling on the swell as the boat was held in to the side ladder by the seaman standing in the bow.

As they came up the ladder into the ship, and were piped aboard, Holland muttered to Rennie: 'It was my own damned pride. In truth I wished him to suffer because I thought he had insulted me. Everything that followed is my own fault, entire.'

'Do not falter now, Captain Holland.' Rennie urgently, in

reply. 'Greer accuses us both of conspiracy to humiliate him, and we must argue the contrary—we must not falter.'

Holland nodded once, to show that he had heard, then turned to lift his hat to the officer of the deck.

'Captain Holland, and Captain Rennie.' Admiral Hollister was seated at his desk in his state room, in plain blue frock coat, and without his wig. He looked older, thought Rennie. He rose as the two officers went to him, and his stoop was more pronounced than when Rennie had last seen him, but his manner was vigorous still, and the pale blue eyes still penetrating as he turned them now on the junior captain.

'Aye, we have met before, Rennie. You had the *Expedient* frigate, had you not?'

'Yes, sir. Near two years ago, her first commission. I am commissioned in her a second time.'

'Yes, yes, I recall—ah, now—yes, I gave you a surgeon out of my ship, I think. A very valuable man.'

'You did, sir.'

'Was he valuable?'

'He died very soon after, I am sorry to say. Within a week or two.'

'Did he? Did he? A misfortune.' He did not say it with sincerity of feeling. They both knew that the late surgeon had been a very unconversable, unlikeable man, a nuisance to the admiral and a curse in Rennie's ship.

Captain Holland now glanced at Rennie. His eyes asked: What the devil was all this about? All this amiable reminiscence? Rennie allowed his eyebrows to rise. The admiral had sat down again, and sipped from the glass at his elbow.

'No doubt you are wondering, Captain Holland, why I have summoned you here, you and Rennie, hey?'

'Sir, I may as well say at once——' began Holland, very stiff, but the admiral interrupted him:

'I have summoned you here to ask you to do me a service.'

'A service?'

'Indeed, a service. It is a matter of—what shall we call it?—of injured pride. Yes, I think that is an accurate description. Injured self-esteem.'

Rennie and Holland exchanged another glance. The admiral motioned to them, indicated chairs. 'Sit down, gentlemen. By the by, you see me taking not wine, but physic. I would offer you some, but it is very bitter.'

The two officers sat down, entirely uncertain of what next to expect.

'It has been brought to my notice that when he was in your ship t'other day, Captain Holland, Sir Robert Greer—who had gone aboard to confer with Captain Rennie on some matter of which I know nothing—Sir Robert was took ill.'

'Sir, I must take full——'

'Was took ill when you was attempting to show him how a ship of the line is worked.'

'Ah. Yes. Well, sir——'

'You cut your cable, as I understand it, and ran down to St Helen's, and fired your guns, and so forth.'

'I must admit that I——'

'Which manoeuvres made Sir Robert sick. The heeling of the ship, the buffeting of the wind close-hauled, and the like. Hold up your hand, Captain Holland, by all means, if I have told any of it wrong.'

'You have not, sir.'

'No, I thought I had not. And then, when you returned to your mooring at Spithead, Sir Robert had to be carried into the boat, so prostrated was he, the poor fellow, by his ordeal.'

'He was put into the boat very pale-looking, but——'

'You went ashore in that same boat, Captain Rennie?'

'I did, sir. However——'

'What was your own opinion of Sir Robert's health at that moment?'

'Well, I fear he was still very unwell, and——'

'Still puking, was he? In the boat? Well, well now, that is what happens when lubberly men get into boats, and go aboard ships, and think that the sea is altogether the same thing as the shore. That it should stand still, and behave reasonable and fair to them. That is what happens to them. They puke, gentlemen. They spew up their innards. And then they have the damned reckless temerity to blame it on sea officers!'

Another wondering, astonished glance between Holland and Rennie.

'Sir Robert Greer is a man of the very greatest probity, I am told, and good works. He is a man, certainly, of very high connection, sufficient to waste the time of the Port Admiral, and myself, on a bloody trifling thing like seasickness. Well now, I have interviewed you, gentlemen, you have told me all the facts, and I am content that we have together done our duty. I am sorry that I am unable to offer you greater hospitality, but I must go ashore myself, presently. Good day to you.'

'Good day, sir.'

'Thank you, sir. Thank you, indeed.' Holland bowed.

James and his bride Catherine were at Weymouth, at the Harbour Inn. It had been suggested that they might go to Bath, but James wished to pay for everything himself, and the expense of an hotel at Bath—or private rooms, in a fashionable part of the town—he had thought beyond his limited means, and so they had come to Weymouth.

The Harbour Inn was a handsome small bow-fronted hotel on the eastern side of the harbour, opposite the stone steps where James had taken passage to join *Expedient* on her first commission. The cries of gulls echoed there over the stone walls and the riding water, the air was pleasant, and their accommodations entirely satisfactory. James had engaged a small suite of rooms, and had arranged for their meals to be brought to them there.

'Should we not go out sometimes?' asked Catherine, late on the third afternoon, lifting her dark hair from her face, and turning to him.

'We shall go out whenever you wish, my darling. Into the world.'

'I meant, I meant not for company, or society, but just to walk a little.'

'Now? This instant?'

'James, I am not dressed.'

'Nor am I, as you observe. How much I prefer that. How much more delightful to be always quite naked.' He poured wine. 'And always a little intoxicated. Entirely, utterly intoxicated. My darling. My love.'

Presently the light faded and night came on. They did not go out. Nearly all of their days at Weymouth were like that, for a week and more, until at last they returned to Birch Cottage and took possession of it, wholly and gladly, as man and wife. And then soon after it was time for James to think about his duty, not to his wife alone, but to his King and his ship.

'I am reluctant,' he said. 'I must admit I am most reluctant. I do not wish to go.'

'You must go.'

'I know that I must. But I do not like it. Oh, Cathy.'

'I shall be all right. Your mother has been very kind in saying I must come to Melton very often, and your cousins will come to visit me, and I shall go to them, in turn. I shall be all right.'

'Yes, I don't doubt it, my darling. But shall I? I may die of loneliness.'

'Then I shall come to Portsmouth with you, and remain there until you sail.'

'You will! Then I am saved. I shall not go mad, after all.'

And he took her in his arms, not to make love to her, but

simply to hold her close to him, to feel her heart beating against his.

Sir Robert Greer had gone to London, so Rennie learned from the Port Admiral, had departed a day or two after his little cruise in HMS *Zealous*. Rennie felt himself free to arrange a dinner for his friends, not at his lodgings, but in the less confining atmosphere of a private dining room at the Marine Hotel.

Had Rennie thought that Sir Robert would retreat permanently to London, taking his extravagant, concocted notions of tropical invasion and piracy with him, he would have been quite wrong. However, Rennie had not entertained this fancy. He knew very well that Sir Robert would persist, that he would return, and summon Rennie to a further meeting—several meetings, all of them exacting. Sir Robert was not a man to allow a little discomforting incident to distract him long, even if at first it had made him determined to hang Rennie and Captain Holland both. When he had recovered his temper, and his icy disdaining composure, he would again be formidable. Rennie knew that he must submit. If his new commission, his position as a sea officer in the Royal Navy, depended on Sir Robert and his secretive, half-revealed notions about Jamaica, then he must submit.

To his looking glass: 'I don't like it, by God, but I shall.' Tying his stock. 'He is a bloodless, stony, overbearing scoundrel, but I shall submit, and do as I am told.'

Attending the dinner were Captain Langton, Captain Holland, and Admiral Bailey—lately arrived at Portsmouth. Rennie would have liked James Hayter to join them, but his lieutenant was still in Dorset. It was a convivial company, entirely naval, entirely masculine, bibulous enough, but not drunken or boisterous. Each man felt that he was among friends, even though their only mutual friend was Rennie. Inevitably, as the early courses were removed and wine flowed, the flow of talk increased, and Rennie—while attempting to join in—found that his thoughts drifted on to the subject of Sir Robert Greer. He had not yet fathomed the purpose behind Sir Robert's other self, Mr Scott. Sir Robert had never been a guest at the Marine Hotel under his own name, nor apparently under the name Scott. Rennie had inquired, and had been met with shaken head and puzzled frown. Sir Robert the black-clad high official lived at another address, Kingshill House, under the brow of Portsdown Hill—a house Rennie knew from a visit years before. Sir Robert had a carriage there, and servants. Admiral Bailey, who had come from Deal to visit his elderly sister at Kingshill, seized upon the name when Rennie mentioned it now:

'Oh yes, Sir Robert Greer. He is often there at Kingshill House, that belongs to the absent Lady Kenton, I believe. My sister Alice lives quite near, and has often seen him in his carriage, you know, coming and going, very grand. He ain't grand, I may tell you. His origins is very humble. His father was an artificer at Chatham Dockyard, and his mother a laundress. Their name was Giss.'

'No!' Rennie, astonished. 'No, it cannot be the same man, Admiral. Sir Robert Greer is certainly a gentleman, even if I don't like the fellow. His manner of speech, his style of dress, his demeanour entire—is unmistakable.'

'I tell you, my boy, with affection and respect—you are mistaken. Greer was Giss. He has invented himself from his shoe-buckle up, by sheer ruthless determination of will. Like an actor in the theatre he trained himself to speak, and hold himself, and disguise himself as another man, and he emerged as that man.'

'Holland, now, you have seen him. And Langton, you have met Sir Robert——'

'No, I have not.' Langton shook his head.

'But surely, you and he talked of my—my letter to Their Lordships, in this very hotel.'

Langton frowned. 'I assure you, my dear fellow, I have never discussed your private business with anyone in this hotel, or anywhere . . . Wait, though, there was a fellow, a fellow that said he knew you, a commonplace, shabby sort of fellow. Scott was his name, I think.'

'But that is the same man! That is Sir Robert Greer!'

'Eh?'

'I tell you, he was in disguise!' Rennie became aware that they were all staring at him. He took a breath, and refilled his glass. 'I did not mean to accuse you, Langton—but did you and Mr Scott talk of me, between you?'

'A word or two only, I assure you. It was in the dining room, as we waited for our coffee. I did not regard the fellow at all. I took him for a clerk, a dockyard clerk, who had met you in the course of his duties.'

'Well,' said Admiral Bailey in the silence that followed. 'Well. He is clearly a man that has not forgot how to deceive.'

'Do you mean'—Captain Holland was clearly still at sea—'do you mean that the fellow who came into my ship was an impostor?'

'No, he is not an impostor, exact, I think,' said Rennie.

'But if he is not, then what the devil was he about, telling Captain Langton that he was a bloody little clerk?'

'In fairness,' said Langton, 'he did not say that he was a clerk. I *took* him for a clerk, by the things he said. He knew of your ship, Rennie, he knew about *Expedient*, he said he was acquainted with you.'

'The whole damned thing is a mystery. The fellow ain't Greer, he is Giss. Then he ain't that neither, he is Scott. My opinion of him does not rise, I may tell you. The more I know of him, the less I like. My understanding of him is this, plain and simple: he is a blackguard.' Captain Holland banged down his glass on the table.

'Admiral Bailey,' Rennie turned to his old friend, 'may I ask how you know that Sir Robert is really called Giss?'

'He ain't called Giss now, clearly. He has been Greer for many years. I know about him through long acquaintance with the business of the navy. The Navy Board, in particular. That is where Giss got his start, and his ambition. He went from Chatham Dockyard to London, at the end of the Seven Years War, very young, and was taken into the household of a political man, Dunbar Greer. This man is now forgotten, but then had some influence at the Admiralty. At first, young Robert Giss was little more than a factotum, but the politician saw something in him, an eagerness and quickness of mind, and he brought him on. Eventually Robert Giss became Robert Greer, a surrogate son to Dunbar Greer, who was a bachelor and had no heir. Well, the old man got him into Cambridge, through influence, and the young man did very well. After Cambridge he began to climb, and climb, and climb. He climbed in Whitehall. He climbed at Court. He learned, and watched, until at last he could become. And he became, during the late American colonial war, Sir Robert Greer, gentleman of standing and power. Quite why he should wish to assume the guise of the lowly Mr Scott, I could not say.'

'At any rate, let us forget him,' said Rennie now. 'We must not allow him to spoil our dinner.'

But Rennie could not forget him. He could not forget his threats, his scheming, and his power to influence careers. No, he could not forget him—and Rennie wondered if, now that he knew these things about Sir Robert's past, he might not be able to use them to his own advantage at some future time.

James came to Portsmouth with Catherine, not to the Marine Hotel, but to a smaller establishment, the White Hart Posthouse, on the road a little way out of the town. It was not altogether convenient; it meant a longish walk to the dockyard; but it was suited to James's purse. He disliked having to be so careful of his money, newly married, but if Catherine was to be comfortable at Birch Cottage during his absence he must not overspend out of romantic recklessness and fond folly. For her part Catherine was perfectly content. She was with her husband.

Expedient had now been refloated, her timbers and copper restored, but she was not yet in a condition to accommodate her officers and people, swarming as she was with artificers.

'What people?' Rennie had asked James at their first meeting for many weeks, after they had exchanged greetings—warmly exchanged them, for they were friends as well as fellow officers. They were in the dockyard, James in his old working clothes, a blue kerchief tied round his head, Rennie in his shabbiest frock coat. 'What people?' said Rennie. 'We have no hands, James. They was all paid off after our last commission, and given their little bit of the reward, so little I was ashamed of it, and they have scattered long since.' A sigh.

'Can we afford a poster, sir?'

'A printed poster, d'y'mean?'

'Yes, large enough to attract the eyes of seamen, bold enough in content. We would very soon fill the ship's books by printing say a dozen copies and displaying them about the town.'

'Aye, certainly, but the men thus encouraged and who then filled my books would not be my own men.'

'Followers? Original Expedients? Surely you have not forgot, we lost half of them in the Pacifick Ocean, more than half. The rest is scattered, as you said. Even if we could find them, we——'

'Well well, I want them found. As many Expedients as may be possible, by the poster. Men we know, and trust, that have been through great hardships with you and me, and willing to trust us again, in their turn.'

'Do you know the whereabouts of Jacob Gurrall, sir?'

'Gurrall is the kind of man I mean, exact.—And the answer, alas, is no. I do not know where he is.'

'We must find him, then. Print our poster, and find Jacob Gurrall.'

Jacob Gurrall, in James's estimation, had been the finest and ablest seaman in the ship's complement her first commission. Captain of the maintop, a petty officer who had the makings of a warrant officer, or even a commissioned officer, taking his watch on the quarterdeck. He had authority of presence, good sense, and was courageous and strong, and well liked.

'Is Mr Loftus to rejoin us, sir?' James, later, as he and Rennie composed their poster at Rennie's lodgings.

'I have every expectation that he will. Why should he not?'

'Well, sir, I had thought that Gurrall would make an admirable master, one day. Loftus is a good fellow, certainly—but Gurrall should have his chance.'

'So far as I know, Gurrall has never been examined by a proper board, nor by Trinity House. I want him in my ship, but not as master, James. No no, Loftus will return, I am in no doubt, when he has got over it.'

James, leaning over the rough square he had drawn in pencil on a sheet of paper, paused and looked up: 'Got over what?'

'Hm? Oh, well. The silly fellow got himself involved with some wench, you know. It is the usual story. Sailors ought not to get involved with women. Bed them, in course, but—Oh, I am very sorry, James. You are newly married, and I have spoke out of turn. Forgive me.' Red-faced with shame.

'You are forgiven, sir. But what happened to poor Bernard Loftus?'

'The girl ran off with his money, I understand. He took it very ill, and is sulking somewhere. He will come back, he will come back.'

'I expect so, yes.' But James was thoughtful as he bent over the paper again. With frequent suggestions from Rennie, he wrote:

EXPEDIENTS!
God Save the King

Pausing again. 'D'y'think God Save the King, sir? Save him from whom? We are not at war.'

'Well well, the King must always be protected. It is a heartening cry, anyway. We must have it.'

'Very good, sir.' He wrote on:

All those gallant & stout hearted
tars that served under
CAPT W. RENNIE RN
in His Majesty's *EXPEDIENT* frigate thirty-six
her First Commission
are urged to rejoin him Without Delay
in her New Commission on Foreign Service
by Repairing to the Rendezvous
at the Cockpit Tavern at PORTSMOUTH
and Presenting themselves to
Lieutenant J. R. HAYTER RN

Huzzay! Huzzay! God Bless *EXPEDIENT*!

Conduct money will be paid.

'I had better take it to the printers at once.' Rolling it up.

'When may I meet your bride, James? I was very sorry to have missed your wedding.'

'We are staying at the White Hart. Will you dine with us there, this evening?'

Rennie found himself greatly taken with Mrs Hayter. Catherine's dark hair, her fine dark eyes, her natural warmth of expression, and her graceful, womanly figure in her low-cut gown made Rennie at first over-gallant. He insisted on taking Catherine into the little parlour—where they were to dine away from the general hubbub of a coaching inn—on his cocked elbow, with a ceremony that seemed to her quite ridiculous, but which she entered into with good grace and a straight face. He then became nearly mute in devotion to her appearance, his eyes fixed on her animated face as she and James talked and laughed and ate and drank. At last, on a point of affable dispute with James she turned and:

'Do you not agree, Captain Rennie? I am in the right?'

'Eh? Yes, certainly. You are right.' Nodding.

'Oh, come now,' James, laughing, 'it is absurd to suggest that boys at sea should be cared for by a governess. An old woman, possibly, boot plain. I have heard of old women in ships.'

'Eh?' Rennie, dragging his eyes from Catherine's face. 'Women afloat? Certainly not.'

'But, Captain Rennie, you have only just now agreed with me.' Catherine smiled, teasing him. 'Are you to be my champion no longer? Why can there be no governess?'

'Well well, it would—it would throw out the balance of the ship.'

'Do you mean that the ship would list to one side, because of the weight of a governess?'

'I meant, I meant—how may I put it?—a young lady in a ship would throw out all the arrangements of daily life, d'y'see. The life of a ship is rigorous, and would not at all suit the sensibilities, or should I say the modesty, of such a young person.'

'Do you mean that the men might cast admiring glances in her direction, Captain Rennie?'

'Well, well—they might.'

'Then I have changed my mind,' said Catherine, turning to James with a playful smile. 'I disapprove entirely of governesses in ships.'

After their dinner Catherine went upstairs to write a letter or two, and James and Rennie were left to their wine.

'By God, you are a lucky fellow, James. Your bride is not only beautiful, she is amiable and engaging and intelligent, altogether a prize.'

'A prize, sir? Like a prize ship, d'y'mean?'

'No no, you know I did not mean that at all. She is quite lovely, and a great asset, is what I meant.'

'I'm glad you approve of Catherine.'

'Oh, good God. Good heaven.' His face anguished, stricken.

James looked at his captain in alarm. 'What has happened? Are you taken ill, sir?'

'No no. No, but I am wracked with guilt. Mortified.'

'Sir?'

'I have forgot to bring you a gift. A wedding gift. I had meant to, particularly had meant to, and it slipped my mind. What must you think of me?'

'Do not, I beg you, think of it again——'

'Not think of it? I must think of it! You are my friend, James, and you have married a most delightful and beautiful girl. How can I neglect my duty? I must make you both a present.'

'Well, sir, if you think so, then I am sure it will make Catherine very happy to accept it, we shall both be very happy.'

'Good. Very good. I shall send it here, at the earliest opportunity. Tomorrow morning.' He lifted his glass. 'And I forgot to make a toast. I had meant——'

There was a rattling at the door, the sound of a deep voice, and another voice, almost bleating in tone. James frowned.

'I made it expressly clear that we was not to be disturbed,' he said, rising. 'It is probably some fellow the worse for drink, that has come to the wrong door——'

The door was now opened, revealing the bowed head of the innkeeper, and behind him a black-clad figure. The innkeeper stood aside, and the black-clad figure came into the parlour. 'Ah, Rennie, I have found you.'

'Sir Robert?' Rennie stood up, startled.

'I must speak to you——' He noticed James. 'Ah. Leave us a moment, will you?'

James stood, but he made no move to quit the room. He was well aware who the visitor was, but felt that, under the circumstances, Sir Robert had behaved ungentlemanlike.

'With respect, Sir Robert, this is a private dinner, and I——'

'Are we acquainted, sir?' Turning his black gaze on James, shrugging off his cape.

'I am Lieutenant Hayter.' A brief, formal little bow.

'Ah, yes, Hayter. You are quite right, we have met, a year or two since. And now, if you will do me the kindness, I need a few moments alone with Captain Rennie.'

James bowed again, and curbed his tongue. He burned to say that as host he did not like to be dismissed like a servant by an uninvited guest, but he curbed his tongue, bowed, and:

'As you wish, Sir Robert.' He nodded to Rennie, and left the table. When the door had shut behind James, Sir Robert sat down at the table and motioned Rennie to sit opposite him, in the chair James had vacated.

'I see there is a third place at this table. Who was the other guest?'

'His wife, Sir Robert. They are newly married.'

'Then it is right he should go upstairs and join her. Newly married couples should be together, and not with older, more cynical men.'

Sir Robert sat back a little in his chair, took a pinch of snuff, and regarded Rennie silently a moment. Then:

'You don't like me, Captain Rennie.' It was not a question.

'I hope that I am always officerlike in our dealings, Sir Robert.' Carefully neutral.

'You don't like me, but I care nothing about that. I am

stone and ice as to what you, or any other officer, might think of me. I have decided to overlook, therefore, what Captain Holland visited upon me aboard the *Zealous*. I had thought that to be private in a naval setting, at sea, would lend weight to what I had to convey to you. I see now that Captain Holland—and perhaps you yourself, as a fellow officer—I see that he thought me presumptuous in dismissing him from his own quarters. He wished to exact punishment.'

Rennie, thoroughly bemused, said nothing. He thought that Sir Robert had been seeking to flatter his own vanity in going out to *Zealous*, and nothing else, and had been brought low by that vanity, but he said nothing.

'He wished to exact punishment—and he did. And I have decided to overlook it.' A black glance. 'For the moment, in least. D'ye know why?'

'Well, I——'

'Because I am not little-minded, Rennie. I care nothing for or about Captain Holland. But you and I, sir, as loyal servants of His Majesty, and the nation, cannot afford to be at loggerheads in that service. You agree?'

'Well, I——'

'You do not agree?' Sharply.

'It is not that I disagree, Sir Robert.' He cleared his throat. 'Perhaps we may both of us have misjudged the other—as to intent.'

'Think you so? I do not know that. However, my *intent*, Captain Rennie, is always to preserve England's well-being. Yours is the same, I think.'

'Just so, Sir Robert. It is my sworn duty.'

'Indeed.' Another long, regarding pause, and: 'Who is this fellow Scott? you have asked yourself. What is the meaning of such a disguise? Alas, I cannot tell you everything, but certainly this much: Scott is a man I become from time to time, here at Portsmouth and in other places, in order to meet certain persons from whom I may gather rumour, speculation, information—and sometimes the truth.'

Emboldened, Rennie ventured: 'Such persons as Captain Langton, Sir Robert?'

'Ah, yes. Langton. I was not certain of Langton, at first.'

'Not certain of him? I assure you, Sir Robert, he is a perfectly honourable——

'Yes, yes, he is a dull fellow, worthy and honourable and dull, and not a single devious nor original thought in his head. Not a spy, in short.'

'A *spy*?'

'There is not an ounce of duplicity in him. He is too dull a man to be capable of such activity, and is therefore above suspicion.'

'I am glad you do not think him a spy.'

Sir Robert took another pinch of snuff, leaned back in his chair and looked into the fire. In a different, quieter tone:

'Have you ever heard of a gentleman, the Reverend Edward Jepp, Captain Rennie?'

'No, sir, I have not.'

'Have you heard of the Secret Service Fund?'

'I have not.' Shaking his head.

'No. That is unsurprising. Why should you have heard of either? However, I may tell you that the fund paid for your ship's first commission, paid for her refit, her manning, provisioning, and scientific instruments, her guns and powder—everything. Paid for her, on your voyage to the Pacifick Ocean, to go out as an experimental ship, an exploring ship, and return a ship full of gold. And that same fund now pays for your second commission, Captain Rennie, to go out to Port Royal.'

'May I ask——' began Rennie, but Sir Robert held up a hand, and continued, all the while staring at the fire:

'I have not forgot the matter of your complaint. Your claim against the Admiralty for what you believe to be your rightful reward. I have not forgot it.'

'You—you said that I would be court-martialled, Sir Robert . . .'

'If you will cease all agitation in your own cause, I have it in my mind to say a word in the right quarter.'

'You mean—withdraw my claim entire?'

'In writing, Captain Rennie.'

'Well, sir, I am not entirely certain——'

'I strongly advise it.'

'Sir Robert, I——'

'I most strongly advise it. The Admiralty wishes it. The fund wishes it. I wish it. Then the question may be addressed quietly, without the hue and cry of open contention.'

'Then I will do as you ask.' He bowed, and: 'You talk of this fund as if it was one man, Sir Robert.'

'In a way that is true. One man controls it, certainly.'

'May I venture to ask—are you that man?'

'I?' Sir Robert turned his gaze from the fire, and looked at Rennie. 'I?'

'Then, if not you—is it perhaps the Reverend Jeffs?'

'Jepp. The Reverend Dr Edward Jepp. And he is not the man, neither.'

'Then who is Dr Jepp? What is his attachment to the fund?'

'He is a cryptographical.'

'Ah. The poor fellow.'

'You find it amusing?'

'Not at all. I am not amused by a man that is crippled, Sir Robert.'

'No no, you have misunderstood. Dr Jepp's work for us—for the fund—is cryptographical analysis.'

'I see—no, I do not, I confess.'

'In little, he is our finest translator of secret codes, enemy codes, which he can discover even in their most innocent and beguiling form. The pages of a charming love letter, as an instance. Or laborious lists of goods upon a bill of lading. A learned scrutiny of the dragonfly. He will find out the code, on all occasions seek and find it.'

'Ah. Like an hog will find a truffle, hey?' Nodding.

'I cannot quite think of Dr Jepp as a pig—he is a very

fastidious man—but the parallel is accurate.'

'Am I to meet him, Sir Robert?'

'In due course. When it is time. For now I will say only this: letters have been intercepted, and translated by Dr Jepp, which indicate to me—to the fund—that such an assault as we have previously discussed, or had begun to discuss, aboard Captain Holland's ship, may already be planning.'

'May I ask—by whom?'

'I cannot tell you that, Rennie.'

'Forgive me, Sir Robert, but if I am to conduct this commission to my greatest capacity, and carry out my instructions, will it not be sensible for me to know as many of the true particulars as may assist me, from the beginning?'

'Sensible? True?' The black gaze became hard, and cold. 'You do not think all I have said to you in this interview sensible and true, sir? You think I would confine myself to trifling and inconsiderable things in these questions?'

'I beg your pardon, Sir Robert.'

'In due course you shall know—a great deal more than at present. That is all I am prepared to vouchsafe to you tonight.' He pushed back his chair, rose, and lifted his cape. 'By the by, I have obliged Captain Langton, and Captain Holland, and your friend Admiral Bailey, to be quiet.'

'To be quiet? They know nothing, I assure you, Sir Rob——'

'They was all at that little dinner you gave at the Marine Hotel, was they not? And they all know about Mr Scott. Each man has been interviewed, and required to be silent, and has agreed. I do not need to iterate that requirement to you—do I?'

Sir Robert fastened his cape, took up his cane, and was gone.

'I can scarcely believe he was ever Giss, the fellow,' murmured Rennie to himself in the firelit silence. 'It just don't seem possible.'

The recruiting poster had produced many applicants—there were great numbers of seamen everywhere in the peace, without employment—but most of them were not men who had served in the ship her first commission, they were not Expedients. Rennie had instructed his first lieutenant to accept into the books only those men who were.

'I have served in frigates, sir, the last war.' An open-faced able seaman, in his late twenties.

'But you have never served in *Expedient*.' James, looking at his papers.

'No, sir, but I am rated able, I am a topman that knows frigates, sir.' And he named three ships, *Penelope*, *Success*, and *Lynx*—the last a thirty-six.

James looked at his earnest, nearly desperate face, saw him as an honest man, very probably an excellent man—and was obliged to refuse him. The dejection and resignation in the young man's face were like an accusation, and James had to harden his heart. There were many such applicants, and even one or two who attempted to deceive their way into a berth:

'You remember me, sir . . .'

'I don't, I fear. You are an Expedient?'

'Aye, sir.' Handing over his papers. 'Foster, sir, afterguard, rated ordinary.' The fingers touching the brow. The name accorded with James's list, and now he recalled Foster—not the man who stood before him. These were Foster's papers, sold on, or pawned, and now in the hands of another man altogether.

'What was our first port of call, Foster?'

'Why—why, it was Gibraltar, sir.'

'And our second?'

'Rio de Jannero.'

'We called at neither place. You are not Foster, even if these papers are his. How did you come by them, hey?'

The impostor snatched up the papers with a curse, and dodged away into the street. James sighed in exasperation. He could only hope that at least some of the original Expedients would find their way to the Cockpit Tavern, and the corner table where he set himself up each day at noon to wait. He had written to Norfolk, to the former captain's clerk, Alan Dobie. He had left word at the Haslar Hospital, on Gosport side, for Thomas Wing—Wing who had acted as the ship's surgeon after the death of Admiral Hollister's man. Word had come from the Admiralty that Tom Makepeace would rejoin as second, and that *Expedient*'s third was to be Lieutenant Richard Peak RN.

'Don't know Peak,' said Rennie later, at the dockyard. 'Never heard of him.'

'Nor have I, sir.'

'What is his background? What was his last ship?'

James glanced at the official communication, with the broad seal. 'Not mentioned, sir.'

'Well well, I hope that he will not be a living replication of Mr Royce. God spare us that.'

Lieutenant Royce had been his third in the ship's first commission, and had caused Rennie endless trouble by his arrogant, clumsy and inept interpretation of his duties.

'Royce was a poor officer, yes, but did not he——'

'Did not he lose his life in attempting to protect my own? He did, and I must not speak ill of him now, since at the end he was very brave, very courageous—but he was a damned young fool, all the same.' Rennie sniffed, drank from a can of tea, and:

'What do we hear of Gurrall? Has he come?'

'No, sir.'

'We must hope that word reaches him. His home is Portsmouth?'

'Yes, sir. He may perhaps have gone into a merchant ship. Such a valuable man would find no trouble in getting himself a berth. Many able men have gone to the Company, after all.'

'Aye, and we cannot blame them, James. Neither them, nor John Company, for taking up man-of-wars' men. The Royal Navy don't nurture seamen in the peace, only in war.'

*

Another summons came from Sir Robert Greer, this time from Kingshill House. Rennie went there in the carriage sent for him.

Sir Robert greeted him in the library, a long tall room in the east wing of the house. A beautiful wide window at the far end overlooked a gentle green sloping sward and an ornamental lake. Tall shelves of leather-bound books lined the side walls, and there was a library step-ladder with a handrail. Urns and busts stood along the tops of the shelves. The curtains, and the walls, were a deep, restful green. Rennie glanced round as he came into this splendid room, and noticed portraits—on either side of the double door—portraits by Reynolds of the late Lord Kenton and his beautiful widow. Sir Robert rose from a wide pedestal desk, which stood on a fine woven Smyrna rug of a red, blue and gold pattern. A wheel barometer behind the desk stood at Fair, Rennie noted from habit. Sir Robert's white stockings contrasted with his black britches and coat, and his black, gleaming, silver-buckled shoes. He shook Rennie's hand, a gesture he had never employed in the past. His hand was, on this mild day, quite cold.

'That poster of yours, Rennie. How many men have you taken in with it?'

'How many men have I deceived?' Taken aback.

'No no, signed on your books?' And before Rennie could answer: 'Remove the poster, will you? At once? Send a man round to all the places where it is displayed, and tear it down. You do not need it. Your books will be filled.'

'With Expedients?'

'Certainly, with expediency.'

'I meant, with men from my ship's first commission. It is customary in the Royal Navy to call a ship's complement after the ship's name.'

'Yes, it was my attempt at a little joke.' Drily. 'I have not seen the poster. My attention was called to it by a report. As I said, Rennie, you do not need such an advertisement. Men will be found in your behalf.'

'Sir Robert, I will like to have in my ship as many of those men that have served with me in the past as may be possible. Loyal Expedients, men I know and trust.'

'You lost a good many of those men, did you not?'

'I did, and I regret it, but it could not be helped. On long foreign service, where great dangers are faced, losing men is the price a captain and the navy must pay.' A hint of acerbity.

'No no, I do not mean to apportion blame. But because so many men was lost, they must of necessity be replaced by new men. You cannot recruit from the dead, hey?' And he smiled coldly. 'We can find them for you, without posters. The others—your surviving crew—will also be found. And it will be better in future, Captain Rennie, that you come to me first with these little exigencies. The fund, you know, prefers to do these things quietly.'

'There is a particular man, he was captain of the maintop, that I am trying to find now, Sir Robert. He could greatly assist us—myself and the fund—in filling the ship's books with good men, both Expedients and others of his acquaintance. He is one of the best petty officers ever served with me. Men follow him naturally, and respect his word.'

'What is his name?'

'Gurrall. Jacob Gurrall.'

Sir Robert returned to the desk and made a note. 'Then he shall be found, your captain of the mainstay, you have my word.' Putting aside his pen. 'A glass of something, Rennie?'

'Thank you, I should very much like tea.'

'Tea? Nothing stronger?'

'Wine is not always my preference, Sir Robert. I am an inveterate tea drinker. It refreshes the mouth, stimulates the brain, and lifts the heart.'

'Ah, does it? I find coffee preferable. I prefer the darker, deeper taste.' He rang a table bell. 'We shall have both.'

The news came to Rennie and his first lieutenant while they were taking possession of *Expedient* for the first time in her newly refitted condition. Rennie had gone into the great cabin, opening the door to a great waft of paint, to inspect the work carried out on what would soon again be his home. James was standing in the waist, at the open main hatch, staring down into the bowels of the ship. A boat came alongside with a heavy bump, uncaring of new paintwork, and a man darted up the ladder. He was not a seaman, nor did he have the appearance of an artificer. He looked like a slightly shabby professional man, perhaps a clerk.

'Where is Captain Rennie?'

'Who are you, sir?'

'I am come from the Haslar. For God's sake, now, where is the captain? Quickly!'

James saw that he was agitated in earnest, with a hint of desperation in his voice, and bit back the rebuke that rose on his tongue. 'Come with me.' And he led him aft to the great cabin.

Rennie was critically examining the panes of the stern gallery windows, making certain of the exactitude of the fitting in the not quite vertical central frame, bending forward, peering.

'Sir! This gentleman has come on urgent business from the Haslar Hospital.'

'The Haslar?' Startled, turning. 'Have we found Mr Wing?'

'Captain Rennie, you must come with me at once!'

'Go with you? What the devil d'y'mean? Who is this fellow, Mr Hayter?'

They went to Gosport in the boat, rowed by two ferrymen, and from the wharf to the Haslar Hospital in an open carriage. The messenger was indeed a clerk, a registrar's clerk at the hospital, sent to fetch Rennie to Admiral Bailey's side. The admiral had been visiting an elderly seaman who had served in his ship during the Seven Years War, and had there himself been taken ill. It was thought by Dr Stroud and colleagues, the clerk had explained in the boat, that the admiral would not live another day. He had something he wished urgently to say to Captain Rennie, had insisted on Rennie's coming to him, before it was too late.

The admiral had been carried to an upper room, with a window opening on a view of the sea, a private room, and was lying on a cot there, deathly pale. The attendants had removed his clothes, and put him in a plain white nightshirt. Rennie was greatly saddened by the fragile appearance of his old friend, and knew at once by his sunken cheek and shallow, bird-chested breathing that he was certainly dying. The old man's eye brightened as Rennie came to the bed.

'Thank God you have come'—a huffling breath—'come in time. There is something I must tell you.'

'I am very sorry that you are ill, Admiral.'

'Bring the chair. Sit close.' His hands, lying on the white coverlet, were blotched and shrivelled, the fingernails tinged blue. Rennie pulled the single chair and sat down, leaning forward. He smelled stale, sour breath. 'Are we alone?'

'Yes, sir, we are alone.'

'Good. Good.' A sighing, catching breath. 'There is something I want to say to you about that fellow Greer.'

'I am here.'

'Do not trust him.'

'Well, you know,'—gently—'I did not trust him, at first. However, I have come to view him as——'

The admiral lifted his hand, and clawed at Rennie's sleeve, and turned his head painfully and slowly to look Rennie in the eye. With the last of his strength he tried to be fierce:

'Do *not* be deceived—hhh—by his blandishments. Do not *trust* him. He is a demon.'

'A demon, you think? Naturally I am anxious to hear whatever you wish to tell me, sir, but do you really——'

'No, no, *no*—hhh—he is duplicity itself. He is incapable of anything—but deceit. You must not allow him to—escape. Pursue him—but for God's sake—beware—beware . . .'

The hand slipped from Rennie's coat sleeve, and fell limp on the coverlet.

'Sir? Admiral?' Rennie took up the hand, and felt there at the wrist. There was no pulse. Rennie held his open hand to the open mouth. There was no whisper of breath upon his palm. He sighed, and turned from the bed.

'Doctor? Dr Stroud?'

Footsteps in the corridor. Rennie went slowly to the open window, and looked out at the sea, his heart full, and his head echoing with those last breathed, taxing words.

The admiral's sister Alice Bailey had been sent for, but was too frail herself to make even the short journey from Kingshill to Gosport, and Rennie was relieved. Doctors in course were used to such things, but Rennie was relieved that he did not have to face her, and mouth the expected sentiments and untruths about a peaceful, untroubled death, &c., &c. That he did not have to comfort and console when his mind was so distracted. His relief was short-lived.

'Where shall we send his things, his effects?' the registrar's clerk inquired, as Rennie prepared to leave.

'Effects? Surely his dunnage is at his sister's house, at Kingshill.'

'His pocket watch, his snuffbox, his signet ring—his money.'

'Ah, personal things, yes. Well, if you like I will take them to his sister. It ain't strictly my business, you know, but if it will save her the inconvenience of claiming them herself, I am willing.'

'Just, yes, if you will sign the personal effects book, sir—here at the bottom of the page, and the date, today's date.'

Rennie signed, the pen slipped in the well, and his fingers were steeped in black ink. 'What are the arrangements for burial?'

'Well, sir, I expect that his next of kin will be informed, as to that. His sister. That is the usual.'

'Very good. I should like to attend, myself.' And he gave the address of his lodgings in Portsmouth to the clerk, took up the items and made his way outside into the air. The smell of the sea came on the wind, the eternal smell of his chosen element, and Admiral Bailey's, and all that race of men whose lives are drawn there.

'Captain Rennie?' Dr Stroud, coming down the steps after him.

'Stroud, I do beg your pardon, I had meant to say goodbye to you——'

'I hear that you go to the admiral's sister. I am glad. It is better such news should come from his friend, rather than an official.' A pause. 'You wished to find Thomas Wing, did you not?'

'I did, yes. I do. I want him as my surgeon.'

'Then you will be pleased to hear that he has got his warrant from the Sick and Hurt, and is now on his way to join you.'

'I am pleased. I am very pleased indeed.'

'It is a great pity I cannot have him here with me, I wanted him to return, but the sea is in his veins now, I think.'

'Aye, it is a powerful drug, the sea. Hey, Doctor?' They shook hands. Rennie knew how sincerely Dr Stroud had valued his young disciple Thomas Wing, who had come into *Expedient* here at Portsmouth two years ago; he knew in addition that Wing had wished always to go to sea, and to return to it as soon as he might, when *Expedient* was again commissioned.

In returning to *Expedient*'s mooring through the traffic of the waterway—hoys, wherries, lighters—to the clamouring cries of herring gulls, with the towers and fortifications to the east, and the spires of cathedral and church beyond, Rennie was thoughtful and troubled, unseeing and unhearing in the stern sheets of the boat. The ferryman steered north to the dockyard, past the stench of the Point, and Rennie scarcely noticed their progress. It was not until the boat nudged in that Rennie was aware of the sheer hulk alongside *Expedient*. The ship's masts were being got into her, the great ringed trunk of the foremast hoisting in the sheer tackles. Rennie roused himself from his reverie, and became again a sea officer with duties, jumped on to the cleated side-ladder on the lift, and up into his ship.

He met James in the waist, dressed in his working clothes. Rennie had never wholly approved of these clothes, which in his opinion gave to James a roguish, buccaneering, piratical appearance quite unsuited to an officer serving His Majesty; but he felt unable to reprimand his lieutenant, who was always a vigorous and resourceful officer, and had worked miracles at Deptford their first commission in getting the dockyard officers and artificers alike to make *Expedient* ready for the sea—wearing this same corsair's costume.

'Do you mean to live aboard now, sir?'

'Eh? I had not thought——'

'It is only that if you was intent on it, I should alike be obliged to live in the ship myself, and——'

'And in course you do not wish to abandon Catherine at the White Hart. Never think of that, James. We will continue to live ashore for the present. That damned stink of paint in the cabin gives me a headache.'

'Thank you, sir. I had hoped that would be your decision.'

'What is your estimation of the ship's condition, her present condition?'

They went forrard to inspect the work in progress there, and then below. By now, in the ordinary way, hands would have been aboard, assisting the dockyard men. Rennie had no hands as yet, aside from the few landmen servants and boys who were berthed in the ship to aid the standing officers. The carpenter Mr Adgett, the boatswain Roman Tangible, the gunner Mr Storey, and the purser Mr

Trent were all obliged to remain aboard now that she was refloated.

Mr Trent was very busy, very stout and puffing as he made his way from storeroom to slop chest and up the companion ladder. Coming on him Captain Rennie said:

'By God, Mr Trent, you are very red in the face. Is it wine, or only bursting good health?'

'It is neither, sir. It is work, effortful work.'

'Very good, very good. I will like to see your books presently, when you have been able to get back your breath.'

'Today, sir?' Harassed.

'Well well, perhaps not today. I must go ashore.' Turning to James: 'May I leave everything in your capable hands, James? I must go ashore while it is still daylight, and call on the admiral's poor sister. I said to Stroud I would convey the news to her. And afterward, I shall need cheering and lifting and so forth—will you and Catherine have supper with me at the Marine Hotel?'

'We shall be delighted.'

'Eight o'clock, then.' And he went ashore.

Rennie engaged a private parlour for his supper at the Marine Hotel, and hired a gig from the ostler in the yard behind. He drove to Kingshill from the crowded High and along the Cambridge Road in a heavy shower of rain, which came down in a long drenching curtain from Portsdown Hill. Thus he was made wet in addition to his already downcast condition. He did not like this duty. He had not wished it—in fact, dreaded it—but felt he must oblige Dr Stroud, who had aided him in the past; also that he must perform this last kindness for his late friend, and bring the news of his passing to his only surviving relation.

Miss Alice Bailey's cottage was at the edge of the village, not far from the gate of Kingshill House. It was small, with a thatched roof, not one of a terrace but a separate dwelling, with trees behind and a garden with a fence. Miss Bailey was very old, older than her late brother, and was now nearly infirm, but she held her back straight, so that although she was small she contrived to be taller.

'He is dead?'

'I am afraid so. I am very sorry, Miss Bailey.'

She sighed, sagged a little under her lace cap and shawl, her hand on the back of a chair to steady herself. Rennie reached out a hand.

'It was very kind in you, Captain Rennie, to come all this way in the rain, when you could so easily have sent a message.'

'I thought it right to come, Miss Bailey.'

'Will you sit down by the fire, and warm yourself?'

'I should not wish to impose at such a moment.'

'Tss, tss, you do not impose, he was your friend. In truth, Captain Rennie, I was expecting something to happen. I knew something would happen. He was ill, had been ill I think for some little time. He tried to keep it from me, tried to conceal it, but I was not deceived. His appetite had gone. Poor Harry.' She sighed, and sank into her chair by the fire, in that small stuffy room with its careful ornaments, and fire-screens, and faded needlework rug. Blue curtains shut out the daylight, and candles had already been lit. Her serving maid—nearly as old as her mistress—brought tea.

Gratefully, Rennie drank two cups. Miss Bailey sipped at hers, then put the cup aside.

'I must tell you something, Captain Rennie. You was Harry's friend, he often spoke of you, spoke fondly of you.'

'I shall feel his loss very deep.' Truthfully.

'I must tell you that Sir Robert Greer, who has taken Lady Kenton's house, is not the man he pretends to be.'

'Indeed, your brother——' then checking himself: 'Admiral Bailey was of the same view, the same opinion. He thought that Sir Robert was, well, not quite an honourable fellow.'

'Not quite honourable! He is a very sinister man, Captain Rennie. My brother told me that you had been obliged to involve yourself with Sir Robert's dealings. He wished to warn you, but did not quite apprehend how he might, without offence. Now that he has gone, I feel that I must warn you myself.'

Rennie did not like to say that her brother had indeed been warning him about Sir Robert at the moment of his death. Instead, he said:

'Please do not trouble yourself, Miss Bailey. I am well aware of Sir Robert's shortcomings, I assure you. He is——'

'I do not think you can be, Captain Rennie, else you would already have entirely disengaged yourself from all his works.'

Rennie was bemused. He was very damp, he was performing a difficult duty, and he did not wish to be put out of temper by disagreement with a frail old gentlewoman. He nodded politely, drank a last mouthful of tea, and rose.

'I will like, if you will permit it, Miss Bailey, to attend the service.'

'Service?'

'The burial service for Admiral Bailey.'

'Yes. Oh. I expect that must be arranged. I had not yet brought myself to——'

'If you would like, I am willing to make such necessary arrangements with the hospital, your local clergyman, and so forth.' It was a rash offer, but Rennie felt better able to cope with such a burden than with further disputation about Sir Robert Greer.

'No, Captain Rennie, you have already been more than kind. When the arrangements have been made, I shall send word to you. Oh, but I do not know your address.'

Rennie gave it to her, and took up his hat, his still very wet hat, relieved not to have to bear a burden after all, and was about to take his leave, when:

'But, but, my dear sir, you have not heard me out.' And Miss Bailey beckoned him back to the fire. 'My brother had come into possession very recent of certain information about Sir Robert.'

Rennie reluctantly again sat down in the chair opposite Miss Bailey, and put aside his hat.

'You know that he lives at Kingshill House?' she continued.

'Indeed, I have been there myself.'

'Was you aware that he had acquired that house?'

'Acquired it? Does not Lady Kenton own Kingshill?'

'She did. Until a year ago she did own it. It came to her when she was widowed in the year '83. Sometimes, after Lord Kenton died, she lived at Edinburgh in Scotland, her birthplace, and the house was empty months together. Then Sir Robert Greer took a short lease on the property, and he came there occasionally, with guests from London. Well. Well. He then contrived to meet Lady Kenton frequently when she came to London from Edinburgh for the season, and he was able—I do not know how, since she was a Scotchwoman and very astute—he was able to persuade her to invest in a plantation in the West Indies, a sugar plantation, which enterprise very soon, shocking soon, drained every shilling of her fortune, and she was ruined. By devious means, preying upon the unfortunate lady in her predicament, a predicament for which he was in least partly responsible, Sir Robert persuaded her to part with Kingshill for a trifle of its worth, and the money—2,000 pound—was at once swallowed up by her debts, and fees to lawyers and the like. She is now reduced to living in rooms at Edinburgh, in penury, and Sir Robert refuses to communicate with her. Nor would he see her in London when she went there to plead with him to aid her. He has cut off all connection. The poor woman is very wretched, but he will do nothing for her.'

Rennie was silent a moment, grave and silent, then: 'Miss Bailey, what you tell me is indeed distressing. Greatly distressing, for Lady Kenton. She is your friend?'

'No, she is not. We did not move in the same circle at all. But she is a lady in great need, without a champion. It was my brother learned all about it, just in these last weeks. He had it from his connections in London.'

'At the Admiralty?'

'It was the Navy Board, I believe.'

Rennie nodded. Admiral Bailey had been given, when he retired to Deal, a sinecure there as inspector of naval stores, which brought him an hundred a year from the board: Officer of the Keys.

'Aye, the board. Well well, it is very distressing to hear of it. However I do not see, Miss Bailey, what I myself can do to aid Lady Kenton.'

'You cannot aid her, I think—except in one thing. What you must do is break all connection with Sir Robert, and expose him.'

'Expose him!'

'My brother thought so, he wished to do it himself, with your help, since his acquaintance at the board would do nothing. But now that he is dead the task must fall to you alone, Captain Rennie. I know that you are an honourable man.'

Captain Rennie sat in his hip bath, in the grateful warmth of a coal fire and of hot water on his naked body, allowing that warmth to dissipate the oppressive chill of the afternoon, and ease his mind. He reached and poured the last of the hot water from the ewer, and sighed as it sluiced over him. Steam rose and there was the restful lulling sound of languid drops and driplings as he lifted the sponge to his neck and shoulders.

It had been a most testing and difficult day. A saddening day, and his visit to the admiral's sister had ended in dismay—dismay and consternation. How could he possibly accommodate her wish that he should attack Sir Robert Greer, and expose him for a scoundrel? Sir Robert was far too powerful a man to allow himself to be bested by a mere post captain

RN, a post captain moreover that was entirely dependent on Sir Robert's good intentions, through the Secret Service Fund. And even if he took it upon himself, in a burst of rashness, to attempt to wound Sir Robert, how could he prove anything against him?

'I know nothing of investments,' said Rennie to himself, 'and plantations, and grand houses. I have never met Lady Kenton. Supposing she has fabricated the entire thing, and Sir Robert is innocent of any wrongdoing. A damned fool I should look, charging at him, sword drawn, on the word of a person I do not know. Do not know, and do not wish to champion, good God.'

He scrubbed at the black inkstains, stubborn on his fingers, staining the minute cracks in the skin. And abruptly remembered, and cursed, dropping the scrubbing brush:

'Hell and fire, I did not give her the admiral's things! His snuffbox and ring! What a damned fool I am. Now I must return with them tomorrow, and listen again to her wild accusations. Damn and blast!' He smashed at the water with his fist, and glittering droplets flew across the room to hiss into steam at the grate.

At supper Rennie told the story of his visit to Miss Bailey to James while Catherine was out of the room, swearing him to secrecy, and asking his opinion as to the proper course of action:

'Shall I put my helm up and bear away, James? Or must I run straight at him, and open fire as soon as I am in range?'

'I should stand off a little, and wait.'

'My sentiments, exact. Do nothing.'

Catherine returned, looking slightly pale in the candlelight.

'My darling.' James, anxiously, half-rising. 'Are you quite well?'

Catherine sat down. 'It is nothing. It was the rabbit, I think. Perhaps the sauce, a little rich.'

'I am sorry for that,' said Rennie. 'These damned hotels, you know, pretend that their cooks are the best in the world, Frenchified and so forth, smothering everything in glutinous rich sauces, when all the time it is simple dishes we want. Juicy roasted meats, plenty of roasted potatoes, steamed plum pudding, and good, flavourful English cheeses——'

'Oh dear——' Catherine rose hurriedly from the table, and hurriedly left the room.

'I am sorry if the supper has made Catherine ill, James. I had thought that rabbit would be a good beginning. I shall certainly complain to the——'

'Do not think of it, sir. It is not—it was not the supper.'

'Oh. Ah. Perhaps she has caught a chill. I am very sorry.' Discomfited, glancing at the closed door.

'It is not a chill neither, I think.'

'Ah. Mm.' Rennie was unconvinced that it was not the food to blame. He had gone to some little trouble in ordering their supper in advance, and selecting the best wines the Marine Hotel could find in its cellar, and engaging a pleasant little private dining room. He had wished to lift himself, after his lowering day, in the company of friends. That Catherine was now made unwell by reason of his efforts was a most unhappy conclusion to the evening.

'It is not the supper, please do not think that,' repeated James. He sat back in his chair. 'As to doing nothing at all about Sir Robert Greer, I had not meant quite that, sir. My sense is that you should take no action at present, but that when you are able to know all the particulars, you must pass them to others.'

'Pass them to others!'

'Aye, sir. In little, you are a single ship in this, a private ship. What is needed in this case is a careful plan, and a fleet action. A line-of-battle sea action, with the advantage of the wind gauge, to run down the enemy flag, rake his stern, and smash and destroy him.'

'Yes. Yes, you are right, James. I had not seen it in that

example, a fleet action, but you are right. I must assemble my ships first, hey?'

Catherine now returned, paler still, and attempted to smile.

'I must take you home,' said James at once, rising. 'The fresh air will do you good, it will revive you as soon as we are outside.' Turning to Rennie. 'Thank you, sir, for a most pleasant and enjoyable evening, very jolly. I am sorry we must leave you so soon, but as you see——'

'No no no, James, you must look after Catherine. Goodnight, my dear. I do hope that you——'

But they were already out the door, James throwing a cloak about his wife's shoulders.

'Damn that cook,' said Rennie to the wall. 'The showing-off villain.' And he poured himself a bumper of claret from the decanter, and drank deep.

'I should like to give these things to Miss Bailey myself,' said Rennie to that lady's maidservant. Again he had come to the cottage in a hired gig, in the morning, a bright, clear, fresh morning, and now here he stood at the door with the admiral's watch and other effects in his hand, ready to counter anything his sister might say about Sir Robert Greer with a reassuring smile and stout, bluff, uncommitting phrases.

'The mistress is unwell, sir. She has taken to her bed.'

'Oh, I am very sorry to hear it.' Greatly relieved. He composed his face into a properly grave expression. 'Will you convey to her my kindest wishes for her rapid recovery?' He gave the watch and ring and snuffbox to the maidservant. 'Please to give them to her. Her brother's effects.'

'Well, sir, she is asleep at present. I shall leave them on her side-table.'

'Very good. Tell her—well, just say that I called.' And he went down the short path to the gate, and got into the gig. With any luck that would be the last he would hear of her crusade against Sir Robert, so that his fleet action could remain a theoretical fancy, and nothing at all need be done.

A ferryman brought to *Expedient* at her mooring a diminutive figure, which climbed the gangway ladder with more certainty and agility than a mere boy, and came into the ship. Captain Rennie was more than happy to receive that figure in the great cabin, and to peruse the freshly written warrant he produced from his new blue coat.

'Mr Wing, how glad I am you have come. Doctor, I should say. A glass of wine?'

'Sir, I think you will recall—I do not take wine.'

'I am a damn fool to have forgot. Tea, then?' He poured tea for them both. 'You have seen Dr Stroud?'

'No, sir, not yet. I have wrote to him, when I was in London. I wrote to you, sir, also.'

'Did you? Did you? No letter came.' Puzzled. 'In fact I have expected daily to hear from Mr Dobie—you remember our schoolmaster?—and nothing has come from him, neither. The first lieutenant wrote to him, on my instruction, but there has been no reply.'

'Is Lieutenant Hayter well, sir?'

'He is excellent well, doctor, he has just got married. A very beautiful bride, I may say. They are a fortunate couple.'

'If he is newly married will he not wish to remain behind then, Captain Rennie? Surely he will not wish to come with us in the ship, and leave his bride alone?'

'Good God, Doctor, he cannot stay behind just because he is married, you know. Marriage confers on sea officers no particular benefit nor advantage. They must do their duty, and it cannot be helped if they pine a little, and their wives pine, hey?'

'Is there no provision made for it, in the navy? Could not quarters be fashioned or found in a ship, for wives?'

'Married quarters afloat? Well well, I have heard of it for captains, sometimes; rarely enough. I suppose they have got the privacy of the great cabin, after all, sleeping cabin, coach, and so forth. But for lieutenants, in the gunroom? Certainly not.'

'No, I suppose not.—You have never been married yourself, sir?'

'No no, I have not.' Brusquely. 'Is your dunnage aboard, Doctor?'

'I have left it in the safe keeping of the inn at Broad Street. The Drawbridge Inn.'

'You left your things there?' Appalled. 'Christ's blood, Mr Wing, that was muddle-headed! That is the most notorious damned den of wretches in Christendom. You must get your dunnage out of there at once. Your medical chest is there?'

'All of my things, but never fear. I know the Drawbridge well, you see. When I was at the Haslar I tended to many seamen that was wounded in brawls there, and came to know the proprietor, one Sawley Mallison. He looks very fierce, but in truth he is only play-acting, to preserve his person from injury and subdue his more boisterous customers, his clients.'

'Clients! That bilge-dwelling barbarian rabble? Swilling his poisonous gin? Christ in tears.'

'I am in no doubt, sir, that my things are safer in his hands than anywhere else in Portsmouth. He is my friend.'

'Then I must not malign him in your presence, I suppose. However, the sooner your things may be got into the ship the better, Doctor, the sooner the better. We go to the West Indies, where there is fever, you know, and you will need all of your drugs and potions, all of your physic and pills.'

Thomas Wing's sea chest and hanging cot, and his medical chest, were duly brought from the Drawbridge Inn to a boat, and brought in the boat to *Expedient*. As the boat was rowed away another boat approached, and in it came a thin young man in a green coat, and a large collection of books. Rennie, standing at the break of the quarterdeck, saw this young man's head appear at the gangway as he climbed—unsteadily climbed—into the ship, his shoes slipping on the ladder cleats.

'Mr Dobie?'

Alan Dobie stumbled on the gangway, and approached. 'As you see, Captain Rennie, I am come.'

'You had the letter, after all? I had almost given you up. Why did you not reply, Mr Dobie?'

'I did reply, sir, as soon as I received your very kind offer to rejoin the ship.'

'Well well, no matter. You are here, and very welcome too. By God, are all those books yours?' Peering as dozens of volumes, bound up in leather straps, were hauled up and into the waist by a ship's boy, who then with the help of the boatman and an artificer brought up the rest of Alan's dunnage by parbuckling ropes.

'Well, yes. I have been attempting to make a study of navigation, and have acquired also a great many other texts, if I am still to be schoolmaster. I hope that is so, I understood that it was so.'

'Navigation, Mr Dobie?' said Rennie as he took Alan into the great cabin. 'Navigation?'

'I understand that under the regulations a schoolmaster in the navy is required to teach it, sir.' Stepping neatly round a pile of timber and pots, and at once stumbling over a case of wine.

'We are yet refitting, Mr Dobie, as you see. I am having lockers added, and so forth. Racks and lockers. You will need a warrant to teach middies navigation, you know. You have not got a warrant, I think.'

'I have not. Only books.'

'It is of no consequence, Mr Dobie. I will like you to undertake the same duties as our first commission, and the master and Mr Hayter will take care of navigation. It is as my clerk I am most in need of your services.' Indicating papers scattered across his desk and table. 'We must get to work as soon as may be possible. You are well?'

'I am, sir, thank you.' A little deflated, hiding it.

'Very good. Then let us make a start.'

The time had come. James knew it and was downhearted, but endeavoured to be cheerful with Catherine, so that she would not be discouraged. The time had come for her to depart the White Hart and go home, and for James to go into *Expedient*. Catherine was no longer ill, but a change had occurred in her, a change of which she was aware but not quite consciously certain. This confusion of feeling was not lost on James.

'Are you sure you are well enough to make the journey?' Dressing.

'I am in perfect health.' Glancing at herself in her glass.

'I think perhaps you should go to Melton, rather than Birch Cottage.'

'James, I shall go to Melton soon, but for the present I shall go home to Winterborne. The house is empty, except for Tabitha, and there are things to be arranged, and completed. Furniture, linen, and——'

'Yes, empty is the word I don't like. You go home to an empty house, in your present condition, and——'

'What on earth can you mean, James? My present condition?'

'Well, I—I had assumed, because you had been ill, and are now a little changed——'

'Changed? How am I changed?' Turning to look over her shoulder. 'I am the same.'

'I think you are not.' Gently, turning her round, taking her hands in his. 'You have married a plain-speaking sea officer, who must speak plain. I think you are with child.'

'Oh.' Looking at him, then away, distracted. A moment, then: 'Yes, I think you are right, James. I think you must be right.'

'You must see a physician, when you arrive at Melton. My

mother's doctor there. You should be cared for in a proper household, where every precaution may be taken.'

'Precaution, James?' Smiling at him. 'I am perfectly all right, I have already told you. In very good health. I shall not go tumbling down hills nor climbing trees at Winterborne, neither.'

'My darling, I will like you to be at Melton at first. Perhaps for the whole time, if Dr Hall thinks so.'

'And leave Birch Cottage empty? What will become of poor Tabitha?'

Tabitha had been her father's housekeeper at Shaftesbury, and had come to Winterborne when Catherine became mistress of her own house.

'Bring her to Melton with you. There is plenty of room in the house.'

The arrangement was made, and soon after Catherine left to go to Dorset, with great sorrow in her heart at their parting, but a brave smile on her face. James tried to smile, but it faltered on his lips and he clasped her to him, his dearest love, and held her a long moment.

James shifted his dunnage from the White Hart into *Expedient*, to his newly refurbished cabin, and became again a sailor in a floating world.

Having been a nearly empty ship for all of her repairing and refit, *Expedient* began to fill quite rapidly. Great numbers of men appeared, none of whom had served in the ship her first commission, but all of whom were sober, and their papers in correct order. In addition each man was able to present a signed chit, issued by the Port Admiral's office, saying that he was recommended to serve in *Expedient*. Jacob Gurrall was not among them.

'Well well, it seems we must weigh without him,' said Rennie to James. 'We must rate all these new hands, and I don't know a single one of them. They have been foisted on me by the Admiralty, and no followers allowed to me. I have not seen Mr Peak, and I have not heard anything of Mr Loftus, neither. Where are my mids, hey? And where is Mr Makepeace, for the love of Christ, that was due here weeks since?'

'Tom Makepeace had some family business to attend to at Cambridge, sir. I think I told you of it. His father was entangled in a legal dispute, and had been threatened with eviction if he did not settle, or something of that sort. Tom thought it was his obligation to——'

'Damnation to his thoughts, Mr Hayter!' Harassed and severe. 'His obligation is to his King and his commission! He had better present himself right quick, or know the consequence!'

'Very well, sir. I will see what may be done to get into touch with him——'

'Mr Dobie!'

'Sir?'

'Pen? Paper?'

'I am ready, sir.' Pen poised.

'Dictate your letter, Mr Hayter, and make it plain to Mr Makepeace that if he don't get his arse into my ship within the week, his arse—and the rest of him too—will be left behind in England!' And the captain stamped aft, kicked a rope, found fault with a tackle block, glared into the rigging and shouted for his steward to bring him a can of tea.

'The captain is very fierce today,' murmured Alan Dobie when James had finished dictating the letter.

'He is hard pressed. We are to get our final instructions at any moment, and we are not ready.'

'Will he sail without the other officers, d'y'think? Without the midshipmen I am supposed to teach?'

'I hope not, Alan, else I shall be taking all the watches myself, and never get a moment's rest.'

The ship was crowded round by victualling craft, boats

full of great casks of meat, and beer, and water. Mr Trent, permanently red in the face, puffed and sighed and heaved himself up and down ladders, lists in his hand. James was busy with divisions, quarters, stations, watches. Slops were issued, mess numbers allocated, hammock numbers, gun-crew numbers. The ship began to fall into a steady routine as the last of the running rigging was rove up under Roman Tangible's fussy supervision, her sail lockers filled, her rope and cable taken in, her twine, Swedes tar and paint stowed.

'I cannot wait another day without a master in my complement,' fretted Rennie. 'She must be trimmed. Our guns are to be got in, and our powder, and she must be trimmed.'

Very late on that same day, rowed out to the ship by a ferryman, Mr Loftus made his appearance. He had been, when Rennie last saw him, a strong, well-made man with an open, pleasant face and a quietly competent manner and bearing. The man who now came to the great cabin and presented himself was unrecognisable to the captain, at first. His hair had begun to go grey at the temples, his cheeks were hollow, and his eyes had a flat, diminished look. His coat hung loose on him, and his britches, and he looked nearly shabby. His hat was not held smartly under his arm, but hung in his hand at his side.

'Who are you, sir?' Rennie peered at him in the glow of the deckhead light.

'Don't you know me, Captain Rennie?'

'I do not, sir——Good heaven, can it be you, Mr Loftus?' Rennie had been prepared, strongly prepared, to rebuke Bernard Loftus upon his eventual arrival for his long absence from the ship without explanation. The master's sad appearance caused him to change his mind. As he walked into the cabin he was perceptibly slower in his movements, like a man lately injured, or reduced by malady.

'I must beg your pardon, sir.'

'Are you ill, Mr Loftus?'

'I am not ill any more, sir. I am all right, now.'

'But you have been ill? Why did not you write and tell me? I should have done something to help, if I could.' His tone entirely free of rancour.

'I had meant to, often I had meant to, but——'

'Will you sit down?' Pulling a chair. 'You had better sit down. Here, a glass of wine.' Rennie poured generously. Mr Loftus took the glass and sucked down the wine in one long draught. He sat down, his hand on the chair-back to guide himself.

'Thank you, sir. You are kind.'

Rennie refilled his glass, and again saw the wine disappear in a long gulping swallow.

'Have you had supper, Mr Loftus? Probably you are hungry, after your journey. I assume you have made a long journey?'

'It is a long story, anyway—and a long journey, to say the truth.' Tears formed in his eyes, and spilled on his cheeks. 'I must beg your pardon.'

'You are not yourself, Mr Loftus. Do not think of apologies, now. We must—we must see that you recover. You are much needed, Mr Loftus.'

'That is kind in you, very kind.' More tears, to Rennie's great consternation. It was difficult enough for a man like Rennie to deal with women in tears—thank God it had happened seldom—but to have to console a weeping man was quite beyond his capacities. He went to the cabin door and said to the sentry—marines had now been drafted into the ship from the dockyard barracks—that he was to pass the word for the doctor. Presently Thomas Wing came to the great cabin.

'You sent for me, sir?'

'I did, Doctor, come in.' Quietly, pointing to the seated man, whose back was to them. 'I should like your diagnosis, if you please.'

Wing approached the seated figure, and now recognised him. 'Mr Loftus.'

The master looked up, saw the diminutive surgeon, the well-remembered, well-liked face, and was further overcome. His face crumpled and he was wracked, tears dripping down his cheeks. The doctor reached and took his hand, felt for the pulse at the wrist, then felt the shaking master's forehead. Looking past him to Rennie:

'This man has a fever. He must be put into his bed without delay, and there kept warm when he shivers, and his brow cooled when he sweats.' He sniffed close at the master's face. 'Has he been drinking? I smell wine.'

'Yes, I gave him wine. He was sorely in need of it.'

'Captain Rennie, he was not. Most emphatically not.'

'Eh?'

'With respect, he should never have been given wine. Fever is not best treated with alcohol. Broth, I will permit, or plain water.'

'Ah, oh—broth. Just so, Doctor, very good.'

'I shall need two strong men to carry him to his cabin, and his cot must be hung for him.'

'Yes, yes, we must get him below.'

Mr Loftus caught his breath and effortfully sat up straight. 'Gentlemen, I must beg your pardon. I am all right, now. I am quite well.' His face was for a moment unnaturally calm and composed, then a further spasm of weeping engulfed him and he slumped once more, shaken by sobs.

Later, when the master had been put to bed and given a draught to help him sleep, Thomas Wing came again to the great cabin to make his report.

'Do you know the story behind this, Doctor?'

'I do not, sir. Mr Loftus tried to explain something to me as I was tending to him, but his words was not very lucid. I think he said the word "betrayed" several times.'

'Did he? Did he? Yes.' Rennie scratched his head, then ran his fingers through his receding hair, and rubbed the back of his neck. 'Betrayed. Yes, I think that he may well have been betrayed.'

'By whom?'

'Well well, I do not know that for certain, altogether. A woman, I think. A young person of dubious character.'

'That explains a great deal.' Nodding, a sigh.

'She stole his money, I believe.'

'Something more than his money.'

'Mr Storey said the same thing, when he first heard of Mr Loftus's difficulty. But what could the wench have took, I wonder, aside from his purse?'

'Surely it is obvious?'

'Mm?'

'His heart, sir. She took and broke his heart.'

If James was not utterly broken-hearted at being parted from his beloved Catherine, he was certainly not bursting with joy. He fulfilled his obligations with his usual vigour and efficiency, he did his duty, but Rennie noted in his lieutenant, when they dined together, a tendency to long silence and distracted looks. They had been expecting their final instructions daily, had been warned to expect them by Admiral Bamphlett, the Port Admiral. They had not come. Nor had Rennie received any further communication from Sir Robert Greer. He was either absent from Portsmouth, or keeping very low—perhaps in the guise of Mr Scott, lurking in the taverns of the Point, or skulking about the dockyard, watching and listening for God knew what. Sedition? Treason? Evidence of pilfering?

Rennie, as had been his habit in their first commission in *Expedient*, confided in James. He trusted him, they trusted each other, and nothing was held back. When James had heard all Rennie had to tell him about Sir Robert, he shook off his despondency and asked:

'Who is the Reverend Jepp? You mentioned that name.'

'Yes, I did. He is a cryptical graphic, apparently employed by the Secret Service Fund.'

'Cryptographical, perhaps? He works with ciphers, with codes?'

'You have it exact. However, I have never met the fellow. What Sir Robert has told me is that Jepp has intercepted messages in code which bear on our commission, directly bear on it. He has not declared to me our enemy. I do not know who sent these messages. The plan he outlined to me, James, sounded entirely fanciful, I'm bound to say. Take Jamaica by stealth? Landing parties, creeping ashore to take the island? Good God, James, it is a schoolboy story, invented by buffoons.'

'His life may principally be concerned with treachery, sir—but Sir Robert is not a buffoon, I think. He is far too acute to be called a buffoon.'

'That ain't to say Jepp is not.' A sniff.

'Cryptographical analysis is not the province of fools, neither—with respect.'

'Well well, I don't like it, though. It don't sit right with me, James. We are sea officers in a fighting ship, not bloody little clerks.'

'A charting survey is hardly the work of clerks. Captain Cook was not a clerk, certainly.'

'Aye, well said.' Laughing. 'He was not a clerk, James, you are quite right. And nor are we.'

Captain Rennie did not contrive to get into his complement a single one of the midshipmen from *Expedient*'s first commission. One of those midshipmen, Mr Pankridge, had been killed in the Pacifick, and the others had scattered into England's counties upon the ship's return. Six new youths appeared, and with them in the wherry came the third lieutenant, Mr Peak. There was one consolation to Rennie: Randall South, his old coxswain, who had gone into an

Indiaman, had lately returned to Portsmouth and heard of *Expedient*'s new commission, and he now came to her.

'Randall South, I am glad to see you! I will like to shake your hand!' Grasping the horny hand with enthusiasm.

'I am right glad to be with you again, sir.' Warmly, his voice vibrating as his hand was pumped.

'Shipmates, hey? We are precious few from the last cruise, original Expedients, and we must thank God we can still be together. Tell me now, Randall South, what d'y'hear of Jacob Gurrall?'

'Ah, well. That is a story.'

'I will like to hear it.'

'No, sir. I think you will not. Jacob signed on with me in the *Bellflower*, and he died at Calcutta of the bloody flux. Strong as he was, he could not mend when the flux got him in its grip, and tore out his guts.'

'That is sad tidings, indeed. He was a right seaman, a good man all altogether.'

'Aye.'

'Well well, we must not dwell on things we cannot alter. He has gone to a better place, and we must make the most of this one, hey?'

'I am ready, sir. I am here.'

'I want you as my coxswain again. We must get you on to the books.' Briskly, pushing away all lowering thoughts. 'Mr Hayter!'

Expedient's guns and powder had now been brought into her, she was now fully victualled and watered, and Bernard Loftus busied himself in trimming her. He was now nearly recovered, though a trifle thin and drawn still, and his energies and strength returned as he supervised the shifting for weight of casks in the hold, and got the ship a little by the stern—her captain's preference, and his own. *Expedient* now lay at a new mooring, at Spithead.

Captain Rennie had interviewed Mr Peak, prepared to

be critical, and had found him to be an admirable young man, who answered the questions put to him promptly and intelligently. There was still no sign or word of Mr Makepeace. Nor had Rennie's final instructions been given to him. He had no firm date of sailing. He had begun to fret, and grow fractious:

'What is the point, James, of getting her ready for the sea without she *puts* to sea, hey? Are we to lie here at Spithead the rest of our lives?'

'I hope not, sir. I wish to see my wife again.'

At last a cutter came out to the ship, dashing before, white at the cutwater, came about very smartly and hove to.

Captain Rennie was to attend on Sir Robert Greer and the Port Admiral at Kingshill. The cutter dashed away, carrying despatches to Plymouth.

'Why not the Port Admiral's office?' Rennie complained to James. 'Why must I make my way to Kingshill? You had better come with me, James, as my second-in-command. Or no, perhaps that will be unwise.' Hesitating.

'As you please, sir.' Formally correct.

'You remember an earlier occasion, James, when we went to Kingshill together, with that fellow from the Admiralty, what was his name? Snoad? Was it? Sole?'

'Soames, sir.'

'Soames! Yes, a holding-back, disapproving fellow. And we got into trouble about it afterward, hey?' Laughing. 'At the Marine Hotel?'

'I do remember it, yes, sir. You was attacked in the night, in your bed, was you not?'

'Christ, so I was. Yes, I had forgot that. Well well, perhaps it will be better that I go ashore alone. I'm sorry, James.'

'Do not think of it, sir.' He watched the captain descend to the boat, Randall South at the tiller, and oarsmen newly selected for his crew, double-banked, and one of the new mids, Mr Lamarr, to shout the commands in his breaking, disconcerting squeak and basso. Rennie stepped neatly into the boat on the lift, the seaman in the bow shoved off, and the oars began to dip and pull. James was regretful, he acknowledged in his breast. In going ashore he could be no nearer to Catherine than he was at Spithead, but he would have been treading on a part of England, and thus connected to her by common ground, no matter the miles between them. Now he would not tread on English soil again for many months, and Catherine was alone, with child. He swallowed, turned from the rail, drew a deep breath and composed himself. She was not alone; Catherine was at Melton. He had twice written to her, and had received her reassuring replies. He would send another letter ashore before they weighed. Catherine was safe, she was cared for, all would be well. He took another breath, and caught sight of——

'Mr Abey? Are you indisposed?'

Richard Abey, thin and small, and at twelve the youngest mid, hastily brushed at his face with the back of his hand, and held himself erect.

'No, sir.'

'This is your first ship?'

'I have been entered in two other ships, sir.'

'Aye, well, entered. But you was not afloat in neither, I think? You was entered on the books years since, so that you might be rated midshipman now, in *Expedient*.'

'This is my first time in a ship, yes, sir,' admitted the boy.

'Where is your home?'

'In Norfolk, sir. At Little Barsham.'

'Mr Dobie our schoolmaster hails from Norfolk. He is from Burnham, which is near to your own home, I think. I will say a word to him. Pay close attention also to Mr Loftus, the master. You will be all right, Mr Abey. At present you are a little lost, a little afraid—there is no shame in it. In a week or two you will begin to feel yourself an Expedient, and you will be all right.'

'An Expedient, sir . . .?'

'That is the most important thing at sea. Not that you serve in the Royal Navy, but in your ship—this ship. She is your whole life, pretty near. You are part of her, and she is part of you, part of us all. We are all Expedients, together. You see?' Kindly.

'Yes, sir, thank you.'

At Kingshill, in the library, Rennie was met by Admiral Bamphlett and Sir Robert Greer, and was introduced to the Reverend Dr Edward Jepp. Dr Jepp was a man with sharp but not quite delicate features, small white hands, and a plain, nearly austere appearance in his dress and wig. He wore small oval spectacles that caught the light as he turned to shake Rennie's hand.

'You have seen the letters, I expect, Captain Rennie?' His voice was a carrying tenor, a little fussy at the edges.

'I have not.'

'Ohh, I had thought . . .' Glancing at Sir Robert.

'Captain Rennie has not yet seen them, because I have not permitted it.'

'Ahh, I see. D'you wish to permit it now, Sir Robert?'

Sir Robert made no reply to that. They were drinking Madeira, Rennie saw. Sir Robert offered him tea.

'Thank you, I should prefer wine today. The same wine you gentlemen drink.'

They sat down. Rennie observed that Admiral Bamphlett was not altogether at his ease. He drank off his glass, took up the decanter, unstoppered it and poured—without asking or being asked. He sucked down fully half of this second glass, and:

'If I am to provide Captain Rennie with his final instructions, Sir Robert, his sailing instructions, I think it my duty, you know, to apprise myself of their content. Nor do I know in what these "letters" consist. Have they come from the Admiralty? Have Captain Rennie's instructions come from Their Lordships, indeed? I have not had sight of them, if they have. I have been asked to come here——'

'Admiral Bamphlett, you was asked to come here as a matter of courtesy. Captain Rennie is in course under the command of Their Lordships, in large, but in particular he is——'

'In *large* under their command, Sir Robert? I know of no sea officer in the kingdom, sir, that is not *altogether* under their command!'

'I beg your pardon.' A cold smile. 'He is altogether under their command, and in particular he engages in a task that is a question of—how shall we say?—of artifice, and stratagem.'

'Trickery, d'y'mean?'

'If you like, if you like. We must certainly outwit our enemies, sir, in any way that is open to us.'

'And you, Dr Jepp.' Admiral Bamphlett turned to him. 'I hear that it is signals occupy your days. I have heard of sea officers that compose signal books, but I confess, never yet a chaplain.'

'I am neither a chaplain in the navy, Admiral Bamphlett, nor a flag officer of any kind.'

'*Flag* officer!'

'Dr Jepp is a translator,' interposed Sir Robert smoothly. 'His work does not entail signal flags. He interprets and translates only documents.'

'Like a tutor in Latin, d'y'mean, or Greek?'

'That is not quite——' began Dr Jepp, but Sir Robert again interrupted:

'Something like, Admiral, something very like.'

'Very good—but I am still unclear why you use the word "enemies". What enemy? Who is it that we seek to defeat, with "letters"? From what source d'y'obtain these documents. Hey?' He now glanced at Rennie, and raised an eyebrow, and Rennie saw that the admiral was determined to give these damned landmen a lesson in naval tactics.

'If you will indulge me a few moments longer, Admiral. All right, Jepp, show the letters to Captain Rennie,' nodded Sir

Robert. To Admiral Bamphlett: 'They have been obtained from confidential sources—abroad.'

Dr Jepp removed three folded sheets from his coat, carefully unfolded them and handed them to Rennie. 'These are written out in my own hand, and are the—the extracted passages that bear directly on your task.'

Rennie took the pages, glanced at them briefly, and: 'May I know which sources abroad . . .?'

Dr Jepp looked quickly at Sir Robert, who gave an almost imperceptible shake of his head. 'I—I have interpreted the code by analysis, and written out the result in plain language,' was all he said in reply.

If Rennie was slightly puzzled by this hesitant and avoiding explication, and the glances exchanged between Dr Jepp and Sir Robert, Admiral Bamphlett was thoroughly bemused. He was losing the wind gage, and he did not like it. He attempted now to change tack:

'May I have sight of those letters? As the senior officer present?'

'I am afraid that will not be possible——' began Sir Robert, again smoothly, but he was not quite prepared for the broadside that followed.

'Not be *possible*! Not be *possible*! Sir Robert, you have wasted my time on a previous occasion, but you will not waste it again, now! *Be quiet, sir!* I will decide what is *possible*! This is a naval matter, an Admiralty matter, and I will like to see all of the papers relating to it! You will give those letters to me, Captain Rennie.' And he held out his hand.

Rennie made to pass the sheets to the admiral, but Sir Robert stepped in front of him and took them from him—swiftly and smoothly snatched them, and thrust them away in his coat. He then turned to face the admiral. Slowly, almost languidly, he brought open his bloodless eyelids and blackly met the admiral's blue furious glare.

'Do not overstep your authority, Admiral Bamphlett,' he said in a tone of such quiet, unlaboured menace that the admiral was momentarily astonished. That moment was fatal. 'You are not in your own domain here. You are in mine. And here, sir, here I am in command.' Still very soft, his eyes unblinking.

'Oh, oh very well,' said the admiral at last, and he turned away and put his glass on the table in defeat.

'Yes, James, I got my final instructions all right, and had sight of those letters,' said Rennie later, having returned at dusk to *Expedient*. 'Admiral Bamphlett saw neither, and was so aggrieved to find himself merely a courtesy presence that he uttered no further word to anyone, not even in farewell at the end.'

'He will likely make trouble about it for Sir Robert, will he not, sir?'

'I do not think so, I do not think so. He was humiliated, and no doubt very angry, but when he reflects he will see that Sir Robert is a man connected at the highest level, while he himself is a man with no power beyond Portsmouth, and very little in it.' He sniffed, and nodded. 'At any rate, James, we have got our instructions at last, thank God.' Tapping the papers on the table. 'And at last we can set our course, and make sail.'

'Without Lieutenant Makepeace? We sail without Tom?'

'I cannot wait for him any more, James. He has had his chance, and he has not come. Well well, it cannot be helped. Mr Loftus may take his watches for the present, and I will like to bring on one of the older mids to act as third, and move Mr Peak up to second.'

'Very good, sir. When shall we weigh?'

'At first light.'

The ship beat into a gradually strengthening westerly wind, and Captain Rennie was obliged to tack more often than he would have wished, to board short, the topmen aloft all the watch, the ship pitching heavy, smashing her cutwater into brute solid seas, straining to lift her head, then plunging, abruptly plunging into steep troughs, yawing and groaning and sighing. On the quarterdeck braced legs, a feet-apart stance, were not enough to keep a man upright. He must from time to time clap on to something—the rail, a backstay—else stumble and measure his length.

The ship was not quite herself, Rennie felt. She was sagging off, a little sluggish in her responses. He would have to consult Mr Loftus about this, to see if she might be further trimmed, otherwise the tiers of the hold would likely begin to shift, and if they did, provisions would be spoiled, water lost, when they were not yet out of sight of land. The Lizard lay to the north.

There had been the usual cases of seasickness. Poor Dobie was prostrated, and young Peak was pallid and wretched, although he had insisted upon taking his watches. Well, they would mend, presently. The ship would not, unless she was aided.

'Mr Loftus!' Into the whipping wind.

'Aye, sir?' Attending.

'She is unhappy. I feel that she is telling us so.' Looking aloft, bracing himself. She was carrying topsails, reefed, forecourse, reefed, headsail and spanker, her main course in the brails. 'She is yet a little by the head, I think, and she needs too much lee helm. I will like a spoke or two of weather helm, Mr Loftus. I will like her ardent by the wind, so we may curb her eagerness, not sluggish and unwilling, you apprehend me?' His voice raised, a hand cupped.

'Aye, sir. It may be the extra weight of her guns. We carry a greater weight of metal this commission, and maybe she wants retrimming, a little.'

'Well well, so it must be done then, Mr Loftus. The sooner the better.' Endeavouring not to sound testy, with his voice raised against the wind and the crashing of the sea. 'I don't want to shorten sail more than I must, more than I absolutely must. We must make headway.'

'Very good, sir.'

At supper, Rennie was alone. He had asked his lieutenant to join him, but James was assisting the master in the hold, a crew of the strongest men shifting casks, making them secure, bilge and cuntline, in the rolling, heaving gloom, the stink of the bilges wafting and seeping round them. James in his working clothes, Mr Loftus also, so that in the swaying lantern glow they were all but indistinguishable from the men they supervised. James, like all good sea officers, was not averse to getting himself dirty in the interests of the ship, for he could drown in her with the humblest man, the least significant boy, if she foundered—the sea permitted no distinction of rank when it chose to make mischief.

They worked all through both dogwatches, and when James came on deck at last it was into violent darkness, and welcome blasts of wind. He let the wind tear the odours of the hold from his nose and throat, and fling spray across his grimy face. Thank God, he was not seasick, had felt no hint of queasiness or nausea at all since they rounded the Foreland two days ago.

'Mr Peak! I will relieve you! You might ask the mess steward to send up a wedge of pie, and a flask of wine, will you? I've had no time at all to eat, and I'm famished.'

'Very well.' A grimace, and Richard Peak with awful determination forced down his rising gorge, indicated his glass-by-glass notations, muttered the course and the ship's speed, and hurried below. James had not heard a word he said, and smiled to himself: 'Poor bugger.'

His pie and wine did not come—clearly iteration of this hearty request had been too much for Mr Peak—and James sent one of the mids below, Mr Delingpole, a tall, whippet-thin, oddly clumsy boy. When he returned, the glass had just been turned and the bell sounded. While James ate his pie and sucked down welcome draughts of wine, Delingpole and his much smaller colleague Abey ran out the logline, read off the knots by the half-minute glass and gave him the speed of the ship.

'Six knots, sir.'

'Six, Mr Delingpole? The retrimming has done her good, then. She makes excellent speed in the conditions.'

James made the notation in the light of the compass binnacle, the last piece of pie jutting from his mouth as he bent over his book, shielding it from wind and slashing spray. As he straightened his back again a cry came from far aloft on the mainmast.

'D-e-e-e-ck! D-e-e-e-ck! Ship afire!'

'Where away?' James flung away the pie, fumbled and found his speaking trumpet, and bawled: '*Where away!*'

'Three points on the larboard bow!'

James jumped into the mizzen shrouds, ran up, and peered into the darkness. Away to larboard a glimmer, lost on the fall, then a shimmering burst of flame on the rise, showing faintly the hull of the stricken ship, and her sails, about a league distant. James jumped down and nearly lost his footing on the deck as the ship lost hers. To the weather helmsman:

'Keep her head up, now, Michael Haynes! Keep your luff!' And to the younger mid: 'Mr Abey, kindly go below to the great cabin and tell the captain we approach a ship afire. Jump now.'

Presently Rennie came on deck, his boat cloak wrapped round him over his nightshirt, his nightcap perched on his head. The burning ship was now clearly visible to larboard, gouts of fire shivering and writhing up from her, the sails reflecting the orange glow and beginning to catch. A shudder of sparks, followed by a thudding bang on the wind. Another, and another. Loaded guns were beginning to explode.

'Should we send boats, sir? Heave to, and send boats?' Knowing the answer, but feeling himself compelled to put the question.

'No, James. The conditions do not permit it. Too close in,

and we should fall aboard her, or she aboard us. Sending boats will only drown men. I cannot risk my people in these seas. Her magazine may blow up at any moment, beside.'

'Aye, sir.' Nodding, very subdued, as they both stared helplessly at the doomed ship.

Presently Rennie shook his head, took a deep breath, and turned, glancing at the binnacle:

'Weather helm!'

'Sir?' Michael Haynes, braced at the helm, his mate on the lee.

'How does she lie?'

'She is true, sir, she don't pitch near so bad no more.' And he gave the heading.

'Very good. Hold her so, just so.'

James continued to stare at the burning ship as *Expedient* ran past her, holding to her course; he could not drag his eyes from the stricken vessel as she fell away on the beam and quarter. Rennie did not look at her again, but kept his eyes aloft, standing silent by the wheel. At last:

'James.'

'Aye, sir.'

'Note the time, if y'please, and enter it.' A nod, a sniffing sigh, and he went to the companion.

At midnight, as James handed over the watch to Bernard Loftus, and went below, Rennie sent for him. James went to the great cabin and found Rennie sitting up in his nightshirt, his boat cloak hanging on the back of his chair. He was drinking tea, poured from a quart pot.

'I had turned in early, James, I was tired. But now I find I cannot sleep.'

'I doubt that I shall sleep, myself.'

'Sit down a moment, will you? A glass of wine?'

'Thank you, no, sir.'

'Tea, then?'

James accepted tea, and cradled the cup in his hand. 'Thank you, sir.'

A moment of silence, then:

'Yes, we are both troubled by that burning ship. The thought of those wretched men in her is very hard to dismiss. Very hard, with the attendant thought of ourselves in the same circumstance.'

'I cannot get the great pillars of sparks out of my head. It is a picture seared in my mind.' A brief shiver.

'Aye, that is the picture, exact. However—however, there was nothing to be done, James.'

A brief silence, except for the creaking of timbers and the seething rush of the sea. Rennie shifted in his chair, and his boat cloak slipped off the chair-back to the decking canvas. He did not notice it. His nightcap lay beside the teapot on the table, and now Rennie scratched his head, rubbed his chin, and took a breath:

'There is something I must tell you, James, in addition.'

'In addition, sir?' Puzzled.

'Well well, in case you had thought me overly callous, overly cold and cruel in not even attempting to help them.'

'I had not thought anything of the——'

'Even had I wanted to, I could not have tried to rescue those wretched men. Even had I wished it. My instructions forbid it, forbid any speaking or communication with any other ship, until we reach the West Indies.'

'I have neglected my duty in many and several ways,' said Rennie, and shook his head sadly. 'I did not attend my old friend's burial service, because I feared his sister's exhortations about Sir Robert. I did not investigate her complaints against him, I did nothing. And I failed to present you and Catherine with a wedding gift, it escaped my mind and I have only now recollected it, when it is far too late.' Days later, during the afternoon watch of a washing day.

'We shall bear it, sir, and live,' said James. 'Do not think of it.' Holding lists of divisions.

'But it's a damned disgrace! I abhor slovenliness of mind, James, promises broke and vowed intentions cast aside through neglect. It is like neglect in a ship, hammocks unwashed, or the deck left—— By the by, we must pump ship as soon as we run clear of this blow. The hold is getting abominably foul. I will not have a stinking ship, James.'

'Very good, sir.'

'I must find something at Jamaica, that will suit.'

'To counter the smell?'

'No no, good God. That will suit you both as a gift.'

'Ah.' Nodding, compressing his lips, fighting back a smile.

'At any rate I am glad that I did not attempt anything against Sir Robert. To have attacked, even to have attempted to attack, so ruthless a fellow would have been damned folly, hey? Beside, he is going to intercede in my behalf—in our behalf—at the Admiralty, about our reward.'

'Do you anticipate success, sir?' James did not. He had accepted long since his meagre part of the awarded money, and put it to use. Privately he thought that Rennie was both naive and over-ambitious in his pursuit of greater riches from that source; that the first commission was long over; that their new commission should and must govern their thoughts.

'Naturally, I do, James. Sir Robert has given me his assurance, solemnly and absolutely given it, and I have accepted it.' A sniff. 'And now I must write up my journal, James.' He drew the journal towards him. 'I must also look at the ship's books. Did you happen to notice Mr Dobie in his little hole, when you came in?'

'I did not see him, sir. I shall look in there as I go out, and send him in, shall I?'

'If he is there at all. I expect he is not.' A sigh. 'He is a very good clerk, you know, and so forth, but his guts don't settle at sea. A clerk that don't appear at my side, pen in hand, when I want him, ain't of the slightest use to me.'

'Perhaps one of the mids might be able to assist, in a temporary way——'

'One of the mids! Christ in tears, do not let them, any of them, near to my books! That would be the end of everything. Ink spilled, pages lost, figures destroyed, blots and smudges and ruin. Mr Trent would never forgive me. He is most particular, Trent, you know. He even had the—well well, he even asked me about my store of tea.'

James, at the door: 'About your *tea*?'

'Aye, you stare. He did. Had duty been paid upon it? he asked. Everything in the ship, he said, had to be accounted for. Good heaven, James.'

'I expect you told him to mind his own business?'

'I bloody well did, too.'

Alan Dobie was in fact in his little half-hole of a working cabin, immediately forrard of the coach, shut in with his papers. As James looked in he lifted his head, and the ghastly pallor of his face was apparent, and his vermilion lips, tinged with blue at the edges.

'Ah, Mr Hayter.' A hollow smile, bravely assumed.

'Good heaven, Alan. You had better see the surgeon at once.'

'I am all right. He can do nothing, anyway. When the wind—the wind moderates I shall recover.'

'Have you been able to eat anythi—— Oh, my dear fellow, I am sorry, I should not have asked that.' As Dobie turned away and dry-retched into his kerchief. When he had recovered, James told him that the captain wished to see him. 'But only if you are well enough to attend.'

'I must make the attempt.' Dobie rose to his feet, steadied himself against the bulkhead, and took up his notebook, pen and inkwell.

West of Finisterre, and beating close-hauled into the prevailing westerly wind, south-west-by-south, towards the ease of the great trade winds, and running before day after day, into warmer latitudes. The deck washed and smoke eddying and wafting away through the rigging from the cowl of the galley stove on the forecastle. Hammocks up, and the hands ready for their breakfast. Eight bells.

A heavy crash, a great shuddering scrape below the waterline, a second, nudging concussion, and *Expedient* yawed heavily, steadied, and sailed on. Shouts. Rennie jumped up the companion ladder and ran aft to the taffrail. 'What in God's name was it!' Peering down and astern.

No sign appeared in the churning wake, nor in the darker water rushing and curving away astern, no splintered timbers, no wreckage, nothing untoward.

'It might probably have been a whale,' ventured Mr Loftus, 'don't you think so, sir?'

James joined them now, coming aft from the waist. 'No, not a whale, I think. We saw no spout of air, neither before nor after the shock.'

'The shock could have killed it,' said Loftus. 'A whale is heavy, but we are heavier, and stouter.'

'Then where is his blood?' puzzled Rennie. 'You cannot kill a whale without blood. It is a mystery.' Turning round. 'We fell on something, I heard the sound of it scraping along our copper.'

'I had better go below, and look for damage,' said James, but at the same moment the carpenter's mate Huish Racken appeared at the break of the quarterdeck, his narrow face fierce with alarm.

'Captain, sir! Mr Adgett says: we are taking water terrible quick below, amidships—she is flooding!'

'Good God.—What depth of water in the well?'

'It is over four foot, sir, and rising quick.'

'Hands to man the pumps!' bawled James at once, without waiting for Rennie to speak. Rennie ran forrard to the break, down the ladder into the waist, and went below.

The damage had been done to her copper and hull timbers deep amidships on the starboard side. Water was pouring into the ship, into her hold; her copper either pierced or torn away, the bottom timbers fractured, perhaps even the square frames of her keel affected.

'I think her frames and bilge strakes is sound, sir,' said Mr Adgett, holding a lantern in the sloshing gloom, attempting to be an optimist. It was evident to the captain, horribly and immediately evident, that the water sluicing and streaming into the ship, pouring through the cuntlines of casks, rising round the shot lockers, rising round their feet as they peered aghast, could sink the ship. The stark truth of that shock, that collision, was that she might already be lost. Mr Adgett passed the lantern without ceremony to the captain, and joined his mate and crew. Huish Racken and his men were attempting to shore, and stem, and plug, with timber, hammocks, canvas, working with desperate concentration of purpose—but the fracture was mischievous, several punctures, a great intermittent scar on the ship's underside, twelve foot long at least.

'We must fother this!' Rennie, on deck. James in his sodden shirt came from the pumps, each double-manned and frantically working in half-glass shifts.

'Aye, sir.'

'We must fother right quick, or she will founder. Christ's blood, the quantity of water flooding in is prodigious. It is very shocking.'

Already *Expedient* was wallowing and growing sluggish, heavy on the lee helm. Rennie made his decisions, and gave his orders. They would shorten sail, and heave to. The wind was no longer forceful, and they could ride head to it. Mr Peak, made aware that the ship would sink if he did not perform his duty, quite miraculously found himself free of nausea and the urge to vomit at every step, and went into the cutter with midshipmen Abey and Lamarr, Randall South and hand-picked men. A great square of number two canvas—thrummed across and through, and smeared with dung from the animal pens—and quantities of hawser-laid rope and tarred twine were rigged, secured at the corners and deployed, and the canvas draped down the starboard side amidships. The boat was rowed round the stern in the heaving swell, guided with skill by Randall South, ropes paid out and under the ship, and brought to larboard, and the heavy canvas then hauled under the ship, to the great wound below the waterline.

Shouted commands, relayed, and the carpenter's crew in the hold released their makeshift barricades, the water cascaded in for a moment, then was abruptly shut off with a great sucking gasp as the thrummed canvas fothered in against the hull without, and held.

When it was clear to Rennie that the ship was safe, at least for the time being, he had the ship's complement assembled in the waist, and addressed them:

'You are wondering what we struck today, why the ship was damaged when we are so far from land, from any shoals or reefs, and the lead cannot find the bottom. Mr Loftus thinks it was a whale. Mr Hayter don't quite agree. He thinks a whale would have come up spouting in triumph had he struck us such a blow.' A murmur of laughter. 'For myself, I think it was something like a great log, suspended below the waterline, which has floated out of the mouth of a wide river far away, a place of forests, and it has been borne out into the ocean by currents, to lie in wait for seamen such as ourselves, intent upon drowning us. Well well, it has not done so, it has not succeeded. Thanks to quick and practical measures taken by Mr Adgett in the hold, and by Mr Peak in the boat, *Expedient* is safe, and we are safe in her, Expedients all.'

'It was a lamentable address, a wretched dull speech, you do not need to tell me, James.' Rennie refilled his glass, pushed the bottle, and took a deep draught of wine. The sound of the chain pumps came to them in the great cabin, over the washing of the sea.

'You made light of the whale, in least, sir.'

'My intent was to hearten them. A man that can smile at misfortune ain't fearful.'

'Indeed.'

'I am not sure the log was a happy invention, though. "A place of forests, far away", like a damned mincing curate. Good heaven, I should have contrived something more persuading, hey?'

James was silent a moment, the bottle untouched before him on the table, then:

'What *do* you think we struck, sir?'

'We might sit here all night guessing, as to that. It might have been a whale, I suppose. It might even have been something like that great half-sinking tree, waterlogged . . . a water log ha-ha-ha! Yes yes, a water log, by God, ha-ha-ha! Hmm, I feel a little better now about that fanciful sermon, James. A water log it shall remain—in my journal, if not in the *ship's log*.' And he chuckled again.

'Aye, well, if we hold steady on our present heading we should sight Madeira in two days, sir, three at most.'

'Madeira? Surely you do not suppose I mean to stop at Madeira? I merely head south for——'

'That fothering sail will not hold for ever, though. Should not we make landfall there, at Funchal?'

'No no no, James. We must get her into calmer waters, certainly, and make repairs as we may, at sea. My instructions forbid my making landfall anywhere, until Port Royal, as I have explained to you.'

James pushed away his glass with a dismayed frown. 'Forgive me, but will not an attempt to repair her at sea loosen her hull timbers further? Loosen and weaken them? Will not the——'

'Pish pish, James. We have today survived a great concussion, great damage to the ship, survived with flying colours. The leak is fothered, and stopped, and I will like to hear no more nonsense about weakened timbers and so forth when she swims so handsome, and the pumps have done their work so well. She is damned near dry.'

'Very good, sir.'

'Fill your glass, James.'

'Thank you, sir, I think perhaps I have drunk more than enough tonight.' Making to rise.

'Come now, James.' Frowning in turn. '*Expedient* is afloat. She swims, for Christ's sake. Ain't it enough that we have had one calamity in a day, without you wish another one upon us for the morrow? Hey? Fill your glass!'

'You—order me to fill it, sir?' Carefully polite.

'That would be ungentlemanlike, Mr Hayter.' Restrained, and furious. 'Goodnight to you.'

'Goodnight, sir.'

But *Expedient* was not dry. Within twelve hours the fothering sail had proved inadequate to prevent the leaks from again asserting themselves, and water began again to trickle and seep in to the hold, so that she could not be tacked properly, for fear of loosening the sail further on the weather side, the wind still steady from the west.

Captain Rennie—without conceding anything to his lieutenant—said to Mr Loftus:

'I have decided that we will alter our course and make for Funchal, Mr Loftus. Beating down to the trades don't answer, in her present condition.—Mr Adgett!—Pass the word for Mr Adgett!'

'Sir?' Arriving on the quarterdeck.

'What depth in the well?'

'It is gaining, sir. Four foot.'

'Hell and fire.' Muttered. Aloud: 'Very good, Mr Adgett, thank you. We shall soon reach Funchal, and you may repair there.'

'Thank you, sir. I am glad.' Greatly relieved, Mr Adgett

removed his hat, shook it free of shavings, and allowed himself a cautious nod. 'As I say, I am more at ease now, sir.'

Captain Rennie glanced aloft, was critical of backstays, and the ship's inclination again to allow her head to dip wallowing low, and said to the helmsman: 'How does she lie?'

'She sags off, sir.'

Rennie looked into the binnacle. 'You are south by west. I will like her south by west, and a point south.'

'Aye, sir, and a point south.'

At noon they lay at 36 degrees and 14 minutes north, 15 degrees and 28 minutes west. They were still by the wind, and the ship was beginning to struggle. The pumps manned, again in half-glass shifts, not gaining on the water in the hold, not quite holding their own, and the water measured in the well at an inch or two under five foot.

The senior midshipman was a sixteen-year-old youth named Martin Cross. Rennie had spoken before they sailed of bringing this boy up to acting third, since the ship was lacking one lieutenant, but had thought better of that arrangement, and now the watches were divided between James Hayter, Richard Peak, and Bernard Loftus. However, Mr Cross was expected to behave towards the junior mids as an elder brother, to chivvy them when they deserved it, and aid and enlighten them in matters of seamanship. Now he and the two most junior mids were in the main topmast cross-trees. Mr Abey was the youngest and smallest, the other boy was called Mayfield, and he was thirteen. They were both of them clinging and fearful, at this swaying height, the deck very narrow and small far beneath their braced feet, the ocean immense all around, rolling and immense under an immense and windy sky. Sails bellied, bowlines taut. Today the ship carried no t'gans'ls, and all the canvas was below them.

'Tell me which are the lateral ropes in the standing rigging, at the level of the futtock shrouds where they are made fast to the lower shrouds? Mr Abey?'

'The—the fixings, Cross?'

'Do you ask me, or tell me?'

'The fixings, then.' Clinging as the ship dropped her head.

'No. Mr Mayfield?'

'The catharpins.'

'Aye, the cross catharpins. Excellent. And where are we stood, at present? Mr Abey?'

'The main topmast—topmast top.'

'No. Mayfield?'

'The main topm'st cross-trees.'

'Indeed. Very good. Now, Mr Abey——'

'If you please, Cross, I think I am going to be sick.'

'No, you are not.' Firmly.

'Oh, please'—closing his eyes—'I am going to faint.'

'Mr Abey! Look at me!'

Fearfully opening his eyes. 'I shall fall.'

'No, you will not. Hold my gaze, do not look down. Give me your hand, now. Your right hand.'

'I—I dare not let go.'

'Give it to me!'

The junior midshipman, in an agony of fright, nausea, and wretchedness, pulled his right hand away from the stay to which it clutched, and extended it trembling. Cross took it firmly in his own.

'Now then, Mr Abey. If you faint, and fall, we shall both plunge to our deaths. Either into the sea, as she heels, or to the deck.'

'Ohh. Ohh.'

'Hold my gaze! You will not fall! I forbid it!'

'Very good, Cross.'

'Now then. Was there a sail set upon this mast, superior to the one below, what sail would it be?'

'The—topgallant sail, if you please.'

'There you are, you see. You knew it all the time. T'gans'l. On which mast are we aloft?'

'The mainmast.' A reviving breath.

A bawled order from the deck below: 'Hands to make sail!'

Rennie had decided that in spite of the increased risk to the already failing fothered sail, he must increase his speed to reach Funchal as soon as he could. To do otherwise, and limp there slowly, would in his judgement put his ship at even greater risk. This judgement was not altogether shared on the quarterdeck; Mr Loftus thought it foolhardy, had tried to say so diplomatically, and had been curtly overruled. James Hayter, not having been asked his opinion, said nothing.

They sighted Madeira, that mountainous island, the day following, swung south-west, and approached Funchal from the extreme western tip. By now the pumps were palpably losing the battle with the leak, there was a further foot of water in the well, and Rennie determined to run east through the night. At first light *Expedient* ran past the formidable cliffs of Cape Turnabout, and wallowed into Funchal in the forenoon watch, nearly fell on board a departing merchantman, somehow negotiated flotillas of fishing vessels and other small craft, and dropped anchor in Funchal Roads. A doctor and his assistant came to the ship, and determined that she was free of smallpox and fever, and Rennie was given permission to remain, and to go ashore. There then ensued a consultation with Mr Adgett, who gave his opinion—reluctantly gave it—that heeling the ship for repair would not answer, since the damage was too far below the waterline to be brought above the surface by that method. *Expedient* would have to be careened.

Preparation for that difficult exercise began at once. A great deal of work was needed, and the help of various authorities in the island, including the governor, the British consul, and the port agent. Her guns, her stores, and part of her ballast had to be taken out of her, and secured ashore. She had in her stores most of the materials required for repair, excepting copper. It was decided that since no wharf existed at Funchal, and no hulk, the ship would have to be moored adjacent to the mole, and a platform constructed there for the ship to be hove down to, by her masts.

The business of heaving the ship down on her larboard side by application of strong purchase upon her foremast and mainmast, properly supported by bedded shores, and the deck shored up also, to withstand the strain upon it, was both extremely troublesome, and extremely dangerous. The gun-ports had to be sealed up and caulked, and pitched over. The lights of the larboard quarter gallery had to be removed, stopped with deal, and caulked. Everywhere in the ship that was suspicious of leaking had to be stopped, sealed, caulked, &c., and then watched over by an appointed man when the heaving-over began. The upper masts were sent down, and all but the standing rigging struck. Capstans were rigged on the platform, to which the falls of the purchase cables were brought. Thick pendants, with double purchased tackles, were also rigged, to strengthen the shores and rigging at both foremast and mainmast. As the heaving down at each capstan began, all the ship's pumps were in full use, and those of the people not employed direct in the operation, or getting stores secured ashore, were ready with oakum, tallow, pitch and sawdust to fall at once upon any leaking place, and stop it.

The operation of heaving her down took an hour, and at last the great tearing wound was exposed, and the terrible extent of the damage revealed on the glistening hull. Rennie marvelled that she had stayed afloat long enough to bring them to Funchal. And now that she was hove down, she must stay in that position for days together, perhaps a week, until the work of repair was completed. Mr Adgett became agitated in the matter of new copper—over-agitated—and Rennie was obliged to be firm with him:

'Yes, thank you, Mr Adgett. You make your view abundant clear to me. We cannot sail without new copper, extensive new copper, at the place of injury to the ship. However, I must sail, d'y'see? Just as soon as we are repaired. You may look forward to the dockyard at Port Royal. There is copper there, I am in no doubt. In the interim, Mr Adgett, we must make do, and repair the torn sheets of copper, beat them flat, renail them in position, and proceed.'

'Sir, that very simply will not do. It will not suit. We *must* have new copper, when new timer has been artificed. I cannot have worm getting at new timber, and ruining all the work we——'

'Christ's blood, man! Do not I make myself plain to you! We should not be here at all! I mean to leave as soon as I can! We careen and repair, and sail, all within the week!'

'Aye, sir. Very well.' His hat off and on. Then, muttering: 'And very likely founder the week after, as I say.'

'What! What d'ye say!'

'I shall hound my crew, and never weaken.'

'Hm. Well. Just so.' A glaring nod, a dismissing sniff, and he stamped away down the mole.

Mr Denning Hapgood of Funchal, an Englishman by birth and education, a Madeiran by virtue of his trade, was a vintner and wine-shipper. His vineyards near Funchal, and west of Cabo Girau, were the finest producers of grapes for the delicious wines of the island—Malmsey, Bual, Sercial—and by dint of shipping and selling thousands of barrels annually in the Americas, Portugal and England, Hapgood had made himself very rich. His house in Funchal, in the Rua da Carreira, was the most splendid in the capital, renowned for its formal gardens and ornamental ponds and fountains. His hospitality—at a time when the poor of Madeira were very numerous, and conditions in the old town very low—was lavish and legendary, frowned upon by the lesser clergy, discreetly tolerated if not welcomed by the Portuguese authorities, and by the British consul, Sir Hendle Dawes. Dawes was a fellow merchant and friend of Hapgood's, and a frequent guest at his less flamboyant dinners. The larger, grander parties, masked balls and the like, inclined to be bibulous and extravagant, he did not attend. He did not disapprove—but he wished to maintain the decorum of his office.

As a post captain RN, whose ship lay in the harbour at Funchal, Captain Rennie was invited to the Quinta de Santa Francesca as a matter of courtesy. In time of war Hapgood's convoy ships had been accorded excellent protection by the Royal Navy, and Hapgood wished to pay tribute to that service. Naturally the other officers of HMS *Expedient* were included in the invitation.

Captain Rennie called on the consul at his residence, paid his respects, and asked a question:

'Do you go to Mr Hapgood's dance, Sir Hendle?'

'Unfortunately, no. I am called away into the country, you know, to the quinta of another gentleman, an earlier commitment. Otherwise, no doubt Lady Dawes would have insisted upon my going, and dragged me along there to dance. I am not much of a dancing man, to say the truth. My legs ain't what they was.'

'I am sorry to hear that, sir.' Mildly surprised. Sir Hendle was a well-made man in healthy middle life, not in the least infirm-looking, or bent, or crippled.

'But I think you should attend, Captain Rennie. Was that what you wanted to know? Whether I should approve of your going?—The Reverend Pembleton has been at you, has he?'

'Well, he—he did say a word of caution, discreetly warn me, when I visited his church.'

'Did he? Did he? I expect he did, yes. He is an admirable fellow, Pembleton, decent and upright, a pillar of the English community here. But he is not by his nature inclined to smile very often, I think, nor to take the world lightly. Why should he? His business is with the After-life, and due preparation for it. Very solemn work. Hey?' And the consul refilled Rennie's glass.

'You are kind, sir.'

'Where do you stay while you are at Funchal, Captain Rennie?'

'In usual I should live in my ship, but she is in course careened. I am staying at an hotel.'

'I will not hear of it. You and your officers must come to me, and stay here at the Residence during my absence up-country. My staff will look after your needs, and the stables are at your disposal.'

'That is very kind in you, sir. Very kind indeed.' Rennie was beginning to warm to Madeira, in spite of his determination not to. He knew that he should not be here, that his instructions forbade it; and he would not have come had he not been obliged to do so—absolutely obliged to do so, to preserve the safety of his ship.

The Quinta de Santa Francesca in the Rua da Carreira, in the English district of Funchal, was a very grand house in the neo-classical style, built for Mr Hapgood in extensive grounds, which included acres of fragrant, vividly blooming gardens and a series of ornamental ponds and lakes linked by a winding stream and gravel paths under wide-fronded trees. The teeming enterprise and bustle of the port and the old city were not greatly removed by distance from the house, but the long wall and the foliage, and the wide gardens, gave the house an air of perfect seclusion, half-hidden deep in its coloured shadows.

The dance for which Mr Hapgood had sent out invitations before the arrival of HM *Expedient* frigate, had since then assumed the importance of a ball. Captain Rennie had been invited, all of *Expedient*'s officers indeed, and Rennie found himself, when he came to the house on the appointed evening in his dress coat, uncomfortably the centre of attention. Rennie did not see himself as a public figure, deplored the very notion—but that was what he had become. The ship's guns, held now in the port under the guard of the ship's marines, who in turn were under the command of the ship's marine officer, Lieutenant Duggan, the ship's guns had commanded the attention of nearly the entire population.

The capital's children had come flocking to see them, and a good many of their older relations. The ship's stores, tiers of casks and piles of ropes, sails, &c., were also held there under canvas awnings on the cobbles, but it was the guns that drew and fascinated the crowd. Funchal was an old-established port, long used to ships, ships' stores, loading and unloading, all the paraphernalia of boats, tackle, nets and ropes and cables—but ships' guns ashore, great guns, naval guns, were not a usual thing. Such guns as were in the island stood in forts, largely away from the public gaze, and unremarked. Here were dozens of gleaming cannon, with shrouded flintlocks, and barrels of powder close by, massive metal things, redolent of power, the smashing tremendous power of a real ship of war.

Even the most sophisticated gentleman or lady of Funchal, well dressed, above the scuttering poor and their gapings, could not but be a little thrilled—a hidden thrill, certainly—by the glossy black menace of those guns. Thus Rennie found himself focused upon as their possessor. A man regarded not merely as a man, but as an officer in uniform, a man of action come here by chance, and all the more glamorous for that. It was a role he abhorred, and loathed, that made him quiver with embarrassment and something very like shame—at first.

'Look here, James, do not think me womanish, and timid, and so forth, but pray do not leave me alone, at the mercy of all these flashy-dressed people. Stay by me, support me as my second-in-command. Hey?'

That nervous 'hey' made James smile, but he contrived to be loyal: 'Very good, sir. However, there will no doubt come a time quite soon when we shall be separated, you know, by reason of the dance.'

'What? Dance? D'y'think I shall be expected to dance?' Alarmed.

'Oh, certainly. You are the guest of honour.'

'Christ's blood, James!' Muttering, smiling bravely, nodding his way across the room. 'I am not a dancing man!' And he thought of Sir Hendle Dawes, who had wisely fled to the mountains.

'I should drink some wine, sir, if I was you, and assume an easiness of mind about the whole evening. I am a married man, so it don't engage my interest, but had not you noticed the numbers of very pretty women that are here?'

'What? No, I had not. Where?'

'All about us, sir. Ah, thank you.' Taking a glass of sillery, and quaffing it.

Presently, a glass in his hand, Rennie felt that perhaps he could begin to take his lieutenant's advice, and attempt to enjoy himself.

'Captain Rennie,' said his host, striding towards him, a hand wide held, 'there is someone I want you to meet.'

Rennie met a great many people, merchants and officials and their wives, also numbers of the apparently unattached young women his lieutenant had noticed as they came in. It was a large, gay gathering, with a string quartet in a corner, sumptuous decorations, and plentiful wine. Rennie drank a great quantity of sillery, not by design but because his glass was constantly refilled; each time he brought it to his lips the chilled, refreshing liquid brimmed within, prickling agreeably at his nose, and he sucked it down with relishing pleasure. He endeavoured to be sociable, by entering into what he would in usual regard as entirely pointless discussion: gardens, fashions, furnishings, the price of wine, &c. He danced, if not nimbly then at least with enthusiasm. He had by now, after an hour or two, certainly noticed a particular young woman, in her middle twenties; dark-haired, dark-eyed, exquisitely dressed in such a way as to show off her figure to alluring advantage. He thought that she was attentive to his conversation, that she wished to make herself charmingly amiable, that indeed there was more than a hint of invitation in her sometimes prolonged glances before she averted her eyes, and hid them under long lashes.

Presently, as James came from another room to take leave

of his host, and his hostess—who was not, so he had been informed by another guest, the host's wife, but another lady—presently James looked about among the crowd of revellers for his captain, and could not find him.

'You leave us, Lieutenant?' said Mr Hapgood. 'But the night is hardly begun. Look, let me introduce you to——'

'Thank you, sir, you are very kind, but I must make an early start tomorrow. The work of repair must be overseen, and I must do my duty.'

'Ah yes, repair, of course. But you must come to us again, Lieutenant. In more intimate circumstances, a quiet dinner, and agreeable feminine company—you take my meaning?'

'I think I do, sir, and I must tell you that I am a married man.' Smiling so that he would not seem too much like a prig.

'Good God, sir, so am I. Are not we all? But you are far from home, and a man don't cease to be a man simply because he travels, eh?'

James thought that it would be impolite to disagree with so generous a host, and so he merely bowed, and repeated: 'You are very kind to us.' He glanced about. 'And now I must find Captain Rennie, and——'

'Pish pish now, Lieutenant,' said the lady by Mr Hapgood's side, 'there is no need of dragging your captain away quite yet.' She smiled at James. 'If you must go, you must, but Captain Rennie need not go with you, so early. He is quite safe with us here, I assure you,' she added with another smile. James had not quite heard this lady's name, when they had earlier been introduced.

'Now, Clara, do not bully the young man,' said Hapgood. 'He is a serving officer, with responsibilities.' Turning to James. 'But Clara is right, you know. No harm will come to Captain Rennie here.'

And James came away from the house without the captain, and without Lieutenant Peak, and Mr Loftus, neither of whom had he seen since they came up the steps under the torches. He walked back to the Residence through the balmy darkness, the fragrance of the gardens hanging on the air. He had drunk just enough wine to make him aware of the seductiveness of this place, but not enough to distract him and make him inattentive to his vows. Yes, certainly, there had been present at Quinta de Santa Francesca some delectably pretty young women, and he had danced with several of them, but none was nearly as beautiful as Catherine. And with that consoling thought he nodded goodnight to the servant at the door of the Residence, went upstairs, unbuckled his sword, undressed and went to bed.

In the morning he found that both Peak and Loftus had come back, and sat now upon the shaded terrace palely drinking tea—but that Captain Rennie had not.

The warm, balmy weather continued, and the work of repair at the end of the mole. The carpenter Mr Adgett, with his mate Huish Racken and their crew of artificers, aided by local boat-building men, worked from the ship's boats at the hove-up hull, stripped away torn and broken copper, and repaired fractured and splintered timbers. The frames of the ship had not been affected, to Mr Adgett's frequently expressed relief:

'As I say, was we to've had damaged frames, well—calamitous ain't too strong a word to describe that, Mr Hayter. Is the captain about, sir, or is he at the governor's Residence?'

'Not the governor's house, you know, Mr Adgett. The consul's house. There is no British governor here.'

'As you say, sir. Only I would like a word with the captain, on the matter of our copper——'

'I will convey to him that wish, Mr Adgett. He does not like to be disturbed at present.'

'Thank you, sir.' And Mr Adgett returned puzzled to the boat, to the sound of mallets and the swishing sluice of the pumps, required to keep water out of the ship in spite of all precautions of caulking and sealing with pitch. Black-backed gulls added their echoing, scolding clamour.

Other than the men required to be with the ship, at the pumps or in the boats, the bulk of Expedients were ashore with nothing to do, except get into mischief. They had been billeted at various inns and rooming houses in the old town, and could not altogether—under these circumstances—be trusted to attend muster at the place in the port where the stores and guns lay under guard, near the mole. At each muster men were missing, sometimes as many as fifteen or twenty, and Lieutenant Duggan's marines were sent into the old town to fetch them out. Drunkenness, in an island whose chief enterprise was the production of strong wines, was a daily occurrence, and there had been complaints in the town about lewd behaviour.

James had continued to live at the Residence, and Sir Hendle and Lady Dawes remained out of Funchal. Perhaps, thought James, the presence of a British man-of-war, and her troublesome complement, was an embarrassment to His Majesty's representative, one that he preferred to avoid.

Both Lieutenant Peak and Mr Loftus repeatedly inquired what had become of the captain. James did not know. Mr Hapgood did not know, when James called on him; or if he did, did not care to say so. The Reverend Mr Pembleton could cast no light on the matter; he had not seen Captain Rennie after his brief courtesy visit on the first day.

Then word came to the Residence: would Lieutenant Hayter kindly attend upon Senhora Maria Vicente at a house in the Calcado do Pico, where she would explain something to him? He did attend, climbing the hill to a large stone house with a coat of arms carved in stone at the gate. Seclusion, a wonderful view away to the east over the bay, Ponta da Garajau majestic in the distance. Ruddy turnstones and wagtails flitted and squabbled over the shrubs and trees of the garden as James came up the broad steps and lifted the iron knocker. He let it fall once, twice, and turned to the view as he waited. The door opened, a maidservant admitted him, and James gave his name and—on an intuitive assumption—Captain Rennie's. A broad hallway with a cool stone floor gave on to a curving stair and an elaborate gold-painted balustrade. A very singular woman came down that stair; not tall, but holding herself tall, with a fine head, and white hands held out in a gesture of—what? Welcome? Anxiety? Grief? He could not quite tell. Her beautiful face, the hair swept back from her forehead and caught behind with a ribbon, her face was inscrutable to him. What was the word? A mask. Her dress was truly gorgeous. She came with a faint rustling to the foot of the stair and advanced, her hands still outstretched. Good God, he thought, she is exactly like an actress, an actress entered upon a stage and come down to the lights to make her speech.

'Lieutenant Hayter, you are welcome to my house. I am so glad of you to come.' The faintest of accents, her voice thrilling and surprisingly deep.

'Senhora Vicente.' He bowed, bussed the extended hand. 'I think we was introduced at Mr Hapgood's house.'

'I remember you very well. You naval officers look so very fine in your dress coats.'

'Ah. Yes.—Captain Rennie? Is he here, in this house?'

She led him into a drawing room, with long windows shaded by fronds on the terrace to the rear. They sat down.

'Captain Rennie is staying here?' repeated James. He was nearly certain, now.

Senhora Vicente rang a bell. 'That is what I wish to explain. The captain is—he is unfit.'

'Unfit? You mean he is unwell?'

The maidservant reappeared, and Senhora Vicente said something to her, a rapid instruction in Portuguese, and the girl withdrew with a curtsey. Before James could again put his question Senhora Vicente turned her beautiful head and:

'I do not put it quite so, how I should. He is—he is injured.'

'Badly? He is badly hurt?' Concerned, half-rising.

She waved him down into his chair. 'No, no, it is not so very bad.' But something was happening to her mouth as she spoke, a peculiar distortion which soon affected her whole face. 'It is—it is——' And what James had thought was an expression of grief he saw now was suppressed laughter. This displeased him, and bewildered him.

'How is it funny? How was he hurt? You have left me behind, madam.'

'He—he fell backways—backwards—into a cardoon. His *behind* is very painful—hhhhhhhh—I am sorry.'

'Cardoon?' Shaking his head.

'It is a plant of spines. Of spikes.'

'Cactus! He fell into a cactus!'

'Yes, he did so. It is very painful for the poor captain. He had a little too much wine, I think, and he slipped in the garden, and fell hhhhhhh—I must not laugh. It was very shocking.'

'I must see him. I must ascertain when he may return. A doctor has attended him?'

'Oh, yes. All the spines was removed from him. He is quite safe, only very sore. And now he is resting, he is asleep. I sent for you to come because he wished it, to reassert you.'

'Reassure me, yes. Thank you, you are very kind, madam. I am very happy the captain is in good hands, and that he is not lost, as we had all feared. And now——'

The maidservant brought in a tray with coffee, and brandy.

'Will you take coffee, *Tenente*? Or cognac? Or both?'

'Neither, thank you. You are most kind, but I really must return to my ship. There is much work still to be completed, and in the captain's absence——' Rising.

'Oh, please do not rush away, *Tenente*. Stay a little minute, will you?' Her voice thrilling, her expression pleadingly earnest as she leaned forward, emphasising her decolletage.

'Naturally, as you wish.' Politely, sitting down again.

She sipped coffee. 'Tell me, *Tenente*, you know the theatre in London? Captain Rennie says that you are interested in the theatre, in literature.'

'Well, I have not been much at the theatre in recent days, I confess, and I have neglected my books. I am recently married.' He smiled.

'But you know Drury Lane? You have been there?' Without waiting for a reply: 'Oh, how I should love to see it. To see Sheridan, and Goldsmith, and Sibber.'

'Cibber? Colley Cibber? He is out of fashion now, I think. He is long dead.'

'Tragedy. Tragedy. But how I should love to see Garrick upon the stage!'

'Alas, he too is dead.'

'Dead? All these great theatricals are dead? Tragedy.'

'Well, not quite all of them, you know. Sheridan is alive. And Mrs Siddons lives, certainly.'

'Oh, how I should love to go to London!' A sigh. A glance at him.

'Your—your husband is not here at Funchal?'

'He is in Lisbon. He does not come here very often. He prefers that I should remain here, however. A prisoner.' Turning away to the window and lifting her hand to her neck.

'Ah.'

'Yes, a prisoner. This house, you will say, is not a prison, it is a beautiful house, with a beautiful view to the sea. But I will tell you, *Tenente*, it *is* a prison.' Dramatically, turning to him. 'It *is* a prison!'

'I am very sorry to hear it.'

'Captain Rennie has made an offer to me.' Another glance.

'Yes?'

'Yes, he has said to me: Maria, I will like you to come to London, when I am returned to England. You must come to me.'

'You and your husband?'

'No no no no no. My husband will remain at Lisbon. The invitation, the offer, is to me alone. My husband does not know of it, and then when I am gone—he may do what he will wish. I shall be gone away. I shall be in London.'

'You mean—you mean that Captain Rennie wishes you to join him in London, to *live* with him there?'

'He wishes for me to be his wife.'

'Good God.' Involuntarily. 'I do beg your pardon, Senhora Vicente. It is—it is certainly a most curious proposal, when you are married already. Do not you think?'

'It is a very joyful proposal, for me. I have said yes. With all my heart I have said yes.'

'Ah. Have you?'

'It is very joyful, but you do not smile, *Tenente*.' Her head on one side, her eyes upon him.

'It is most interesting news. Astonishing news, indeed.'

And shortly afterward he took his leave.

At the Residence he said to Mr Loftus: 'We must weigh and put to sea right quick, Bernard.'

'Put to sea?' Rising from his chair on the terrace. 'The repairs ain't complete. Adgett has not even begun to restore her copper.'

'We must get the captain out of that house, and back here. We must take in our guns and stores, weigh, and sink Madeira far to sternward. We must save him.'

'Save him from whom? What house? With respect, you ain't at all making sense, you know. Thank you.' To the boy who had brought his coffee.

'We have grown far too comfortable here at the Residence, we have not been rigorous in getting the ship ready for sea, and we have allowed the captain to be inveigled into a very desperate position. He has been plied with drink, injured, and ensnared by the most unscrupulous creature in the island.'

'Surely you cannot mean—at Mr Hapgood's dance? Yes, I remember her.' Mr Loftus had grown grave. He put down his coffee cup. 'Did he say whether or not his purse was safe? Did he look to his purse?'

'I was not permitted to see the captain, nor even to look at him. She has him ensnared there.'

'Drugged, d'y'think?'

'I had not thought of that. You may perhaps be right. At any rate, we must have him out of it, and away. We cannot waste any more time.'

'I am with you.'

'Mr Peak!' Looking to the far end of the terrace. 'Richard Peak! Get your arse out of that chair, sir, and present yourself for duty!'

And roused from his doze the junior lieutenant joined them, and together they formed a plan.

Alan Dobie, who had been living with the ship's standing officers, including the purser Mr Trent, in a rather low, grim old inn in the Rua de Santa Maria, in the old part of the town, a much dilapidated building, the white lime peeling from the walls, smelling foul at the rear—Mr Dobie had been sent for, and now left the inn to climb up the hill. He had complained to Mr Trent about their accommodations, and had been rebuffed:

'This is a untoward circumstance, Mr Dobie. It must be accounted for in my books. Expenditures of this sort must be found, they don't contrive to appear, miraculous, out of the air. This ain't a British port, you see, and there is no usual method, neither, of accounting for a careening repair, when alls of the people are took out of the ship, and housed ashore. It is most unusual altogether. You don't like your accommodations, Mr Dobie? Then do not blame me. Do not blame me, that is only trying to do my best for you, when there is no funds to spare.'

Alan had an ally in the lieutenant of marines, Mr Duggan, who had been—he thought unjustly—excluded from the party of officers housed at the Residence. Captain Rennie had decided that it was appropriate for all the marines, their corporal, sergeant, and commissioned officer to be housed together near to the ship's complement, in order to maintain discipline, and prevent drunken debauch in the town. Mr Duggan had resented this, not without good reason. One evening, returning from a foray which might easily have been managed by his sergeant, to bring back a dozen drunken seamen, he had had his scarlet coat repulsively besmirched when a chamber pot had been emptied from an upper window into the narrow street, and its contents of turds had fallen on his shoulder and back. Alan thought of this now as he climbed the hill to the Residence, into the sweeter-smelling air. He hoped that the other gunroom officers would ask him and Lieutenant Duggan to join them there, out of kindness.

He was soon disillusioned; the thought had not entered their heads. What was in their heads was the captain's plight, and how to relieve it. The doctor was with them. Thomas Wing had not been living at the Residence, but had found for himself a place in the lower town, where he had made himself daily available—as he would in the ship—to any and all ailing Expedients. Hearing of this, hearing of the diminutive Englishman who could cure and succour, local people began to come to him, bringing their sick children. It was with great reluctance that he had had to turn the bulk of these poor people away, for lack of time and space to deal with them.

'You and the doctor are to go to Senhora Vicente's house, Alan,' said James, 'and make it clear to her that she must allow the captain to be examined. Say that it is a matter of regulations. Produce an official document—one that I shall dictate and you will write out. If she makes excuses, or attempts to deflect you from your object, do not threaten or coerce her. Withdraw, bow and withdraw, politeness itself. The other part of our plan will then be brought into operation tonight.'

'Other part?' Thomas Wing turned from one to the other, looking at them all in turn. 'Other part?'

'Aye,' said James. 'You will present yourselves a second time at the door, this evening, you and Mr Dobie. You will iterate your earlier request: the captain must be examined by his own surgeon. Engage her in conversation, seek to be persuasive, politely and insistently. Keep her there. Mr Loftus, Mr Peak, and myself will deploy to the rear of the house, and gain entry through the kitchens or such quarters as is there. We shall then separate, and search the entire house until we find the captain. Mr Loftus thinks that he may be lying drugged in a remote room.'

'Drugged!' Alan and Thomas Wing together.

'I have met this woman, and conversed with her,' said James. 'She is amiable, plausible, and very beautiful—a fatal combination.'

'How is that fatal?' asked the doctor, shaking his head a little. 'Let me understand you, Mr Hayter. You think that she has kidnapped Captain Rennie, and is holding him there in her house against his will, has possibly stupefied him with a drug?'

'Yes.' A nod. 'I do.'

'Do not think me impertinent, Lieutenant, but—for what purpose?'

'To make him marry her! She told me that Rennie wishes her to go to London with him. She is already possessed of a husband, yet she sees no difficulty in marrying a second time, the devious creature. I believe she means to make him marry her before we depart the island.'

'Does she mean to bribe a priest to perform a bigamous marriage?' asked Alan incredulously. 'While the captain is in a stupor?'

Thomas Wing cleared his throat. 'May I ask what we are to do, Mr Dobie and I, if when we arrive at the house we discover that the captain does not *wish* to leave? That we find him quite well, in possession of his faculties, and determined to remain there? What then?'

'I had thought of just such a possibility,' said James. 'We

will execute the second part of our plan tonight, find the captain in the house, overpower him and bring him back to the ship.'

'Is not that mutiny?' ventured Alan. 'To assault the captain?'

'It will damn well be mutiny if you don't obey me, the pair of you!' said James now, getting fierce. 'The captain must be saved. Saved from that woman, and from his own folly, and brought back to his proper condition of an officer serving His Majesty. D'y'have me?'

'Well, I suppose so, Mr Hayter.' Reluctantly. 'You are in command.'

James, relenting a little: 'You will say, I expect, that I should take Mr Duggan and his marines up to the house, and simply demand that she release the captain forthwith. It is all well and good allowing marines to bring back a few drunken seamen in the lower town. The authorities look kindly enough on that. But I cannot deploy marines in the respectable district of Funchal. They would not be welcome. We are not in a British port, we are guests of a foreign power, and we must be discreet. That is why I employ you and the doctor, because you are not fighting men, you are merely meek underlings, carrying a message, and making a request.'

'Meek underlings?' wondered Mr Loftus, when the pair had gone away.

'Well, that is what they are,' said James. 'There is moments when only plain language will do.'

When Alan Dobie and Thomas Wing, carrying their folded and sealed 'document', had presented themselves at the door of Senhora Vicente's house, and the maidservant had gone to find her mistress, Captain Rennie strode to the door—wincing as he came—and demanded to know what the devil they meant by coming there at all, when he was in the house by invitation, and it was none of their damned business, nor anyone's in the ship, or out of the ship. Alan was prepared to be submissive, and subservient, and to go away without demur, but the surgeon saw through the captain's bluster, saw straight through it, and found underneath—if not fear exact, then a degree of apprehension, and discomfort. The captain knew, in little, that he had made a fool of himself, was making a fool of himself still, and did not quite know how to extricate himself from that lamentable condition without dishonour.

'Go away at once,' he said. 'When I want you, either of you, I shall send word.' Turning away from the door.

'You are limping, sir,' said the doctor.

'What?' Turning again to him, irritably. 'Kindly do not——'

'I have brought with me a salve, and something for you to ingest, that will ease the discomfort.'

'A salve?' Hope of relief in his face, instantly replaced by a frown. 'I have no need of unguents, nor physic. I am perfectly sound, perfectly well.'

'Sir, I think you are not. I will not feel quite content until I have made sure of your healing. The cactus spine is a pernicious interloper; if not entirely removed it festers and corrupts, under the skin.'

'What d'y'know of cactus!' erupted Rennie. 'I have said nothing of cactus!' Wincing again.

Thomas Wing came inside, that small, determined man, and took the captain by the elbow, unbidden. Firmly: 'You do not wish to be crippled for life, sir. As your surgeon, with only your welfare in my mind, as is my sworn duty, I am going to examine your backside, and treat your injury. If you please.' Guiding him to a door within. Rennie allowed himself to be taken into the room beyond, and the doctor shut the door behind them.

Alan stood alone on the cool stone floor of the hall, and was nonplussed when Senhora Vicente appeared, looking cross, her maidservant hovering behind.

'Has Lieutenant Hayter sent you? Who are you?' Noting his plain green coat, and his hat held in his hand. 'You are not a naval officer, I think?'

Alan bowed. 'I am very sorry to intrude upon your, upon

your, into your house, madam. I am come upon Mr Hayter's request, upon his instruction, to inquire——'

A muffled gasp of pain from behind the closed door, across the hall. Senhora Vicente darted a look there. To Alan:

'Is Captain Rennie in there?' Making towards the door. 'Who is with him?'

Alan ran in front of her, and stood with his back to the door. 'If you please, madam, his doctor is attending on him. He is examining the patient. If you please.'

'Doctor? Why, my own doctor has cured the captain. He has been cured. What is this new doctor, that comes into my house? Who is it!'

'He is the captain's own doctor, madam, from the ship. A naval doctor. Who must, by order'—waving the document the lieutenant had caused him to write out—'by order examine him.'

'But I have not permitted it! I have not asked such a person to come here, to my house! How dare you to come here!' Senhora Vicente had grown very imperious, and Alan knew that he could do nothing more to persuade her, to dissuade her, in her own house. He stood aside. She pushed past him, grasped the handle of the door, and flung it open.

Thomas Wing looked over his shoulder, a bloody instrument in his hand, an open tweeze-case on a chair, the captain's bare backside behind, bent over. 'Have a care now, madam, lest I slip, and cause a dreadful accident to his nether person!'

Captain Rennie was persuaded—his buttocks freed of the remaining, concealed spines, and duly salved and bandaged, and his discomfort further alleviated by alcoholic tincture of opium—the captain was persuaded to return to the Residence.

'I must keep you in my care a further four-and-twenty hours,' insisted Thomas Wing.

Rennie took his leave of his hostess, briefly and in private, then went away with Wing and Alan Dobie, compliant but out of temper, to the Residence.

'Thank God you are safe, sir,' said James in greeting.

'Safe, Mr Hayter? Safe?' Brusquely. 'I was never not safe. What the devil d'y'mean?'

'We had been very worried and concerned, sir, when you did not return, that you had perhaps been set upon by footpads——'

'Footpads! In Funchal? Don't talk womanish, Mr Hayter. I sent word that I have been a guest a day or two at another house. Why should I not be a guest at another house, as well as in this? Hey?'

'Indeed, sir, there is no reason at all. We are becalmed, as it were, and nothing to be done until our repairing is completed.'

'Just so.'

'However—however, perhaps it might have been prudent in you, sir, had you informed me a day or two earlier, as your second-in-comm——'

'Prudent! Who are you to tell me to be prudent! Good God!'

'I beg your pardon, sir.'

'Stop fussing about behind me there, Mr Wing, for Christ's sake! Have you not cut and pricked my arse enough in one day!'

'You are bleeding, sir, through your britches. I did warn you that excessive agitation——'

'What! I am bleeding! What have you done to me, you damned dwarf!' Turning angrily, craning his neck to look at his behind.

The doctor froze in the act of opening his small leather bag, and stood very still. Rennie became aware of the sudden uneasy silence, and observed the small, contained figure of the surgeon, his back to the room.

'What have I said?' Rennie sniffed, and looked at the others, who looked away. 'Have I said what I oughtn't?'

James coughed, and cleared his throat.

'Well?' Rennie looked at them—James, Mr Loftus, young Peak—and none would meet his eye.

'Mr Wing.—Doctor.'

The doctor turned slowly round. He met the captain's gaze, and waited, his face without expression.

'Doctor, I think that I may have said something, just now, that—that was ignoble in me. Something to which you might perhaps have took offence, was you to have took it wrong.'

'Wrong, sir?' Quietly.

'Well well, it was wrong. I apologise, Mr Wing. Doctor. You have done your best for me, in removing the wretched spines, and I am very sorry.'

'Thank you, sir.' A bow.

'Good. Very good. Well now, gentlemen'—turning to the others—'what d'y'say to a glass of wine?'

'You will take no wine, sir, until I permit it,' said the doctor behind him, in an implacable tone. 'Nor will you leave this house.'

At sea, 31 degrees 46 minutes north, 22 degrees 17 minutes west. The wind on beam and quarter, and *Expedient* under all plain sail, a flying jib to keep her head up, making a steady nine knots. Well victualled, fresh produce taken in, wine, water, wood—from that wooded island—and killing beasts in the manger. Her repair, in timber if not in copper, entirely sound, and the ship nearly dry. The torn and buckled copper, at the place of injury, had been prised off, beaten flat and renailed, but there were gaps in that protection, inevitable gaps, since parts of several sheets had been torn away and lost. It could not be helped; the deficiency of metal could only be remedied at Port Royal, where there was a proper naval dockyard. Mr Adgett, although less than wholly content, had been reconciled to the insufficiency. Mr Trent, greatly troubled by additional costs, had not become reconciled. It was not only the cost of victuals, and the local boat-building men for their labour, but of the accommodations in the lower town at Funchal, while the ship had lain hove-up, careened.

Captain Rennie dismissed these concerns.

'It ain't a question of moneys, Mr Trent.'

'Ain't a question of *moneys*!' Genuinely shocked. 'Then what is it a quest——'

'It is a question of time. I have lost near two weeks of time.'

To James, with whom he had restored equitable relations, he said: 'I know that I may rely on you, and the other gunroom officers, to say nothing of my little misfortune at Funchal.'

'It is already forgotten, sir.'

'Just so. Thank you.—However, however, some little inkling of it may have crept into the ship, elsewhere in the ship.'

'I think that is improbable, sir. No one was aware of it, outside the consul's Residence.'

'I suppose so. Thank God the consul himself was not there. And his servants are discreet, you think?'

'Their palms was crossed, crossed generous.'

'Indeed, just so.' But the agitation in his breast remained, the fear of dire consequence should the truth reach London, and the Admiralty. 'I have lost weeks of time. Should Their Lordships hear of it, or Sir Robert Greer, God knows what fate might——'

'There is no question of consequence, or fate,' James earnestly interrupted. 'Sir, we was obliged to go to Madeira, else allow the ship to sink under us. Their Lordships know that anything may happen at sea, that sea officers and their people must make the best of things when an accident happens, and their ship is damaged. Good heaven, if we did not have that leeway no man would ever venture beyond sight of land.'

'Yes, yes, yes, you are right.' A sigh. 'I meant—I meant the other accident.'

'You are quite healed now, sir? It is no longer painful?'

A sharp glance at James, then, seeing no mockery: 'I am sound again, in that place. Like the ship, hey?'

'Like the ship, sir.' A smile.

'Well well, I shall not speak of it again, after this—but do you think that the lady herself——'

'That lady will not make trouble for you, sir. She is married, with a position in the island. Even in that island, where much goes unremarked as a matter in course, she would be foolish to jeopardise her position by pursuing you beyond. No doubt her husband is content to let her lead her own life when he is not there, as very probably he leads his own life in Lisbon—but beyond that? I think not. I think you are quite safe, sir.'

'I think that I have had a lucky escape, then. I damn near made a fool of myself.'

James was silent.

'And I have you to thank for effecting my rescue, James. You and Mr Wing.'

'We did our duty, sir, nothing more, in restoring you to—to health.'

'Yes, to health. Of body and mind, hey? Of body *and* mind. I will like to give a dinner, tomorrow, now that the doctor has permitted me again to take wine. Wing shall be my guest, one of my guests. Will you join me as another, James?'

'With pleasure, sir.'

'In the interim, we will clear for action and fire the great guns. We must not allow our people to think that the interlude at Funchal makes the pattern for the entire cruise. They have got soft, lolling about, whoring and drinking. They must be brought back to their proper work, as hands in a fighting ship.'

'Very good, sir.'

Damped flannel cartridge ready, and shot boxes; tackles loosed, hand spikes laid out, sponge-rammers taken down.

'Run out your guns!'

The cries of the gun captains to their tackle men, and the heavy rumbling of trucks.

'Prime!'

Gun captains forward with their horns, the goose-quill priming tubes filled with fine mealed powder mixed with spirits of wine.

'Point your guns!'

Handspikes and crows, gun captains crouched ready behind the flintlocks, and:

'Fire!'

Lanyards pulled in a long ripple, and the broadside of guns erupted in smoke, blasting flame, and huge, concussive shocks of sound

BANG BANG BANG BANG BANG

and the solid two-ton masses of black metal jerked back against the breeching ropes. One breeching rope, spring-loaded, snapped at the button, flew wide in a flail of untwisting strands, the gun ran back unchecked—and under the gun was a man. His scream cut off at once. In the hanging, vaporous incense of powder smoke, along the sanded deck, a sudden silence, except for the hissing seethe of the sea along the wales.

'We are cursed in this ship.' As he said this Rennie did not turn to look at Mr Storey, the ship's gunner, who stood in the great cabin behind him. The captain faced the stern gallery windows, blindly faced them, for his eyes were shut.

'I do not know how nor why the breeching rope broke, sir. All breechings and tackles has been checked regular since we weighed at Spithead. All ropes was new, fresh issued, I saw to that myself, with Roman Tangible.'

'We are cursed.' Barely above a murmur.

'Ropes do fail, sir. Cables fail and part, stays and shrouds. It is not our privilege always to know the reason. Only the Almighty knows such things.'

'Damnation to that, Mr Storey.' Rennie opened his eyes, and turned round. 'Nor God, nor the lower fellow neither, had any part in what happened today.—Yes, Mr Wing?'

'Steep is dead, sir.' At the door.

A nod. 'Thank you, Doctor.'

'He never did open his eyes again, and so he did not suffer.'

'I am glad of that, in least. I am glad of nothing else.' Bleakly. Another nod, of dismissal.

'I have caused new breeching to be sprung and rigged at the gun, sir.'

'Yes, Mr Storey, thank you. I shall not trouble you further, now.' Then, as the gunner made to depart: 'I must tell you, I do not blame you, Mr Storey. Let me make that plain. Neither you, nor the crew of the gun. It was not your fault. You apprehend me?'

'Thank you, sir.'

'It is the ship. We had it the first commission, with those damned Waterfield patterns, and now the same curse has risen from the bilges, wafting and stinking, and caught us about like invisible seizings, like a miasma of unsighting twine.' He shivered, as if to shake himself free.

Mr Storey could think of nothing to say, nothing that was permissible, and he put on his hat and went away. Rennie shook himself again, sniffed deep, and went on deck.

'Mr Hayter.'

'Sir?' Lowering his glass and attending.

'We will conduct the burial service when we are rigged for church tomorrow.'

'Very good, sir.'

'The crew of Steep's gun is to have an extra ration of grog. Say so to Mr Loftus.'

'Very good.—May I make a suggestion, sir?' His glass under his arm.

'What is it?'

'By the quarter bill in course they are a crew, sir, number six starboard gun. But their mess numbers differ. Will it not be better to give all the hands extra grog, sir? Rather than a few men scattered across different messes?'

'No.' A glance. 'It is not a matter for celebration in the ship that a man is dead.'

'I did not mean it in any way as a celebration, sir. The opposite. A way of lifting the spirits of the people against dark——'

'Lifting their spirits? That ain't possible after what has happened. It is fitting their spirits is low. I wished only to benumb the men that was present, but I will belay that instruction. There will be no extra grog for any man in the ship. It ain't fitting.'

'Very good, sir.' Regretting now that he had spoken.

Rennie stood closer to the wheel and spoke to the weather helmsman: 'Robert Marston, how does she lie?' Glancing aloft.

'She is lying well free, sir. Five points large.'

'Mr Hayter!'

'Sir?'

'We will haul up the weather clew of the main course.'

The speaking trumpet raised, the order given. The sun reddening now in the canvas towers as the ship made south-west-by-west, flying and slowly flying across the vastness of the sea.

'D'y'see, they gave me the first commission in *Expedient* because I am a dull fellow. Dull, and worthy, wishing to be a gentleman, and most unlikely to abscond with the gold.'

'Wishing to be a gentleman, sir? You have left me behind.'

The night of the following day, a Sunday. The burial service over and done, prayers read, the Articles read, and the ship inspected by divisions. The Sunday dinner that Rennie had proposed cancelled, because he thought it wrong to entertain after a solemn occasion, the memory of Steep's weighted shroud plunging over the side still sharp in the mind of every man. Rennie and James, as they had so often their first voyage, sat together in the great cabin, contemplatively drinking wine and talking, talking as informally and intimately as it was possible for two sea officers to do in a crowded ship, with only bulkheads and decking to shut them away from 250 men nearby.

Rennie did not answer the question, and James let it sink away astern in the washing of the sea. He had written a letter to Catherine at Funchal, which he had intended to send home by a merchant ship; Rennie had learned of the letter and forbidden him to send it, on the grounds that they should not be there, that there could be no communication from the ship to England until they had reached their official destination at Port Royal. James had resented this at first, keenly felt it, thinking it a quibbling, foolish, petty, mean-spirited interpretation by Rennie of his instructions. However, he had complied, had come to see that Rennie was probably right; and now the matter was no longer one of contention between them. Now they were again easy one with the other, they could talk as friends, in familiar surroundings, and Rennie could relieve the loneliness of command and unburden himself.

'And because I brought them back their great prize,' he continued, pushing the bottle across the table, 'they have now given me my reward: a second commission. A second commission, in the peace, when dozens of other post captains, poor devils, lie on the beach on half-pay.' A hint of irony in his voice.

'It is more than simple reward, sir, surely. Else why would Sir Robert Greer involve himself with us a second time?' He poured wine. 'You said, I think, that he gave you sight of certain letters, cryptographic letters, translated? Surely these do not concern only a charting survey?'

'Yes, yes, I have thought it all out, you know, James. I did not see it clear, at first, but now I am perfectly convinced. It is all a damned hoodwinking scheme, d'y'see. An artifice.'

'Eh?'

'It is all dishwater, the whole contriving plan. So that I would not pursue them.'

'Is it . . .?'

'Yes, look, it is the most transparent thing. I have made a claim against the Admiralty, which they know to be just. Which they have known all along to be just. I would not give it up, I would not desist, even when they sent Sir Robert to dissuade me, and intimidate me. I would not.' He slapped the table, and sniffed. 'Therefore, they knew they would have to invent a whimsy, a fantastical whimsy, about an invasion of Jamaica by hobgoblins in the night, or wild dogs, or stray porpoises—who knows what was in their heads! Hey? Damned foolishness, and coded documents, and that sinister chalky-faced fellow to peddle it all, whisper it in my ear as a wondrous and noble duty "in the nation's interest". In the nation's interest? Swill, James, and hog's piss. It is in nobody's interest excepting their own. So they send me far away on foreign service, in pursuit of tropical faeries, to *stop my claim*.'

James sat mute, caught himself openly staring at his captain, and hastily took up his glass. He swallowed the wine in one draught.

'Well, it is obvious, is it not? Don't you think so, James?'

'Well, sir, well—I am not in command. You know all of the facts, in all distinctions.'

'I know no more than you do, James. Oh—but in course you have not seen the letters.'

'No, sir. I have not.'

'You must see them now, James. Then you can be in no more doubt than I am myself.'

As he stood up and stepped to his desk the ship dipped her head into a sudden trough, and Rennie steadied himself with a long reaching hand. Was he drunker than he seemed? wondered James.

'Here are the letters, copied out in Dr Jepp's hand.' He passed a fold of documents to James. James opened the fold, and withdrew the sheets. Attached to the top of the first sheet was a note in a neat hand:

> There is strong reason to believe that this man is Pierre Henri Lascelles, Comte d'Argenton, of the Château de St Felix, which lies in the dry, stony and impoverished region between the ancient towns of Lodève and Clermont l'Hérault, west of Montpellier and the Golfe du Lion. His estate is impoverished, & he is heavy in debt.

James folded back the note, and began to read the first of the letters, which bore the heading, in capitals:

E.J. DISENCRYPTED & TRANSCRIBED

> You are to take ship at Marseilles, & proceed to the Caribbean, calling as arranged at Martinique; then you are to proceed to Jamaica, under the arranged alias. There you will contact M.L. He has the highest connections in the island, & is entirely respectable. His advice & intelligence will be invaluable to you.
>
> You will establish yrself as agreed as a person of business—according to the abilities you have described to us. Bank drafts will be written in yr name, so that you may find premises, and do so at once.

The second letter, which he now turned up, gave a great number of details of the leading sugar estates of Jamaica—the families, holdings, districts, numbers of slaves, income, &c.

The third letter addressed a particular purpose:

> Your object is to discover how—and how soon—it may be achieved, without raising the slightest

suspicion nor engendering alarum, until afterward, when the bird has flown. When you have established yrself, & are known & unremarked among them, proceed as arranged.

There is ample opportunity, at Spanish Town, to gain admittance, and keep yr ears open. You may well hear significant things, by virtue of being unnoticed—for these high persons speak freely among themselves in private. In wine-loosened talk they may let slip all manner of indiscretion—not merely of a scandalous nature, but matters of moment—politics, defences, &c. Be discreet in your occupations, always discreet, & listen—and learn what is vital to yr success.

James finished reading, then sat forward in his chair, frowning, and holding the several sheets in his hand. He looked at Rennie.

'You have read all of these letters, sir?'

'Yes, James, indeed I have read them. It is a most remarkable and elaborate ruse, ain't it? Carefully rendered to persuade me that we face a clever villain, a remarkably clever spy, that has crept into the bosom of Jamaican society, is even now lurking there. Hm. Well well. No doubt when we reach Port Royal there will be additional such papers, designed to persuade me further. No doubt I shall be required to kidnap the fellow, spirit him out of the island and back to England, so that he may there be cast into a dungeon at Windsor Castle, for the King to gloat over, and tip the royal piss pot over his head. By God, they must think me very gullible, James!' Sniffing, shaking his head. 'But they have wasted their time, hey? I shall not desist in my claim—Sir Robert Greer, subterfuge, damned foolish letters, Frenchman spies, and all!'

'Sir, may I speak plain?' Earnestly.

'You are free to do so, my dear James. By all means.' Rennie refilled his glass.

'This is not a deception, sir.'

'What?' Putting down the bottle, a disbelieving smile.

'This is not something fraudulent, invented to hoodwink you. It is entirely true, entirely serious. And we are caught up in it.'

'Come now, James, good heaven ha-ha-ha, you jest eh?—Surely, you have not been taken in?' Frowning.

'I do not jest, sir. You see, I know this name.'

'What the devil d'y'mean?' Half-bewildered, half-cross. 'It is an invented name.'

'No, sir, it is not. This man, Henri Lascelles, Comte d'Argenton, lost a large sum at cards to a friend of mine, Jack Torrance, and then contrived to provoke a quarrel, which became a duel. I was present. It was at Cambridge, when we was all undergraduates. I acted as my friend's second in the matter, and saw the whole thing. Lascelles fired before my friend was ready—he had not even cocked, nor aimed—and he took the ball in his eye, and fell dead. Lascelles then made his escape to France, and was never made to answer for it.'

Rennie stared at him in the creaking quiet, and the bell sounded forrard, echoing through the ship. Rennie tapped his fingers on the table. 'I should take it very ill if you *was* in jest about this, James. It is far too——'

'Sir, it is not a matter for jesting. I saw my friend Torrance killed. Lascelles is the worst kind of damned scoundrel——'

'Yes. Yes. I am sorry.' Rennie pushed away his glass. A nod, a sniff. 'Well well, I see that I must reconsider. Perhaps I have been too dismissing of the Reverend Jepp and his crypts, too hasty altogether. We shall not know for certain until we come to Port Royal. If Lascelles is in the island, we shall discover what Sir Robert wishes us to do with him.'

'He will not be living under his own name there, but under an alias, surely?'

Rennie lifted his head, nodded wisely, and took a breath. 'Yes, I am in no doubt.' As if he had already been thinking the same. 'I am to consult with the Port Admiral, and other officials, upon our arrival. Perhaps the Governor himself. Who knows what intrigue awaits us?'

But he could not rid himself of the sense that he was being deceived, all the same, that he should never have accepted this commission, that he should have stayed at home in England and pursued his claim. Intrigue, and spies, and plotting, was not business satisfactory nor becoming to a sea officer.

'Is the ship lucky, d'y'think, or unlucky?'

'*Expedient*, sir?'

'Aye, *Expedient*.'

'There can be no other answer excepting "lucky".' Confidently.

James said to the surgeon, when they were briefly alone in the gunroom: 'Doctor, I must ask your candid opinion.'

'You are unwell?' Closing a book.

'No. It is—that is, I wish to discover whether or no someone else is unwell.'

'Should not that person himself consult me?'

'No. That is, I do not wish to discommode him, you know. I do not wish to interfere with his peace of mind. However, it is his peace of mind, or the lack of it, that troubles me.'

'Troubles *you*, Mr Hayter?—Ah, yes, I see. It is the captain.'

A glance, a nod. 'Yes.'

'You think that he is losing his reason? That he has lost it? Already, has lost it?'

'Not quite that, you know. It is only that—well, he is not always quite entirely cogent in his thoughts.'

'Ahh. In other words, you think he *is* mad.'

'No. No, I do not think that. But I am mindful what he suffered our first commission, in the Pacifick Ocean, at the hands of the savages upon the island. Perhaps he has recalled that terrible experience, and——'

'And is *going* mad, because of it?'

'No. Well, perhaps a little. This is very hard, very taxing, to say such things about my commanding officer is——'

'Mutiny? Treason? Surely if the captain was mad, and we did nothing, you nor I, to save ourselves and the ship from his depredations, *that* would be treason, would it not?'

'It is certainly our duty to aid him in all things.'

'Lieutenant, you cannot aid a madman in anything, if neither your nor he will acknowledge the fact of his madness.' Patiently.

'Well, well, I suppose so—put like that. Put like that, I must do something about it. Which is why I have come to you. I cannot say to his face that he is unwell. But you could say it, Doctor. You could cause him to examine his own condition, so to say, and—and confront it.'

'I do not think the captain is mad,' said the doctor. 'He is a man much given to speculation, and deep thought, in personal questions. Many sailors are like that, I think. They have a great deal of time for reflection, after all.' He picked up his book. 'Say this to him: "Sir, you are pallid, a little. Should not you see the doctor?" '

'Hm, yes, I know what he will say to that: "I am perfectly well." '

'Yes, he may very probably say that. But then afterward he will think on what you said, and he will come to me. I must look to the sick list, Mr Hayter.' And taking his book he went from the gunroom.

James had no time to ask the doctor what treatment he might propose, even if Rennie did ask for his attention. Had he done right in saying anything at all? He did not know that, either.

He did say something to the captain, the next day. Not: 'You are pallid.' He said instead: 'Are you quite sure the doctor removed all those troublesome spines, sir?'

'Eh? Why d'you ask that?' As they went over the ship, a routine inspection.

'I read once, in a book, that if such things cannot be entirely removed, after an accident such as you suffered, they may produce illness months afterward.'

'But I am not ill, I am cured. They was all removed.—You have replaced the wooden tallies on all sails?' he asked the sailmaker. Massed sails lay before them in the lockers.

'Aye, sir. As instructed.'

'Point to the fair-weather fore royal, if you please.—Very good. I am satisfied.' They moved on, and up the ladder. When they were on the lower deck, Rennie paused and looked at James again, shaking his head. 'Why did you ask me about those damned spines just now, James?'

'It is nothing, except you had the look of—well, no matter.'

'No matter? No matter? What had I the look of, hey? Speak plain, now.'

'Well, sir, you had a slightly flushing look, as if something might have got into your blood.'

'Good heaven, what nonsense. Nonsense, James. I am perfectly well.'

But the captain did consult the surgeon, in his little dispensary in the orlop.

'Good morning, sir. You come with me to look at the men on the sick list? I am glad——'

'No no. In least, I will like to see the sick men presently. First, however, I must—I must consult your opinion.'

'You wish me to prescribe a draught? To help you to sleep?'

'No no. I am feeling—I have felt not quite myself these last days. I wonder, can it be those damned cardoon spines?'

'I can say beyond doubt that those spines was all removed, sir. I took great care, peering through a lens, took great care to see that your posterior was entirely free of them, at the end. It cannot be that.' Firmly.

'Ah. Hm. Well well. Then it must be something other, that has caused——'

'Please to sit down, Captain Rennie. Or perhaps you would prefer it, was I to attend on you in your quarters?'

'No no. No, here in the orlop is more convenient.' He took off his coat, and loosened his shirt.

Thomas Wing took the captain's pulse, listened to his breathing, and looked into his eye. He made him put out his tongue. 'Your bowels is opened daily?' Sharply.

'Indeed, Doctor, indeed. Defecation ain't a difficulty.'

'You pass water without discomfort?'

'I piss freely, excellent free.'

'Appetite?'

'And I eat hearty, Doctor. Stamp's replacement is altogether a better cook. You remember Mr Stamp. That made pies so——'

'Shh, if you please.' Tapping his chest, then his knee. Then: 'There is no physical manifestation of illness. Your colour is good, your pulse steady, no wayward nor malignant humours is present. However—hmm.'

'Yes? However?' Beginning to be concerned.

'May I speak freely?'

'I hope that we may both speak freely, Doctor.'

'I detect in your eye a certain sideways quickness, a jumping look, that betrays disturbance. Something is causing you anxiety.'

'Anxiety? Nay, Doctor, there is nothing remotely like. I am perfectly well, you said so yourself, just now.'

'Then why have you come to me?' Again sharply.

'Why? Because I had not felt quite well. Since I have learned otherwise, thank God, I am entirely hale.'

'I think not.'

'What? What the devil d'y'mean?' Jumping up.

'You are agitated, sir. Something is troubling you.'

'Good God, man, there is an hundred things and more which the captain of a man-of-war must attend to, day upon day. Yes, I am troubled by many things, little things. Lists, and books, and the condition of the ship, and punishments, and grievances, and divers stupidities in the lower deck. It is endless. However, I am able to deal with all such distracting things, by method. Method, and regulation, and discipline. And so they do not grow large in my mind, nor defeat my purpose. Now, then.'

'I think you know very well, Captain Rennie, that we are not speaking of little, usual things.'

The captain put on his shirt, and his coat, and glared straight ahead very severe as he did so. Without another word he left the doctor's quarters, and climbed the ladder.

In his cabin he sent for the cook. His steward was a competent-enough man, who could provide him with tea, and snacks, and his breakfast. However, as on the first voyage, he had now to rely on the ship's cook to provide him with his meals, rather than a cook of his own. Mr Pleasance, the present ship's cook, was a one-legged man, and Rennie heard his stumping, peg-legged approach along the deck.

'You sent for me, sir?'

'I did, Pleasance, I did. I will like to give—come in—I will like to give dinners. There has been a deficiency of dinners, a wanting in number.'

'You has not been getting your meals regular, sir? I am very shocked to hear it. I has sent them by the steward, my mate has sent them——'

'Nay, Pleasance,' shaking his head, 'I have had my own dinners, do not rebuke yourself as to that. And very tolerable, too. Excellent. No, what I require of you is captain's dinners, you apprehend me? Gatherings.'

'Ahh. I see, sir, yes. Courses. Removes. Wine aplenty. *Puddings*. With the other officers.'

'You have it exact.'

'I shall do my best, sir. When will you wish me to prepare the first?'

'Tomorrow.'

*

His guests were the three junior midshipmen, Abey, Mayfield and Lamarr, the master Bernard Loftus, Lieutenant Peak, the purser Mr Trent, and Alan Dobie. Neither the doctor nor the first lieutenant had been invited. Thomas Wing was not surprised by this apparent slight, nor unhappy. He did not greatly care for formal dinners, since they were invariably bibulous. He had found in the past at such dinners, after the first course had been removed, and the second decanter of wine had been replaced by the third, and fourth, that not much sense was talked; that what was discussed was repeated, point for point, in ever more emphatic and insisting tones, as faces grew red, and redder; that conviviality was in truth loud, sweaty, over-indulging, a lesson in brutish consumption, like hogs squealing and grunting at the swill trough. Lieutenant Hayter did feel his exclusion, though. He did feel it as a slight, a deliberate bringing-down slight. He knew why he was slighted: because he had spoken to the doctor about Rennie, and Rennie knew it, and resented it. And now James felt his displeasure.

He had been meant to. He had the deck as the dinner proceeded beneath his feet. He heard the muffled clinking of decanter and glass, the clatter of removing plates, the raised voices and laughter; and he busied himself. He would not allow himself to be brought low, nor filled with resentment. He found out the speed of the ship, glass by glass, as the middies on watch ran out the logline; he stood at the weather rail and conned the ship, eyes aloft, speaking trumpet held in his hand; he made his notations at each striking of the bell; spoke to the quartermaster, the marine sentry, the afterguard petty officer; he required the lookouts to report to the deck. He busied himself, and smelled the wind, heard it sighing and humming in the rigging. He heard the sea, the seething rush of water along the lee, and the wash of it astern. And he saw the seabirds hovering wing-stretched at the high yards, keeping pace with the running ship. He busied himself, and his spirit lifted as men's spirits have always lifted at sea, when they are handling ships in fair winds.

Rennie reflected, after his dinner, that Thomas Wing had become quite a different fellow, a changed man, since *Expedient*'s first commission. Then, at the last moment before weighing, he had come aboard with his dunnage, that diminutive figure, and had been almost pathetically grateful to have been taken into the ship without a proper warrant, to have achieved his life's ambition of going to sea. Then he had had to suffer—as the entire ship's complement had had to suffer—the imposition of a warranted surgeon by Admiral Hollister. Had had to vacate his quarters, and hand over to an overbearing, incompetent, wretched fellow all of his instruments and potions, and watch while these were incompetently inflicted upon sick and injured men. All of this had been a great trial to Thomas Wing, until the sudden—and merciful—death of the pestilential surgeon, Mr Lancing. Wing had then, to the relief of all, resumed his rightful position as the ship's medical man. He had grown throughout the commission, if not in stature then certainly in status, through all the ship's ordeals and tribulations and alarums, had grown and earned the respect of every man aboard.

But now, in this new commission, his new warrant under his arm, there was a new appearance to Thomas Wing, a new confidence of manner and bearing and speech, a new maturity in the way he looked the world in the eye, and was not bemused or intimidated or dismayed by what he saw; and Rennie was not entirely sure that he liked this new Wing. A ship's surgeon's business, Rennie thought, was illness, and injury: stubborn constipation, seasickness, fever, the pox; broken bones, gashed flesh, boils. It was not the workings of men's minds, their private concerns and anxieties, and unresolved conflicts of the spirit. Those were surely the province of the Almighty.

However, there was no chaplain aboard to whom Rennie might turn for solace. Even had there been such a person aboard it was doubtful—very doubtful—that he would have consulted him in such a question, or for such a need. Prayer was the only fitting answer. Prayer, and purity of thought. Good God, how had he permitted himself to be lured into that woman's house, at Funchal? How could he have been so foolish as to risk his entire career on such damned recklessness, like an over-eager quivering virgin boy, or a dog snuffling at the rump of a bitch? What had possessed him?

'Sillery,' he said aloud. 'Intoxication. Wine.'

He resolved henceforth to be sober.

'I am not sober, now,' again aloud.

And then he thought of his first lieutenant, who had gone behind his back to the doctor, had sought to influence the doctor in the whole question, the cardoon spines, &c., and the adjacent folly. He thought about James and was once again vexed by what his lieutenant had done, was glad that he had excluded him from the dinner, and the doctor also. Meddlers. Meddlers. Well well, they would not undermine him, the pair of them, they would not succeed.

A further troubling thought came to him, in this troubling reverie: had the death of Steep, the gun captain, been visited upon the ship in retribution for his own offence?

'No! No, that is too much!' He shook his head to free his mind of such pious idiocy, and to clear it of fumes; sneezed, and heard:

'D-e-e-e-ck! D-e-e-e-ck! Ship's boat adrift, on the starboard bow!' and ran up the ladder.

As he came on the quarterdeck he missed his long glass, left below. James Hayter, lowering his own glass, saw the captain's lack, and handed the glass over with a composed, polite, but neutral expression. Rennie took it, and brought it to his eye.

The boat lay sluggishly riding the swell half a league from the ship.

'We will heave to, Mr Hayter, and lower a boat.'

'I can see no sign of life, sir.'

Briefly raising the glass again, and lowering it: 'Nor can I. That don't mean there is no life, lying prostrated in the bottom of the boat, and only awaiting Christian rescue.'

The cutter was lowered, and rowed to the drifting boat with Mr Peak in command. Rennie's remark about life lying prostrated proved prophetic. Of the three bodies lying in the boat, one was not quite dead. He was brought back limp and emaciated in the cutter, his scrawny skin blistered by the sun, his clothing in tatters, and carried carefully below to the surgeon's quarters in the orlop. The boat, towed to the ship by the cutter, lay alongside with its noisome burden.

Mr Peak made his report: 'The boat had a mast stepped, which has snapped off, the sail and rigging gone by the board with the pole. There are no oars aboard, sir, only thole pins remaining. The tiller has been repaired, but steering must have been near impossible. No water, no victuals. The two corpses lie under the thwarts, very black and stinking.' He swallowed, and took a deep breath.

'You left corpses lying in the boat, Mr Peak?'

'I thought it my duty to bring only the living man aboard, sir—to preserve his life if that were possible.'

'You did right, but we cannot leave the dead to rot, Mr Peak. They must have a proper service, and a decent burial.'

'Very good, sir. You wish me to——'

'Is the boat marked? Does it carry a ship's name?'

'No, sir.'

'Very likely the ship foundered in a storm, and the bulk of her crew was lost. Was she an English ship, I wonder? We shall only know that when the rescued man recovers his senses, and his powers of speech. I will like to be informed of his condition, watch by watch.'

'Very good, sir. You wish me to—to carry the corpses into the ship?'

'I do, Mr Peak, if you please.' Firmly, a nod. 'We are one of His Majesty's ships, a Christian ship, and we must likewise assume they was Christian men. I require their remains to be treated accordingly. We must do what is right.'

Mr Peak bowed and put on his hat, and went down, reluctantly, to the boat. When the grisly remains had been brought aboard *Expedient*, and the sailmaker instructed, Rennie gave the order to scuttle the boat. He did not care to repair and tow it; he wished to be rid of it.

Two days later word was brought to him that the survivor was returned to consciousness, and able to speak. Rennie went below to see for himself. The emaciated figure lying under Thomas Wing's assiduous care was called Nathan Derrick, and he was master's mate of a slave ship, the *Olympus* 350 tons, out of Bristol. The *Olympus* had suffered a great calamity. Derrick told his story in a thin, barely restored voice, with frequent pauses. Fever had broken out below, in the tiers where the transporting slaves were housed. The master, Captain Welland, had ordered the dead put over the side. Some of the remaining slaves had contrived to escape their bonds.

'Bonds?' said Rennie. 'You mean, they was chained up, below?'

'Aye, always chained, otherwise they would make mischief. And they did make mischief.' A pause, and he licked his cracked lips. The surgeon wiped his lips with a moistened cloth. In his breath-taxed voice Derrick continued, pausing frequently and closing his eyes.

'Captain Welland ordered us to fire on them with muskets, and pistols, but we was fewer in number, and it did not suffice. We was driven aft, and forced to defend ourselves from the captain's quarters, firing through the bulkheads. After the passage of one glass, or a little longer, we ran low in powder and ball, and began to despair. And then we smelled fire. The galley stove had been torn open in the mêlée, and had set fire to the fo'c's'le, and soon the whole ship forrard was burning. We forayed on deck, firing ahead of us into the smoke, and contrived to hoist out one boat. Only Captain Welland and myself, and his steward Daniel Fife, ever got into the boat. The others was cut down on the deck by the escaped slaves. We pushed clear, stepped our mast and made sail, and wore away—and shortly after, the ship's forrard magazine blew up.' He closed his bird eyelids, and lay breathing shallowly, his burned and blistered skin grey behind.

'He must be taxed no more,' said the doctor with authority. 'He is yet very weak.'

Afterward, on the quarterdeck, as the ship ran with the wind on her quarter, the air growing balmy, Rennie said:

'I found what he said about chains abominable.'

'Chains, sir?' James had not been present below.

'Yes, James. I had heard that slaves was kept chained, you know, but never before from the lips of a slaver himself.'

'Ah, so he was a slaver, was he—the man we saved so careful?'

'It was our duty to save him. There is no choice in such things.'

'We did not save anybody from that other ship—you recall it, sir, before Madeira?'

'Well well, that was a quite different circumstance, as a moment's thought will reveal to you. Beside, I could not know he was from a slave ship, the poor wretch, when we took him aboard.'

'No, sir.'

'Even *had* I known it, it would have been my duty to save him. As it was my duty—our duty—to give his two dead companions a Christian burial. One was the captain, that we buried.'

'Ah. Then he has got better than he deserved, don't you think so, sir? I fear I cannot mourn the loss of a man that involved himself in that trade——'

'I do not ask you to mourn him, Mr Hayter.' Vexed with his lieutenant, with whom he had wished to restore amicable relations. 'We are sea officers in His Majesty's service, and we follow the Regulations. Personal conviction don't come into it.'

'I beg your pardon, sir.' Politely corrected.

Rennie stepped away to the rail, and made plain by his demeanour that he wished not to be disturbed. He did not actively attempt to conn the ship, or give instructions of any kind, but his presence on the quarterdeck was felt by every man there. At eight bells and the changing of the watch he stood observing the bustling activity, the hurrying of men along gangway and deck, the shouts and calls echoing through the ship, and then he went below, having exchanged no further word with his first lieutenant, nor spoken to the relieving officer. In maintaining this silence, this aloofness, he was not doing anything unusual or contrary. He was merely following a long tradition.

In her first commission HM *Expedient* frigate had carried many innovative scientific instruments, among them two chronometers bespoke of Plenitude Tyndale, lately apprenticed to Mr Arnold. These admirable sea clocks—shaped like large pocket watches—had worked with such accuracy that there had been few occasions when Rennie was unaware of the ship's position. He had written highly favourable reports of the chronometers, and had been able to prevail upon the board to allow him the chronometers a second time. Others of the instruments, like Mr Baragwanath's wind-measuring scale, and Mr Hetton Barkworth's Patent Perpetual Log—a new, intricate and inefficacious rotating logship—he had happily left behind. Similarly he had been happy to learn that he would not again have to take into his ship Waterfield pattern guns. Two of these lighter, shorter guns had fractured in routine great-gun-firing exercises, one explosion causing great loss of life. The new powder designed for these guns, charcoal cylinder, had also been excluded from the gunner's stores this commission, thank God. Charcoal cylinder gunpowder was certainly very powerful, and less inclined to deteriorate on long foreign service, but in Rennie's opinion it was devil's dust, unfit to be stored in any ship's magazine in the Royal Navy.

He was a cautious man, he reflected, which did not mean that he was a coward. In least, he hoped it did not mean that, good God. He was cautious in anything new. He believed in the traditions of the Royal Navy, and the slow, evolutionary changes brought into the service since the great and necessary reforms under Anson forty years since. Anson's time as First Lord had brought uniforms to the quarterdeck, new Regulations, new Articles, and much greater system and organisation into the daily management of men in ships. The refurbished Regulations, of the past year, had improved things further.

There were other valuable things which had come into ships. Dr Lind's anti-scorbutics, first absolutely proved as prophylactic by Cook, on long voyages. And Dr Stroud's further work in following Lind: the necessity for cleanliness in the people, and in their living quarters between decks; the need to pump and sweeten the bilges; the need to wash and smoke between; &c.

'And copper,' said Rennie aloud. 'Copper has been a boon to all seafaring men, in keeping the toredo worm out of ships' timbers.'

'You wish me to make *coffee*, sir?' His puzzled steward, attending.

'Eh? Coffee? Sppppfff, to coffee. I never drink the dark loathsome gut-troubling muck, for God's sake, Cutton. Do not you know my habit by now, man? Tea. Tea, by all or any means. Jump now.'

'Aye, sir.'

'I am contradicted at every turn of the glass.'

'I am very sorry, sir.'

'No no, Cutton, it ain't your fault. I am weary, and out of sorts. Tea. Tea will refresh me.'

Why was he weary? he asked himself. Why was he out of sorts? The surgeon had declared him perfectly fit, had he not? Well, except for that damned dishwater about his anxious eye. That was something he and the first lieutenant had concocted between them. Cardoon spines, and poisoned blood, &c.

Could it be the business of his claim, his claim against the Admiralty? He shook his head, leaned forward on his desk, and shook his head. Lieutenant Hayter had revealed that the man named in the translated letters was a real man, and not an invented one. Which had in turn made Rennie realise that they were not involved in a wild goose chase this commission —in least, not entirely, as he had at first assumed. He still had very grave doubts about the veracity of those letters, even if the man to whom they were addressed was real enough.

Cutton brought his tea, and he drank two cups at once, gratefully sucked them down, and his headache diminished.

'I did have a headache,' he said, pouring himself another cup.

'Would you like me to bring you something to eat, sir? A snack? A cut of pie?'

'What? No. No thankee, Cutton, the tea is aiding me, and refreshing me sufficient, I think.'

'Aye, sir.' Withdrawing.

Rennie sat at his desk, and pulled towards him his journal, and opened the inkwell. An hour and a half later, as the bell sounded, he woke in his chair.

The rescued man, Nathan Derrick, had nearly recovered his strength, and Thomas Wing made the suggestion in the gunroom that perhaps when he was strong enough to walk, and move about the ship, Mr Derrick should be invited to join their mess.

'Join our mess?' James was severe as he asked this question, frowning and severe.

'Yes, he is really a very genial man, an easy man to know and converse with, and after all he was an officer in his ship.'

'That carries no weight in the Royal Navy.'

'You know about such things, Mr Hayter, and I must not dispute facts with you, but surely it will be simple good manners to invite him?'

'Good *manners*? To invite a person engaged in that particular trade to eat and drink with us, and be our daily companion? I think you cannot be in earnest.'

'Well I—I had not looked at it in that light. I had simply thought, since we have rescued him, and I have brought him back to health——'

'I cannot bring myself to sit at the same table with such a person,' said James very stiffly, aware even as he said it that he sounded like the worst kind of parsonish prig.

'But what have you against him, Hayter?' asked Richard Peak, with a hint of asperity. 'Yes, he was in a slave ship, and there is some ill-informed objections to slavery in political circles, but we are practical fellows in the navy, and we know that——'

'Yes, what do we know?' James interrupted him, keeping his temper bowsed taut.

'I hope that we may speak openly and freely in our own mess, Hayter,' said Peak in a subdued voice, subdued but not submissive.

'It ain't for me to issue edicts as to what may or may not be discussed. Speak, by all means.'

'Thank you, I will. I should say, I think, that my own family has interests in the West Indies, in large estates. I think you must acknowledge that no plantation may be worked without slaves. That is so, whether it be sugar, or cotton, or tobacco, or coffee that is grown. How will England prosper, unless we may grow things, and engage in trade? And so we must always have slaves, just as we must always have ships.'

'You make your case with eloquence, Mr Peak,' said James, wiping his lips with his napkin. 'One day, I am in no doubt, you will make your way into Parliament, and become a political man yourself. Hm?'

Richard Peak flushed, and his whole face tightened. He took a breath through his nose, and composed himself, his eyes fixed on the table in front of him.

'I hope you do not mean to insult me, Hayter.'

'I do not. I merely speak free and open, as you had wished for all of us only a moment since.'

'I had not wished to be insulted.' Very deliberately, his eyes still on the table, his hand gripping his glass there.

'And I do not insult you, Mr Peak. Have a care, now, before you say anything else.'

Richard Peak lifted his gaze to James, and his eyes were burning in his head. 'Have a *care*? It is you, I think, that must be careful.'

'Come now, gentlemen,' said Mr Loftus uneasily. 'It is pointless to quarrel over nothing, when——'

'It is not *nothing*.' Peak had now grown very pale, his mouth had set, and the muscles of his jaw flexed and bunched in his cheek. 'I have suffered a deliberate slight.'

'Mr Peak, do not be foolish——' began the surgeon, turning to him, and attempting to put a hand on his arm.

'I am not *foolish*.' Furiously, shaking off the hand. 'I have been insulted, and I demand——'

'You will make no demands, Mr Peak,' said James, coldly and firmly. 'It ain't your place, as a junior sea officer in the service of His Majesty, to make any demands at all in this ship. Only to do your duty.'

Peak rose from the table, knocking over a glass, and stood quivering. 'I do demand! I demand an apology, or satisfaction!'

James sighed. 'Mr Peak. I cannot accept your challenge, in one of His Majesty's ships, at sea. However, was you to be willing to wait until we make landfall at Jamaica, I am at your disposal. In the interim, gentlemen, if you decide among you to invite the rescued man to join you, I will not object. However—however, I would not any longer dine in the gunroom myself.'

He rose and went on deck.

'We cannot go against the wishes of the first lieutenant,' said Mr Loftus, who had found the whole incident profoundly uncomfortable. He was mess president this commission.

'Why do we not put it to a vote?' demanded Peak. He had sat down again, but the muscles of his face still worked.

'I do not think that would be wise.'

'In our own mess it is up to us to decide, together. It is not for one man alone.'

'Very well, then. I am opposed.'

'Doctor?'

'I know that I made the suggestion—but I agree now with Mr Loftus. I cannot oppose the lieutenant. And so I am opposed to the invitation, after all.'

'Mr Trent?'

'Eh? Opposed.'

'But good heaven, why? It is absurd, when you have nothing against the fellow!'

'Begging your pardon, Mr Peak, but it ain't usual that we must give our reason, in a gunroom vote. Only vote.'

'Oh, very well. What do you say, Dobie?'

'As a matter in fact I agree with the lieutenant, entire, so naturally I am opposed.'

'Good God, are you all so hopelessly enslaved to him! Is there not one of you that will stand up to him!' Unaware of any irony.

No one answered, and with a furious sigh Mr Peak flung down his napkin and banged away into his cabin.

The captain, by what means he did not say, had heard of this dispute, and thought it sufficiently serious to ask his first lieutenant to attend on him in the great cabin and provide an explanation.

'Good heaven, Mr Hayter. Politics, at dinner? Politics, in the mess? What was you thinking of?'

'You have left me behind, sir.' Politely, a slight shake of the head.

'Come, come, come now, Lieutenant! Do not play the innocent with me, sir. You and Mr Peak was at each other's throats, over politics. A challenge was issued, and accepted. Christ's blood! As if I have nothing at all to concern me, nor take up my time in the ship! Yet you, a long-serving sea officer, allow y'self to be drawn into a damned dismal pot-house quarrel with a foolish boy! Over nothing! Over politics!'

James stood silent, his hat under his arm, his back straight.

'Well?'

'I have nothing to say, thank you, sir.'

'Nothing, in your own defence?'

'Neither in my defence, nor otherwise.'

'You do not deny to my face that such an altercation took place?'

'I would only iterate, sir: you have left——'

'Yes yes, left you behind. Well well, this is a damned foolish business. Quarrelling, challenging, calling out, however you like to dress it up it is against the Regulations, and the Articles. I will have no duelling in my ship, you apprehend me?'

'You need have no fear of that, sir.'

'Hm. You will settle the matter between you, upon this day.'

'Settle?'

'Whichever man made the challenge must withdraw it, and the man that provoked it beg his pardon.'

'Sir, I do not see——'

'Do not *see*? Do not *see*? I will make you clear-sighted, sir! You will settle this today, or take all of your watches together the remainder of the commission! You have me?'

'Very good, sir.' Bowing, and withdrawing. As he reached the door:

'Do not think it may be settled behind a closed door, Mr

Hayter. I will like you to come here to me in the great cabin, and shake hands in my presence.'

Another bow, and James went on deck. The master was taking the watch, and James stood with him, then enjoined him to pace the quarterdeck, away from the wheel and binnacle.

'Bernard, I am very sorry you had to see that damned wrangling nonsense in the gunroom. I know it embarrassed you. No, hear me out. I know it did, since you are our mess president. I was on my high horse, and at fault. If you have decided to invite Mr Derrick to join the gunroom mess, I——'

'We have not. We decided against.'

'Ah. I see.'

After a moment, as they braced themselves on the heeling deck, Mr Loftus said: 'Surely you will not fight him?'

'I have given my word to the captain that the quarrel will be settled today. I must apologise, and Mr Peak must withdraw.'

'How did the captain hear of it?'

'Captains know everything in a ship, do they not?'

'Aye. In the end, they always do.' A wry smile, a nod.

'At any rate, I wished particularly to say a word to you, Bernard, and——'

'I have already forgot all about it.'

James and Richard Peak stood in the great cabin, hats off, in front of the captain. Rennie sat at his desk. He did not rise.

'Very good, gentlemen. I understand that a dispute arose between you, which has led to a challenge. I understand further that you have decided, between you, to settle that dispute. That is so? I am correct?'

'Yes, sir.'

'Yes, sir.'

'Very good. I will like to hear an apology, if you please, and then I will like to see you shake hands.'

Awkwardly the two officers faced each other. James, as

the older man, felt that it was his obligation to set the example.

'Mr Peak, I was at fault in our quarrel. I ask your pardon.'

'Thank you. I accept your apology, Mr Hayter.' Very pale, very stiff.

'Will you shake hands?' James held out his hand. A brief hesitation, a half-second only, then Peak held out his own hand, and formally shook the proffered one. The captain saw the hesitation, and was very dismayed. Clearly young Mr Peak did not feel placated, had not accepted the first lieutenant's apology with anything but the greatest reluctance. This would not do.

'Now, Mr Peak. I will like to hear you beg Mr Hayter's pardon, in your turn.'

Richard Peak looked at him in either astonishment or momentary defiance, and was silent.

'Mr Peak?'

'I—I had understood that I should only be required to *accept* an apology.' Setting his jaw.

'Had you? Ah. But that will not do, Mr Peak. A quarrel must be settled equally willing on both sides. By both parties. Hey?'

'As you wish, sir.' Facing James again. 'Mr——' clearing his throat 'Mr Hayter, I will like to beg your pardon.' His temple twitching, and his eyes flicking away from James's face.

James bowed. 'Thank you. I am happy. I am content.'

'Very good, very good,' said Rennie. 'And now, gentlemen, a glass of wine. Cutton!'

The ship now at 22 degrees and 12 minutes north, by 37 degrees and 42 minutes west, and the wind—the constant, steady, day by day great trade wind—brought *Expedient* closer and closer to her destination, under all plain and the main course partly in the brails, to aid her fore course. Rennie entertained Mr Derrick at dinner in the great cabin.

Having discovered why James Hayter and young Peak had quarrelled he did not invite his first lieutenant, but he did invite the junior lieutenant, with whom Derrick now had a long conversation. This conversation touched on many—most—aspects of the sugar trade, and its concomitant trade to and from Africa. Captain Rennie, in spite of his determination not to allow himself to have opinions as to these matters, since he was a sea officer whose only business was in fighting ships, in spite of this intention he found himself at first mildly dismayed by what he heard, then more than a little shocked. His other guests—two midshipmen, the contentedly guzzling Mr Trent, Mr Dobie, and Mr Loftus—also found themselves, severally and over time, increasingly discomfited.

'Yes, I have even known, once or twice——' nodded Derrick, swallowing wine and putting down his glass, 'I have known captains——' and now he paused, glancing round the table, sensing perhaps that he was venturing into uncharted waters.

'Yes, Mr Derrick? You have known captains——?' Rennie raised his eyebrows, endeavouring to be polite.

'Ah, hm. I have known captains that——', unsure of himself, now, 'that is to say, I have known *of* captains that have had to throw slaves over the side.'

'*Living* slaves?' Rennie stared at him.

'Only those that was sick, you mind me. Only to prevent further illness spreading below.' He nodded reassuringly. 'No captain in his senses would put strong healthy Negroes over the side. Good heaven, no, that would be folly, when a good price may be had at the block for every one of them. Every one that is healthy.' He nodded again, and gave them a confident smile.

'You have witnessed this yourself, Mr Derrick?' Rennie was still staring at him in wonder.

'Well now, hm, I have not seen it myself—above once. Only once.'

'Was it your late captain did this? Captain Welland?'

'Well, it was. I did not myself have any say in it. No no, I was not a party to the decision. Captain Welland was a very particular man as to the question of command. He would countenance no——'

'You are saying to me, entirely in earnest, that your commanding officer threw living beings into the sea? Are you, Mr Derrick?'

'Well now, he did—but they was sick, you see. Only because they was too ill to live, and could infect all the ship below. They was a severe impediment to their herd, their entire herd, and he could not allow it, could he?'

'Yes—yes, I see. Thank you, Mr Derrick, for enlightening me. I had—had never known, nor heard, of anything quite like it before.'

'I hope I do not shock any of you gentlemen by what I have said? We are sometimes, in the trade, aware of how the world sees us. That is, the world don't see us in a wholly favourable light, if they regard us at all. But trade is trade, and money is money. Eh?'

'Indeed, exactly so,' nodded Lieutenant Peak. 'There is many that prefer to be ignorant as to how England makes her money, and is prosperous. They had rather turn their face away from fact.'

'I am glad you see that, Mr Peak, very glad. Because it *is* fact, sir, it *is* fact.' Turning. 'A glass of wine, Captain Rennie.'

Rennie inclined his head, and smiled with his mouth, and half-raised his glass, but his eyes would not let him show approval of what he had heard today. Soon after, the dinner broke up, and Rennie settled at his desk to catch up with and defeat his paper work. Presently:

'Mr Dobie!'

Alan Dobie came through from his cramped working cabin forrard of the coach.

'Mr Dobie, I wonder if you was shocked by what you heard today?'

'You mean, about the living slaves thrown overboard, sir?'

'I do mean that.'

'It disgusted me. *He* disgusted me.'

'Then I am not alone, thank God. You was disgusted, and so was I. Christ Jesu, what a story.' Shaking his head. 'However, there is nothing can be done—not by the navy, at any rate.'

'It is the kind of thing that will always happen so long as that abominable trade continues.'

'Hm. Hm. We in the King's service must not have opinions about trade, Mr Dobie.'

'I fear that I do have opinions, sir. I do not think it the navy's business to teach me my opinions.'

'You are on the wrong tack, I think. The Royal Navy don't *teach* any man his opinions. The navy says, merely, he must not *express* opinions, detrimental to the standards of the service.'

'I have never heard that, sir. Where is that wrote out? In the Regulations?'

Rennie glanced at his clerk very sharply, and frowned. 'Have a care, Mr Dobie. It ain't fitting you should talk to your captain in that tone.'

'I am very sorry.' Flushing.

'However, we have all been disturbed in our thoughts today, by what was revealed to us by that scoun—— by Mr Derrick. I must not malign him when he is our guest, in course, and neither must you, Mr Dobie, whatsoever opinions you might hold as to the damned wretched infamy of something, or someone. Hm?'

'No, sir.'

'We will make a start, if you please.' A long, sniffing sigh. 'Letters, I must write letters.'

Rennie sat late and alone in the great cabin, slowly drinking wine, and thinking. He knew that it was not advisable for him to think in this way, ruminatively, since almost certainly, almost inevitably, his thoughts would grow dark. At such moments he reflected not upon his good fortune in having got a second commission in a fine ship, at a time when many other officers on the list were not treading a quarterdeck, but kicking their heels ashore, writing letters to the Admiralty, or hanging about in side rooms there, waiting to be interviewed, knowing even as they waited that there were no ships to be had. He thought about his case of complaint, about Sir Robert Greer, about the near-disaster at Funchal, and groaned to himself, groaned and cursed himself for a fool. His steward, who wished to retire but had not been given leave to do so, attempted to bring the captain's reverie to a conclusion.

'You called me, sir?' Coming into the cabin.

'Eh? No, I did not.'

'I'm sorry, sir. I could of swore I heard your voice. It must of been a stray seabird, which give its cry, and I heard it——'

'It is night, Cutton. You will hear nothing at night, excepting the sea.'

'Yes, sir, I dare say it was that, sir. May I clear away for you now?'

'Eh? No no, I shall sit a while yet, I think. Leave the cheese, I may eat it. I am not inclined to sleep for the moment, thankee.'

'Yes sir. Only——'

'You may go to bed yourself, Cutton, I shan't need you again. Oh, Cutton——'

Turning at the door: 'Sir?'

'I may very probably go on deck, presently. Just fill me a flask, will you, and leave it at the binnacle?'

'Aye, sir.'

'Am I drinking more than is good for me?' Rennie murmured to himself when his steward had gone. 'It don't help me to sleep, I know that.'

On deck James was taking his watch, in the pattern established the first commission. In usual in a fifth-rated frigate the first lieutenant would not take regular watches, but Rennie had instituted the change when there had been a difficulty about his third lieutenant; now, short of a lieutenant in the ship, Rennie had reintroduced his earlier system, and James trod the quarterdeck in turn about with Mr Peak and Bernard Loftus, with an occasional watch taken by one of the older mids. James did not mind. He would rather be active than lie in his cot, tossing and turning and fretting about Catherine. He took a long breath, sniffing it into his lungs, and looked aloft.

The sky, when he saw it now above the sails, was dark and brilliant, and when he lowered his gaze the black sea all around flickered and sparkled with phosphorescence, beyond the little island of the ship. The wash of the sea, the hum and whisper of the wind, the creaking of timbers emphasised the loneliness of their progress, and now he felt a strange detachment, as if he were not quite contained within himself, but was someone other, some separate, separate-minded being floating with the ship, above it, above the sea, between the great broad watery darkness, and the brilliant infinity of the night sky far overhead.

Rennie came quietly on deck, and found his flask at the binnacle. His form hid the glow of the light a moment.

'Mr Hayter.'

James, startled at the rail, turned round. 'Sir, I did not know you was on deck.'

'I have only just climbed the ladder. How does she lie?'

James gave him their course and speed, the direction of the wind, &c. The captain spoke to the helmsman, and inquired about backstays and sails. He was conscientious, but both he and his lieutenant knew that what he wished for, in coming on deck late at night, was not information about his ship, routine information as to her working—but company.

'Are you a lover of birds, Mr Hayter?' he asked presently.

'D'y'mean seabirds, sir?'

'No, I was—I had in mind ordinary birds, you know, on land. Blackbirds, curlews, starlings, jackdaws and the like. Rooks. The finch.'

'Which finch, sir?'

'Eh?'

'There is a great many finches, I think. The red poll, the twite finch, the green, and the gold, and the haw——'

'The whore? Surely there ain't such a thing as a slut finch, good God?'

'H-A-W. It is the largest of the finches.'

'Ah. Hah. Not a tart among birds then, James? Hey?'

'No, sir.' A smile in the darkness.

'Just so. Hm. There is a great many pretty birds at Jamaica. Hummingbirds, and the like.'

'Yes, I had thought to sketch some few of them, up-country, should the opportunity arise.'

'It will, it will, I am in no doubt.'

Thus were friendly relations restored between the two sea officers, to the great relief of both, and they fell to talking, pacing back and forth and talking, as loneliness fell away astern.

Heat was now increasing, and with the heat came flashes of temper, fighting below decks, and occasional outright defiance. At six bells of the forenoon watch, a day or two after Rennie's reconciliation with James, hands were assembled to witness punishment. An ordinary seaman of the larboard afterguard, Thomas Yardley, had been drunk at his station the day before, and had refused to obey an instruction from one of the midshipmen, within the hearing of Mr Peak, who had then admonished the man. Yardley had stared at Mr Peak, and had then turned his back with a shrug. The captain had heard the evidence and had come to his decision at once.

'Stopping his grog will not suffice in this,' he had said. 'He is to receive one dozen lashes, Mr Hayter.'

'Very good, sir.' Entering it in the book.

And now Yardley was seized up to a grating in the waist, his shirt stripped from his back. The drum-roll sounded, and the bosun's mate removed the cat from its red bag. He stood wide, and swung the knotted lines.

'Please, sir!' A boy's voice.

A murmur of surprise and consternation. Rennie, standing at the break of the quarterdeck, was very severe: 'Silence on deck! Who spoke!' The drum-roll ceased.

Richard Abey, the junior midshipman, quaked and steeled himself: 'If you please, sir, I wish to say that——'

'Be quiet, sir!'

'Oh, please! It was my fault! He did not understand me!'

Rennie slapped the rail with his hand, glaring down. The bosun's mate stood still, the cat trailing on the deck.

'Mr Duggan!'

The lieutenant of marines, very stiff in his red coat and cockaded hat. 'Sir?'

'You will escort Mr Abey below, if you please.'

'Very good sir.' His hat off and on.

Richard Abey continued desperately to plead and protest, and was marched by the embarrassed Lieutenant Duggan from the waist down the ladder into the midshipmen's berth on the lower deck.

'For the love of Christ, have you no sense at all?' demanded Mr Duggan as they reached the gloom of the berth.

'But I was in the wrong, sir. Yardley did not understand me. He did not properly hear what I said to him, and now he is being punished. Because I did not speak up. I should be bolder in giving instructions on deck, but I am not yet strong enough.' In a gabbling, high-pitched tone.

'Be quiet!'

'Oh, please——' Near to tears.

'Sit down, now.' Less harshly, removing his hat. His sandy hair glistened with sweat. 'Just calm yourself, lad.'

The boy sat down on the bench. The lieutenant put one foot up on the bench and leaned forward. 'You may not interrupt punishment. Good heaven, the youngest scut of a ship's boy knows a thing like that. You are a quarterdeck man, in a blue coat. You, most of all, must realise that there can be no leniency in discipline, no hesitation, when one of the people is at fault. He defied Mr Peak.'

'Oh, but he only——'

'Tut-tut-*tuh*, Mr Abey. This is the Royal Navy, and the soft rules of governesses, and nurseries, don't answer here. Not at sea.' And Lieutenant Duggan put on his hat, climbed the ladder, emerged into the waiting hush, and took his place at the head of his column of marines. Captain Rennie nodded, scowling, and the drum-roll rattled across the deck over the rushing wash of the sea.

'One dozen lashes! Commence!'

Mr Abey was requested, with the captain's compliments, to present himself at the great cabin. Rennie had eaten his dinner, and drunk a glass or two of wine, and had asked his first lieutenant, who had dined with him, to remain there when his other guests had departed. Richard Abey climbed the ladder with trepidation, caught the sentry's eye at the door, took a deep breath, and entered.

'Ah, Mr Abey, yes. Come in, come in, sir. Explain, if you please, to the lieutenant. Explain to him why you made a disturbance on deck. Perhaps you was took ill. Pray proceed, I shall listen at the side.'

'Thank you, sir. I was not—I had not——'

'Your voice is very indistinct, Mr Abey. Have you caught cold, sir? Is that it?'

'No, sir.'

'Then clear your wind, and speak up.'

Poor Abey cleared his throat, lifting his hand timorously to his mouth a moment. Then he lifted his head and spoke in a clear voice:

'I was at fault, sir. I was very rash, and behaved foolish.'

'Is that all?' Again it was the captain who spoke. The lieutenant as yet had said nothing.

'I should not have said anything, when punishment was about to commence.'

James turned briefly to Rennie. 'With your permission, sir?' Rennie nodded. James turned again to the midshipman. 'I think what we wish to understand is *why* you made so rash an interruption, Mr Abey. Hm?'

'I had—I had thought that Yardley did not hear my request to him, that he did not mean to be defiant to Mr Peak, but had only heard indistinct what I said, and thus—thus could not be blamed.'

'You thought that, did you?'

'Yes, sir.'

'You thought it your duty, therefore, to say so?'

'I did, sir.'

'I see, yes. Perhaps it will aid in your future understanding, Mr Abey, when I tell you several facts. Hm?'

'Yes, sir. Thank you, sir.'

'Very good. Yardley was drunk. That is an offence, *which he knew*. Yardley turned his back deliberate upon an officer, when that officer was addressing him. That is an offence, *which he knew*. Further, in committing these offences, he laid himself open to punishment, *which he knew*. From the instant he pretended not to hear what you required him to do, Mr Abey, that man *damned well knew* that he would be *punished*. You have me, thus far?'

'Yes, sir.'

'Further, every man in the ship *damned well knew* that Yardley would be flogged, *why* he was to be flogged, that he deserved and merited nothing *but* a flogging—every man, excepting one. Only you, Mr Abey, did not know. Only you, Mr Abey, thought otherwise. However, unless

I am much mistook, I think that you do know now. I am correct?'

'Yes, sir.'

'Very well.'

'Thank you, Mr Hayter. And now, Mr Abey, will you step to the table, sit down, and drink a glass of wine with me?'

'Thank you, sir.'

'By the by, Mr Abey'—lifting the decanter—'there ain't such a thing as a "request" when a quarterdeck officer is addressing a member of the crew. Orders are given, and orders are obeyed.—Your health.'

To the quartermaster Lieutenant Hayter said: 'Thank ye, Daley Wragg, I will take the conn.' To his charge, Richard Abey, of whom he had decided that the mid must be made over into a seaman, lest he lose all sense of the ship under his hand and eye and leg, necessary to all sea officers, lose the sense before he had ever gained it, to him he said:

'Stand to the wheel now, Mr Abey.'

The helmsman stepped aside, keeping his face expressionless, as this scut of a boy stepped half-dwarfed to the spokes that he was now called upon to grasp.

'Take the spokes firm, now, in both your hands, if you please.—You have her?'

'I—yes, thank you, sir.'

Attempting to brace his feet, feeling the ship in his whole body, his whole frame of flesh and bone as he had never felt her before, as a part of himself, and he a part of her, this living creature moving through the sea, guided by the great fin of the rudder, a fin over which he was now master.

'What d'y'feel, Mr Abey?'

'I—I feel her swim, sir.'

'Aye, do you? Then we shall make a seaman of you, if you

can feel that.' A glance at the quartermaster, and a brief nod exchanged. 'You have the ship, Mr Abey. Any question you wish to ask, you may put to the quartermaster, or to me, do not hang back.'

'Thank you, sir.'

'She is wandering a little, bring her back.—No, you are too soft. Be firm with her, be decided, she don't want coddling and caressing, Mr Abey. Make her obey you, and she will like you for it.—She is wandering a little to larboard now.' Extending a hand, closing it over the boy's on the spoke. 'Bring her back, now. Just so, hold her just so. Excellent.—How does she lie, Daley?'

The quartermaster gave the course from the binnacle. To Richard Abey James said:

'Now you must look aloft, and see what your canvas does. Do we harness the wind well? Is there a question in your mind?'

'A question, sir?'

'Aye.'

'I—I do not think so, sir.' Anxiously, looking aloft at the mizzen topsail, and t'gan'sail.

'Look forrard, now, and again aloft. Will not she carry weather stunsails, profitably?'

'I—I do not know, sir.'

'Then ask the quartermaster's opinion, will you?'

'*D-e-e-e-ck!* Two sail of ship, three points on the starboard bow!'

James jumped into the starboard mizzen shrouds, focused his glass, and found the ships. Hove-to together two leagues distant, emerging from the haze the morning airs had not yet quite dispersed. 'They are speaking, I think.' Holding both ships in the lens, steadying himself, an arm looped round a shroud. 'Merchant ships, I am nearly certain.'

Mr Loftus was now on the quarterdeck, and had brought up his own glass to his eye.

'What d'y'think, Bernard?' James, over his shoulder.

'I am not sighted—ah, yes, now I make them out. The larger ship is a frigate.'

'A frigate?' Peering again, focusing. 'Is she a British ship? That ain't a Union flag . . .'

'Neither ship wears British colours—although, in the haze, I cannot tell which flags . . .'

'That is French lines, if I am not mistook,' said James now. 'The frigate is French. Mr Abey!'

'Sir?'

'Y'may stand away from the wheel. Go below and say to the captain with my compliments that we approach two ships to starboard, one of them a French frigate. Jump now.'

'She don't appear to carry French colours, however,' puzzled Bernard Loftus, holding his glass to his eye at the rail and bracing himself there as the helmsman, returned to the wheel, brought the ship true.

'Have they seen us, Mr Hayter?' Captain Rennie, coming on deck from the companion, carrying his glass.

'I do not think so, sir. There is haze, considerable haze, and we come from the sun.'

'Just so. I am minded to give them a gun—merely as a courtesy, you know.' Raising his glass.

'A gun, sir?' Exchanging a glance with Bernard Loftus.

'A signal gun, James, just to announce ourselves, you know. So that we do not come at them all at once out of the sun. It is a courtesy.' Still peering through the glass.

'Very good, sir. You wish to speak with either ship—or both?'

'Neither, thank you. My orders don't permit it. On second thought, belay that gun. Do not fire. We shall simply hold to our course, and if—when they see us—they decide to give us a courtesy gun, then we shall acknowledge with one of our own. It is gentlemanlike to acknowledge, after all. But I ain't inclined to be *overly* polite to a Frenchman—Mr Loftus!'

'Sir?' At his elbow.

'Ah, there you are.' Lowering his glass. 'I will like weather stunsails, high and low, if y'please. Smartly, if y'please. Let us show the Frenchie how we work our ships in His Majesty's service, hey?'

'Very good, sir. Mr Tangible! Hands to make sail!' The calls.

James smiled to himself. Rennie had evidently forgotten, in his desire to show off his seamanship, that the French frigate had not yet seen *Expedient*, foreshortened as she sailed from the haze; and that the setting of *Expedient*'s stunsails, however smartly booms were run out, and canvas loosed and sheeted home, would thus go unnoticed.

As *Expedient*, steady on her course, half a knot faster now with her weather stunsails, as *Expedient* drew closer to the two quietly riding ships, both those ships burst abruptly into activity. A boat could be seen between them, double-banked oars pulling frantically from the smaller vessel to the frigate, both ships unbrailing canvas, bracing yards, and preparing to get under way. A flash of reflected light at the frigate's taffrail showed that an officer there had brought up his long glass and was observing *Expedient*'s approach. Both Rennie and James, observing in turn, thought the figure was likely that of her captain.

Rennie lowered his glass a moment, raised it again, and: 'What colours are those?' he puzzled. 'I thought ye said she was French, Mr Hayter. If I am not mistook—that is a Dutch flag. Aye, a Dutch flag, and pennant.'

'Yes, you are right, sir.' Peering through his own glass, focusing. 'He is a Dutchman, by his colours. But that is not a Dutch ship, she don't have Dutch lines. She has French lines . . . and the name on her transom is . . . "Bernadette".' Lowering his glass. 'That is not a Hollander name, exact.'

'Well well, there is nothing to say the navy of the Netherlands may not buy in French-built ships, eh, Mr Hayter?' Mildly. 'There is French-built frigates in our own navy.'

'Indeed, sir. Very probably she is a private ship, like ourselves, detached from the Dutch fleet.'

'Hm. Hm. What are the other ship's colours, can you see? I could not make them out.'

'Nor I, sir.' Peering again briefly. 'I don't think she can be Dutch, by her lines.'

'Well well, we certainly cannot give them a gun, now. They would take fright, I expect.' Peering. 'Perhaps they have took fright, already, hm? They are certainly in very great haste, between them.'

'What can they fear from us?'

'Don't know, James, and don't care, neither. It ain't our affair why they are here, on the open sea. I am under strict instruction to mind my own business, and speak to no one.'

He paced the quarterdeck, fore and aft, glass under his arm, then from the top came a shout:

'The merchant ship wears away south! And the frigate swings nor'east by the wind, crowding sail!'

Rennie came to the rail—he did not venture into the mizzen shrouds—and raised his glass to look again at the frigate. As he caught the ship in the lens there was an orange flash and a ball of smoke rushed out from her starboard mizzen chains. A moment, and . . . *BOOM*.

'Why has he fired a gun?' Rennie lowered his glass in surprise. 'Is it for us?'

'No, sir, I think it was a signal to the other ship.' James, at his side. As he spoke there was a second flash, and moments later another *BOOM*.

'Two guns? From his starboard battery, when the other ship is away to larboard? I tell you, Mr Hayter, when a man-of-war of another nation fires her guns in direct proximity to one of His Majesty's ships, twice fires, I am not inclined to ignore it.'

'Should we perhaps fire a brace of guns ourselves, sir?'

'No, thank you. We will clear for action, Mr Hayter.'

'Surely, sir, the——'

'Did not you hear me, sir! We will clear the ship for action!'

'Aye, sir, very good. Mr Tangible! Beat to quarters!'

Calls were sounded and gun-crews assembled at their batteries in all the hectic activity of preparation: decks sanded, handspikes and rammers brought down, cartridge brought up. As the clatter of bulkheads being struck below echoed the roll of the drum through the ship, Rennie bellowed: 'Put your helm down!' and *Expedient* swung to starboard in pursuit, in a long lace-creaming curve through the broad sea, the last of the haze burning away and the wind freshening as the ship heeled into it close-hauled.

The other frigate, with the advantage of her graceful French lines and a few minutes' start, was a match for *Expedient*, and more. *Expedient* was a sturdy, well-built, weatherly ship, but she was not a fast-flying one. The leading frigate drew away. An hour passed. Another. At last, as six bells of the forenoon watch sounded, and the glass was turned, James asked:

'Should we fire a gun in acknowledgement, sir?'

'What? What?'

'In course, he may not hear it, since he is well clear of us, but it has been good sport, and it would be gentlemanlike to——'

'Good *sport*, Mr Hayter! What the devil d'y'mean? We are not at the hunt in Dorsetshire, amiable over the bloody stirrup cup! We are at sea, sir!'

'Sir, I did not mean——'

'I don't give a damn what y'meant, Mr Hayter. You will recall yourself to your duty as a sea officer. Mr Loftus!'

'Sir?' Attending.

'Royals, Mr Loftus. I will like royals bent.'

'The wind—very good, sir.'

At noon, when the official ceremonies of the naval day were due—sightings, declarations, &c.—Rennie still paced his quarterdeck, and peered through his glass, and glanced impatiently aloft. The other frigate was now two leagues ahead, and drawing inexorably farther away. Eight bells sounded, the glass was turned, and James thought it opportune to say:

'Shall we declare noon, sir?'

'What? Yes yes, declare it to me, and then let us get on, if you please. We are in a chase, and we cannot waste time with trivial things.'

'Very good, sir.'

At four bells of the afternoon watch, the French frigate fading into the distance far ahead, Rennie turned from the rail, sniffed, put his glass under his arm—and relented:

'Mr Hayter, the hands have not had their dinner. We are all hungry, no doubt. We will stand down, go about, and resume our course for Jamaica.'

'Very good, sir.' With great relief, evident on his face.

'There is nothing good about it.'

James could think of nothing to say to that. As the captain turned on his heel and went to the companion James sighed, and caught Richard Abey looking at him.

'Yes, Mr Abey?' A slight tilt of his head.

'Oh, no, sir.' At once looking away.

'Your eyes asked a question, I think.'

'No, sir. I—that is, I did not mean——'

'Well, never mind.' Brusquely. 'Go below and eat your dinner.'

At supper that same evening in the gunroom, Alan Dobie, passing the cheese dish to James as requested, said:

'I am a little concerned about Midshipman Abey.'

James cut cheese, picked a maggot from the piece with the tip of his knife, and pushed it to the side of his plate where it lay wriggling.

'Yes, concerned? Are you?' A frown, as he selected a biscuit.

Alan stared in queasy fascination at the maggot, that tiny writhing creature, and felt his lately amenable stomach quiver uncomfortably in its pit. James tapped his selected biscuit sharply, and pushed a weevil aside to join the wriggling grub. He munched biscuit and cheese with satisfaction, and through the saliva'd crumbs said:

'What concerns you about him? Hm? Strikes me he comes along handsome.'

Moist fragments scattered from his mouth as he spoke, falling on his napkin where they lay in glistening flecks. Alan stared at them, stared and was unable to link his thoughts.

'Um. Um. Will you excuse—excuse me a moment? Very sorry. Cannot quite——' And abruptly he pushed back his chair, breathed very deep through his nose, rose rigidly and went rigidly from the gunroom, his hand half-raised to his mouth.

'What on earth have you said to Dobie, I wonder?' Lieutenant Peak peered at James. 'It has clearly upset him. He is a very sensitive soul, you know.'

'I said nothing.' Mildly, munching, shaking his head and lifting his glass. He washed down cheese with wine. 'Nothing at all.'

'It was certainly the cheese,' said the master, reaching and cutting a piece for himself. 'Living cheese don't suit every appetite. I've seen it often, in the heat in particular.' He wiped his neck with his kerchief, and sighed. 'We shall have nothing but sticky, close-clinging, sweating heat from now on. For myself I hope that we may keep the sea nearly always at Jamaica, on our surveying duty, rather than spend time ashore. Spanish Town, dear God.'

'Yes, I quite agree with you, Mr Loftus,' said the purser. 'A very oven-like place.' Mopping his face in turn, and pouring more wine.

'Aside from the heat, have you an objection on principle to Spanish Town?' Peak now inquired rather tartly of the master.

'Objection? Oh no. No objection, excepting it is the least comfortable place I have ever been in. It is badly built, and ill-looking, and the heat is unendurable. Sleep is near impossible, so that people are exhausted all the day and all the night too, and fall sick of the fever, and die like flies. There is no seasons, only hot, and hot and drenching wet. Dear God.'

'Come now, Mr Loftus.' Lieutenant Peak, frowning and acerbic. 'Come come. It is a tropick place, and certainly it is hot, but it is also perfectly civilised. People there lead a civilised life, they go to dinners, and the theatre, there are concert parties and entertainments of all kinds. You make it out a dismal city, much worse than is actually the case.'

'Do I? You think so? In the late American war I was at Jamaica many times, on convoy duty in the *Alarum* thirty-two. We was often invited to dinners at Spanish Town, official dinners, you know. Lord, the memory of those dinners.' He pushed away his plate, the cheese untouched. 'Six and eight removes, fat men in coats, purple in the face, dripping into their wine. Ceaseless loud talk, shouting talk, and terrible bursts of loud laughter. The candles along the table fiercely increasing the heat, dripping hot wax. And musquitoes. Horrible infestations of musquitoes, worrying and biting flesh without pause, everywhere. Dear God.'

'You grow quite poetical in your loathing, Bernard.' James, with a wry smile. 'Perhaps you should not have come with us, this commission.'

'The men you so despised at those dinners,' glared Lieutenant Peak, 'might very probably have numbered among them members of my own family, which has large interests throughout the island. Cousins of mine sit in the Assembly. I would take it very ill was you to continue to suggest that all these men was buffoons, and puffing dolts, good for nothing but filling their bellies like swine at the swill trough.'

'Mr Peak,' said the master, the look of grumbling levity fading from his face, 'Mr Peak, I meant no insult to any member of your family. I was talking in a general way, in fun. Good God, the fellows I spoke of was minor officials, no more. The tables we was placed at, as mere warrant officers——'

'You deliberately described entire dinners of bellowing pigs,' said Lieutenant Peak. 'Really, I don't know why it is, but whenever Jamaica is discussed it is made out a filthy excrescence among British possessions, instead of a great and glowing jewel.'

'You are quite wrong, I assure you. Jamaica in large is very beautiful, and I am the first man to say it. It is a jewel. In talking of Spanish Town as I did——'

'Perhaps you had better not talk of it any more. It is very difficult to speak from plain ignorance on any subject, after all.'

'As you wish, Mr Peak.' Bernard Loftus inclined his head in an icy bow over the hot, embarrassed, silent table.

No mention had been made of the long pursuit, of Captain Rennie's stubborn insistence upon that pursuit, and its failure; but James knew that the unease round the table, his own unease—reflected in that exchanged glance with young Abey on the quarterdeck—came from it, and was growing in the heart of the ship. The unspoken, only half-acknowledged sense that Captain Rennie was . . .

'What?' murmured James to himself later as he swung into his hanging cot. 'That he is what, for God's sake?' He took up a book, riffled pages, cut some with his penknife, then threw the book aside. 'He is captain of the ship, he is fully enabled by the Articles, and the Instructions, to command her as he sees fit. He need consult neither me, nor any member of her complement, nor take any advice that he does not like. Does one problematic chase, one abortive pursuit, make him a madman, or a tyrant? Does even his curious early view of the commission, and those secret letters, does *that* make him a Bedlamite?' Aloud: 'No, it does not, by God. None of it. I will not believe it.'

And having thus admonished himself he lay back and closed his eyes. He could not sleep. He wriggled and squirmed, beat his pillow, and could not become comfortable. He thought of Catherine, and his heart grew tender as he pictured her at Melton, she and his mother cutting flowers together in the walled garden, or sitting at their embroidery before the fire in Lady Hayter's withdrawing room. But what if that was a false picture? Supposing that Catherine's progress was not quite smooth and easy, with bees in the blooms and birdcalls echoing soft across the roof? Supposing that Dr Hall was anxious, calling daily in his gig, hurrying in, making his grave examinations, shaking his head gravely to Lady Hayter as he emerged from the sickroom.

Sickroom?

Good God, what was he thinking? What foolish disasters and calamities was he conjuring in his head, to no purpose? Catherine would be perfectly safe. She was in safe hands, loving hands, she was healthy and strong and sensible. She would do nothing untoward, take no risks in her comportment, such as running upstairs, or down, instead of walking. Their child, his child, was safe. His son. He was certain that he was to be the father of a boy. What to christen him? What names should he be given? James Rondo, his own names? Or Charles, after his own father? Charles Gordon Hayter?

He would teach the boy to ride. Aye, he would manage that himself. That task should never be left to a groom, when the groom might well be a fellow like Padding. Padding he had never liked, he was not a pleasant fellow, a warm companion; there was in his face and posture and voice a sly, humble, simmering contempt for his betters, his younger betters. 'Now then, master, grip with yrr *knees*, what did I say? If you is not inclined to lissen, how may you learrn, izzen it, eh? Boy? *Think*, Master James, you stupid little bugger. *Knees*.'

The ship dropped into a passing trough, and was briefly and heavily shaken. James's cot swung with the creaking, rolling movements as *Expedient* righted herself, shook water from her scuppers, and regained her footing. The bell sounded on deck.

'I must get my sleep,' James sighed to himself. 'I must take divisions tomorrow, and listen to grievances. There is punishments to convene, too. And I must listen once more to Adgett's damned vexing complaints, good heaven. Much to be done, wearying things, routine wearying things.' He felt suddenly and miserably alone in the darkness. He missed his love, his sweet companion, his soul, his life, missed her with a yearning so cutting deep he nearly gasped with the pain of it. 'Oh, Cathy,' he whispered, and felt tears on his cheek. 'How I wish we could be together. How I wish you was here by my side.'

He lay on his back, and swallowed, and sighed. His cot swung with the ship, swung back, he took a further breath and a thought came to him. It was not a comforting or consoling thought, but a lucid realisation. The reason for Rennie's peculiarities was that he had never married. He had lived alone all his adult life, so far as James was aware, without companionship of any kind. Yes, certainly he had had friends, like the old admiral, but never anyone with whom to share his life. Never anyone with whom he could share his heart, open it, surrender it. Save what he had in ships, which for a captain could never be more than close acquaintance, he had had no companionship at all.

'Well,' murmured James, 'I suppose I am his friend. We have been through much together, certainly. But that ain't the same thing at all. He has had no *intimate* connection, the poor fellow, and has suffered for it.' Another sigh, and oddly, curiously—for it should not have relieved him—that thought did console him, and he turned into his pillow and drifted into dreamless release.

On the morrow, as the ship's complement went about its business—decks washed, hammocks up, breakfast, divisions, inspections—Rennie gave no hint to his lieutenant that he recognised the folly of the pursuit, and the loss of a full day in time and distance, which must now be made up. He gave no hint, and James in turn was determined not to show disapproval. He wished, for the remainder of the passage to Jamaica, only to aid his captain, aid and assist him in everything, and where possible lighten the burden that command placed upon that lonely man.

In ten days, a fortnight at most, they would be at Port Royal, and the full import of their duties would become apparent. Until then James must make himself a model second-in-command.

However, *Expedient* did not arrive at Jamaica for nearly three weeks. A difficulty arose with the rudder—a loosened spectacle plate, and upper pintles—necessitating minor but troublesome and time-consuming repair. There followed a long period of calm, the sky cloudless, the air windless, the surface of the sea so flat that the merest flickers of flying fish, far distant, were like the quills of invisible gods, scribbling the mysteries of the infinite upon an immense page of glass.

PART TWO: PORT ROYAL

'That is Yallhas Point to the north, sir.'

Expedient, in light airs, approaching her destination. The island along whose southern coast she was now sailing was spectacularly beautiful. Hills reared up from the fertile green of the coast, and great ranges of mountains behind. Rocky points and outcrops abounded, against which the surf could be observed—in a focused glass—rolling in and exploding. Great heat, even in the sea breezes, under a steamy, haze-glaring sky.

Mr Loftus, conning the ship, consulted a chart covered in close-written instruction.

'Steer west-by-north and a half north!' he instructed Daley Wragg. 'Chains! What mark?'

The depth, sounded at the forechains, came back to him from the seaman with the lead line. 'Twenty fathom and a half, sand and shell!'

The master's mate, Martin Cross, was busy with his sextant, taking readings and conveying them to Mr Loftus. An hour passed, and the heat of the day increased. Loftus kept up his attentive, not quite anxious, briefing of the quartermaster.

'We will steer to this course until we are abreast of Lime Key!' And now as Captain Rennie came on deck: 'Good morning, sir.'

'Morning, Mr Loftus. Damned hot, hey?'

'Aye, sir. All the time we are here, from now on, it will be hot, I fear.' To Wragg: 'We will take her through the Middle

Ground, a point south, at seventeen fathom, with Great Plumb Point to our north.'

'Very good, sir.'

'We must keep the marks on all the while. There is many keys that we can see, but almost as many that is not quite visible.' This last half to himself. 'Shoals and the like. We do not want her copper damaged further, nor her timbers.'

The ship made slow but steady progress through the glittering tropical sea, encountering now more and more boats, and the occasional canoe. Ahead a scattering of keys, and beyond, clearly visible now, rising out of the diamond fire of the water, the heights of the fortifications at Port Royal, with the standard fluttering at Fort Charles.

'I will like to salute the fort as we round the point,' said Rennie, straightening his back, and lifting his head. 'Pass the word for the gunner, if y'please.'

'Mr Storey,' as the gunner came to the quarterdeck, 'let us give 'em plenty of smoke, as we fire our starboard battery. Worm and reload with blank, and your secret ingredient in the cartridge, which produces such wonderful smoke. I will like to show them that even although we are a survey ship, we are a fighting ship too, by God, that can fire her guns with spirit.'

'Very good, sir.'

Mr Loftus guided *Expedient*, with great care and skill guided her from Lime Key to Rackham's, then between Rackham's and Gun Key, keeping to the narrow mid-channel, then steered for Port Royal Point.

'Stand by to fire!'

BANG BANG BANG BANG BANG BANG
and a glory of smoke.

'No, sir,' said Captain Rennie in reply to a question put to him by the Governor, Sir Compton Merrick, 'we did not call at Antigua, nor did we have any communication with the fleet at the Leewards. We made direct passage, sighted St Lucia, then St Domingo—very mountainous—a few days after, then two days after that, Jamaica. My instruc——'

'You did not make your duty to Sir Jendex Lyle?' The Governor, tall and ruddy-faced in the candlelight. 'Is not he your commanding officer, in these waters?'

'Not quite, sir,' said Admiral Pearson, the Port Admiral, who had accompanied Rennie and Lieutenant Hayter to Spanish Town. '*Expedient* is a private ship, under direct instruction of the Admiralty.'

The Governor nodded, and exchanged a quick, telling glance with his aide-de-camp Colonel Hepple, the only other man present in the room. They were in the Governor's private study on the upper floor of the King's House, adjacent to his dressing room, and used when he wished to read or write despatches, or write up his journal. It was not a confining, small room, and the tall windows provided some little circulation of air, but the air was very hot, and they all felt it in their dress coats. A moth whirled at a candle, and its giant shadow flickered on the panelled wall. They were drinking Madeira, and Colonel Hepple smoked a cheroot.

'We shall very soon be summoned to dinner,' said the Governor. 'Lady Merrick has told me that she will not tolerate my absence very long, gentlemen. She will not permit serious interruption of her *placements*, since we are eighteen going in. As her humble servant I must obey her in all particulars of etiquette, hey? May I suggest we continue our discussion afterward?' And he glanced round at them all, to show how reasonable was this request, and what a reasonable fellow he was.

'Well, Your Excellency,' said Rennie, ignoring the admiral's warning frown, 'I think I must just say—and I am most grateful that you have invited us here this evening—I must crave your attention a moment, as to certain documents that I made certain to deliver at once——'

'Ah-hm-yes-well,' interjected the admiral, embarrassed.

'No doubt His Excellency will wish to peruse them at his leisure, Captain Rennie. They are—are they not—confidential, after all?'

'Confidential?' The Governor exchanged another glance with Colonel Hepple, who puffed at his cheroot.

'Yes, indeed, sir,' said Rennie. 'They concern a particular fellow, and his plan to——'

'You are privy to these documents yourself, Captain Rennie? You know their content?'

'When you have had a moment to read them, sir,' said the admiral, laying a hand discreetly but firmly upon Rennie's arm, 'afterward, you will perhaps——'

'Yes, very well, thank you, Admiral Pearson.' Over him, nodding. 'And thank you, Captain Rennie. I shall read them—read them afterward, with keen interest. And now . . .' as a black servant entered, and murmured something to him '. . . and now we must go down and dine.'

The servant, a young man, was dressed in the uniform of a page of court, with bare feet. Captain Rennie stared at those feet in astonishment. The Governor stood up, and mopped his sweaty forehead. He was in the dress uniform of his regiment, the Royal Irish, and now took up his cockaded hat. The servant brought his dress sword from the back of a chair, and made to assist the Governor in buckling it on, but the Governor sighed impatiently, abandoned his hat, and grumbled:

'No no, Joseph, I will not clank and clatter my way down stairs and in to dinner wearing the damned thing, only to have to remove it again before I sit down. Leave it, leave it.'

'Clank clank,' said Joseph, and laughed, 'clatter clatter, ha ha ha, yes, all right.' He put the sword back on the chair, and they all followed the Governor downstairs.

'Extraordinary behaviour in a steward,' muttered Rennie to James, as they descended. 'Did you see his feet, good God?'

'His feet make perfect sense to me,' murmured James. 'Would that my own was naked as his.'

At dinner James found himself seated between two ladies, both very ample-bosomed, in low-cut gowns. They ate and drank with extraordinary appetite, and talked freely. James, after the rigours of the sea, was at first reticent in his manners and his replies, and uncomfortably sticky in his dress coat, shirt and stock. He glanced frequently down the table towards his captain, who sat near to Lady Merrick at the far end. James wondered if Rennie was as impressed as he was by the splendour of the great dining room, the beautiful shield-backed Hepplewhite chairs, the gilded mirrors on the walls, the tall candelabra slowly leaking wax. The table was noisy, hearty even—in spite of the heat—and bibulous.

'Have you been at Jamaica before this, Lieutenant?' inquired the lady on his left.

'Yes, indeed, madam. Twice, during the late war.'

'Then you have been up-country, I expect, into the mountains?'

'I have not. My duties confined me largely to the coast, you know.'

'Then you have never stayed upon one of our great estates here? Up-country?' She bit into a slice of pork, and succulence ran down her chin. Without embarrassment she brushed it away with a finger, and licked her fingertip.

'I have not yet had that pleasure, madam.' Determined not to stare at the glistening dribble still on her chin.

'You must come to us as soon as it may be arranged. Mr Debus! Mr Debus!' To her husband on the opposite side of the table; he nodded at his neighbour, laughed, and turned his attention across the table. 'Mr Debus,' said his low-cut wife, leaning fully forward, 'Lieutenant Hayter is to come to us at Hyatt Hill.'

'Splendid, splendid!' The gentleman raised his glass to James, and James saw with a hazy astonishment—he had drunk two glasses of Madeira, and three of claret—that Mr Debus's fingers, straying into the dish in front of him, were black at the nails, and his hand dirty right up and under his dirty lace cuff. There were wine stains on his shirt-front, and gravy stains on his sleeve. His face shone with sweat, and sweat dripped from the end of his nose into his glass. 'Yes, splendid, sir. Welcome at any time. Open house, ain't it, madam, at Hyatt Hill?'

'He is very drunk,' said Mrs Debus gaily, 'and he will almost certainly wet his britches before the night is done, but he enjoys himself, and is amiable, and what more can a man do for his wife, than that?'

'No, indeed, I think you are quite right,' nodded James, and remembered to smile.

'Other than that he should make money, that is to say, and keep horses.'

James hid his face in his glass a moment, then glanced round the table. The other guests were a couple of military men and their wives, an official or two, ditto, and a preponderance of merchants and estate proprietors like Mr Debus. James nodded politely once more to Mrs Debus, and turned his attentions to the lady on his right.

Captain Rennie, for his part, although he was seated on Lady Merrick's right, who was a civilised, moderate, conversable woman, was in large appalled by his fellow guests. On his one previous visit to Jamaica—in '82, after the Battle of the Saints—he had been a lowly master-and-commander, not privy to greatness, great men and the high social life of the island. He had lived in his ship at the anchorage at Port Royal, then he had been interviewed—briefly and cursorily interviewed—by Admiral Rodney, and had almost at once been sent home to obscurity. His ship decommissioned from under his legs, he had been set free to wander disconsolate upon the beach, literally on the beach, at Deal. He had always imagined, since that brief first visit years ago—the green lush hills and mountains beyond the harbour, the boats coming and going from Port Henderson, filled with ladies and their parasols—that high official life in Jamaica was one of splendour. In his head he had conceived of marble halls, with great swaying fans worked by teams of boys, glittering appurtenances, cool shining floors, beautiful women and brilliant conversation at table, and afterward the well-tailored gentlemen—not foppish, but dignified, and assured—talking of the Stock Exchange, the price of goods, and ships, and horseflesh, over their port wine. He had imagined these elevated people, had almost loved them, because in his heart he wished to be one of them. One day, he would himself be a gentleman of means.

What he saw now, at the King's House—the centre, presumably, of high Jamaican life—was a stuffing, slurping, dinning, guffawing and vulgar disgrace. Good God, these 'gentlemen' proprietors, and their over-assertive wives; those stout, sweating, red-coated officers; the slovenliness of the servants, who presumed to address everybody, regardless of rank, in the most unsuitable and familiar tones. Was *this* Jamaica? The whole place, everything, was a disappointment to him. He had expected to discuss his commission—his instructions, the letters about the Frenchman Lascelles—with the Port Admiral and the Governor. He had been met, as he saw it, with insouciance and indifference, even in spite of this early invitation to dine. He had expected to make his duty to, and consult with, Commodore Hamish Blethen, who commanded the Jamaica Squadron. Commodore Blethen was with Lyle and the fleet at the Leewards, and all but two sloop ships and a cutter gone with him.

'I am small beer,' Rennie said to himself. 'I am a person of no consequence, at Jamaica, or anywhere.'

He was certain, now, that his original estimation of his commission, and of those damned secret letters about Lascelles, had been correct. He had been sent here to be got out of the way, so that he could not pursue Their Lordships in his rightful, vexing claim upon them, his claim to thousands of money and the chance to lift himself. Lift himself, and become a man of substance, with a house and a carriage, and a silver vinaigrette. If that damned fellow Greer could lift himself—his opinion of Greer had again sunk low—why should not he?

'And do they sing, Captain Rennie?'

Rennie became aware that Lady Merrick, handsome in her gown, her ringleted head inclined towards him, her face politely inquiring, was addressing him.

'Do they—erm, do they what, Lady Merrick? I did not quite catch——'

'Your crew. When they are set free of their duties, do they sing?'

'Ah. Ah. Well well, they do—sometimes. Sing and dance, you know, on the forecastle.'

'The sailors in our ship, when we came here from Ireland, was not permitted to sing very often, by the captain. He was inclined to be severe. Captain Boland, perhaps you know him?'

'I have seen his name on the list. He had the *Rampant* seventy-four, I think.'

'Yes, *Rampant*, we came here in her. Are you so severe as Captain Boland?'

'I hope not, Lady Merrick, if he was. A happy ship is what a captain wants. Yes, we have singing, and the jig, in *Expedient*.'

'I am very glad to hear it. Sailors seem to lead a very rigorous life, after all.'

'Mind you,' endeavouring to be amiable and confiding, 'I won't have chanting.'

'Chanting, Captain Rennie? Do you mean sea-shanties? You disapprove?'

'Not shanties exact, Lady Merrick. I meant chanting, in a rhythm, you know. At the capstan bar, or clapping on to a fall. I will not permit that.'

'Whyever not?'

Rennie glanced at her again. Was there perhaps a very little hint of ridicule in her smiling, inquiring expression? He decided there was not.

'I believe chanting ain't conducive to good discipline, ma'am. Words is slipped in, unsuiting words, of-of—— Well, we need not examine them here, I think.' Sniffing, nodding, slightly embarrassed now, wishing he had not mentioned it.

'Insulting words, you mean?' The same polite expression, inquiring, smiling, uncontrived. 'Insulting to the officers?'

'Erm, well—not quite.' He cleared his wind, and was very uncomfortable, the heat prickling at his neck, and in his armpits.

'I am greatly intrigued,' persisted Lady Merrick, and Rennie did now see that she was teasing him, gently and affably teasing him, and that had he been a quicker fellow, a more sophisticated fellow, he might have thought of a witty response.

'All I can tell you, ma'am, is that they are not words a lady should hear.'

'Ahh. Ahh. Then it is very wise in you, Captain, I am in no doubt, to suppress them.' And with a playful smile she turned to her left, and began a conversation on that side.

Rennie felt great inner relief, and took a pull of wine. As he glanced down the table he caught his lieutenant's eye, and gave him a quick, mirthless grimace. And was gratified to see a brief, according nod, which showed the lieutenant's own suffering.

Soon the ladies rose, and the gentlemen were left to their wine. Both Rennie and James, used to sea manners and rough language, were nonetheless surprised by the barnyard flavour of the jokes and anecdotes that followed, as decanters circulated, and cheroots were lit—Jamaica was an earthy society, earthier by far than any gunroom.

No further mention was made by the Governor, or the Port Admiral, of Rennie's duties, and he and James returned very late in the Port Admiral's carriage to Port Henderson, upon an ill-lit road, and were rowed across to Port Royal in his launch, the admiral snoring beside them.

In the morning both sea officers had business ashore, Captain Rennie at the Port Admiral's office—although he was unsure what exactly that business might entail, given the Governor's almost dismissive attitude of the night before—and James at the dockyard, with commissioner and master shipwright, in the company of Mr Adgett, who would talk of nothing but copper, and decay.

When he came on deck at first light, in the comparative cool of that hour, James found Rennie already up and dressed —at least, he was in clean shirt and britches—and standing at the rail. He had trained his glass on the high fort above Port Henderson, the Apostles, just visible to the west-south-west, beyond the heights of the Port Royal fortifications. He swept his glass north to Port Augusta on the point, peering in the still imperfect light, then across to Kingston and the riding merchant vessels in the harbour there.

'Good morning, sir.'

Rennie did not at first reply. His scalp was visible through his thinning hair as he stood, wigless and intent, peering through his hand-supported glass. Then:

'Yes, James, stand with y'back to me just forrard, will ye?'

James did as he was asked, and Rennie grunted his thanks and rested the tube on James's shoulder. He peered again, focusing. A moment, a breath sniffed in and held, and:

'I am sure of it. I am certain.' He removed the glass from James's shoulder. 'What d'y'think, James? Eh?'

'Think, sir? Of Kingston, d'y'mean? It is not a place I know at all, excepting to——'

'No no no. The *ship*. *There*.' Pointing.

James looked in that direction, and saw at anchor in the harbour, perhaps a mile distant, a merchant ship of four hundred tons, her canvas in the brails, and a boat or two tethered alongside her.

'May I borrow your glass, sir?'

Rennie gave it to him, and obligingly stood so that James in turn could steady the tube on his shoulder. The ship came into focus in the lens. A boat with water-casks was alongside, the casks hoisting into the ship. Another boat was under her stern, and her carpenter's crew was at work with tools, and paint-pots. In consequence he could not make out the name on her transom.

'She is a merchantman, I should estimate four or five hundred tons burthen. Perhaps she will take in sugar, at another port, when she has revictualled here.' He lowered the glass. Rennie frowned at him impatiently.

'No no no. Cannot you see, good heaven? It is the ship.'

'I do not——'

'The ship that was speaking to that frigate, James. You are not yet awake.' A sigh.

That this was a just rebuke James felt keenly. His head was thick, and his tongue was thick and furred. He had drunk deep the night before, to get himself through the ordeal of that dinner. He rubbed at his eyes, brought up the glass, and looked again. Well, it might be the same ship, he could not be certain. They had concentrated so absolutely upon the frigate that the other ship, bearing away to the south, had been given no more than a perfunctory glance or two. He doubted that she was accurately described in either Bernard Loftus's log or the captain's own journal. Her flag, in any case, was not the Netherlands merchant colours. The flag was limp in the still air, but James thought he could discern the barred red, white and blue of the United States merchant ensign.

'She ain't Dutch, anyway.'

'What? Not Dutch?'

'No, sir. She is an American ship.'

'No no. It is the same ship.' He took back his glass, snatched it from James's grasp. 'I tell you—her lines is unmistakable. The single quarterlight, her bow, the rake of her foremast.'

'Well, yes, sir. But would she not—was she indeed Dutch—be more like a flute, very bluff? Her lines, I should say, is more Danish, or Swedish. Or American.'

'She is not an American ship, for Christ's sake! You saw her yourself, at sea, with a Hollander's colours!'

'I beg your pardon, sir, with respect we none of us could make out the colours of the merchant vessel we saw at sea—and then she bore away right quick, and we——'

'Yes yes, all right, all right.' Rennie's own head was not quite sparkling clear today, nor his temper. He checked himself. In a quieter, more amiable tone: 'I am very sorry, James. I should not have spoken hasty. We had better drink a quart of tea together, and refresh ourselves, before we go ashore.'

The rhythmic sounds of holystones, swishing and grinding on the forecastle and in the waist as the decks were washed, and the clanking of the chain pumps, were not amenable to Rennie's ear. He was already beginning to be over-hot, and sweaty. James had a headache.

'Thank you, sir, I should very much like tea. May I join you in a few minutes? I have a notion to sluice my head under the pump.'

'Yes yes, very good. Five minutes, then.'

He glanced briefly to landward, at the great mountain range rearing purplish blue in the slight haze away to the north-east, the sun's rays already beginning to burn away the mist. He was aware of the astounding natural beauty of this place, its dramatic landscape, vividly green, and the enchanting tranquillity of the early morning water, glassily stretching away across the harbour. A last glance at the merchantman, then he took a long sniffing breath, nodded, and went below. James yawned, stretched, shrugged off his shirt and made his way forrard into the waist, and the reviving pump.

At seven bells of the morning watch, now properly dressed, both officers were rowed ashore in the cutter, and went about their duties.

The first thing Rennie noticed, as he made his way to the Port Admiral's office, temporarily located near the dockyard whilst his permanent quarters were being renovated, the first thing that came to him was the smell. Port Royal was not a sweet-smelling place, and Rennie had to swallow twice, blow out his cheeks and tug down firmly on his waistcoat to quell his undisciplined gorge.

He paused a moment, getting his bearings, took off his hat, and put it back on. Would that he had a silver vinaigrette now, that he might fill his nostrils with clean, invigorating pungency. The streets and lanes near the dockyard were filled with activity, of people coming and going, hand-carts trundling, drays hauling—here in Jamaica much was accomplished early in the day, to avoid the energy-sapping heat that rose and hung over everything after nine o'clock, hung foetid and oppressive all the day. Smells, stinks, rose all round him, of fish and tide and human waste. His head swam, his stomach nearly rebelled. He made himself think of other things as he came into the High Street.

When they anchored, Lieutenant Peak had said at once that he could be of great use—had indeed been saying so for a week and more before they made landfall. His connections, he had said, his connections in the island were numerous and influential. He had cousins in the Assembly, two of his uncles owned great estates of five thousand acres; his family and the Governor's family were intimately acquainted both here, and in Ireland; &c., &c.

There was more than a hint of arrogance in the junior lieutenant's self-estimation; he was inclined to be both prickly and over-assertive. Certainly he was a fine seaman, no fault could be found with his working of the ship, nor with his quarterdeck manners. It was his tendency to assume his family was superior to anyone's in the ship that grated. What Lieutenant Hayter thought about this Rennie had never discussed with him. James was not at all assuming or arrogant about his own connections—but they were considerable in Dorset, and elsewhere.

An immediate message had come to *Expedient*, inviting her captain and first lieutenant to dine with the Governor. Peak had offered to accompany them. Rennie, offended by this pushing assumption in so young a man, had put him in his place.

'One officer must stay in the ship, Mr Peak.'

'Oh, but, sir—I can be of great service to you here. My family, you know——'

'Mr Peak.' Firmly. 'Your name is not on the invitation. I cannot presume to put it there. When we have been here at Port Royal some little time, I am in no doubt you will make your own private arrangements as to your social life. For now, sir, for today and tonight, you will remain in the ship.'

'Oh, very well.'

'What! What did y'say!'

'I am very sorry, sir. I meant only——'

'You meant to be insolent, sir! That is what you meant! Make your back straight, sir, and be quiet!' And so forth, until Mr Peak, thoroughly brought down, had been permitted to bend his back in a bow, and make his obedience.

Rennie had also decided there was to be no immediate shore leave for the men. Until he had learned from the Port Admiral the full extent of his duties, in least. He had discovered very little, last night. *Expedient*'s complement could not be confined to the ship indefinite, when she must be taken into the dockyard to have her copper repaired. Billets would have to be found in the town during these repairs, or in Kingston. Mr Trent would not like it. He would complain about the cost of revictualling, too. Rennie's head pained him as all of these details became jumbled within. He found the Port Admiral's temporary offices, the entrance in an inconveniently narrow lane, nodded to the marine sentry, and climbed the stair. At the top he was already in a sweat.

*

Admiral Pearson had been in his office half an hour already, and was now—as Rennie was shown in by a clerk—taking a glass of sillery.

'Will ye join me, Captain Rennie?'

'At this hour, sir?' His head throbbed.

'Ohh, this ain't early by Jamaican standards, you know.' The admiral contrived to be cool by sitting in his shirtsleeves, wigless, his hat and coat lying on a settee by the window. He was a man in late middle years, once naturally lean, whose position and mode of life in the island had made him stout. He was not yet, so early in the day, red-faced and sweating, but as Rennie had observed on the previous evening he would almost certainly grow rubicund and moist as the day lengthened.

'You are sure?' Offering sillery again.

'I am, sir, thank you. I should like tea, if that were possible?'

'Certainly, certainly it is. Hulton!'

'Sir?' The clerk, reappearing.

'Tea for the captain, if y'please.'

'Very good, sir. *Hot* tea, sir?'

The tea came, and Rennie drank a cup, and mopped his brow. The admiral put down his glass, glanced out of the window, and came to the business of the day:

'Now, Captain Rennie, let me be clear in my mind. Your task here—do remove your coat, sir, if you will be more comfortable without it—your task here is to make a new survey of the southern coastline?'

'That is so, sir.' Struggling free of his coat.

'Notwithstanding there has been a number of such surveys done, in the not very distant past, by Mr Moore, and Lieutenant Cranmer, and others.' The admiral stood up, and rolled down one of the charts that hung on the wall. 'This is Cranmer's chart, as you observe. You are to make your survey from Point Morant, in the east', pointing, 'to Negrile Harbour in the west. Yes? And you are to take particular note, as I understand it, of such several places—bays, river-mouths and the like—where an hypothetical enemy force might mount an invasion. In least, attempt to do so. I am correct?' Turning his head.

Rennie cleared his throat. 'That is correct, sir.'

'Hm.' The admiral sat down, and took a contemplative pull of sillery. 'And now we must refer to those letters.' Admiral Pearson had had sight of the letters, because he had asked—demanded—to see them. Certainly, Admiral Bamphlett had been prevented from seeing them, at Portsmouth, but Sir Robert Greer was not here at Port Royal, and Rennie was a mere post captain. He had shown the admiral the letters. 'This fellow Lascelles, that is apparently some kind of poverty-struck French nobleman—he is going to mount this invasion, is he?'

'That I do not know, sir. It might be something like. That is, his task could be to discover which place on the coast might be most vulnerable—however . . .' A sniff, a shrug, as the admiral cocked his head to one side. 'However—I cannot quite grasp how ingratiating himself with the important men of the island will accomplish that. It don't seem sensible tactics. In least, that is my own opinion.'

'Is it? Is it? Hm.' The admiral swallowed the last mouthful of wine in his glass, again looked briefly out of the window towards the wharves, then: 'All this is something of a surprise to me, Captain Rennie. I confess I find it difficult to credit. The implication is that France, a country with whom we are not at war, a country with whom we have reached extensive accommodation, to general satisfaction, in the Caribbean, is going to attempt to invade and take Jamaica. Fffff. Well. I think the thing is fantastic—quite fantastic, the whole thing. What is your view, Rennie?'

Rennie hesitated. Should he tell the admiral, whom he did not know, whose attitudes and temperament he did not know, should he risk telling him what he really thought and felt? The admiral saw his hesitation, and prompted him:

'Speak plain, Captain Rennie. One sea officer to another.'

'Well, sir, well—I cannot say I am persuaded, entire.'

'No?'

About to take the plunge, endeavouring to protect himself: 'Certainly, I am only one man in this, a simple post captain, doing his duty as instructed. I cannot hope to know everything, in all particulars, and it ain't my business to presume. However——'

'Yes yes, go on—however?'

Again Rennie hesitated. Had not Admiral Bamphlett at Portsmouth been ruthlessly snubbed by Sir Robert Greer, on these very questions? Well, they were not at Portsmouth. Rennie sniffed in a breath, and plunged:

'My commission was arranged by the Secret Service Fund, a body I had never heard of before, but with great power and influence. Sir Robert Greer is involved, and the Reverend Dr Jepp.'

'I have never heard of this secret fund, neither. Nor do I recognise the names you mention.'

'My lieutenant, Mr Hayter—you met him last night—knows something of this fellow Lascelles. He knew a man that was killed by Lascelles in a duel, in a most cowardly, blackguardly way. Clearly he is a scoundrel, a murderous scoundrel. Which need not surprise us, many a Frenchman is a scoundrel, after all. However, that don't mean the rest of it makes any sense, that it is not all just puff and dust.' He had gone as far as he dared.

The admiral's face had set in a frown as he listened, and now he sat upright in his chair. 'If there is one thing I have learned in the Royal Navy, Captain Rennie, it is to go wholly by the book upon the shore. I will like you to come with me, today, to Spanish Town, and lay before the Governor everything you have told me—the fund, those two gentlemen, and Lascelles. The whole thing may be nonsense, but that ain't our business, as sea officers. We will leave it all in his hands. Then you are to put to sea, as soon as your ship has been repaired, and make your survey as instructed by Their Lordships.'

'Very good, sir.' Feeling himself relieved of the need to think for himself, relieved altogether.

'Hulton! Pass the word, I shall want my launch!'

James stood in the dockyard, looking across the new careening wharf, where *Expedient* would soon be taken in, her upper masts and running rigging sent down, and everything removed from the ship—her guns, powder, water and stores—everything taken out but her ballast, and the whole troublesome business of sealing, and stopping, and caulking up would have to be repeated, so that she could be hove down and her copper restored where the great injury to the hull had occurred.

Mr Adgett had been anxious for weeks past, since before they left Funchal, about her copper, and her timbers. He had fretted that there would be no copper to be had at Port Royal. He had fretted that on the way there worm would get in and damage her. He was fretting still, as he interviewed the Master Shipwright in his office, on the far side of the yard.

James was feeling very flat, not just because he was hung over, but because he had found no letters waiting for him at Port Royal, when he had inquired. Had there been a packet, in recent days? There had, bringing despatches, and other letters. No letter had come for him in the packet. Had there been letters brought by merchantmen? There had, but none for Lieutenant J. R. Hayter RN. Surely Cathy had not neglected to write to him? The delay at Funchal should have meant that letters would await him now.

Had something gone amiss with Cathy? The question alarmed him. If nothing was wrong she *would* have written, by now. Certainly, he had not wrote to her. Not that he had not attempted it, and been prevented—prevented by Rennie's damned stickling rectitude, concerning his orders. 'In course, he cannot understand how a married man might feel about such things. No tender thoughts rise in his head, nor in his breast, neither, the unfeeling bugger. He is alone in the world, and selfish, and unconsidering.' James sighed, and walked back towards the dockyard offices, along the wharf. The careening wharf was empty, and silent, but here in the dockyard proper two supply ships were being refitted in the slips, and there was the usual swarming activity, the usual crack-crack-crack of mallets, and sharp odour of tar, and the loud voices of men, their whistling, and snatching songs. Why was it that, the world over, men at work contrived to be as yelling in their speech as if they stood a chain apart, instead of side by side?

'Christ, the din,' muttered James to himself. 'But I must not blame these fellows, that must earn their bread, work hard for it and earn it. Why should not they shout, and sing? And I must not be unfair to Rennie. I must rather think of him as a man deprived, not unfeeling but deprived.' He had a sudden image of Cathy in his head, stumbling at the top of the stair at Melton, stumbling, reaching out a hand in vain to the banister—and falling headlong, tumbling over and over, her dress tearing as her shoe caught in it, and then her form flopping over lifeless at the bottom, and her dark hair spreading unpinned as her head lolled and was still.

'God! Cathy!' Aloud.

'Are you quite well, sir?' The marine sentry, at the door of the Commissioner's house.

'What? No. Yes, thank you. I was coughing, you know, in the morning air. The smoke.' And he made a show of coughing into his hand, and blowing his nose, and clearing his throat loudly—and felt himself a fool.

'You wish to call on the Commissioner, sir?'

'Eh? Oh, yes. Yes, I shall do him that courtesy, if I may.' He adjusted his stock, and was shown inside.

The Commissioner, Captain Hall, gave him coffee, and

asked sensible questions about their passage, what repairs the ship would need, and so forth, and said that the officers of *Expedient* could always count on him, should they need anything.

'Do you need anything, Lieutenant Hayter? I am at your service.'

'Well, sir, unless you are able to bring my wife on a winged chariot, from Dorset to my side, then I do not think so.'

'Ah, I fear I cannot do that.' Shaking his head, smiling. 'You are newly married?'

'I am, sir. Very recent.'

'Aye, it is hard, Lieutenant, very hard. I know it is, because I have been in your position, exact, years since. The life of the sea officer, hey?' And again he shook his head wryly, and shook James by the hand. 'You must come and dine with us, I shall send word.' At the door.

'That is a kind fellow, a kind man,' James said to himself, as he went in search of Mr Adgett. He would busy himself, and lift himself with vigorous work. As he found Mr Adgett, and listened to him haggling for twenty new sheets of copper from the stores, James's mind was no longer filled with horrible imagined scenes, nor did he think about the dinner he and Rennie had attended at Spanish Town, nor the dismaying invitation from Mr and Mrs Debus to their estate, nor the Governor and Lady Merrick, nor the letters Rennie had carried to the King's House. In truth his mind was not on the business of the commission, either. He would do his duty in the dockyard, see the crew billeted ashore, and the ship careened, and then he would ask leave to travel into the high country, alone. He would hire a horse, take his sketching book and a few provisions, and make his way up there, into the cooler air. No doubt there were inns, or farms where he could spend the night—pens, they were called, he thought. He longed to be out of the ship, away from his daily responsibilities in her, free to breathe in the mountain air, and be his own master for a time.

'No no no no, Mr Adgett. Christ Jesu, *twenty sheets*? My dear man, that is nearly all of the copper I have got here. This ain't Portsmouth, nor Chatham. This here is thousands of leagues from limitless stores of everything—nails, rope, number one and number six, and copper—that you will find in England. No no, certainly not. I might manage a few, a very few.'

'How many?' Intently, rubbing a trickle of sweat from his cheek.

'Well—three or four, maybe.'

'Whhhh, that will never do, that will never suffice. The least number, the very least I could use to cover the place, is sixteen sheets. There, now. That is fair.'

'Ha ha ha, you are a very humorous fellow, by God. Ha ha ha, *sixteen*?' Throwing a pencil on the desk, and standing back a little, dismissively.

'We shall require one dozen sheets,' said James firmly. '*That* is fair. Otherwise we shall be unable to carry out our surveying duties, which is why we are here. My captain is even now with the Port Admiral, and——'

'Yes yes yes, very well, Lieutenant.' The Master Shipwright sighed magnanimously, nodded, took up his pencil, and made a note. 'One dozen sheets of new copper, the *Expedient* frigate, agreed. It will nearly strip me of copper, but agreed.'

'Well done, sir,' said Mr Adgett quietly to James, as they came away. 'Werry well done.'

The admiral's carriage, a sociable kept for him at Port Henderson, with horses stabled there, carried him and Captain Rennie to Spanish Town on the sometimes rough road. The admiral, in whom Rennie had already noted a tendency to be instructive, and prescriptive, pointed to things as they went past, things that they had not seen in the darkness last night.

'That is the Twelve Apostles Battery, high on the point, covering the entrance to the harbour.' Rennie glanced up, and nodded. 'With Fort Charles the battery gives us very good defences.'

'I notice hedges by the road, dense hedges,' remarked Rennie. 'They are like country hedges at home, a little, excepting——'

'Yes, excepting there is bamboo in them, and berries. You see, Jamaica is very lush, everything here is very lush. You see the red berries? Never touch them.'

'Ah.'

'They attract a minuscule ant, a black ant, that swarms in the hedges and has a powerful sting.'

'Ah.' Nodding, mopping his face and removing his hat.

'No, do not remove your hat, Captain Rennie, I beg you.'

'I have a headache.'

'It will grow worse if you expose your head to the sun.' The vehicle bounced in a rut, and Rennie winced. 'The sun is your enemy in Jamaica,' continued the admiral, 'and you must never venture out without a hat. Take sugar and water, mixed, when we reach Spanish Town.'

'Eh?'

'Drank straight down it will cure the headache.'

'Very good, sir, thank you.' Dubiously, putting on his hat, feeling the already stifling heat of the day all round him, the progress of the sociable creating only the most trifling breeze, not enough to relieve him. Was it the admiral's damned business to coddle him, at all? Good God. Presently he said:

'Who are all these people on the road, sir? Are they slaves?' Pointing to knots of people, clad in white, and bright colours, carrying bundles. Some of these people had stopped and made little campfires, and were cooking snacks.

'Aye, some of them is slaves, and others—the older fellows, grey-haired—have been made free by their proprietors. They go to market at Spanish Town, or take the road by the swamp to Kingston. They may take to market the produce they grow, surplus to their own needs, and sell it. They grow all kinds of foods on their provision grounds in the hills, and come to town on a Saturday, and sell it.'

'In course, I had forget that it is Saturday. Perhaps the Governor will not wish to receive us, on a Saturday.'

'He will receive me,' said the admiral briskly. 'Come on, Mellow!' to his driver. 'Whip them along, now!'

'I do not wish to injure the beasts, sir. It is very——'

'You will not injure a horse by showing it the whip, you will make it go swifter. Do so, do so.'

'Be it on your head, then.'

The admiral ignored this riposte from his driver, who pretended to be vigorous with the whip, but in truth merely swung it high above the horses, without touching them, and presently they came to the King's House in the great square at Spanish Town.

The Governor was not at home, said his secretary, Mr Fielding, but would return in the early evening from an official visit to the Rock Fort, where he was inspecting the garrison. Would the admiral and the captain wait for him, or would they perhaps prefer to return on another day? Lady Merrick, having heard that the admiral was come to the house, made the decision for him.

'Of course, you must stay and have dinner here, Admiral Pearson. You and Captain Rennie. I am in no doubt that Captain Rennie's crew may sing and dance contentedly, in his absence.'

'Thank you, ma'am.'

'Thank you, ma'am.'

Lady Merrick took them through to her own quarters, her day quarters, where they were introduced to a pale, retiring-looking man in a grey coat, of whom her ladyship was clearly very fond. 'May I present Monsieur Lange, who is my great friend and tutor in French.'

The sea officers made their duty to M. Lange, were seated,

comfortably seated in the tall cool room, and to Rennie's great relief given tea, which cured his headache at once. The admiral, however, declined the tea, and was given instead more sillery. How was the fellow able to drink like that, all the day? wondered Rennie. They were joined after half an hour by the Governor's chaplain, the Reverend Laycock. If anything, Mr Laycock was even more retiring than M. Lange. He had not wished to intrude, he said, and would not stay with them long. His Excellency had asked him to preach at the church in the country tomorrow, and he must look out his texts. He was a stooping man, with something of resignation and defeat in his manner. Had he been brought low by circumstances in England? mused Rennie. Had he lost his living there, ignominiously lost it, and been offered this tropick opportunity, as a saving measure?

'You have a chaplain in your ship, Captain Rennie?'

Rennie, startled by this sudden question from the very man whose life he had been belittling in his head, stumbled in reply:

'Good God, no. That is, that is, I beg your pardon—*Expedient* is without a warranted holy man, at present.'

'I see.' The Reverend Laycock smiled, and was not offended, or embarrassed. 'I think perhaps the Royal Navy is not altogether fond of "holy men", at sea.'

'Well, well now, I don't know that is altogether true, sir. Hm. Prayers is read, church is rigged, and so forth. It is just that we ourselves, in *Expedient*, have not been granted a chaplain of our own.'

'Ah.' And soon after: 'With your permission, ma'am, I will leave you and go to my texts.'

When he had gone Lady Merrick did not quite confirm what Rennie had suspected: 'Poor Mr Laycock. I fear the climate here does not suit him. I am sure he has only accepted his position here at Jamaica because he had not been able to make a success of his appointment at the Windward Isles, where he was attached to the fleet.'

'He was a naval chaplain?' Rennie, in surprise. 'Did he serve in the flag? That is, was he the admiral's holy man?'

'I think that his duties kept him chiefly ashore, Captain Rennie. He travelled about a great deal, I think, among the islands.'

'Did he, indeed? A queer kind of chaplain, if he did.'

'The Governor appointed the Reverend Laycock, when he came here, because there was a distant family connection.'

'I meant no offence, ma'am,' said Rennie hastily.

'No apology is necessary. Sir Compton himself was at first prepared to be amiable towards him merely out of good manners—Mr Laycock is a very self-effacing, retiring man—but in course they have become great friends, and conduct long, intimate discussions in seclusion. I expect the same thing happens often in ships, does it not, between officers thrown together by circumstance, and necessity?'

'Sometimes it does, ma'am,' said Rennie. 'Not always, however.'

'How very distressing it must be, when you do not rub along comfortably together, in such a confining place as a ship.'

'A captain may shut himself away in his own quarters, ma'am. That is his privilege.'

'Is it a privilege, altogether?'

'Oh, but it is, ma'am.' Admiral Pearson, holding up his glass so that the servant could refill it. 'A captain, or a commodore, or an admiral, must be permitted his privacy—a very necessary privilege, since he must make all pertinent decisions at sea, must think things out, and decide. He is both commander, and judge, and monarch, in his ship.'

'That is three things, Admiral Pearson.' Lady Merrick, smiling. 'Is not that too many, for one man?'

'Aye, and a kind of deity, too,' nodded the admiral, oblivious. 'When a commanding officer has hundreds of men dependent upon him entire, he is a kind of god, by God.' And he sucked down half a glass in confirmation.

So the day passed at Spanish Town, in idle talk, and waiting. The waiting guests were given a light luncheon, in the Jamaican manner, of soup, and four meat dishes, and puddings, and fruit, and a choice of wines and punches, and then Lady Merrick retired upstairs to her bedroom, and slept through the heat of the afternoon. The two naval men were left to themselves in a reading room downstairs. The admiral dozed in his chair, and snored. Rennie, who had drunk very little wine, was disinclined to sleep, felt that he was wasting time rather than just waiting, and wandered restlessly through the house. Upon opening a door he found himself in the long splendour of the ballroom, with tall windows, tall columns, a wide polished floor, chandeliers, and a woman servant arranging flowers in the far corner. The smells of the flowers, and beeswax, hung on the air.

'Who you want?' inquired the servant, peering at him.

'No no, I am just looking.'

'You look for somebody, please?'

'No no, nobody.' Rennie backed out of the door, feeling foolish. He was not at his ease in such a place. He wandered on, and opened the door to the square outside, and was driven back by a wave of heat.

'You go outside, sir?' Another servant, an elderly man, appearing at his side. 'Ver' hot there, outside, sir.'

'Yes yes, I am in no doubt, as to that. Thank you.' Closing the door against the glare.

'Will I bring you somet'ing? Tea? Hock wine?'

'Tea, yes, indeed. I will like tea. When does the Governor return?' Looking at his pocket watch.

'Presently, sir. He come, presently.'

'Presently, yes. Very good.' And to himself: 'Five minutes, or five hours—presently, good God.' And drank his tea in the reading room, to the sound of the admiral's grunting snores.

The Governor, when he arrived at seven in the evening, was very tired. The exertions of his day had been great. He and his entourage, including Colonel Hepple, had ridden to Rock Fort, on the far side of Kingston Harbour, and back, and they were all fatigued. One of the horses had collapsed as they approached the stables, throwing its rider, and had died of heat exhaustion. This had distressed Sir Compton because the horse had belonged to him, and had cost him 150 guineas only six months ago.

The secretary Mr Fielding came to Admiral Pearson and Captain Rennie in the reading room, where they had waited all the afternoon, and was apologetic. His Excellency was very sorry, but he was quite done up by his journey, and asked his visitors to excuse him this evening. He would not dine, but would take refreshment in his private quarters, and turn in. Would it be convenient for the admiral and the captain to come back tomorrow?

What could the visitors do, but accept? They had come there uninvited, had been cordially entertained by Lady Merrick, had been given all the hospitality and comfort the house could offer. That their object in coming in the heat to Spanish Town had not been achieved could not be helped. They came away.

When Rennie returned weary and fractious to *Expedient* in the admiral's launch he found a cutter moored alongside, and saw the painted name on her transom in the glow of the lantern: *Snipe*. Her commanding officer was in the ship as Rennie came aboard. Lieutenant Hayter brought him on deck.

'May I present Lieutenant Cobbett, sir, in command of the *Snipe* cutter, lately arrived from the Leeward Islands.'

'Mr Cobbett.'

Hansard Cobbett bowed, and the captain shook his hand.

'D'ye carry despatches, Mr Cobbett? Have you dined? Let us go in, shall we, and sit down?'

'Indeed, sir,' as they went through to the great cabin, 'I carry a despatch, in the singular, for the Port Admiral. And Mr Hayter has fed me handsomely in the gunroom, thank you, sir.'

'Cutton! Wine! Hm-hm, very good, Mr Cobbett, you have a despatch.' Flinging off his coat, and hat, unbuckling his sword, tearing off his already loosened stock. 'By God it is hot in this place. Cutton! Let us have some air circulating, for God's sake, before we all suffocate. Sit down, gentlemen, sit down. You have delivered your despatch, Lieutenant?'

'No, sir, not as yet. The——'

'Not as yet? Not as yet?' Staring at him, as Cutton opened gallery windows, and brought a tray with wine and glasses, and biscuits.

'The Port Admiral was not there, sir, when I came ashore.' Hastily. 'I was instructed by the admiral—that is, Sir Jendex Lyle—to deliver the despatch only into the hand of Admiral Pearson himself.'

'Well, the Port Admiral is there now, sir, at Port Royal. I have just left him. You had better go to him at once, had you not?'

'Tonight, sir?'

The bell was rung on the deck, and Rennie peered at his watch.

'Eight bells? So it is, so it is. Eight bells of the first watch, and midnight, by God.' A sigh, and he rubbed his face. 'A long day.'

'We are keeping only an anchor watch, sir, at present,' James reminded him.

'Yes yes, just so—we shall not be disturbed by pounding feet. Very good.' A brief pause, a sniff. 'Now then, Mr Cobbett, a glass of wine?'

'Thank you, sir. You—you do not think, then, that I should disturb the admiral tonight?'

'At this hour? No no, most certainly I do not. When he is exhausted by his excursion to Spanish Town? Certainly not.' Lifting his glass. 'Your health.'

'Your health, sir.'

'James, you are not drinking.'

'I fear I have had a surfeit of wine, sir. Lieutenant Cobbett and I are old acquaintances. We was middies together, long ago, and have drank deep in renewing our acquaintance.'

'Middies together, hey?' Glancing at them in turn, indulgently. 'Well well. What ship?'

'The *Gargoyle* seventy-four, sir.' Lieutenant Cobbett.

'*Gargoyle*? Who had her?'

'Captain Bright, sir.'

'Bright. Haven't seen his name on the list. Don't know *Gargoyle*, neither.'

'She foundered during the late war, sir, in a storm at Cawsand Bay. And Captain Bright is dead.'

'Ah. Ah.' Another sigh, and a hint of melancholy as fatigue began to overtake him. 'Time passes, hey, gentlemen? Ships are lost, and men die, and we are no longer young.'

The sound of water sucking at cables drifted in through the stern gallery window, combined with the easeful creaking of the ship, and quiet descended over the three sea officers.

James reined in and turned in the saddle to look away to the south. His chestnut horse snorted, tossed its head, and twitched at flies with its tail. Lieutenant Cobbett ambled to a halt on his grey, and mopped his face. They were beginning to climb into the mountains now. The plain below them, stretching to the coast and harbour, dotted with pens and cane pieces, was verdant and vivid in the morning light. Above them, to the north-east, mist hung in the mountains and across the valleys. The road they had travelled climbed gradually along the sides of steep gorges, sheer rock-faces tall above them, and across a wide gravelled river-bed, climbed again with glimpses of magical valleys, little houses teetering on the sides of high slopes, and all around them the astonishing greenness of the island. Bamboos overhung the road, and great spreading cotton trees, and picturesque shrubs, bright with flowers. Up here, where they had reined in, the air was already beginning to be free of the heaviness, the moist, clinging, feverish heaviness of the atmosphere on the plain below. To James the air itself was like a release. Release from his duties in the ship—now lying careened in the dockyard at Port Royal, her complement billeted in the town as artificers worked on her—and from his lowering mood of the last days. He had written a long letter to Catherine, and without consulting Rennie's opinion, or asking his permission, had sent it by a returning packet, the *Kestrel*, bound for Portsmouth with official despatches. It was a release to have unburdened himself to her, tho' he had not filled his letter with puerile complaint, nor even with manly regret at the great distance between them, but had sought to be reassuring, and amusing in detail, and loving, and fond.

In these last days Rennie had gone again twice, unsuccessfully, to interview the Governor with Admiral Pearson, and to James he had seemed to be particularly cast down by these excursions to Spanish Town, and bemused. There had been a vexing incident involving the man they had rescued from the slave ship's open boat, and put ashore at Kingston, Mr Derrick. He had been arrested for affray at a bawdy-house, where he had struck a mulatto woman so forcefully that she had had to be removed to the infirmary.

'We should have left the fellow in his damned boat,' said Rennie, when he had been obliged to vouch for Derrick by the magistrate, as a nominal member of *Expedient*'s complement. 'Left him rotting there with the corpses of his worthless companions.'

'Was it not our Christian duty to rescue him, sir?'

'Damnation to that, James. He is a blackguardly, worthless, wife-beating wretch.'

'It was not his wife that he beat.'

'Well well, if the villain had a wife he would damned well beat her, I am in no doubt.'

Rennie had with great reluctance paid the fine, and given Lieutenant Duggan fierce instruction:

'If ever that man attempts to come aboard, indeed if you ever have sight of him again, anywhere, you are to *run him through*, you have me?'

James smiled grimly at the memory. He would have liked to run Derrick through himself. Shortly after this incident he had made his request. Rennie shuffled papers, sighed, and:

'You may as well go on this riding expedition of yours, James, I expect. There is nothing pressing for you to do ashore, while the ship is repairing, that cannot be managed by Mr Peak. Nothing for me, neither, but books, charts, and Mr Trent's endless vexing expostulation about the billeting, good God. I would gladly go with you, except I am not a great riding man.'

'May I take Mr Cobbett with me, sir?'

'Mr Cobbett? Good heaven, I don't know. He ain't under my command, James. He is under the command of Sir Jendex Lyle. He had better return to the fleet, and his flag officer, unless Admiral Pearson has something for him to do here.'

'*Snipe* is revictualling, and undertaking minor repair, the next day or two, and cannot yet return to the fleet at the Leewards.'

'I wash my hands, James. If Admiral Pearson don't want him, it is none of my business.'

And so James and Hansard Cobbett, on horses hired from stables at Kingston, had set off.

As a matter of fact, what Lieutenant Cobbett had been instructed to do—in the despatch brought to Admiral Pearson—was to bring *Expedient* to the Leeward Islands, where she might join the fleet. Commodore Blethen was already there with the Jamaica Squadron. Word had come to Sir Jendex Lyle, from a passing ship, that a British frigate had come to the Caribbean and sailed direct to Jamaica, without making her duty to him at Antigua. This had angered him, incensed him, and he had sent Lieutenant Cobbett in *Snipe* to discover what the devil the captain of the frigate had meant by this slight, and to order him to join the fleet without further loss of time.

Admiral Pearson in his turn had written a replying despatch, to the effect—politely and dutifully to the effect—that *Expedient* was at Jamaica as a private ship, under the sole discretionary instruction of Their Lordships, and could not be released to the fleet under any circumstance. Rennie had been informed of this, but not consulted; he could not, and did not, expect to be consulted. Until *Snipe* had revictualled, and repaired, the despatch could not be carried.

'You need not rush, Mr Cobbett, I think,' the Port Admiral had said. 'There is no great urgency in this, since *Expedient* will not accompany *Snipe*, anyway.'

And so matters stood, as the two old friends rode on into the mountains.

'Well, Han, we have escaped.'

'Aye, so we have. I am damned glad to have got out of my ship a few days.'

'And I, out of *Expedient*.'

'Very probably, however, you would prefer your bride to me as your companion, hey?'

'Certainly I should. Catherine ain't getting bald and fat, and old, after all.'

'Old! Fat!' Laughing. 'In least I ain't a self-satisfied married man, by God. The girls still look on me favourable, and I am fancy-free.' He sang a snatch of a bawdy song, dug in his heels, and cantered ahead.

Rennie made a third attempt to see the Governor; however, this time Admiral Pearson did not go with him.

'You must argue the case, Rennie. It is your affair, in the end, and not mine. I know that I am welcome at the King's House, but I cannot in conscience call on Lady Merrick's hospitality three times in a week.'

'Well well, sir, if you think it is not your business, as well as my own,' said Rennie with some asperity, feeling slighted, 'then in course I must go there alone. Will you permit me to use your carriage, at Port Henderson?'

'My dear Rennie, by all means. Do not think me indifferent to your business, your commission, but as you will apprehend it is not the only matter I have before me, as Port Admiral.'

'Yes, sir, in course I understand you.' Politely, but still feeling slighted. What had caused this change in Admiral Pearson's attitude? It was almost as if . . .

'That *is* what has happened, by God!' Rennie said to himself afterward, and banged his fist into his palm. 'He has been told by the Governor to tend to his own business here at Port Royal. And I'll stake my warrant they will tell me to follow my orders, and mind my own business, in *Expedient*. There is a peculiar stench underneath this whole thing, and it is getting into my nostrils. Cutton!'

Cutton came along the narrow passage of the inn where Rennie was lodging while his ship was careened, and put his head round Rennie's door. 'You called, sir?'

'Tea!' And he sneezed, to get rid of that smell. But when he had sneezed, and blown his nose, and drunk his tea, he was no less determined to go again to Spanish Town. There was a question he wished to have answered there.

When he arrived at Spanish Town he found the Governor willing to see him, but for a few minutes only—there was a pressing matter he and Colonel Hepple and Mr Fielding were dealing with. The Governor received Rennie in his shirtsleeves, and was already florid-faced.

'I must see a great many officials today, Captain Rennie. The custos of Montego Bay has come here, with his own party. I must see him, and I must preside at a dinner for the members of the Assembly afterward. But above everything else I must conduct an urgent inquiry into a domestic matter.' Glancing towards the door. 'I do not wish to appear abrupt, or brusque, or to be in any way ill-mannered towards you, sir, and I hope that I do not give you that impression.' The Governor clearly was preoccupied, and clearly did wish to give an impression of being so—in order to get rid of him right quick, thought Rennie. That was Rennie's estimation of things. The Governor thought him a nuisance, and he did not like it.

'I will come to my point at once, sir. I hope that you have had time to consider what the Port Admiral and I have concluded, namely that this man—named in the letters—Pierre Henri Lascelles, the Comte d'Argenton——'

'Yes yes,' the Governor interrupted him, glancing in his looking glass, and frowning, 'what is it that you *have* concluded, exact?'

'Well, sir, well——'

A knock, and Mr Fielding came in without waiting, and whispered in the Governor's ear.

'Ah, yes. Thankee, Fielding. Say that I will come and see him presently.' Turning to Rennie: 'I am very sorry, Captain Rennie, but I must interrupt this interview. We have had a disturbance to the household during the night, and that and its aftermath must now take precedence.'

'A disturbance, Your Excellency? I hope nothing very serious?'

'I'm afraid it was serious. An intruder has broke in and attempted to steal Lady Merrick's jewels. Poor Mr Laycock was injured when he very courageously tried to apprehend the man. Perhaps there was more than one man, we cannot be certain.'

'I am very sorry to hear it. Was he badly hurt?'

'A blow to the head. He was lucky not to have had his skull fractured. Dr Stroud has been with him all the morning.'

'Stroud?' Surprised. 'You cannot mean—Dr Stroud of the Haslar Hospital, at Gosport?'

'There is a connection. Our Dr Stroud is his nephew.'

'Ah. Ah. Then the Reverend Mr Laycock is in safe hands, I am in no doubt.'

'Indeed.' The Governor laid his own hands flat upon the desk, sniffed in a long breath, raised his eyebrows, and smiled.

'So you see, Captain Rennie, that I must—— Ah, Hepple, come in. You know Captain Rennie, in course.'

Colonel Hepple bowed. Rennie bowed quickly, and rushed on. 'My principal purpose, sir, if I may impose on your time thirty seconds longer, is to discover the real reason *Expedient* has been sent here.'

'Yes, forgive me, Captain Rennie.' A frown, a nod, a half-smile. 'I know that I must have seemed to thwart you in these questions before this, and I do not wish to deflect your inquiry now, entire. Will you indulge me when I tell you that in due course—in due course—more will be made clear to you?'

'May I ask—when, sir?'

'I must crave your indulgence, Captain Rennie, and ask that you be patient a little longer. Your task in the immediate, as I understand it, is to conduct a navigating survey of our coastline. Will you aid us in all our endeavours by undertaking that task, now?'

Rennie saw that he had no real choice. The Governor was endeavouring to be accommodating and gentlemanlike. 'Very good, Your Excellency. However, if I might just——'

'Thank you, Captain Rennie. And now, good morning to you.'

'Will your Excellency permit me to ask——'

'Good *morning*, Captain Rennie.'

Colonel Hepple extended an ushering hand at the door, and smiled not quite patiently, as he might have smiled at an errant boy who had overstayed his moment in the headmaster's study.

'Damned supercilious fellow, Hepple,' muttered Rennie as he stepped into the carriage, and sat down forcefully, so that the vehicle rocked.

'Port Henderson, sir?' said Mellow, turning his brown face. Mellow was a quadroon, the product of a union between an overseer on an estate near Kingston and the overseer's mulatto servant. As a quadroon he was freeborn, and cheerful.

Rennie found it impossible to remain ill-tempered in the face of that inquiring smile.

'Aye, thankee, Mellow. There is nothing to keep me at Spanish Town, apparently.'

James and his friend Hansard Cobbett had put up at an inn on the lower slopes of the mountains, near an estate—one of the many estates—owned by Mr William Grice, the island's richest man. This was at Cleeston Hill, and the estate was approached up a long and winding mountain road, on which the two sea officers had ridden the preceding day. They had passed the gated entrance to the estate, at the front of which stood a long fence, and had stood in their stirrups to catch a glimpse of the great house. A quarter of a mile in they saw—surrounded by flowering shrubs, fruit trees, and a thick lime hedge, with the fruits tinting yellow and green like baubles on a Christmas decoration—they saw a plain low wooden building, with open windows, which was connected with another, smaller building by a kind of covered walkway.

'That cannot be the great house,' Cobbett had pronounced. 'There is nothing great about it.'

'No, you are right.' James shook his head. 'It is a stable, or servants' quarters.' But as they rode on, and got a clearer view of the estate, they saw logwood trees, orange trees, avagado, mangoes, pomegranates, shaddocks, and a variety of vivid cherry trees, all proximate to the buildings, and James began to doubt that first opinion. Surely this was too luxuriant a garden for servants?

'Perhaps it is the great house, after all.'

'Eh?'

'Houses here in the island are not built of stone and brick as we would build them in England, I think. They are built to suit the climate.'

Mrs Leslie, a woman of startling bulk, rich decoration and effusive personality, had confirmed this. Great houses, she said, were not at all like country houses in England. They were great only in the sense that they were bigger than any other dwelling on the estate. Mrs Leslie had owned a small inn in Devonshire, on the edge of Dartmoor, and years ago had come out to Jamaica to visit her brother, who managed an estate in St Thomas in the East. She had then married an overseer, who had died soon after, and the widow had again taken to inn-keeping to make ends meet. Her small establishment was adequate in the provision of meals, but primitive as to bedrooms, and other facilities. The linen in the bedrooms—simple wattle and daub rooms, with a verandah—the linen was not clean. James and Hansard Cobbett had protested.

'Oh, we don't mind about that kind of thing in Jamaica, look. It is only a night or two, and then you will move on.' Cheerfully.

'How many other travellers has occupied these rooms before us, Mrs Leslie, that slept on the same linen?'

'Ha ha ha, I don't know. I must look in my book, to know that. The rooms is comfortable enough, ain't they, gentlemen? As nice as you will get in Jamaica, and better than any at Kingston at the price.'

'Yes, well, that's as may be, Mrs Leslie. We will like clean linen, if you please. Eh, Han?'

'Indeed.' Nodding.

'For which you is happy to pay additional?'

'How much?'

'Let us say, let us say—a *maccarone*? Each?'

'How much is a *maccarone*?' whispered Cobbett.

'It is one shilling and eightpence, I believe.' James, quietly.

'For clean linen! Each! Above the cost of the rooms!'

'Take it or leave it, gentlemen, take it or leave it.' With a beaming smile, her chins chuckling. 'I manage an inn, not a parish poorhouse.'

Reluctantly they had paid. The changed linen—when they returned to their rooms after their dinner—proved to be no cleaner than the linen it had replaced.

'Damnation to the woman!' James, undressed, was outraged as he peered at his bed in the candlelight. He pulled on his nightshirt, and knocked on Cobbett's door, and when there was no reply opened it and went in. Lieutenant Cobbett was already soundly asleep, fumy with wine and oblivious of his new, soiled linen.

'Damnation to the woman,' muttered James, sighed, and was resigned. He returned to his own room, sprinkled a little cologne water on his pillow, blew out the candle and lay down.

In the morning Lieutenant Cobbett was not himself at breakfast, and could eat nothing.

'I wonder if that damned linen was verminous,' he said, pale and sweating.

'That would not make you ill, old fellow, only itching. Will not you take something? Coffee? Tea?'

'Perhaps a little tea.' His hand trembled as he took up the cup, and what he drank made him vomit. James helped him to his bed, where he lay trembling and sweating all the morning, as the heat of the day increased, and even the sounds of birds in the trees seemed to be hushed by the burning sun. Mrs Leslie came to see the patient for herself, then met James as he came from his room to look in on his friend.

'He has got the fever. He cannot stay here.' All laughter and smiles and effusiveness absent today. Her face was grim, her voice cold, her manner uncompromising.

'Cannot stay?' James stared at her. 'What'd'y'mean, cannot stay? He cannot get up and go out, when he is ill. We must send for a doctor, don't you think so?'

'I will not allow fever in my premises,' said Mrs Leslie harshly. 'You must get him out of this, right quick.'

'And I tell you he cannot be moved!'

'I will have him moved, look. I will not allow fever in my house. I am a widow woman, that must earn her living, and fever will frighten travellers away. He must go, or be thrown out!' Menacing now, in the doorway.

'Madam, should any of your people attempt to throw my friend out, or go near to him at all, they will know the consequence.'

'Don't make threats to me, sailor boy, in my own house!'

'It is no threat, madam.' Buckling on his sword, and opening his pistol case. 'It is plain fact. Any person that attempts malign action against my friend, I will run that man through. Or pistol him. Or both. You apprehend me, madam!' Equally menacing.

'Now, now, now, now, Lieutenant—let us not be hasty.' Her fierce bulk, her quivering menace, suddenly melting into a show of feminine acquiescence, all smiles and placatory gestures. 'I did not mean immediate, that he should be taken out of his bed immediate, and left to the vultures, no no no no. Hhhhhh, you are quick-tempered, you seafaring men, hhh-hhh.'

'You will allow him to remain, until a doctor has looked at him?'

'Yes, yes, yes, I will allow it, in course I will. I am not an unfeeling wretch, that I would put the poor fellow out in the heat of the day.'

'Tell me, who is the medical man in this parish?'

'There is Dr Harald, at the Ridge, or—let me think—yes, there is Dr Berry, at Whitefield.'

'Which is the better man? How far are these places?'

'As to the better physician, I could not say, exact. I am seldom ill.' A girlish laugh, which made her great bosom heave and shudder.

'Which is the nearer place, then?'

'Oh, the Ridge, the Ridge. Dr Harald.'

'Then send someone there at once, will you? And in the interim you must tell me what to do.'

'Do, sir? Do?' Alarmed now.

'Aye, madam. You know the fevers of this island, else you would not have been so fierce just now. I do not ask that you go anywhere near my friend, only tell me what I must do to relieve him, until the doctor may come.'

'You must bathe his head, and keep him cool.' Standing away from James as she spoke, as if the mere suggestion of his touching his sick friend had already contaminated him. 'Do not allow him food, only fluid. I will send water in a can, and a cordial, should he wish that.'

'Is there nothing else? No physic, that is usual?'

'Some of the Eboes say that chewing bark is benefissal, sir.'

'Eboes?'

'Slaves, sir.'

'Ah. The bark of which tree?'

'Oh, I don't know that, I fear. It is only something I have heard, in passing.'

'Hm. Very well, kindly bring me a basin, and cloths, and water. Leave them here, at the door of my room. Who will you send to fetch the physician?'

'I will send one of my girls, that can ride a pony. However, I must tell you—Dr Harald may not arrive here before dark, if he is able to come at all.'

Dr Harald did not come before dark, and poor Cobbett fell into a writhing fit, sweat pouring from every part of him, his eyes stark mad, and his voice babbling—of home, of sweet girls, of a horse he had ridden as a boy, of a terrible storm in the Chilterns, where entire orchards had been torn up, and hailstones as big as fists had smashed through roofs. His ravings were sometimes loud and shouting, and he started up in the bed before James could restrain him, and lay him down gently on the sodden covers. Sometimes his voice grew soft, and wheedling, as if he was talking to a kitten or a puppy, and his eyes became glazed and unfocusing. He wept, and sighed, and his hands fidgeted purposelessly at the covers, or at the buttons of his shirt. Twice he half-sat, twisting, clutching at his throat, and vomited noisome green bile, then fell back exhausted, his eyes rolling into his head.

As the afternoon wore on James began to be fearful.

Although the air up here was clearer than on the plain, the heat of the day was still considerable; only in the early morning and at night was the atmosphere cool. Three or four times James emerged from the sick room to inquire whether or not the doctor could be seen approaching up the mountain. At dusk he tackled Mrs Leslie, who stood well back from him, with a handkerchief soaked in vinegar at her nose.

'Why has the doctor not come?'

'I did tell you, sir, that he might not—I did say that.'

'Where is the girl you sent on the pony? I will like to speak to her.'

'Little Jancice? Why, she has gone to her bed. I could not disturb her now. She was hixhausted by her journey, sir.'

'She spoke to the doctor herself? To Dr Harald?'

'I believe she did, sir, yes.'

'Believe! Do not you know for certain that she did?'

'Yes, yes, in course she did speak to him. Please not to shout at me, sir, when I am only a poor widow woman, that is doing her best for you.'

'I beg your pardon, madam. It's just—I am fearful for my friend—he is really very ill, you know. Very ill indeed. Perhaps I should ride for the doctor myself. It is too far to go back to Port Royal, else I should go there and fetch our own doctor, from the ship.' Distracted, staring out towards the last glimmering glow across the mountains to the east.

'You had better stay here, sir, and wait. That is all we can do.'

Dr Harald did not come in the evening, nor at night. James sat up with Hansard Cobbett all the night, in a chair by the bed, wiping off the sweat from his forehead and face, bathing him in cool water, and attempting to restrain him in his moments of agitated, jerking torment—which grew less frequent through the long hours of darkness. In the small hours the air grew distinctly chill in the little bare room, and James attempted to throw a warming cover over his friend, but Cobbett threw it off in a strengthless flailing frenzy, gasping and panting, his candled shadow long across the wall.

At dawn James woke, hearing a sudden movement in the bed, a fitful gasp. He stood, bent over the bed, and found that his friend was lifeless. He felt at the neck, and at the wrist—as he had seen Mr Wing do in the sick bay in *Expedient*—and felt no pulse.

'Han! Han! Wake up!' Shaking him.

He did not wake.

James returned alone to Port Royal, having seen Hansard Cobbett buried in the graveyard of the local church in the mountains the day following his death. The clergyman, the Reverend Starlight, had been most insistent:

'In Jamaica we bury the dead at once, you know. It will not do to have the deceased left lying. It is the climate. I do not say anything untoward when I tell you that. Nothing unfeeling nor untoward. They must be interred. The service performed, and the correct things said, and the deceased put in the ground. Hm?' His grey eyes over the tops of his spectacles, under his wide dark hat, as he spoke in rapid, rapped-out sentences, urgently spoke, and then immediately wondered if James was in funds?

'Funds?'

'Well, hm. Burial costs. The service. The digging of the grave. A simple stone.'

'In course I am willing to pay whatever is necessary. Cannot I send for some of his shipmates, and do the thing honourably?'

'Send for them? Oh, no. They could never attend in time. I repeat, time is of the essence, in this climate.'

So James had stood in the sun, his head bared, as the Reverend Starlight spoke the solemn words, his own head protected from the sun by a parasol held there by a youth.

There were no other mourners in the little churchyard, which offered a stupendous view of the Blue Mountains, framed by spreading trees. Mrs Leslie did not come, no one from the estate came, and the Reverend Starlight stood well clear of the simple wooden coffin as the black grave-diggers lowered it into the ground.

As they came out of the churchyard, and James gave to the clergyman the sum in coins he had asked, the clergyman murmured:

'They was not told it was fever. Otherwise, they would never have dug the grave, nor touched the coffin.' Jingling the coins, and putting them away in his cloth purse. 'Practical measures must be taken, Lieutenant, in this climate. May God bless you. Good day.' Putting on his hat.

James returned to Port Royal with Hansard Cobbett's effects, arriving two days later, and carried them himself to *Snipe*, where he gave them into the care of the senior midshipman, a youth of seventeen called Rigby.

'Who—who will command us now, sir? Are we to return to Antigua?'

'That is for the Port Admiral to decide.' Then, kindly, seeing the youth's distress: 'He did not suffer greatly. The end was very peaceful.' A lie which seemed to stiffen the youth's resolve.

'Should we burn his things, sir?' Affecting now a callous pragmatism.

'Burn them?'

'His clothes. Because of the fever.'

'I had not thought of that. No doubt his family will wish to have his other effects, his sword and glass and books, and so forth. I will leave the matter in your hands, Mr Rigby.'

Expedient's damaged copper had been fully restored, and she was now back at her mooring, where she was being revictualled, and her guns and stores got back into her. Lieutenant Peak, to his great discontent, had been given the very considerable task of supervising these procedures, and in consequence had not been permitted to pursue what he saw as his pressing family and social obligations ashore. Captain Rennie had been insistent that his junior officer should attend to nothing but his naval duties while the first lieutenant was away from Port Royal. When Mr Peak was not occupied at the dockyard, and the storehouses, Rennie had taken him upon an inspection of the Port Royal defences. They had visited the fort, the six, ten, twenty, and saluting gun batteries. They had dined at the fort, and they had dined with the Port Admiral. It would not be wholly accurate to say that Rennie took a malign pleasure in thus occupying his junior lieutenant, nor would it be wholly inaccurate.

James's appearance, when he came to *Expedient*—his expression and demeanour—shocked Rennie greatly.

'What has happened? Are you ill? All right, Mr Peak, you may leave us, if you please. Sit down, James. You had better drink some grog. Cutton!'

'You had not heard anything, then?' Removing his hat, sitting down.

'Heard? I have heard nothing.'

'Lieutenant Cobbett is dead.'

'Good God. Good God. His horse threw him?'

'No, sir. He died of a fever, in the mountains. I had thought the news would have come to Port Royal by now. I sent a messenger days ago.'

'No message came to me, nor I am certain to the Port Admiral. How very distressing for you, James. Cutton! Where the devil is the villain when I want him!'

A boy came to the door. 'Colley Cutton is ashore, sir. He has arst me that I should take his place today, sir. May I——'

'Ashore! I have not given him permission to go ashore! I am very sorry, James. Will you drink grog, or a glass of wine?'

'Grog, thank you, sir. I am a little done up, I think.' Running a hand across his forehead, and staring at the sweat that glistened on his palm. 'It is only now—only now come home to me, that he is dead. Poor Han.' Staring at his hand, closing it slowly to a fist. 'I could do nothing for him, at all. He fell ill in the morning, and grew worse through the day, and early next morning he died. Poor Han.'

'Are you ill, yourself? Are you fevered?'

'No, sir. Just a little done up.' He took the pint of grog the boy had brought, but did not drink. 'I must return to my duty.' He put the tankard aside.

'No, James. No, no, you will do nothing of the kind. Lieutenant Peak may——'

'I am quite well. Just a little done up.' Standing. 'I must attend to my duty.' He turned, and fell forward senseless on the canvas squares.

'Boy! Fetch the surgeon, at once! Jump!'

James woke in his cot, thinking himself at sea, for he had heard the wash of waves. When he pulled himself up in the cot he saw at once that he was not in his narrow cabin, but in a much wider space, a room with a window. Sea-reflected light rode and danced across the ceiling. He felt himself well, moderately well, but warm. He was dressed not in his familiar nightshirt but a flimsier garment. By his cot stood a chair, and on the other side a cabinet, on which there was a pitcher covered with a gauze cloth. What was this place? An inn?

A shout, and the sound of wheeled vehicles, and horses. 'Make way, there!'

Now, that shout had a naval ring to it. He was in a naval place. He looked for a bell, to attract the attention of a steward. No bell was there. But again, there were no bells in ships, neither. Only the bell itself, to tell the progress of the watches. A slight dizziness asserted itself, then his head cleared.

'Must I shout?' Aloud. He was saved further effort by the appearance of a very fat man in his shirtsleeves and britches.

The sleeves of his shirt were splattered with blood. His black hair clung sweatily to his scalp.

'Ah-hah. Ah-ha-hah. So you are a-wake? Mr Hayter is a-wake.' To someone behind him. 'Fetch Riddle, at once. Riddle must assist me.' To James, smiling and revealing wide-spaced yellow teeth: 'And now, sir, it is time you was bled.'

'Bled?' So the fellow was a surgeon. A bloodied surgeon. 'Is this—is this place a hospital?'

'Indeed it is, Lieutenant, indeed it is.'

'The Haslar, is it? I am at Gosport?'

'Good heaven no, sir. No no no, you are at Port Royal. Do not you recall it, when you was brought in here?'

'Port Royal. Ah.'

'You do not recall, I perceive. Ah-hah-hm-hm-hm. Not unusual, sir, that. The memory is briefly upset, in many fever cases.'

'Fever!'

'Now now now, now then.' A plump restraining hand. 'Settle yourself, Mr Hayter, allow yourself to lie back upon the pillow.' Regarding him benignly. 'You was fortunate. You are alive.'

'Have I been so ill? I do not quite collect how I—how I came to be here.'

'No no no, why should you, hey? You was poorly, sir, when they carried you here, very poorly. How shall we say it? You was not yourself, entire. Only half yourself, shall we say. And now you are whole a-gain. Or nearly so, so nearly so as makes no matter. Riddle!'

'You say it was fever?' A breath, the dizziness returning, then receding. 'Do you know Mr Cobbett? Lieutenant Hansard Cobbett?'

'I do not, sir. Riddle! Where are you?'

'Well, he—he's a friend of mine, you know. He has the *Snipe* cutter, ten guns. I should like to see him, if that can be arranged.'

'*Snipe*, is it? I shall inquire—or rather, I shall cause an inquiry to be made. Now that you are nearly well, visitors may be permitted, I think.'

'Yes, thank you. I should also like to send word to my commanding officer, Captain Rennie.'

'Captain Rennie, the *Expedient*, thirty-six? Well, sir, your ship ain't here.'

'Not *here*?'

'No, sir. *Expedient* has put to sea a week since. And now—ah, there you are, Riddle—and now, before anything else may be considered, you must be bled.'

'Is it necessary, d'y'think, when I am only now recovering?'

'It will aid that recovery, sir. It will en-vigorate that recovery. Hold the basin now, Riddle, will you?'

James saw Riddle, a thin, pot-bellied, meek, nearly cretinous creature of indeterminate age, and recognised the type. Here was a loblolly boy, the lowliest surgeon's assistant.

'You will feel a little pricking, Lieutenant, and then nothing. If the sight of blood disturbs you, then by all means turn your head a-side.'

James felt the dizziness rise again, and did turn his head away, felt the prick as the blade cut the vein, and heard the rinsing squirt of his blood as it ran into the basin. With his arm still gripped firmly by the surgeon, and held there over the basin, he succumbed to the dizziness and sank down into a choiring black void.

'Is he conscious?' he heard later, how little or long later he did not know. 'Ah, his eyelids flutter, I see. He is conscious.'

'Is Han come?' James asked with an effort, opening his eyes, hoping for a glimpse of his friend's amiable face. 'Has he brought my letters? He carries letters from Catherine.'

'Who is Catherine?'

'She is with child. It is imperative that Mr Cobbett should be brought to me, d'y'hear! Why—hhh—why do not you allow me to see him?'

'Now, sir, now then.' The surgeon, gently pushing him

down. 'Your blood was a little frothed, considerable frothed, and you must not become overly en-vigorated, all at once.'

'Blood? What blood? Where is Mr Cobbett? Han! Han! I am here! Bring the letters to me!' Attempting, in a tangle of arms and restraining hands, to sit up in the cot.

'Ho, dear. Ho, dear oh dear. The bleeding has over-excited him, I fear.'

'Who is bleeding? Damn *your* blood! Let me go, d'y'hear me!'

'Tincture, Riddle, tincture! Yes yes, give it to me. Now then, sir, will you open your mouth? No? Then I shall be—obliged—to force it—open.'

James felt his lips prised apart, attempted to clench his teeth, and found them opened by a cold instrument, and liquid poured into his throat. He choked, swallowed, struggled briefly, and then was afloat. Gently and blissfully afloat, far out upon a tranquil sea.

When Lady Merrick learned that HMS *Expedient* had sailed without her first lieutenant on surveying duty, and that that lieutenant was lying ill of the fever at Port Royal, she sent word that it would please her to take him with her to Government Penn in the hills, to complete his recovery and regain his strength. There had been a severe outbreak of fever at Spanish Town, where the yellowjack was a regular and unwelcome visitor, in the steamy heat of the plain.

The Port Admiral himself brought this invitation to the hospital at the corner of New Street and Lime Street, above the Bathing House.

'I would say—would have said, long since—you must come to Admiral's Penn, but I am in no doubt Lady M would protest that Government Penn is a pleasanter place, altogether.'

'It is very kind in Her Ladyship, and in you, sir, in bringing this message to me.'

'You are recovered from the worst of it. I am glad. It has

been very bad at Spanish Town, very bad. They have lost eleven dead there.'

James was over the worst of it, and had quite recovered his senses and his equilibrium. He knew that his friend Cobbett was dead, and was reconciled to it. During his delirium a packet of letters had been delivered to the hospital, from home—from his father, his mother, his cousins, and most joyfully from his dearest Catherine. He had opened first the letters from Catherine, then the other letters, and had called for pen and ink and paper, and written lengthy replies. With time on his hands he found the task pleasurable, and lifting. In his long letter to Catherine he had made light of his illness and recovery, and said nothing of Hansard Cobbett's death. He pretended that duties ashore had kept him from sailing in *Expedient* on the survey. He wrote of his impressions of the island, the uplands, the climate, the great beauty of the place, &c., &c. He told her that soon he was to be the guest of the Governor and his wife, and had been treated with the greatest kindness everywhere. The tone of his letter, light and easy and good-humoured, had been made the more possible by news of Catherine's progress, which was all favourable: she was strong, healthy, and engaged in placid, useful occupations, and was living entirely now at Melton, where her child would be born.

Two days following the invitation to Government Penn, James was rowed in the Port Admiral's launch to Port Henderson, conveyed thence in the Port Admiral's carriage to Spanish Town, and from the King's House in Lady Merrick's sociable to the country house in the hills. There he found, as the carriage rounded the flank of a slope, a large, part-timbered, part-stone-built house, with an entrance framed by a double stair. A covered walkway, open at the sides, connected the great house with adjoining buildings. This, he was later informed, was called a piazza. Parakeets flitted squealing in the trees—logwoods, palms, spreading cotton trees—and the ubiquitous staring black grackles hopped and pecked and scolded. Domestic animals lay panting in the shade, and chickens, ducks and geese spread their wings, their beaks agape, among the shrubs and fruit trees that circled the house. The air, thought James, was not appreciably cooler up here than it was below. His buoyant mood was a little deflated by this discovery. Had he made a mistake in coming here?

Lady Merrick was already in residence; the Governor himself remained at Spanish Town on official business. Monsieur Lange was at Lady Merrick's side, as James was shown in. The Frenchman was solicitous, as to Lieutenant Hayter's health. Was the lieutenant mending? Was his strength returned? His appetite? &c., &c. If there was anything M. Lange could do for him, he had only to ask.

'You are very kind.' Bowing.

'Monsieur Lange is the kindest man in Jamaica,' declared Lady Merrick. 'There is no doubt of it.'

Dusk came abruptly, as always in the tropicks; the mountains to the east were lost in gloom, the sparkling coastline to the south disappeared, and with the departure of daylight came nearly instant relief from the heat. James was pleased to find his earlier buoyancy restored, and was putting on his coat when he heard the clopping of hooves to the rear, and Lady Merrick's voice, raised a little:

'No, no, you must return tomorrow, without fail. Go now, quickly.'

The sound of a horseman clicking his tongue, and of hooves retreating. James peered from his window, but horse and rider had already disappeared into the night. When he joined Lady Merrick for dinner James found to his surprise that they were to dine *à deux*.

'I hope you do not mind, Lieutenant. I hope we are not too dull for you, here.'

'Dull! Indeed no, Lady Merrick. I am flattered that you should think a mere invalid your suitable dining companion.'

Had he gone too far, in saying this? Her eyes, turned on him, said not.

'You have not the appearance of an invalid, Lieutenant, nor the demeanour, nor the hoarse, halting voice. I find you quite suitable.' A playful smile. 'M. Lange insisted upon returning to Spanish Town, because he had forgot his books, without which in course he cannot aid me in instruction. He is so very kind, and would not hear of delay. So tonight we alone are the revellers.'

This explication puzzled James, since it did not accord with what he had heard from his window. Lady Merrick had certainly required M. Lange to depart. He had not been acting out of kindness, but under obligation. Well, mused James, it was not his business—and he put it from his mind as they went in.

The dinner was very tremendous, when it was begun to be served. To his further pleasure James found that for the first time in many days he was hungry. Certainly he had attempted to eat the food brought to him in the hospital, had pretended that his appetite was hearty, but in truth he had addressed the unappealing concoctions of the hospital cook simply by pushing the congealed ingredients this way and that on his plate, to give the semblance of having dined. Even the more appetising dishes sent to him by the Port Admiral, from time to time, had not greatly tempted him. Nor had he been inclined to suck down the tumblers of grog prescribed for him by the fat doctor, Dr Hodding.

'Now then, you must pre-serve your strength, sir, by taking grog, which stimulates the heart and the lungs.'

'I had thought you was stimulating me quite enough already, Doctor, by bleeding me.'

'In a sense, in a sense. But grog builds, sir, while bleeding re-lieves.'

'I see.' He did not see, and was indeed relieved to have got out of the clutches of Dr Hodding.

Although he was hungry, James did not wish to give the

appearance of gluttony. Lady Merrick ate with such evident relish herself, however, that he soon forgot to be careful, and consumed everything put before him with seamanlike gusto.

They ate land tortoise, roasted; pigeon pie; mountain mullet; barbecued pig stuffed with peppers and spices; a great variety of shellfish; yams, Lima beans, plantains; then granadelloes, shaddocks, and bananas. They drank at first sillery, then claret, then sillery again. All the while Lady Merrick kept up an amusing and informative discourse, her eyes flashing on him with flattering intimacy as she talked—about the island, about officials and members of the Assembly, about custos and judges and magistrates, about the broad class of proprietors and their wives, some affecting grandeur, while others were slovenly and careless in their manners.

'I do not object to men that do not read books, nor live at all in their heads, if they are amiable. But in the tropick heat even high men, men that think themselves high, lose all apprehension of their duty to be washed, and clean in their persons, and amiable. They are brutish, and dirty. Oh well, I must not be so particular, I expect. We are not in London, after all.'

'There is many men in London, Lady Merrick, not altogether sweet-smelling.'

'That is true, certainly. There, however, one may avoid them. Here that is impossible.'

'You remind me of my commanding officer, ma'am. Captain Rennie is a great one for insisting upon cleanliness of the person, in both body and mind.'

'I hope that I am not like Captain Rennie, altogether. No doubt he is a very admirable officer, but he is not handsome.' A smile.

'Oh, I had not meant to make any comparison of appearance. Forgive me. I had meant only similarity of attitude, and belief.' At once he felt himself clumsy and inept in this reply.

'Had you? Am I like Captain Rennie in strictness, do you suppose? In rectitude? In my sense of duty, and discipline?'

James was aware, as she regarded him a lingering moment, then lowered her lashes as she drank from her glass, that he was being teased, and very probably flirted with—but he was out of the habit of feminine company, and incapable of the easy banter between the sexes that Lady Merrick so clearly enjoyed. He must make an effort, he told himself, to be witty, and civilised, and urbane—but nothing came immediately to his mind.

'You are a married man, lieutenant?' An inquiring smile, relieving him.

'I am, ma'am.'

'And you have children?'

'My wife is now with child, her first. We was not long wed when I was called to this duty.'

'You must miss her very much, I expect.' Softly.

'Indeed, I had much rather be at her side, than far away.'

'You do not like Jamaica? You find it backward, and uncongenial?'

'Oh, no. Never think that. I meant only——'

'Do not distress yourself, Mr Hayter.' Putting a hand on his arm, and letting it rest there a moment. 'I know very well what you meant.' She rang the table bell, and the last dishes were removed. Again James felt himself at a disadvantage. The pressure of her fingers, now removed, her glancing eye, hinting at intimacy, the smile that hovered at her lips—all left him clumsy, awkward, tongue-tied.

'Will you drink coffee? Or do you prefer to drink your wine in solitude?' Rising.

James rose, and bowed. 'I hope Your Ladyship does not wish to leave me all alone?'

'To say the truth I do not know what is the correct thing, when I am dining *à deux* with a gentleman. It is most unusual here, nor at Spanish Town, nor at any of the island estates, for so small a party as two to be found at dinner.'

'Do not you dine alone sometimes with your husband, ma'am?'

'My husband?—Seldom.'

'Then if you do not object I will gladly join you for coffee.'

She glanced at him again, and he was aware in the candle-light of another little flicker, the merest suggestion in her eye, of the desire for a more intimate connection between them. Or could he be mistaken? No, he was not. He must be careful, very careful, and behave very correct.

They sat in a parlour, smaller than the dining room but with windows open to the night air, except for latticed blinds. As they sat down a large centipede fell on the coffee table and writhed there in the candle glow. James leaned forward to flick it off the table, but Lady Merrick at once reached and gripped his wrist.

'No—do not touch it with your unprotected hand.'

He was aware, acutely aware, of her hand at his wrist, staying there a moment longer than was absolutely necessary, of her soft presence leaning forward, and the curve of her breast, and her peculiarly heady cologne. He withdrew his wrist, gently withdrew it—and felt a familiar pulsing in his veins, and a shameful and urgent desire to pull her into his arms. Instead he seized the sugar nips and flicked the coiling creature to the floor, and there crushed it lifeless under his foot.

'I fear we are greatly plagued by insects, even here in the hills.'

'Can nothing be done to keep them away?' He said it only to make conversation, to fend off all thoughts of intimacy, and bring himself to his senses. By God, he must be careful, now—very very careful, and true to Catherine.

'The servants sweep out the rooms, but the creatures lurk everywhere . . .'

'Could not you wash and smoke?' Blurting it, for something to say—anything.

'Wash and smoke?' A musical laugh, and a mischievous glance. 'Lieutenant, what can you mean? Do you mean bathe ourselves?'

'Not yourselves. In—in ships we wash the decks below with vinegar, then smoke the air with sparked gunpowder and burning pitch. It purifies the air, d'y'see, and keeps infestations away. That, and chamberlye.' Firmly.

'Chamberlye?'

'That is, that is—for washing linen, and hammocks.'

'Dear Lieutenant Hayter,' laughing again, 'we are not a ship at sea.' She lifted the coffee pot, and poured. 'Will you take sugar?'

'Thank you, ma'am.' Formally, correctly. Surely, all sense of intimacy was now quite destroyed? Banished and destroyed?

'Tell me, Lieutenant . . .' after a moment, '. . . when must you rejoin your ship?'

'That I do not know, ma'am, exact. The Port Admiral has kindly given me leave to remain ashore a day or two longer, and Captain Rennie left no instruction. However——'

'Fever is a very deceptive affliction. You must not rush into the world so soon as the early danger is past. You must convalesce, slowly convalesce. I will like it very much, Lieutenant, if you will convalesce here.'

'You are very kind, ma'am. I must not forget, however, that I am a commissioned sea officer, and that——'

'I think you will never forget that, Lieutenant.' Leaning forward and touching his hand. Her touch burned him, and he was again acutely aware of the cleft between her curving breasts, and of her soft mouth, the lips a little apart. 'When you are quite well again, you will in course return to your ship. Until then, you must stay here.' Lifting her eyes to his, and gazing at him. 'Will you make me that promise?' Softly, her hand remaining on his.

He did not make the promise, he did not say anything; but he did pull her into his arms, almost roughly pull her, and kiss her. Kissed her with a passion that briefly astonished him, and then consumed him—until he was utterly and headily and willingly lost.

'Surely you do not wish me to take the ship inside, sir?'

'I do, Mr Loftus. I mean to anchor in the bay.'

'The charts is most specific, sir, as to the risk for any ship above four hundred tons burthen.' Showing Rennie his annotated chart. Rennie sighed, clasped his hands behind him, straightened his coatless shoulders and stared shoreward a moment, at the green mangroves falling down to the bay's edge in the distance, the thick trees and rocky inclines behind, and the purple dark mountains rearing up from verdant slopes inland. Then:

'This is just such a place, Mr Loftus, where an invader might seek to outwit the island defences. At just such a place might a new fort be built. You have the list of existing forts?'

Mr Loftus found the list, lying on the flag lockers, and gave it to the captain. Aloft the courses were in the brails, the maintopsail backed, the mizzen and foretopsails braced round and bellying full, and the ship lay stationary on the swell, turned into the westerly breeze. She lay just beyond the narrow, rocky, treacherous channel. Rennie raised his glass. Above the mangroves ashore, in the little settlement of Black River, lattice-windowed houses nestled in shadow under the trees.

'What are those trees, Mr Peak?' Rennie, in a demanding tone, pointing. 'You have a wide knowledge of the island, I think.'

Mr Peak raised his own glass. 'They are logwoods, sir, very plentiful.'

'Hm, very good. You have deliberated long enough, Mr Loftus; you may take us in, if y'please.'

'Sir, with your permission,' allowing the chart to fall to his side, 'with your permission, the chart indicates very specific——'

'That is Mr Cranmer's chart you have in your hand?'

'It is, sir. Lieutenant Cranmer made his survey not ten year since, in the *Nymph* sloop.'

'And we are to make a *new* chart, Mr Loftus, a *new* survey. We are a surveying ship, for God's sake. What did Captain Cook ever achieve by hanging back, standing off, and shaking his head in despair? Hey?'

This was not quite a fair or logical question, and Captain Rennie was himself still greatly vexed by this duty, which he saw as purposeless, and fantastical, but he could not allow his officers and people to perceive any lack of determination on his part, in carrying out his instructions. He would do so with great exactitude, and painstaking draughtsmanship. There would be no finer new charts available to Their Lordships, no more thorough suggestions for improvement of defences, when he had finished. He had required Mr Peak to make observations and sketches of the rocky coastline, and the lines of mountains and hills, from the first hour of leaving Port Royal. Mr Loftus stood waiting, the chart held at his side.

Rennie looked at him, at the chart like an accusation in his hand, and:

'Very well, Mr Loftus,' a conceding sniff, 'you may take a boat, and venture in with the marks on. Far be it from me to force you into risking the ship, with her gleaming new copper. Mr Adgett would never forgive me.'

'Very good, sir.'

'Y'may take the small cutter.' He glanced down at the list in his hand, as he heard Mr Loftus give the orders for hoisting out the boat, and read:

Fort Charles, at Port Royal, and 4 batteries
Fort Augusta
Twelve Apostles Battery } all nr Kingston
Rock Fort in the E
Fort George at Port Antonio (N)
Fort Charlotte at Lucea (N)
Montego Bay Fort (N)
Fort Haldane (at St Thomas in the East)
Fort Dundas at Rio Bueno (N)
Fort Clarence at St Catherine

Leaning on the rail at the break he added in pencil:

A new fort at Black River (S)?
Another at Savannah-la-Mar (S)?—not yet surveyed

A shadow fell over his notes, and he felt a presence at his elbow. Irritated, he straightened and saw Mr Peak.

'What is it, Mr Peak? I am busy.'

'I ask your pardon for interrupting you, sir. May I go ashore in the boat?'

'You may not.'

'Sir, if you please, my uncle Mr William Grice has an estate at Black River. I think that he may be in residence. He would I am sure make all officers welcome there, principally yourself, sir, was I able to alert him of our presence by going ashore in the boat.'

'The boat don't go ashore, Mr Peak. The boat navigates the channel with the marks on, and returns through the channel to the ship.'

'We are not to go ashore at all, then, at Black River?' His expression so disappointed, his demeanour so crestfallen, that Rennie was unable in all conscience to sustain inflexible hardness towards the young man.

'Well well, Mr Peak, I have not said conclusive that nobody should go ashore, you know. It may be that a watering party should land. I should make no objection to a watering party, when the cutter has returned. You may take the launch, Mr Peak.'

'Thank you, sir!'

'Take your sketchbook, in course, and your Hadleys.'

'Very good, sir.'

'Hm, hm,' and a nod. Turning: 'Mr Tangible! You may pipe the hands to their dinner.'

The cutter returned in the early afternoon, Captain Rennie saw the evidence of the soundings in the channel, and was obliged to anchor *Expedient* outside.

'I was quite right to insist on your taking the cutter in, Mr Loftus. A frigate could never enter the bay without great risk. My opinion has been wholly confirmed.'

'Aye, sir. Indeed.' Politely.

'Mr Peak!'

'Sir?' Attending.

'You may choose your watering party and hoist out the launch, with eight casks. Should your uncle be at home at—what is his estate?'

'River View, sir.'

'—at River View, pray give him my compliments, will you?'

'Very good, sir. Thank you, sir.' Hurrying forrard into the waist.

Insects flurried and dived about the candle flames, and were frequently and abruptly sizzled into small angry cinders that fell on the table among the innumerable dishes. The blinds were partly open, and the night air circulated after a fashion, but it was not cool here in the dining room of the great house at River View. The captain and officers of *Expedient* were being entertained, sumptuously entertained, even by the generous standards of the island's estates. Only Mr Loftus remained in the ship, to keep her safe. Mr William Grice, the proprietor of this estate—a 15,000 a year estate—was enjoying himself. He liked the navy, and naval men, not only because his nephew was a sea officer, but because in the late war the navy had protected his ships, and preserved his fortune from the plundering French. He was in expansive mood, after the fourth remove, and the third delivery of claret to the table. His guests had eaten very well, and were beginning to be flown with wine. His nephew *was* flown with wine, as was the young Acting Lieutenant Cross, just turned seventeen and brought up to temporary third.

'If you are not in a great hurry, Captain Rennie, I shall be honoured to escort you over the estate tomorrow. It is important that the King's service should know what very valuable work it does in protecting the riches of Jamaica for England. And we are rich, sir, by the grace of God, and what we have is by God worth preserving. A glass of wine, sir.'

Captain Rennie looked at his host's strong-jawed, intelligent face, with its deep-set shrewd eyes and friendly expression, and liked him. 'You honour *me*, Mr Grice,' raising his glass, drinking, 'and you have treated us handsome, very handsome, but I fear I must return to my ship and my duty, short as I am of officers, and much to be done.'

'You are making a navigational study of our coast, I think you said?'

'Survey, sir, survey—a defensive survey, in case of theoretical attack from the bays and river-mouths.'

'Attack? From Black River Bay?' Mr Grice shook his head and smiled. 'Nay, sir, no enemy might attack us here. Not from the sea, at any rate. The channel is far too hazardous, as no doubt you have discovered in your frigate.'

'Never forget shore parties, sir—in boats—at night.'

Mr Grice's smile faded, and became a slight, disbelieving frown. 'You cannot seriously believe that we are at risk here? From the sea? I think not.'

'There is talk of building a fort.' Captain Rennie had wholly invented this talk, but wine encouraged him—wine, and a desire to assert himself—to expand on that imagined conversation.

'A fort, among the mangroves?' Another sceptical glance.

'No no, upon an eminence somewhere close, you know. With a battery of—say—ten or twelve guns. Perhaps two batteries, to cover the whole of the approaches.' Extravagantly inventing now.

'Good heaven,' mildly, 'I had always thought the danger might come from inland, from vengeful Maroons, joined by escaped slaves in the hills, and descending on us from that direction.'

'Ah. Maroons. Yes.' Rennie drank off his glass, and mopped his neck. 'Marooned pirates and the like. I understand you.'

'No, sir, no no. The Maroons are not pirates. They are the remnants of a rebel slave force, originally fighting in the Spanish cause, that was granted immunity by Governor Trelawney fifty years since. Their leader was a fellow called Cudjoe, long dead but still revered among them. They promised Trelawney, in return for their immunity, they would act as a militia against future rebellion or invasion. But they have been joined by many escaping slaves, with vengeance in their hearts, and they are not to be trusted, sir. Not to be trusted. The talk I have heard at Spanish Town has not been of new forts, but a system of watchtowers, to be built at the boundaries of each estate, able to signal in a line across the country, at the first sign of murderous uprising.'

'Ah. Hm. Well, I have heard nothing of that, Mr Grice. I am a serving sea officer, whose business is ships.'

'Indeed. But tell me more of this idea of forts, and batteries, will you? That speaks to an exterior enemy, an invading enemy. Since the treaty with the French, at the end of the late war, we have no enemies in these islands—that I know of.'

'Well well, I fear that I have already been indiscreet.' Rennie cleared his throat. 'Your—your very excellent claret loosened my tongue. Perhaps I had better say nothing further, as to forts.'

The hour was now too late for Rennie and his officers sensibly to return to the ship. The boat's crew, and the officers, stayed at River View. The crew slept in the book-keepers' barracks, Rennie and his officers in the great house. After their sumptuous dinner Rennie was expecting equally sumptuous accommodations. He was greatly disillusioned by the room he was shown into by a servant. The windows were open, except for a flimsy blind that had stuck on its cord. The bed was little more than a cot, there was no other furniture apart from a chair. The servant placed the candle-holder on the chair, nodding and smiling.

'Goodnight, sir, goodnight, sir.'

'Yes. Thank you. Erm—where might I—is there a commode?'

'Goodnight, sir, goodnight.'

'A chamber pot, perhaps?'

'You want water, sir?'

'No no, I wish to *make* water.'

Et cetera, et cetera. It was not a comfortable night. During the night there was a deluging storm of rain, and Rennie woke to find his candle still burning beside him, the dismal flame flickering in the gusts of air from the open window. He felt water dripping on him from the roof, and sprays of rain swept in over the cot. He rose, and tried to move the cot out of the rain, but a new leak in the roof drove him back to his original position.

'Christ in tears,' he muttered bitterly, his head aching, 'why did not I stay in my ship?'

When at last the rain stopped, as abruptly as it had begun, the room came alive with musquitoes, great bat-like moths, and centipedes, which fell from above on to the bed-covers. The candlelight seemed to attract them, but Rennie was loath to extinguish it for fear of being overwhelmed by crawling, biting, buzzing creatures—in the dark.

'God damn this pestilential place!' he fumed, flailing at the swarms of musquitoes.

In the morning his face and arms were mottled with red swellings, which itched abominably.

'Got bit in the night, did ye?' said Mr Grice, at breakfast. His own face was unblemished. He made no explanation as to how he had avoided a similar fate, but ate heartily, and was cheerful. Only when Rennie had been persuaded to drink several cups of strong tea did his spirit begin to revive. And afterward he was persuaded to look over the estate, at Mr Grice's energetic insistence—for fear of offending his host, and appearing to be churlish, if he had refused.

They saw the whole workings of the estate, and Rennie was duly impressed—his headache receding—by the extent of the enterprise: the stretching cane pieces, with new and ratoon canes; the field slaves bringing great bundles of cut cane on their heads to the watermill; the viaduct and boiling house, with its huge coppers; the trash house; the curing house; the massed casks of sugar, draining; the process of distilling rum—where the stink of the dunder made young Richard Peak retch, and turn away with his kerchief pressed to his nose; the carpenter's shop; the animal pens.

'It is most impressive, sir,' Rennie nodded, at the end. 'A most impressive enterprise.' He looked to the north, pointing to the slopes and dense trees, behind which rose green foothills and purple mountains. 'What are those huts, above the compound? Are they for other beasts?'

'No-o-o-o,' laughing, 'they are the slave houses, Captain Rennie, a great deal better than mere animal pens, I assure you, with little patches of garden.' Pointing in turn: 'Over there, on the rise, is the hospital. The large building, standing alone. There the sick are well tended, and the women delivered. An estate-born slave is very valuable.' A jerk of his head, another chuckle. 'He costs me not a *maccarone*, not a farthing. Aye, that is good value, hey?'

'Hm. Hm.' Rennie nodded politely, and glanced at his watch. He saw that it had stopped, and paused to wind it, but the key would not turn. 'What o'clock is it, Mr Peak?' Putting his watch away, and mopping at his face and neck.

'I have not got my watch, sir.'

Mr Grice obliged him with the time, nearly noon, and said: 'There is a new fellow at Kingston, lately arrived there, Swiss, I believe. You might profitably take your timepiece to him, if it is broke. A Monsieur Darder. Spoke well of, at Spanish Town.'

'Darder? Thank you, I shall remember the name.' Then, almost as an afterthought, with another glance up the hill: 'Tell me, Mr Grice, are your people content?'

'My people? You mean—the slaves?'

'Aye. Are they happy? They work very hard, certainly—cutting and carrying the cane, feeding it into the crushing mill, carrying away the trash, and so forth. It is arduous toil.'

'They are happy enough at River View, I think, in general. As a matter of fact, the reason I came here at all, this time, was to dismiss an overseer. Fellow called Calloway. In usual I am at my coffee estates in the east, in the mountains, but I had to deal with Calloway, and appoint a new man from a neighbouring estate.'

'What had Calloway done?'

'He beat some of the Eboes I had lately purchased. I will not have new slaves beaten. It makes them resentful, and impairs their seasoning.'

'Seasoning?'

'For a year they are seasoned, to allow them to grow used to their new condition. Beating impairs it, and they don't learn the habit of work. At eighty pound an head I cannot afford idle and resenting slaves, Captain Rennie. So the fellow had to be dismissed.'

'He was not punished, himself?'

'Dismissal is punishment enough. Off my hands, he don't cause me losses.'

'Ah, I see.' Nodding thoughtfully. 'It is purely a question of moneys. I see.'

A shout, as they approached the great house. Rennie turned, and saw his coxswain Randall South running towards them:

'Captain, sir!' Nearly breathless, scattering ducks and geese.

'What is it, Randall South?' Alarmed as he saw the stricken look on his face.

'Hhhhh-Jesus! The ship has drifted, sir! Dragged her bowers in the night, and drifted on a shoal! I fear she is holed below the line!'

Lieutenant Hayter sat reading in a deep chair in the summer-house at Government Penn, in near perfect contentment; the only flaw in his mood was a niggling guilt, very persistent under his skin, that he could not quite ignore. When he looked up occasionally from his book he saw the grandeur of the mountains to the east, some covered in forests of vivid green, others craggy, rocky, and blue. Tremendous drops fell from the high ridges, with tufts of green at precarious intervals, and below all of the splendour lay the spreading fertile plain. This morning he had risen from his bed at first light and padded trough the dew to see the fiery ingot of the sun rise bright from behind the peaks, and the silvery mist draped like a delicate cloth across the slopes and valleys. It was a magical place, a beautiful jewel, just as young Peak had said.

'Only he should never have spoke of it in anger,' James had murmured.

He was now quite recovered, and knew very well that he should by this time have made an attempt to rejoin his ship and resume his duty. He knew that he should not have lingered here in the hills, in guilty dalliance, that he should have insisted on returning to Port Henderson, thence by boat to Port Royal, and there requested permission of the Port Admiral to sail in one of the small vessels anchored there, find *Expedient*, go aboard and report to his captain. One of the cutters would do. He did not know what had become of *Snipe*.

Perhaps she had returned to the fleet at the Leewards. The other cutter, then. What was she called? He might very probably have been permitted to commandeer her.

He had voiced these things to Lady Merrick, last evening, and she had been contradictory in all particulars of his proposals. She had pleaded and cajoled, and grown tearful. There had followed a few moments of great difficulty for James.

'I think it very foolish in you, James'—she now called him James—'not to say cruel, even to think of making the attempt to rejoin your ship. She has sailed, and is now far away.'

'Well, you know, *Expedient* cannot be *very* far away, Lady Merrick. She is——'

'Will you not call me Cora, as I have asked you to?' Gripping his arm with something more than affection, something more like desperation.

'She cannot be very far away, Cora. She is near to Jamaica, to the coast, wherever she lies.'

'But Jamaica is so very large. In any case, it will take you days—a week—to find a ship to take you to her. Probably the Port Admiral will not wish to give you a ship, with the squadron away at the Leewards with the fleet. There is very few ships at his disposal, at present. You see?'

'I do not want a ship. I am happy to go in one of the cutters.'

'Oh, why must you go! Your late friend's cutter has gone away, probably. And the other cutter is out of the question. It is always at the Governor's disposal, should he wish to send a message to Port Antonio, or one of the forts. You cannot take the cutter, you cannot.'

'Then I must make the journey by road, along the coast.'

'By road! Good heaven, the coastal roads are dreadful. They are not roads at all, but rutted, dangerous, ill-maintained tracks. The Governor and I, when we first came to Jamaica, was obliged to travel to and visit every corner of the island, as a courtesy. It took weeks of comfortless bumping over those primitive tracks, our carriage nearly upset an hundred times, and the horses half-drowned. I should not even begin to attempt such a journey in your reduced condition, James. Please——'

'Reduced condition? I am quite well——'

'Fever cannot be took lightly,' feverishly, 'nor scorned, nor assumed to be defeated, over-eagerly.' Clinging to his arm, looking into his face. 'Only think what has happened at Spanish Town, a dozen and more dead there of fever. Oh James, do not leave me, when M. Lange has not returned.' She was trembling, and he began to fear that she was ill.

'Cora—Lady Merrick—your husband is there, ma'am, is he not?' Endeavouring to be gentle. 'Do not you wish him here, away from harm?' Gently but determinedly withdrawing his hand.

'Do not leave me all alone. Please, please, do not leave me alone.'

'Lady Merrick—Cora—I am very sensible of your great kindness to me, but——'

'Kindness! You think that love is a kindness! Cannot you once admit to me that you wished for this as much as I did?' Barely above a whisper, a passionate and accusing whisper.

'I am very sensible of everything, Cora, but I must not go on with it. *You* must not go on with it. *We* cannot. That is all I am able to admit, or confess.'

'Ohh! Ohh!' Turning her head away, shielding her face with her hand, her whole body trembling.

'Cora, I have no wish to hurt you, nor offend you—after all that has passed. But it *has* passed.' As gently as he could manage. 'It has passed, and I must go away tomorrow morning.'

She had sat up very straight, lifting her head, very pale and quiet, and touched her lace handkerchief to her lips. She did not look at him now, but stared straight ahead. 'Very well, I have said nothing. Nothing at all has happened, and I did not speak. I have a headache. I—I shall go inside.' And she left him.

It had been a very difficult few minutes for James, in this very summerhouse, last evening. Lady Merrick did not appear at dinner, and James—with a guilty sense of relief—had dined alone. He would not allow himself to think of Catherine. Was not one guilt enough, good God?

'But now I cannot risk a recurrence of yesterday's scene,' James told himself, closing his book. He took a deep breath, and rose. 'I really must go away.' And his brief feelings of contentment were dissolved in the growing heat of the day, and the necessity of making his travelling arrangements.

He went to his bedroom, gathered together his things, and rang the little bell by his bed to summon Daniel, the manservant who had been looking after him during his stay. Daniel did not come at once, and after a moment James rang the bell again. A brief further delay, and Daniel appeared.

'Ah, Daniel,' lifting his sketching things, 'will you tell——'

'Terrible t'ings, terrible t'ings, sir!'

'Eh?'

'Mistress is wailing and crying!'

'Wailing and crying!' A further stab of guilt. 'Why? What has happened?'

'The Frenchman, sir. He dead.'

'Monsieur Lange, d'y'mean?'

'Yes, sir, killed dead, in the Governor's house, at Spanish Town!'

'Good God.'

'Mistress crying her heart out.'

James put down the sketching materials with the other things lying on his bed, and muttered to himself: 'A second attack in the Governor's house? And a man killed?' And he thought of those letters about Lascelles, and felt a chill in his belly, and at the base of his spine. He had best get back to his ship, and report to his captain, without further delay. Else he would find himself adrift, alone, in increasingly dangerous waters. To Daniel, waiting by the door:

'Where is Lady Merrick? I will come with you. How was Monsieur Lange killed?'

'Don't know, sir. Bandits, maybe. T'ieves, in the house.'

The story unfolded. During the night, M. Lange—staying at the King's House—had apparently heard a disturbance, had risen and armed himself with a dirk, and had gone to investigate—this was conjecture, but supported by the logic of events. In the Governor's private quarters there had been a struggle, during which the Reverend Laycock, himself roused from bed, and armed with a pistol, had at first been struck a savage blow in the darkness, and had then fired his pistol, killing M. Lange. A calamitous and dreadful accident.

Lady Merrick was inconsolable, and would not leave her room. When James—feeling it his duty, feeling that he was in some way to blame for her distress—tried to see her, he heard her sobbing and lamenting: 'What am I to do? What will become of me, without him? I am left all alone!' Her maid emerged to say that her mistress could receive no one today.

'Will the Governor come here?'

'I don't know that, sir.'

'Someone should be here, to comfort Lady Merrick, do not you think so?'

'I am here, sir.' Holding up her head, her small chinless face pale with resolve.

The usual callers to Government Penn—local estate proprietors and officials, such as Colonel Missingham, and Mr Delbert, and the Hon Mr Playford, and their wives and daughters, had been turned away, bearing their gifts. The messenger from Spanish Town—a young man on the Governor's staff, Lieutenant McFadden—was preparing to go back, without any lunch. James asked if he might go with him to Spanish Town.

'Go with me, Mr Hayter? Have you a horse? I did not come in a carriage.'

'I have arranged to borrow a horse.'

James packed his valise, and rode away with Lieutenant

McFadden. On the way he questioned him closely. The lieutenant had been commissioned in Sir Compton Merrick's regiment, the Royal Irish, and had come with the Governor and Lady Merrick to Jamaica two years ago. There was a minor family connection; Lieutenant McFadden and Lady Merrick were distant cousins. The young man imparted this information readily enough as they rode through the heat, and James gave him the same kind of information about himself. In between, he attempted to gain more intelligence of the death of M. Lange.

'Do not you think it damned peculiar that two such assaults have been made on the Governor's residence in so short a space of time, both of them involving injury to the Reverend Laycock?'

'Laycock is a very courageous fellow, anyway. It ain't his fault Lange was killed, in my view.'

'No, well, in course it was an accident. Ain't it odd, though, that a clergyman should be armed?'

'I think he acquired the pistol after he was assaulted the first occasion. Can we blame him for that?'

'No no, certainly a man must be permitted to protect his person from injury. But surely—surely there is others in the household, military officers and the like, that might act as bodyguard to His Excellency, rather than his domestic chaplain?'

'D'y'mean me, sir?' Reining in, glaring.

'No no, I do not. You are not quartered there, after all—are you?'

'I am not. I am quartered at the barracks.'

'Quite so. But I wonder, was not it thought necessary—after the first assault, when Laycock was injured, and the Governor's own quarters entered—for a bodyguard to be present in those quarters at night?'

'The Governor would not allow it.'

'Ah. Ah. Then—it was suggested to him?'

'I believe it was.' Shortly.

'Yes, forgive me for seeming to pry, Lieutenant. Lady Merrick has been—very kind to me, and in consequence I feel perhaps closer to these events than might ordinarily be the case, for a visiting sea officer.'

'She is very kind.' Stiffly, his eyes on the road ahead, sitting up in his saddle. He was a well-made young man, a fine figure of a fellow, thought James. Something about that curt reply, and the straightness of his back, suggested to James that young Lieutenant McFadden wished to keep concealed quite how kind Lady Merrick had been to her cousin, more than kind, and James in spite of himself felt a brief quiver of resentment. He dismissed it, and:

'She was very greatly attached to Monsieur Lange, clearly.'

Lieutenant McFadden gave him a sharp glance, and chose not to reply. He dug his heels into his horse's flanks, and rode on at a brisk canter.

Instead of going all the way to Spanish Town, James said goodbye to the lieutenant at a fork in the road, and rode across to Port Henderson. He knew that he must find a means of reaching *Expedient*, with all possible despatch.

Admiral Pearson was decided, and firm. James could not take the remaining cutter, *Curlew*. *Snipe* had indeed returned to the fleet at the Leewards. The *Curlew* was held at Port Royal at the Governor's pleasure, as were the two ship sloops anchored there, *Nymph* and *Ventura*, should the Governor wish to embark and sail with his entourage to another part of the island, many of the island roads being nearly impassable.

'Is no exception ever made, sir?' James asked. 'How else will I proceed to rejoin my ship?'

'I expect you could hire a vessel privately, at Kingston, and a few men.'

'Privately! Could not I take a pinnace, or a launch, out of the boat-house at the dockyard?'

'There is nothing suitable at present, I fear.' Making a face, shaking his head, sucking in a breath. A moment, then: 'If I was you, my boy, I should take my ease at Port Royal, and await the return of my ship in due course. Write letters, read, fill my sketchbook. You are very welcome to stay with me, until *Expedient* returns. In fact, let me send word to the inn, and have your dunnage——'

'That is kind in you, sir, but I must consult with my commanding officer without delay.'

'But—why? Where is the urgency?' Frowning at him. 'Is it something new you have learned at Government Penn, about those letters, and that fellow Lascelles? I should tell you, I think, that my own view—and your captain's, too—is that the matter should be allowed to rest.'

'I have learned nothing new—except what has happened at Spanish Town last night, in course.'

'At Spanish Town?'

'Was you not told, sir? I should perhaps have said something at once. Lady Merrick's French tutor, Monsieur Lange, was shot dead at the King's House. I had thought——'

'Shot dead!'

'Aye, shot. By the Reverend Laycock. He——'

'The Governor's chaplain? Come now, Mr Hayter! Do not make damned idle jokes!' Severely.

'I assure you, sir, it is quite true.'

Admiral Pearson stared at him, and gulped down the mouthful of sillery remaining in his glass.

'He has gone mad in the heat, clearly. Christ's blood, this climate.' Shaking his head again, and refilling his glass. He sucked down half of the wine, mopped his face, stared briefly out the window, and turned again to James. 'Was you at the King's House today?'

'No, sir, I have come direct from Government Penn, where I heard the news. It is thought the shot was an accident, in the darkness. Thieves had broke in, both men went to investigate the sounds, there was an altercation, and——'

'Thieves had broke in—*again*?'

'And again the Reverend Laycock was attacked. That is why he fired, apparently.'

'The Governor was not hurt? Nor Lady Merrick? I should have asked that sooner.'

'Lady Merrick has been all the time at Government Penn, sir. I do not think the Governor——'

'I must go at once to Spanish Town.' Throwing back wine, banging the glass down on the table.

'Very good, sir. With your permission——'

'Hulton! Send word for my boat's crew! Jump, man! Now then, Lieutenant, I will like you to come with me.' Taking up his coat and hat.

'Go with you, sir?'

'Indeed indeed. Ye've been idle these many days, sir. You will accompany me to Spanish Town, where we may be of service to His Excellency.'

'In what particular, sir?' James dared to ask as they went downstairs, the admiral jamming on his hat.

'Eh? How the bloody hell can I be expected to know that, for Christ's sake, until we get there? We are both serving officers, and we must show ourselves willing to serve, by God.'

'Very good, sir.' Putting on his own hat as they emerged into the sun.

Contrary to Randall South's breathless opinion, *Expedient* had not been holed below the waterline. However, that was—in Captain Rennie's opinion—the single happy fact of her going aground. He had been rowed out to the ship from Black River, and had gone aboard expecting to hear and find the worst. He did not hear and find quite that, but she was stuck fast, and he was uneasily aware when he had made a rapid inspection with Adgett and Tangible and Mr Loftus that she would not readily be got free. Mr Loftus made an effort to describe what had already been attempted, but was cut short:

'Was you on deck at the time of the accident to the ship, Mr Loftus?' demanded Rennie.

'I was not, sir, but I am fully——'

'Then who had the deck, sir?'

'Mr Delingpole and Mr Lamarr, sir, and the quartermaster Daley Wragg. I am fully——'

'They will attend me in my cabin, if y'please, Mr Loftus, right quick. You will kindly accompany them.'

'Very good, sir.' His hat off and on.

Rennie went below. In the great cabin: 'Cutton!' he bellowed, and rubbing and scratching at his musquito-pocked face and neck he tore off his stock, and opened his shirt. 'Cutton, damn you!'

Cutton appeared from the quarter gallery, swaying a little. Rennie flung down his hat.

'Where was you when I came aboard? Tea, for God's sake.' A peering glare. 'Are you ill?'

'Nho hir, hi am quite well, hank you.'

'You are drunk.'

'Ho-nnnn, nossir. Teassir.' Nodding blearily, touching his forehead, withdrawing.

'Is no one sober nor capable in the bloody ship?' sighed Rennie. 'Yes yes, come in, Mr Loftus. Is that you, Mr Lamarr, and Mr Delingpole? And Daley Wragg, behind? Very well, come in. Now, then.' Leaning forward, hands flat on his desk. 'What the devil happened, that no one of you saw that the ship was beginning to drag and drift? Hey?'

'I must take the blame for it, entire, sir,' began Mr Loftus.

'But you was not on deck, Mr Loftus. I will like to hear—from one or all of you that was—how *Expedient* has found herself in the present predicament. You, Mr Delingpole.' Looking at him.

'Well, sir, it seemed to happen in a very stealthy way——'

'Stealthy! What fucking nonsense is this! An anchor watch

is kept in order that the ship shall not be permitted to drift on the tide, so that she don't foul her hawses. If such a watch was being kept, why in the name of Christ our Saviour and Comfort was the drifting not *noticed*! You, Daley Wragg.' And he looked at him, now. 'What can you tell me?'

'Tell you, sir?' With every appearance in his expression of a wish to assist.

'Do not be obtuse. Do not be obstructive. If you, a seaman of long experience, had in fact *been* on deck, this calamity would not have occurred. But you was not. You was smoking in the forecastle, or abusing yourself in the head, one or t'other, I am in no doubt.' Grimly.

'Sir,' began Mr Loftus, 'if you please, I had the ship, and in fact should have kept the deck the night through. I will take all blame, and——'

'That is for me to decide, Mr Loftus.' Bluntly. And he was about to continue, but was interrupted by the appearance of Mr Peak at the door.

'Sir, we are going to try backing sail and warping, sir, with shoes on the kedge—to see if she might be backed off, sir.'

'Very well, thank you, Mr Peak. I shall come on deck directly.'

Mr Loftus risked a further intervention. 'Wragg and I have already tried that, sir, and I fear it did not answer.'

'Well well, we must try again, Mr Loftus. She is trimmed by the stern, and we must hope that that is where she is caught.'

But Mr Loftus again was obliged to disappoint him: 'We have sounded right round, sir, and she is firm upon the shoal as far forrard as the main chains.'

'Hell and fire, Mr Loftus.' Dismayed. 'Very well, we must start our water, and get everything else into the boats, that will fit. Swivels, powder, shot, spare bowers, stores. We must strike and send down our upper masts and yards, and get them into the boats, too. Everything that will go into the boats without swamping them, as many trips ashore as it takes. And we must pump her dry, so there ain't even six inches in the well. Then we may perhaps float her off.' Peering over the rail.

'I do not think she will float, sir, even then—unless we can relieve her of the weight of the carronades.'

'Then—then we must lower the carronades into the boats, when they have made all the other trips ashore, and returned.'

When all these things had been done—her water started, stores, bowers, swivels, powder and boxes of shot taken ashore, the upper masts and yards sent down and hoisted out, and her bilges pumped dry—the carronades proved by far the most stubborn difficulty. Each squat weapon weighed seventeen hundredweight, over nineteen hundred pounds. When the first carronade was hoisted out and lowered to the launch, the tackle slipped, the gun swung round heavily, nudged and nearly upset the boat, and had to be hoisted back inboard.

Rennie stared, scratched at his neck, sniffed, sucked down a draught of tea, and at last—as the carronade swung slowly twisting in its ropes inboard—came to his decision. A sigh:

'Pass the word for the gunner, if y'please.' Puffing out his cheeks. 'Ah, Storey. Now then, we are many miles from assistance of any kind.'

'That is so, sir.' Wiping his neck with an already damp kerchief, mopping his forehead.

'Even was another ship able to come to us—she could not in course come alongside.'

'That is so, sir.' Pursing his lips, knowing what was coming.

'We must get rid of these fat fellows, I fear.'

'Yes, I thought you might be going to say that to me, sir. Might I suggest? Why do not we try to float them, with casks? I believe it might be manag——'

'No, no, no—at nearly a ton apiece, Mr Storey? No no, we must lighten ship, and our smashers must go over the side.'

'Very good, sir.' Hesitating, then: 'If I *was* able to save one or perhaps two of them, by floating them on a cradle of casks, would you allow me to do so, sir?'

'Good heaven, man, this is a tropick place. There is squalls, and storms, that whirl up out of nothing, in a moment. We must swim the ship off this shoal, at all cost, and part of that cost must be our carronades. We have saved our swivels, and we shall still have all of our long guns. Now then. Let us get it over and done.'

'Very good, sir.'

'Mr Peak! Vast there, with those carronades! We will not attempt to get them into the boats, any more! They are to go over the side!'

'*All* of them, sir?'

'All of them, Mr Peak. Right quick, if y'please.'

Half a glass later, as the tide came to full flood, the last of the carronades tumbled with a great plunging splash over the side. The breeze had freshened, and *Expedient* stirred under her backed courses, stirred under the taut cable of the kedge and the straining backs at the capstan, stirred with a pale seething of mud and sand along her wales, and:

'*HUZZAY! HUZZAY! HUZZAY!*'

echoed across the bay as she slowly swam free, floated free, and rode the blue swell.

'It was most kind and dutiful in you to hasten here, Lieutenant,' said Colonel Hepple. 'However, everything is in hand, you know, and I think it will be better that you return to Port Royal, since there is really nothing at all to keep you here.'

They were in the reading room at the King's House, where James had been asked to wait—had been kept waiting some considerable time.

'I came at the Port Admiral's request.' Politely. James did not like Colonel Hepple. His manner of speech that hinted at superiority in all distinctions—of education, intellect, social position—was coupled with a drawling fastidiousness of diction that set James's teeth on edge. James in short thought Colonel Hepple a vain, stupid fellow.

'Indeed,' said the colonel, 'and His Excellency wishes me to say that he greatly appreciates and values your sense of duty and loyalty—but in course he is aware that you must have other duties to attend to, at Port Royal.'

'May I ask: where is Admiral Pearson?'

'The admiral is with the Governor, at present.'

'Then—will not the admiral wish me to remain until he himself returns, sir? I came in his carriage, after all.'

'Ah, yes, hm.' A vexed frown, grimacing into a smile. 'Then by all means, Lieutenant Hayter. Wait, by all means. You may be kept waiting quite long . . . but if you don't mind that . . .' Turning towards the door.

'Colonel, may I be permitted to ask, sir: do not you think—does not His Excellency think—that two assaults in the King's House, so close on each other, must be more than mere coincidence? Two assaults involving injury to Reverend Laycock?'

Pausing at the door. 'Do not concern yourself, Mr Hayter. It has all been most unfortunate, but everything is in hand, thank you. You will find something to read, no doubt, while you wait . . .'

As Colonel Hepple left the room, James glimpsed a figure in the hallway beyond, by a longcase clock, with the case open. The man's back was turned, and James had just time enough to see that the cut of his light grey coat was not English. As the door was closing behind the colonel, the man turned a little to let him pass, and part of the man's face was visible in the crepuscular light. It was a pale face, with grey hair tied back behind, not with a bow or ribbon, but a silver clasp, an oval-shaped silver clasp. The glimpse was fleeting, and then the door swung shut, but that clasp had alerted James, and made him curious. The coat was of a particular cut, narrow in the back, but the clasp was more than merely particular; so far as James was concerned, it might only be described as unique. In all his life he had seen only one man wear such a clasp . . . Henri Lascelles. He went quickly to the door, and opened it, and looked into the hallway, but the man had disappeared, and the clock case was shut. James frowned, shook his head, and returned to his chair. No, it could not be. The man he had seen was middle-aged, and greying; Henri Lascelles was James's age, or a year or two older, at most. In any case, the Lascelles he remembered from long years ago, in extreme youth at Cambridge, had worn not only a distinctive silver clasp, but a livid cicatrice that ran the length of his left cheek, a duelling scar. The figure he had seen in the hallway bore no such disfiguring mark, he was sure of it. No, it was absurd. The clock man was exactly what he seemed: a middle-aged mender of clocks.

And yet—that clasp . . .

James felt the beginnings of a headache, and rubbed his forehead. He took up the *St Jago Gazette* from the table by his chair, and to distract his thoughts began to read.

> *Runaway slave*, Socrates Mullen, aged 21 yrs. Missing from the Prospect estate, nr Spanish Town, a reward of £*25* is offered for his capture, in good condition. Attorney, Mr H. Kempson.

> *Missing cattle*—an horse & a cow, strayed from the Twin Palms estate, nr Kingston, a reward of £*20* for said cattle, in good condition. Attorney, Mr J. Filgate.

James sighed, threw the paper aside, and fell to puzzling. His thoughts clashed and spun in his head, and he felt an ominous wave of dizziness, a residue of his fever. He must endeavour to be quite collected, and calm.

Presently the Port Admiral came to the reading room, and James stood up, and felt a further wave of dizziness. The admiral was flushed, and there was the smell of brandy.

'Yes—yes yes, I have been enlightened as to the whole matter, the whole unhappy affair.' He did not look unhappy, but full of good humour, good spirits.

'I am glad, sir.'

'All a dreadful mistake, a dreadful mishap, in darkness. Dreadful, very dreadful.' He came to the table, and sat down opposite James, who resumed his seat. 'Yes—yes. I think one more glass before we depart, to refresh me.' He rang the bell on the table. A servant came, his page's coat unbuttoned, his feet bare.

'A glass of wine, sillery if you have it.'

'Yes, sir, make you ver' red in y'face ha ha. You want wine now, sir?'

'They mean no harm, they mean no harm,' said the admiral expansively, when the servant had gone. 'It is just their way here, you know. One gets used to it.'

'Indeed. I wonder, sir—did you happen to notice a man in the hallway, or on the stair, wearing——'

'I saw no one.' Bringing his watch from his pocket, squinting at it. 'Where is my wine, I wonder? I am parched. We have been here some little time, and I am parched.'

When his wine came, and he had become unparched, the admiral moved his head from side to side with comfortable gravity. 'He was unused to pistols, poor fellow. He had thought, in his commendable haste to discover the intruders, that he had not yet cocked the pistol. Then, when he was attacked in the darkness——'

'Forgive me—but surely he took a lantern, sir, or a candle-holder?'

'The candle was knocked from his hand—I said the same thing, exact—knocked from his hand, and then he was at once assaulted. He attempted to cock the pistol, but it was already cocked, d'y'see? And it was at that moment—dreadful bad luck—that Monsieur Lange entered the room. The pistol discharged—*bang*—he was struck full in the forehead, and killed outright.'

'So—he never saw Monsieur Lange at all?'

'Never saw him.'

'It could not have been Monsieur Lange that attacked him?'

'Eh?'

'Taking him for one of the intruders?'

'No no, good God—the suggestion is fantastic, Mr Hayter.' Sitting back in his chair and frowning at James. 'They was both of them bravely attempting to protect the Governor, in his private apartments.'

'Yes, sir, I suppose so.'

'It ain't a matter of supposition.' The admiral now appeared to have reached a condition beyond mere good humour, and unparchedness; he had become querulously assertive. 'Facts is facts. We are too long here, Mr Hayter, in any case, at a time of tragedy and grief. Let us leave His Excellency in peace.'

James contrived, before he and the admiral returned to Port Henderson—by saying that he must relieve himself, having sat so long—to have a further word of conversation with Colonel Hepple. He went upstairs to the private apartments, and by recollecting them from his previous visit, with Rennie, came to the Governor's quarters and found the colonel seated in an ante-room, his sword unbuckled and a cheroot fixed in his mouth.

'Ah, Colonel—may I ask——'

'What d'y'mean by coming to these quarters unannounced?' Startled, brusque, removing the cheroot. 'These quarters is strictly private, and after what has happened——'

'Yes, sir, please forgive my very precipitate intrusion, but I must ask something of you.'

'Why did not y'ask me downstairs?'

'Forgive me, I ought most certainly to've done so.'

'Well?' A sigh.

'The man that was at the longcase clock downstairs, sir, outside the reading room. Who is he?'

'He is the fellow'—raising his eyebrows as if addressing a stupid child—'that looks after the clocks.'

'How long has he done so, here at the King's House?'

Another sigh. 'Not long—why d'y'ask?'

'A few months, perhaps?'

'No no, not so long as that. A few weeks. He is Swiss, from Geneva. He has lately established a shop at Kingston, and undertakes repair upon all manner of clocks—bracket, lantern, longcase and the like, such as we have here—all manner of clocks, and watches, too. Since it is the only shop of its kind in Kingston, he has found ready employment. And now—is *that* all?'

'May I know his name, sir?' Wiping sweat from his brow with his kerchief.

'It is Darder. Monsieur Gabriel Darder.' With thinning patience.

'I wonder, have you noticed a very distinctive silver clasp that he uses to tie back his hair?'

'Have I noticed a *clasp*?' Incredulous.

'You have not. And may I ask who employed him, here?'

'Why *do* you ask these questions? Good heaven.'

'It is merely a suspicion, sir. I have a—a question in my mind——'

'Another question?' Heavily.

'That this man might be the man mentioned in the documents Captain Rennie brought to the Governor. That he might be Henri Lascelles.' And he explained the circumstances of the duel in which his friend had been killed. Colonel Hepple listened, but he was less and less inclined to hear. And now he interrupted:

'What age is Henri Lascelles? Much your own age, Lieutenant, is he not?'

'Yes, sir.'

'Yes, well, Monsieur Darder is a man above fifty. You spoke of a duelling scar. I may tell you, Monsieur Darder bears no such scar. He is a most peaceable, quiet, industrious man—that mends clocks. He has come with the highest references from the courts of Europe, that I have looked over myself——'

'Are you perfectly certain his documents are genuine, sir?' Sweat trickled into his eye.

'Do you dare to question my judgement, sir! Do you dare to continue in this lunatic inquiry, when I have been more than patient with you! Damn your impertinence!'

'Sir, Colonel Hepple, it is because of what has happened that I ask these questions. The assaults in the night, and a man shot——'

'You persist, sir, in your interference, and impertinence?' Colonel Hepple had risen from his chair. 'You, a junior sea officer, out of your element ashore? You had better go away. You had better go away, before I lose my temper altogether!'

James saw that he could put no further questions to Colonel Hepple. It was possible, beside, more than possible, that the colonel was right, and that he was wrong. He bowed politely.

'I beg your pardon, sir. I shall not trouble you further.'

'Thank God!' Fixing the cheroot in his mouth with a glare, and turning his back.

To the admiral, a few moments later, as Mellow whipped up the horses and they turned out of the square, James said:

'Sir, I have a question remaining in my mind about that man in the hallway——'

'What? Who?' The admiral blew out his cheeks in the heat, and sat back, his hat shading his face.

'The clock man, sir. Will it be possible for us to go to Kingston, instead of to Port Henderson direct?'

But the admiral was already falling into a doze, and only grunted, his head lolling against the back of the seat, tipping his hat further so that it jiggled with the motion of the carriage.

'Mellow?'

'Yes, sir?' Turning, reins in hand.

'We will take the road to Kingston, if you please.'

'Kingston, sir?' Puzzled.

'Aye, Kingston.' Firmly. 'There is something I must learn there, without delay.'

At Kingston James alighted from the carriage, and sent it on by the circuitous route to Port Henderson, with the admiral nodding oblivious in his seat.

'How will you go on to Port Royal, sir?' Mellow had asked.

'I shall take a wherry from Kingston across the harbour. If the admiral should wake on the way back to Port Henderson, say nothing of where I have gone, say nothing of Kingston.' He gave him a coin. 'Say that I wished to stretch my legs in an out-of-the-way place, and thus got down.'

James made inquiries, and was directed to Shaddock Street, in a shabby part of the town, where he presently found M. Darder's shop. It stood opposite the Kingston Playhouse, an old, once imposing theatre, with posters. The shop was quite humble: a narrow frontage, timber-built, a low door and a painted sign:

CLOCKS, WATCHES & INSTRUMENTS
REPAIRED & REFURBISHED
TO THE HIGHEST STANDARDS OF
EXCELLENCE
Proprietor G. DARDER—late of GENÈVE

James went in at the low door, and a bell on a spring jangled above his head. M. Darder was not inside, but there was another gentleman there, waiting for him. He was dressed elaborately, even flamboyantly, in a patterned blue suit, a waistcoat of glittering red and gold, and a black tricorne hat with a great feathery cockade. The buckles of his shoes glistened. The shop was stifling hot, the ceiling low, but the dressy gentleman appeared to be entirely at his ease. From the rear came the insistent fidgeting metallic clamour of timepieces ticking in the fusty quiet.

'He is not here at present.' The gentleman, after a moment.

'Ah. No. Have you any notion as to when——'

'Soon, sir, I understand, very soon.' His voice had a peculiar vibrating resonance in the confined space. 'You are a lieutenant in the Royal Navy, I perceive.' Eyeing the lace on James's sleeve.

'I am, sir.'

'May I know your name?'

James told him, and bowed, and the gentleman introduced himself:

'I am John Vanbrugh Dunkling, manager and proprietor of the Royal Theatre Company of Drury Lane, presently touring in Jamaica. My friends call me Van.'

'Drury Lane—in London?' Surprised.

'Well, I do not say that, I do not specify that, exact.' A little shake of the head, and eyes briefly shut. 'I do not say London, outright. It might be, or it might not, you mind me? It is a distinction unnecessary to make in such tormenting heat, and at such distance, hmm?'

James smiled, and gave a little jerk of his head in acknowledgement. 'Yes, I see.'

'You see before you Vanbrugh Dunkling, and you see also Mr Jerome Garritt, playwright, and author of *The Nobleman's Daughter*.' Sweeping off his hat with a flourish. 'Again, you see Mr Kipton Cimmer, author of *The Officer's Revenge*.' He replaced the hat, and stood back a step with his head cocked on one side, his hand at his chin, and contemplated James.

He asked James: 'Was you ever a player in the theatre, sir?'

'Was I?' Laughing. 'Good heaven, no!'

'Ahh, do not laugh, sir. Do not dismiss the question with

such wanton self-deprecation. You are a fine figure of a man. You have an excellent, carrying voice. I'll warrant you are quick on your feet, with a sword in your hand, and have the agility necessary to avoid falling over the clats.'

'Clats?'

'Furniture, sir, upon the stage. Tables, chairs—the low stool. The low stool is always an high hurdle for the ac-tor, in avoidance.' He brought his hand from his chin to his hip, and peered at James from another pose. 'If ever you contemplate giving up the sea as your profession and calling, come and see me, sir, come and see me, and we shall strike a bargain. Can you master sides?'

'Eh?'

'Sides, sir. Pages of lines.'

'Really, you know, I think it most unlikely that I shall ever——'

The bell jangled behind them, the door opened, and M. Darder came into the shop. At once Mr Dunkling began addressing him in French, taking him by the elbow and complaining that Darder had not yet repaired and returned his pocket watch, that he had left a week ago, &c., &c. James stood back from this, and was able to observe M. Darder in full face. He was indeed a man in later middle life, above fifty, as Colonel Hepple had said. His hair was grey, and his pale face lined about the eyes and mouth. He looked a little like the Henri Lascelles James remembered—the aquiline nose might be the same—but the face was altogether older and thinner, and there was very definitely no cicatrice upon his left cheek, no sign there at all of a duelling scar. He wore the same coat he had been wearing at the King's House, and carried a black bag, very like a physician's bag. He put down the bag on the long table which served as a counter at the rear of the shop, and glanced through the doorway behind, into the rear of the premises. As he did so James was able to observe the hair tied at the back of his head, and the silver clasp. Except for that clasp, James could find nothing in M.

Darder's appearance that would justify his suspicions. This man was not Lascelles that had so callously shot down his friend, could not be Lascelles. The clasp was neither here nor there, James told himself. It was merely a silver clasp, and nothing more.

Apparently reassured that all was well to the rear, M. Darder turned once more to Dunkling, and answered him in French. Dunkling again began to protest, and M. Darder excused himself with a cold smile, and came away from the table to where James stood waiting. With no hint of recognition in his eye or manner he said to James, in accentless English:

'Forgive me, Lieutenant, for keeping you waiting. How may I be of service?'

'Ah, yes.' James fumbled his watch from his pocket, nearly dropped it, and: 'I—I think that my watch may need adjustment. It has not been keeping good time in the heat and damp air . . .' He held out the watch—that had served him well, without losing time, all this commission—and felt a twinge of disloyalty to that maker of fine instruments, Plenitude Tyndale of London, and to his mother Lady Hayter, who had so fondly and generously bespoke it.

'By all means.' M. Darder took the watch. 'It may take a day or two, if you do not mind leaving it that long.'

'A day or two, you say, Monsieur?' interrupted Dunkling crossly, in French. 'I have been deprived of my own watch above a week.'

'Your watch, Monsieur, is not—how shall we say?—of the very highest quality.' Smoothly. 'You will not be offended, I am sure, when I tell you that I cannot make accurate an instrument that is little more than a box of springs——'

'Can you mend the bloody thing?' Forcefully, in English. 'Or is that damned sign outside just tinker's puff?'

M. Darder put down James's watch on the table, and was very still in his person. After a moment he turned, and with another cold smile: 'Alas.'

'What d'y'mean, *alas*? What does that mean, *alas*? Ye've

had the damned thing a week, and now you say *alas*! What does it mean, *alas*?'

'It means,' icily polite, in the stuffy little shop, 'that you must be careful, Monsieur.'

'Careful! Christ's tears, I am Vanbrugh Dunkling, the most celebrated theatrical ever to grace these island shores, and y'tell me to be careful? I have lived all my life for my art, I have risked everything, always, to bring my art before the public. Careful don't describe me, sir. Careful ain't an adjective I care to acknowledge. Give me back my watch, if you cannot mend it, you pallid shiftless mechanical! Hand the bloody thing over!—Unless you have sold it, *alas*!'

During this short histrionic tirade he had again swept off his hat, and waved it about him, his voice booming and distinctive in the confined space, and James was aware that he was witness to a performance. A performance that both amused and appalled him by its violent bombastic bluntness. For a moment M. Darder looked as if he might erupt into violence himself. He quivered rigidly, his cheek twitching, then checked himself, drew a calming breath—and became affable, and smiling.

'Naturally, Monsieur, I have retained the watch. I shall bring it to you at once. I regret that it is in pieces, but all of them are there.'

'In *pieces*? How may I know the time when my watch is in *pieces*, you villain!' Theatrically.

M. Darder did not reply, but repaired to the rear. He soon emerged, without his coat now, and wearing a long apron. In his eye was fixed a jeweller's glass, which he removed. On the table he placed a square of velvet, on which there rested the several pieces of Mr Dunkling's watch—the case, the face, the hands, the internal springs, &c.

'It is all there, Monsieur, down to the last diminutive screw. But as I have said—alas.'

And he smiled with such open, utter, and terrible ferocity, looking up into Mr Dunkling's face, that the theatrical snatched up the velvet, bundled it into the pocket of his coat, and withdrew with a jangling of the bell into the street.

When James himself emerged from the shop a few moments after, Mr Dunkling was standing on the steps of the Kingston Playhouse opposite; he beckoned. James crossed the street. Posters on both sides of the entrance proclaimed:

The Royal Theatre Company
of Drury Lane

presents

THE NOBLEMAN'S DAUGHTER

by the greatly celebrated
PLAYWRIGHT

JEROME GARRITT

'A most uncomfortable fellow, that fellow,' said Mr Dunkling, and James now saw—in open daylight—that he wore powder on his face. Sweat had begun to start through that powder. 'He has destroyed my timepiece, and I should have everything on my side was I to have him arrested. However, however, I have other things that occupy me. My art. My company of players. My public.'

'I wish you good fortune,' said James. 'And now, I must——'

'Have you seen the theatre?' A wide-held hand indicating the entrance. 'Have you been inside?'

'I have not. Perhaps on another occ——'

'Spare a moment, will you? To have a look? It is well worth it, sir. The cathedral of the performing arts. Let us go in, and breathe its incense.' And he took James by the arm.

James allowed himself to be brought inside the building—because he rather liked Mr Dunkling, absurd as he was, and declamatory, and flashy. There was something endearing about him, he thought, in this very absurdity. Inside the theatre was very shabby. The seats were in a poor, tattery, threadbare condition; the red curtains at the sides of the broad stage were tattery and threadbare; the floor was unswept, the stage was unswept, the air was stale.

'Drink it in, sir. Breathe it in.' Sniffing deep. A pause. Then, in a hushed, thrilling tone, gradually rising:

'Here the playwright's words are made real, made flesh and blood, bringing forth tears, suffering, sorrow—and the glorious redemption of the power of love. Here—here is all life extant. Drink it in!'

'Yes, very—very well put,' nodded James, his arm still gripped.

'And now, sir, now I should like to put to *you*—a little proposition.'

'Proposition?'

'An half-share. No! Do not answer at once.' Freeing James's arm, and marching away down the aisle towards the stage. He gripped the boards at the edge, and sprang up. Turned, and struck a pose, one foot forward. 'Allow yourself a moment's reflection. Think on it. Think. An half-share—in all this gloreh!' A hand aloft.

James nearly laughed, and had to bite his lip to prevent it. Recovering, he drew breath and:

'I fear that I am not in a position to be able to——'

'An hundred pound!'

'Alas—no, that is not the word. Unhappily. Unhappily, I cannot assist you, Mr Dunkling.'

'Van, Van, please—to my friends.'

'Quite so. Van. Unhappily, I am not in sufficient funds to——'

'Fifty, then! Fifty guineas! That is more than generous, you must allow! A mere fifty guineas for an whole half-share in a great theatrical enterprise!' Hands clasped, hands held up before him.

'Not even fifty, you know, Van.' Shaking his head.

'Then—then—what *could* you manage to raise?' Eyebrows lifted, in a flaking of powder.

'Raise? Well, look here, you know—I do not think it my responsibility to raise anything.'

'Nothing! Then what have we been discussing, sir? What is the meaning of this conversation? *Hmm!*'

'Van. Mr Dunkling. I must disabuse you of the notion that I am in any way obligated to you. I am not. Good day to you.' And he turned on his heel, having had quite enough of absurdity for one afternoon.

'Mountebank!' shouted Mr Dunkling, and flung his hat to the boards. 'Turncoat! Traitor! Mump, scoundrel, poltroon! *Wretch!*'

On his return to Port Royal in the wherry, immediately upon leaving the turbulent Mr Dunkling, James decided that he must again call upon the Port Admiral, in an effort to get the admiral to change his mind in the matter of a boat. His place was in his ship, James knew, and he must have a boat to rejoin her, a boat in which he could step masts, and make sail.

The admiral, his housekeeper informed James, when he called at the residence, the admiral was resting.

Might he see the admiral?

'He cannot be disturbed.' Her face, under her neat cap, set in a shutting-out expression.

'Could not you tell him that I am here? It is a matter of some importance——'

'He is asleep. He is—he is unwell.'

'Unwell? Is it fever?'

'No, sir. There was an upset in the admiral's boat, returning from Port Henderson. He fell, and struck his head on the thwart. I am afraid—that he was flown with wine, and he fell.'

And James came away, fretful. Fretfully he returned to his inn. What the devil was he to do? Briefly he considered the admiral's earlier suggestion: that he should hire a private vessel, and a few men. But Rennie would never countenance the extra expense, nor would Mr Trent; it would have to come from his own pocket. No, he would wheedle a boat out of the dockyard officers, somehow.

'I must make it a matter of urgency, that I rejoin my ship. They cannot deny me, when it is an urgent matter.' To his reflection in the looking glass. He nodded decisively, turned away from the mirror—and was assailed by a further and more debilitating surge of dizziness, and lurched against the bed. He sat down, and felt his head.

'I must be careful. I must keep my health, that I have only just regained, else fail in my duty.'

He splashed water in his face, and in spite of his best intention, and his determination not to think any more on M. Darder, and Henri Lascelles, Comte d'Argenton—he could not help himself, and did begin again to think of them, and to wonder anew if they might not be one and the same. Leaving aside the absent scar, leaving aside the grey hair and lined face, and allowing the single fact of the clasp . . . M. Darder had arrived in Jamaica only a few weeks since, as Lascelles would have done, according to Jepp's intercepted letters. Darder had certainly been granted access to the King's House as a clock repairer, and might very probably be assumed to know the whole geography of the building as a result. Supposing Darder *was* Lascelles—discarding all evidence against it—supposing he *was*, might not he have been the intruder that struck Reverend Laycock, causing Laycock to fire into the darkness?

But would Henri Lascelles, a gambler, a duellist, a reckless adventurer, really be able to pass himself off as an elderly mender of timepieces, with all the attendant mechanical skill? Aloud, lifting his head from his hand: 'It ain't likely, good heaven.' He sat silent a moment, then: 'But he did give that ferocious smile that terrified Dunkling.' Had he seen that smile before, in dawn light on the field at Cambridge, as Lascelles raised his pistol and fired before poor Jack Torrance was ready? No, thought James, Lascelles had been facing away as he fired, had he not? Well, he had. Had he worn the silver clasp that morning? 'Oh, it is no bloody good, all this!' James thrust all memory of the scene from him, took a breath, a reviving breath, and rose cautiously from the bed. Tipped more water from ewer into basin, and again sluiced his face. Lifted his face, dripping—and paused with the cloth at his cheek, seeing his reflection in the glass. He touched his cheek, and an image came to him of Mr Dunkling as he turned this way and that, lifted his hands in flourishing gestures, and declaimed, and the face powder—the thick layer of disguising powder—flaked from his sweating skin.

'Powder . . .' James stared at himself, and wiped his face vigorously with the cloth. 'Powder and paint, like a theatrical. That is why Darder looks so damned pale. His face is powdered, hiding the scar, and he has painted on the lines of age, and made his hair grey by artifice. His whole appearance is a clever disguise—except he failed to remove that silver clasp! Failed to out of vanity, the blackguard wretch, and now we will come to a reckoning, by God!

He threw down the cloth and it caught the edge of the basin, tipping it and sending a fan of water splashing over the dry floor.

James returned to the admiral's house, determined this time to see him. He must be woken up, given coffee to drink, and told all. But when James knocked at the door he found everything changed. The admiral had woken from his slumber very ill. His physician, Dr Latimer, having been called to the house, had been made anxious by the admiral's colour, his slurred and rambling speech, his palsied hands. The admiral did not know anyone that spoke to him.

'Who are you, madam?' he had asked his housekeeper, Mrs Swale. Mrs Swale had been his housekeeper at Port Royal all the time since he was made a widower five years ago.

'Why, sir, I am Mrs Swale. Surely you know me?'

'Mrs Who-are-ye? Mrs Trinder, is it?'—the keeper of the most notorious bawdy-house in Kingston.

'Ohh! Ohh!'

Dr Latimer gave James all this intelligence, and: 'He can see no one. I have sent word for Dr Stroud, at Spanish Town. I fear his diagnosis will be the same as my own: delirium, induced by concussion of the brain, assisted and compounded by alcohol. I fear it will, aye. However, a second opinion is always advisable, always expeditious—in such circumstances.'

James did not like the sound of that word. 'Circumstances?' Looking at him.

'Aye, aye.' A pause. 'It is very possible he will not recover.'

'Not recover? Good God. I had no idea he was so very ill.'

'He had evidently drunk a great quantity of wine before he fell. That is very bad. I have seen it so often in seafaring men.' Sucking in a breath. 'Aye, very often.'

James returned bemused to his inn. What was he to do, now? Well, he must go to Spanish Town, after all—return and insist upon seeing the Governor himself. Pacing up and down his room:

'But I would have to persuade Colonel Hepple to let me in. Hepple will never believe a word I say to him. And even if he did let me in, very likely the Governor would not wish . . .' Roaring dizziness overtook him, and he fell back on his bed. 'I cannot rush about, everywhere, I must be quiet, and calm. Yes, I must endeavour to think it all out . . .' He lay back, and settled his head on the pillow.

When he woke it was to the sound of the church clock, echoing over Church Street and York Street, and through the window of the inn, as it struck eleven.

'I must go to Kingston.' James sat up in his bed. 'I must go to Darder's shop, and make a search under cover of darkness. I must find something that will damn and condemn him.'

The dizziness and the haziness of thought which had sometimes afflicted him ever since his bout of fever were entirely gone. His head was clear, and he felt strong. He rose, sluiced his head and neck at the basin, and dressed by the light of the moon, which bathed the crumpled bed-covers, the chair, the uneven floorboards, his face in the glass, and gave them ghostly shadows. He dressed in his dark working clothes, clothes Rennie was pleased to call 'those damned piratical slops', and tied a kerchief round his head. He armed himself not with his sword, but with his first acquired blade, his middy's dirk—and with one of a pair of matched pocket pistols presented to him by his father as a wedding gift (to Catherine Sir Charles had given a fine inlaid dressing case; when Catherine had wondered later why he had not made them a gift they might share, James had said: 'My father is a practical man, that thinks men and women are quite separate creatures in their interests and activity, which is the natural order of things.'). He smiled at this now. Would he say something like to his own son, one day? Smiled—and recalled himself to the task in hand.

He went quietly downstairs, let himself out into York Street as the church bell clanged the quarter-hour one street away, and made his way towards the Dockyard. He did not go there; there were always marine sentries on duty. Instead he cut away through an alley to his left, through the silent market—the moonlight pooled over the cobbles—and down to the waterfront between the wherry wharf and Clarke's, where many private boats lay tethered overnight. He was looking for a small boat, something light and easily managed by one man. Wherries, hoys, barges—all the private boats daily employed in conducting the business of the harbour—lay at their moorings. He found a canoe, hollowed out of a single cotton tree log, with a crude paddle lying in the bow, and decided that this would not answer. He must row near two mile across the harbour, and back, before daylight. He found another boat, very small, with a single pair of oars—a jollyboat in miniature. This he could manage. He glanced about him, and murmured: 'Well, old fellow, whoever you are—I am going to borrow your boat. It ain't stealing, because I mean to return it before it is missed.' He stepped into the boat, slipped the knot of the painter, sat on the thwart and shipped his oars. Water rippled in the hot, quiet dark as he pulled away from the shore, through the moored vessels and into the wide harbour beyond the anchorage. The moon stared in the sky. James put his back into his work, pulling in a steady rhythm, and soon he was sweating freely.

An hour later he was in Shaddock Street. The street was flooded with moonlight, and he kept himself concealed in the shadows which fell from the theatre opposite across M. Darder's shopfront.

'I cannot go in at the front.' In his head. He glanced along the street—north, and south—and saw no one, heard nothing. He stayed very still a moment longer, then darted down the alley that ran to the west by the side of the shop, and looked for a side door. There was no door there. He ventured further, in the deep moonless gloom of the alley, and hoped for a gate, or a window. He found neither.

'I must go in at the front, after all.'

He crept back, along the narrow frontage of the shop—and probed the lock with the tip of his dirk. It was fast. He drove the knife deep between the door and the jamb, wedging it in, then gave a powerful jerk. There was a rasping crack, and the door swung open. Jesu Christ, that sound! Surely it must have been heard by someone? He waited, very still in the doorway, crouched down.

Waited a full minute.

And slipped inside, shutting the door carefully and quietly behind him. He put up his dirk.

Listened again a moment, determined that the only sounds were those of clocks and watches in a clamour of subdued ticking in the rear, and moved towards the table by the inner door. Moonlight from the window gave him illumination enough, but here in the front part of the shop there was little to engage his interest. Darder kept nothing here but two chairs for his customers, and the table, and one tall clock. James knew he must go into the rear of the premises to conduct his search, and there he would require artificial light.

He had brought a candle with him and his pocket tinderbox, but dare he strike a light?

Supposing there was some person sleeping in there? An assistant that Darder allowed to live there in return for watching over the place at night? Or perhaps there was a dog kept there, to spring at his throat as soon as he advanced. He crept past the table, paused, pushed open the inner door—and slipped quickly through to the rear. He stood very still, in the multiple fidgeting of springs, spindles, and escapements, could detect nothing else, and let out the breath he had kept trapped in his lungs near sixty seconds. Let it out whhhh—and felt for his tinderbox and candle. And found that he was sweating so heavy, dripping from every pore, his fingers slippery and clumsy, that he nearly dropped everything on the floor.

'Christ Jesu, you fool!' A furious whisper.

And struck his light.

In the trembling glow of the candle, soon made steady when he placed it upon a tall stool by the desk that stood against the far wall, he began to rifle through the drawers of the desk, then through the drawers and shelves of the cabinets that stood on either side. He found nothing but a few papers: neatly written statements of repairs carried out, of others presently to be carried out, and statements of account—all in French. A bundle of quills, a seal and a stick of wax. Ink. He moved to the bench standing away to the left. Upon the bench stood a dozen clocks. To one side were three or four tall clocks, in various stages of undress. Arranged in two wide, neat drawers below was a mass of instruments, of diverse sizes and purposes: pliers, sprung tweezers, little hammers and chisels, tiny wooden mallets, screw pins, &c.—all of the greatest delicacy of manufacture. There were also two jeweller's eyepieces, with magnifying lenses. James brought the candle from the stool, placed it on the bench, and opened the third and lowest drawer. The drawer was lined with velvet.

In it were a pistol case, with two superbly made duelling pistols, the locks signed:

McArdle—Dublin 1781

and another case, a large wooden box. James opened it, and found several soft wax moulds, and a ring of large, newly made keys. Beside the large keys was a set of several dozen skeleton keys, on a brass loop. Also a roll of drawings, bound with tape. James slipped off the tape, unrolled the drawings, and saw that they were the floor plans of a large house. And now he noticed, fixed to the inner page of the plans, a label written in black ink:

La Maison du Roi

James reached for the skeleton keys, lifted them wonderingly to the candlelight—and was struck a tremendous blow to the back of his head. The candle flew out of his hand, the flame streaking and tumbling, and he pitched into blackness.

He woke to the sound of running water, and the strong, sweet, aromatic smell of flowers. He was near water—opening his eyes. By God, he was lying in it, his whole body lapped and sluiced by a wide running stream, and under him the water-worn stones of a river-bed. Somewhere near, behind, a dull roaring sound, the sound of water tumbling over rocks. He tried to sit up, and was appalled by the wrenching pain in his shoulders and back, as if he were pinned by staves to the hard stones under him. He struggled, turned the other way, spluttered as his face was momentarily submerged, and at last succeeded in raising himself to a half-sitting-up position. He stared about him. He was in a deep gorge, the rockfaces rising sheer from the rushing river, and just upstream of him the falls—a line of low ledges with a glassy rim that became boiling white as the river plunged over into a deep dark pool, from which it swirled spreading forth into the wider stretch where he lay now. On the jutting overhang of the bank on the far side, and upon two or three little islands of rock, in mid-stream, massed dense foliage and bright wild flowers—red, blue, yellow—the foliage thick waxy green. Insects danced in frantic knots above the water, in beams of sunlight. The air was temperate and pleasant here in this watery, deep-hidden place.

James realised with astonishment that he was entirely naked. His right arm was covered in bloody abrasions and bruises, as was his right leg. Feeling his face he found it torn and tender to the touch. He had fallen heavily. He was very sore, his head ached abominably, and he was dizzy—turning his head made his vision blur.

'Again,' he said aloud. 'I was dizzy at some recent time, and now I am dizzy again.'

He crawled painfully to the near bank, where there was a stretch of sand, mounded under the cliff. He could not stand —yet. He would make the attempt again in a minute or two. For the present—for the present he would rest. He lay still on the sand, getting his breath, and heard a movement behind him. A stone fell. James turned painfully, his neck strained, and saw on a ledge of rock above him the figure of a man. A black man, in breeches and shirt, shoeless, with matted hair and beard, looking down at him with a watchful eye.

'Y'must be bad hurt, I reckon.' The voice not unfriendly, but not particularly amiable neither, James thought.

'I—I do not quite know. I am a little injured, I think.'

'A little, yes. Cut up all over you. Y'bruised all over. D'y'know what happened to you?'

'I cannot tell, exact.' Dizzy, attempting to focus his gaze on the man standing above him in a shaft of sun.

'This heer is a ver' remote place. How d'y'suppose y'came to be heer?'

'I—I cannot tell, in truth.'

'Wheer's y'clothes?'

'Again—I cannot tell. I know nothing of how I came here, nor how I came to be naked.'

'Will I tell you how?'

'I wish you would. And I wish you would help me to stand.'

'I will tell you, then. Two men brought you to the top of the hill,' pointing up, 'wheer I came upon them. One of them had a knife, and they was goin' to cut your t'roat, and throw you down into the river. I rushed at them, and fired two shots, and yelled ver' fierce, like I had ten men wit' me. And they let you go, dropped you, and ran away. Y'fell like a stone, straight down. No, that ain't wholly acc'rate. Y'bounced heer-'n'-theer, goin' down. And fell in the deep pool. You was lucky.'

He leaned down now, holding out a hand, and James held up his left hand and grasped it. With surprising strength and ease the black man pulled him up on the ledge, where he sat until the dizziness the movement had caused had passed.

'Yes, whichever fellows brought you heer was surely intent on killing you, and t'rowing your corpse down to smash on the rocks. They believed y'would never be found.'

'You know these men? You know their motive?' Touching his head gingerly.

'No no. I have seen them carry you to the edge, yes. *Why* they did it, the dear alone knows—or y'self.'

James stared up the rockface, fighting his dizziness. The cliff stretched tall above, and he saw plants, vertiginously and improbably clinging here and there, their foliage dangling. James made a great effort, and stood up. He was obliged to lean on his companion's shoulder to steady himself, but he stayed on his feet. A moment after he was able to stand unsupported.

'May I know your name?'

'I am Archimedes.' A steady stare, the same neutral tone and expression.

'I am honoured to make your acquaintance. I am James Hayter.' He made an awkward bow, and extended his hand. The other man did not respond, but stood looking at him. 'I will like to shake your hand, Mr Archimedes, and thank you.'

Archimedes continued to stare at him, then burst into sudden hearty laughter.

'Why do you laugh?'

'Two gentlemen—ha-ha-ha!—in the wild rio gorge, bowin' and shakin' hands as if they was about to go into dinner with the Governor himself, at Spanish Town—ah-ha-ha-ha!' Taking James's hand now, and shaking it delightedly. 'I am honoured t'make *your* acquaintance!'

'Yes, thank you. Tell me—what did they look like, those fellows that brought me here?'

'I don't know them at all. Never saw them before, at all. This is wild country, y'know. Remote country. Not many people come heer—that don't have to come.'

'You are here, Mr Archimedes . . .'

'I have to be heer, I must be, unless I wish to be hanged.'

'Ah. Yes. You are an escaped slave?'

'No. No. I am a man living in *freedom*.' He said it fiercely, and lifted his shirt, revealing a brace of pistols tucked into the waist of his breeches. He glared at James, and let the shirt fall.

'Please forgive my asking, it is really none of my business.'

'No, it ain't your business. I could abandon y'heer, y'understand me now?' Again fiercely.

'I am very sorry if I have offended you.' Another awkward bow, fearful that in his present weak condition he could be felled by the lightest of blows. Or shot dead, indeed. Archimedes looked at James a long moment, scratched his beard, then suddenly smiled, and again laughed.

'No no, it's all right, I will not abandon you. We got to find you some t'ing to wear, over your naked self.'

'Yes, indeed. I cannot return in this condition.'

'Return? Return wheer? You cannot return anywheer, just now.'

'But I must return to the port, you know, to my ship. I am beginning to recall, now.' Rubbing his forehead. 'I came up into the mountains, with a friend of mine, Hansard Cobbett. We stayed at an inn, Mrs Leslie's, near the Ridge.'

'The Ridge? That is over twenty mile away, to the east.'

'What is this place? Where are we?'

'Satan's Peak, this heer. It is the wilds, this country. Deep rio country, wild mountains.'

James had no recollection beyond staying at Mrs Leslie's inn, with his friend. They had hired mounts at Kingston, and ridden into the mountains up a steep, winding road. The Blue Mountains.

'Well, I will say it again—this ain't the Blue Mountains. The men that brought you here must've had some damn' pro-found reason to do it, dragging you all this way. They must've carried you on horseback—nor wagon nor carriage can penetrate this place.'

'I cannot understand it. My head aches dreadfully, as if . . .' He felt the back of his skull. There was a lump there, very tender. 'Yes, I have been struck a savage blow.'

Archimedes motioned him to turn round, and looked closely at James's scalp, parting the wet hair. He nodded, sucking his teeth.

'You was struck a blow. You have a strong skull, else it would've killed you. They carried you heer senseless, to kill you and drop you in the river. Not friendly, not friendly by any means.' A moment, then he took James's arm and turned him round.

'Maybe you had a fallin' out wit' y'friend, eh? Maybe he tried to kill you.'

'Han? Good heaven, no. We get along very comfortable, we are old friends. No no, something has happened to him, too. We must have been set upon by thieves, in the night, and—— Ohh, I wish to God I could remember!'

'Are you able to walk?' Peering at him closely. 'Are y'strong enough?'

'Aye, I am able.'

'Follow along, now.'

And Archimedes led the way along the ledge to where the river widened, farther downstream. Here a tributary flowed into the river, and along the bank of the smaller stream a rough track led away into the deep forest. At times James felt nauseous, at other times so weak he feared that he could not continue—but he did continue, barefoot and unaided, for the better part of an hour, as the track slowly rose above the stream, higher and higher, until the sound of the water was no more than a distant murmuring far below. They rounded a great outcropping of rock, and came to a cave. From the mouth of the cave a tremendous panorama of mountains and valleys folded away to the north and west, green upon green upon darker green, and purplish shadow. James stood in wonder, and his feelings of pain and exhaustion began to diminish.

In the cave, which was not very deep, but deep enough to provide adequate shelter from rain and storm, was a proper camp. There was bedding, a fireplace of circled stones, cooking pots, a pail of water; crudely made pieces of furniture, including a chair and a table. A lantern stood on the table, and leaning against the rear rock wall of the cave was a fowling piece, with a powder flask and shot.

James wandered about in the cave. 'You are well provided for, here. How long have you lived up here?'

Archimedes did not answer him, but began rummaging about in the shadows at the rear, and presently produced a pair of frayed yellow britches, and a much-patched shirt. He threw them to James.

'They ain't the flower of fashion, for a gentleman, but they will cover you.'

'I am greatly obliged to you, Mr Archimedes.' James pulled the clothes on, and now felt that he was on an equal footing with his companion—even if neither of them had shoes.

'There is no need for calling me mister, all the time.'

'I beg your pardon. What shall I call you, then?'

'Archimedes.'

'You have a first name?'

'Only Archimedes. That is how I am called, by friend or foe.'

'I hope I may be your friend, Archimedes. And please call me James, will you?'

'James, all right.' He rummaged again, and produced a bottle of rum, and a battered metal cup. He poured a generous measure, and handed the cup to James.

'Thank you, you are very kind. D'y'mind if I add water?'

'Water? To rum?'

'It is our naval drink. Grog, you know.' He scooped water from the bucket into the cup, and drank it off gratefully. Handed the cup back, and at once felt the rum begin its beneficial work inside him, and smiled.

'You are a naval fellow? You talked of a ship. Which ship?' Closely.

'His Majesty's *Expedient* frigate. I am the first lieutenant.'

'Do you return to England, in this ship?'

'Yes, indeed. We are here only upon surveying duty.'

'When d'y'return?'

'When we have completed our duty. Which is why—although you are very kind indeed—I really must begin to make my way back, you know. I must discover what has happened to Han. I must try to find the men who have done this to us both, and——'

'If I show you the way back—will you take me in your ship, to England?'

'In the ship? Well, I——'

'In England I would not have t'live like this. I could live the life of a respectable person, and walk about freely. I might have a house, books, gentleman's clothes, a horse. I would be *free*. Take me in your ship. You could do it. You are an officer.'

'It ain't quite so simple, I fear. You would have to be put on the ship's books, and accounted for.'

'You mean, chained up? Chained up like an Eboe, in the ship?' Staring at him, then looking away.

'No no, I do not mean that.' Then, after a moment: 'Archimedes, let us be frank, one with the other. What is your present condition? Are you an escaped slave?'

Turning again: 'That is my condition.'

'Very well. Then as I understand matters in the island, there would be the very greatest difficulty in getting——'

'Yes, it is difficult! But you could do it! You could hide me in your ship! I am sick to my soul of this damn' life. Look at it. Hidin'. Hidin' away. Plagued by the duppies of the forest. Shootin' wild t'ings to stay alive. Stealin' t'ings. Oh, Christ, you must help me!' A groan of anguish came from deep within him, and broke from his lips, and he stared out at the mountains folding away into the distance.

James was moved by the despair in his face and voice. Quietly: 'Very well then, I will do what I can for you. I cannot absolutely promise anything—but I am greatly in your debt, and I will do my best.'

The sun lay briefly red and gold in the west, and then the sunset was gone, and night fell at once. Archimedes lit a fire, and lit the lantern on the table. He had a small store of food in the cave, and he began to prepare a meal in the large cooking pot, which he hung over the fire. His anguish and despair had disappeared, and he seemed quite cheerful.

'Would have shot a wild hog, if I'd been aware you was comin' to dine tonight.'

They drank more rum, and ate the stew Archimedes had cooked, and for two men perched on the side of a mountain in the middle of the wilderness they were modestly content, and food in their bellies, and rum, and the comfort of the flickering flames, made them talkative. James began to learn something of his companion's history.

Archimedes had been born into slavery upon the estate of a Mr Dowell Kempson, in St Thomas in the Vale. His mother had died soon after, in the estate hospital; his father he had never known. Due to the concern and effort of a local clergyman, the Reverend Marshall, the slave children of the estate, and several of the other estates surrounding, had been given some religious teaching, and fundamental schooling. Archimedes was a clever child, and he took to reading 'as natural as a duck will go down to the pond'. The manager of the estate, Mr Brunson, and the overseer, Mr Hythe, were both reasonable men, neither of them given to treating their slaves harshly. The trustee lived at Kingston, and did not visit more than once a month. Mr Kempson lived in England, and never came to Jamaica at all. Archimedes was marked down for a position in the great house as a servant, or it might be that he could be trained in the cooper's shop. He would never be a field slave—or so he believed.

Then both the manager and the overseer had died within a month of each other, of the yellowjack. There had been a poor season, and the new cane plants had withered and died, and the estate lost money. A new bookkeeper had been appointed, and a new overseer. The bookkeeper was a drunkard, who beat his mulatto housekeeper. The overseer, left to his own devices in running things, had gathered round him a team of the most savage drivers in the island, and a regime of brutality and harsh punishment had been established.

'His name was Dwight. For the rest of my days I will never hear that name without hatred and dread in my heart.' Taking a suck of rum. 'He put me into the cane piece as a field slave, when I was twelve year old.'

'About the same age as a middy goes to sea.' James, nodding.

'Middy? Is he a slave?'

'Not quite. Nearly, but not quite.'

'Y'cannot know the misery of the field slave, James.' Looking at him almost pityingly in the firelight. 'Not'ing in your own life will show you that misery.'

'No.' Quietly. 'Go on . . .'

'Even when there is a good hospital on the estate, he will suffer disease all his life. Cocoa bay, fever, yaws, the chiga fly—makin' him limp, with the cane piled on his back, so the sores never heal. If he gets bit by the galliwasp, he will die. Or get ate by crocodiles in the morass, if he tries to run away. He must grow his own food, on his provision ground, or starve on the poor rations the bookkeeper will allow him. No matter how hard he will work—he will be beaten. If he complain to the magistrate, or the custos, his case will never likely be heard in the court. Why?' Another suck of rum. 'Because he got no rights. He ain't even a human bein'. So, I decided to escape, when I was big enough, and strong enough. Me and some others made a plan to flee, and join with the Maroons in the north. The Maroons is free men. Howsomever, when it came to the time, the other field men would not go with me. They lost heart. I went to the bookkeeper's house, creepin' in at night, and took that fowlin' piece you see theer. I took his pistols, and his gun, and some food in a bundle, and ran away into the hills. I never been back theer. I travelled to the Maroon country, but me and those people—well, we did not see things the same way, not at all. So I came heer, to this place, and from time to time I go down, and steal from estates, and that is how I survive. But I am not even a human bein', livin' like this. I can never know freedom, like this.' Tears formed in his eyes, glistening in the firelight, and he drank.

'Yes, I understand you perfectly,' James nodded. 'I see why——'

'No, you will never *understand* me.' With sudden harshness, glaring at James.

'Well, I am trying to, you know.' Gently.

'You will *never* understand what it is to be a slave!' Vehemently. 'You are a white man, and free to do as y'please! A slave is *nothing*! He is a beast of burden, bought and sold! Or he is *born* a slave, like Archimedes!' He wept, dashing at the tears with furious shame.

'I understand your distress——'

'It is not *distress*! It is not!' Standing, walking away angrily from the fire.

'I—I am very sorry. Let us talk of something else.'

'There is no use to talk! Words is no damn' use! Go to sleep!'

James saw that he could do nothing to placate, or assuage, or comfort—and presently he lay down near the dying fire, and fell into a fitful, troubled doze, his head spinning and aching with rum, and weariness, and deep uncomfortable puzzlement.

When James woke in the morning he was dry-mouthed, bleary-eyed, and in pain. He stumbled to the mouth of the cave, and stared out over the descending track, and the bright, sun-glowing day—insects buzzing, dazing warm—and found himself entirely alone. Archimedes had gone.

James remained all day at the cave, waiting in the hope that Archimedes would return, return and show him the way out of the forest and back to the coast. In bare feet, still weakened and in considerable discomfort from his injuries, he could not hope to succeed by attempting the journey alone. He would need a horse, accurate directions—even a map, if one could be obtained.

While he waited he made a thorough inspection of the cave. He found a store of root vegetables, a little dried meat, flour, and a small cask of rum. There was half a pail of water left. He examined the few oddments of clothing that made up Archimedes's wardrobe: a couple of patched shirts, a kind of jerkin, a battered tricorne hat. And then he made a surprising discovery—surprising at first, until he recalled Archimedes talking of his education at the Reverend Marshall's school: a little store of books. The books were in a shabby condition, with loose bindings and well-thumbed pages, but they were kept under a cloth covering in a dry corner. Locke's *Essay concerning Human Understanding*; Pope's *Dunciad*; Fielding's

Joseph Andrews—very battered; Milton; a Bible; the Book of Common Prayer. Clearly Archimedes had made an effort to keep up his reading, even while living the life of a hermit. James took up the Locke, sat in the cave mouth, and passed his time in philosophical reflection.

As afternoon deepened into evening, and the fast night fell—and Archimedes did not return—James lit the fire, and the lantern, made himself a rudimentary supper, and helped himself to rum. In the morning he would leave here. Bind up his feet with rags of cloth, make his way down the track to the stream, and thence to the river. He would follow the river as far down towards the coast as he was able. Likely he would come to an estate, or a village. He knew the points of the compass by the sun, and the stars at night. He would not become lost. He would go south, and south.

He had eaten his supper, and was swallowing the last mouthful of grog in his mug, when he heard the sharp clatter of a falling stone and turned to find Archimedes standing in the cave mouth.

'You are back! I am right glad! I had thought——'

'I have brought horses. They are down the hill.'

'Horses! That is well done, indeed!'

'Damn bloody handsome, I reckon.' A weary smile. 'I had to steal them, and it took me all day gettin' heer.'

'You stole them? From whom?' Dismay replacing relief.

'An estate. Don't be concerned, I was not ob-served, at all. I got away clear.'

'Yes—but two horses, in Jamaica. I know that horses are very costly here. People are forever complaining of the price of horseflesh.'

'Yes'—a flash of his earlier bitterness—'they cost as much as slaves, near 'nough.'

'No, I did not mean——'

'Listen, now. Y'cannot walk all the way, you are weak from y'hurt. So I found us horses, to take us down to the coast.'

'Surely the estate will send out men, searching?'

'They will not know wheer t'look. And in the mornin' we will be gone, anyway.' A dismissive shrug, then peering: 'Anyt'ing left in the pot?'

'Who is that, wishing to speak?' Rennie, on his quarterdeck, *Expedient* standing just off Negrile Harbour, by the north point. Mr Peak focused his glass and watched the cutter come about. The name on her transom was *Curlew* in smart gold lettering, and the lieutenant informed his captain.

'Ah, yes, that is the Governor's cutter, from Port Royal. Does she send a boat, or does she mean to come in under our lee?'

'The latter, sir, I believe.'

'Very good. Mr Abey!'

'Sir?' With the signal book.

'Acknowledge, and make: Come aboard.'

Ten minutes later the commanding officer of *Curlew*, Lieutenant Dower, was standing in *Expedient*'s great cabin, and delivering the despatch that had brought him to the far west of the island.

'Thank you, Mr Dower.' Taking the sealed packet. 'Let us sit down. Cutton! Will you take tea, Mr Dower, or a glass of something stronger?'

'Wine, if you please, sir.' They sat down.

'Wine it shall be. Cutton!' Breaking the seal of the packet, and opening the folds. He took out the despatch, glanced through it. Stared at nothing a moment. Read the letter again.

'Good God, well well,' half to himself. Looked up, took a breath, noticed Mr Dower waiting patiently, and: 'You made good time, Mr Dower?'

'Very good, I think, sir. *Curlew* is fleet of foot, under a large press.'

'Just so, just so. Thank you, I am very glad to have this—at last.'

'At last, sir?' Puzzled.

'No matter, no matter.—*Cutton, damn your blood!* Very glad, indeed. I have been long in the dark, so to say—or at any rate, in twilight.'

'Ah—very good, sir.'

'I am a little surprised that Mr Hayter is not with you—my first lieutenant, that we left behind recovering from fever.'

'I am to give you that intelligence, as well, sir.' Solemnly. 'Mr Hayter has——'

'Good God, do not tell me he has died!'

'No, sir, in least I do not think so. But he has disappeared.'

When Lieutenant Dower had departed into his cutter, and stood away to the south, and Rennie had sent Lieutenant Peak in the jollyboat to bring back the shore party he had earlier sent away, he entered in his journal that Lieutenant Hayter had vanished, and that he had received the despatch from Spanish Town. He reread the despatch:

> *To be given into the hand of Captain William Rennie RN aboard His Majesty's* Expedient *frigate, in Jamaican waters, westward.—Oct. 1788*
>
> My dear Sir,
>
> By the present opportunity of HM cutter *Curlew*, held at the disposal of His Excellency the Governor, at Port Royal, being available for the purpose, I beg to enclose the following intelligence, *in strictest confidence*, which His Excellency respectfully requests and requires may be always adhered to:
>
> All previous orders, instructions & directions given to you by the Lords Commissioners of the Admiralty, as to the present commission of HMS *Expedient*, yr

duties heretofore described, &c., are in all respects hereby rescinded & removed, and yr work in progress of surveying & charting of the Jamaica coast is to cease forthwith.

From the moment of yr receiving this letter, delivered into yr hand by Lieutenant F. Dower RN, you are to regard yourself & your ship under the direct instruction of His Excellency the Governor in *a matter of the most urgent grave & momentous significance*, concerning His Majesty's interests in the Caribbean. His Excellency is himself acting for & under the authority of HM Secret Service Fund, whose authority in these matters shall supersede all other.

It is His Excellency's wish that you, Captain Rennie, shall be informed as to certain background information, which may aid & assist you in yr understanding of these matters, to wit:

The Reverend Felix Laycock, chaplain to His Excellency, in association with the Rev. Jepp, & the Secret Service Fund, has gathered certain information at the Windward & Leeward Islands, which he brought to Jamaica; and at Jamaica, gathered further information that—together with the aforesaid—made the basis for a Plan of Defence of Jamaica which Rev. Laycock, acting in concert with others, has wrote out in detail; said Plan for use in the event of future conflict with enemies of His Majesty.

Clandestine representatives of Foreign Interests, inimical to His Majesty, are known to be in Jamaica, of whom you will be aware—M. Henri Lascelles, Count d'Argenton, is known to you by name. He & his associates have the intention to obtain the aforesaid Plan by deception, theft, or any violent and forceful means, & a number of attempts has already been made upon the life of Rev. Laycock.

The Plan is to be carried to England, by the Rev.

Laycock's hand, in your ship, as soon as may be possible upon receipt of this despatch.

Accordingly you are to proceed to Port Royal without the loss of a moment, where you will take into your ship Rev. Laycock, his dunnage & effects, and sail for England by the Windward Passage, that is the most direct, swift & expeditious route open to you.

I have the honour to remain, Sir, yr most humble & obedient servant,

D. Lemuel Fielding
Secretary to Sir Compton Merrick

'I suppose I must believe it,' sighed Rennie to himself. 'I have been expected and required to believe so many damned reckless lies and half-lies these many months, good God, that I can no longer quite believe anything that any bloody wretched man in authority may say. But I expect I must believe this—at long last. *Is that you, Cutton!*' Hearing a shuffle of movement in the quarter gallery.

'I am here, sir.' Cutton, emerging.

'Where the devil was you when I wanted you just now?'

'Caught short, sir. Got the runs, like——'

'You will run, by God, the rest of the bloody commission! Tea, man, tea. And wash your hands in vinegar before you put them anywhere near to my teapot, d'y'hear me?' Going to the companion ladder: 'Bring it on deck.' Stumping up the ladder: 'Mr Loftus! We will get under way in half a glass, if you please!'

He said nothing to young Peak, nothing to Mr Loftus, or anyone, about James Hayter's mysterious absence from Port Royal—but it lay heavy on his mind as they hoisted in the returned boats, came to the wind, and followed the now distant *Curlew* to the south. Rennie had questioned Lieutenant Dower closely as to James's disappearance, but had been able to learn only a little:

Lieutenant Hayter had gone with the Port Admiral to

Spanish Town, upon the admiral's learning of the sudden and violent death of Lady Merrick's French tutor, M. Lange, at the King's House. There was some confusion as to the time of their return to Port Royal, the admiral having suffered an injury in his launch. The admiral's housekeeper had apparently seen Lieutenant Hayter at the admiral's residence, but had not seen him thereafter. His things remained at the inn where he had been staying. A small boat had been found to be missing from the private wharf near the Dockyard—although no direct connection between its absence and Lieutenant Hayter's could be established. Beyond that, nothing was known.

'Nothing,' said Rennie aloud. 'It ain't like him, to leave no word.'

'Sir?' Mr Peak, attending, his hat off and on.

'Eh? No no, nothing.' His knees flexing as the ship pitched in the swell, nearing the point at South Negrile. He strode to the wheel as *Expedient* righted herself. 'How does she lie, Daley Wragg?' And allowed the wind to catch his troubled thoughts and whip them away high through the vangs and far astern over the line of the wake. Nothing known—and nothing to be done until they reached Port Royal.

James, dozing blearily in the great heat that enveloped them in the forest—they had come far down the mountain now, and far down river—felt himself begin to fall from his horse, and was unable to check himself in time. As a boy he had sometimes clutched at his pony's mane as he lost his seat, and even now he heard in his head Padding's shouted: 'Knees! For Christ's sake!' as he hit the stony ground with a great winding thud—then nothing.

Archimedes reined in, jumped from his horse and ran back to where James lay on the stones of the extended river-bed. They had reached a bend, and here the river widened in the yearly floods. It had begun to rain, and Archimedes was becoming anxious, now. At any time in this, the rainy season of October, the river might flood and drown them both. They must get up out of the river-bed and on to the higher ground of the track. James was unconscious. He crouched beside him, and presently splashed water into James's face, and saw his eyelids flicker as he came back into the world.

'Who is it? Who are you?'

'I am Archimedes. Don't you know me, James?'

'Why d'you call me James? Are not you a servant?' Attempting to sit up, glancing round, taking in the river, the steep slopes, the thick forest.

'You mean—am I your slave?'

'I should never allow that word to be used. My slave.'

'Would y'not? Ha ha. That is right handsome of you.'

But the ironical tone was lost on James, who clutched at his head, winced, and said—wonderingly said: 'I remember, now. I was at Kingston, at night, in the clock man's shop. I went there, and found—found evidence, by God. Evidence against him.'

'Against who?'

'Darder! The clock man! Listen to me, I must return to Spanish Town, at once.' Staring round again, and frowning. 'Where the devil is this place? How am I come here?'

'We came here on horses, these horses. From the cave above the river, back yonder. Don't you recall none of it?'

'I—I do not. My head hurts—oh Christ, how it hurts. I am very confused. Help me up, will you? I must get on my legs.' And very unsteadily, with Archimedes to aid him, he did rise on his legs, and stood swaying. 'Have I fallen? Was I thrown? What *is* this bloody place?' Growing fractious, clutching his head. 'Will you for the love of Christ tell me what has happened?'

'You was not t'rown from y'horse. You was t'rown in the river, way upstream, by two men that did not wish you well.

You was naked when I found you. I have clothed you, and brought you down.'

James stared at him, and something like recognition came into his eyes, something like recollection. A moment, then:

'Yes—yes, I mind it all, now. In least, nearly all.' A pause. 'The cave! And books, there. Your books, Archimedes.'

A smile, a pleased nod. 'You have remembered—good, good, you make me happy.'

'How far have we come down? I am in a very great hurry, you know. There is not a minute to lose. Will you help me to mount? I am a little sore, still. Thank you.'

And soon—James urging his horse, which was inclined to amble in the drizzling, pressing heat—they rode on down the river track, to the clacking rattle of hooves on stones and the echoing rush of water. Presently from the distance, reverberating down the rocky gorge, came the irregular booming broadside of thunder. The rain increased from a light pattering to a steady, drenching downpour, hissing all round the two horsemen, pouring down their necks and their faces, and blotting out everything but the stony track immediately ahead.

'We must get to a higher place!' Archimedes, turning to shout.

'Higher? I have no time! I must go on down!'

'Then you will drown! The river will flood, and you will drown!'

'Do not talk womanish, Archimedes! We are above the river on this track, and we must proceed!'

'You proceed, y'damnfool white man. I will go to higher ground.'

'Oh, very well! If you will not, then I must go on alone!'

He kicked his horse's flanks, vigorously kicked, the beast snorted and roused itself into a trot, and soon James passed out of Archimedes's sight into the curtains of rain. As he rode on, James heard another sound—under the rumble and boom of thunder—a deeper, more consistent booming sound, a roaring din. He heard it, sensed the horse under him become unwilling, then wildly fearful, and before he could grip with his knees, before he could control the horse's head, the animal reared and threw him, and galloped in whinnying panic away into the forest.

In another moment the flood was upon him, he felt himself lifted up, as if borne on a giant wing, lifted up and flung forward in the torrent, then buried in a brown blur as he was submerged. He took a noseful of water before he could shut off his breath, choked, and thrust himself upward, swimming and kicking, fighting the terror that flooded in his heart. Again he was flung forward, tossed and flung headlong, still submerged, his strength ebbing by the second. He must breathe, or be lost. He bounced heavily off a rock, thudded sickeningly off another, felt his belly scraping over a rill of stones—and abruptly his head was above the surface, he could suck in air, and all around him was the terrible noise of the river, the crashing, roaring, seething power of an immense mass of water.

'I shall die!' he cried aloud, but could not hear his own voice. 'I am a dead man! Oh, Cathy, I am drowning!' Expecting at once to be sucked down into the roiling maelstrom, his breath snatched from him and his body dashed to pieces against a jutting rock. Instead after a moment he found that he was still buoyant, still breathing, that it was possible after all that he might survive in the whirling flood—and he began to concentrate all his strength, all his determination, upon reaching up and grasping one of the tree branches that he could now see flashing and fleeing by above him. He must reach up, grasp a branch, and pull himself bodily clear.

He saw the branch, kicked up from the swirling water, with all his strength kicked up, grabbed and felt leaves and sticks in his fingers, slithering through them, tearing at his palms. Gripped for his life, found the body of the branch, the knobbled hardness of wood, and clung there. All his experience as a seaman now came back to him, from his first moments as a midshipman aloft in a storm in *Gargoyle*, all those moments of weathering and surviving, clinging to yards, clinging to ropes, clinging and clinging and telling himself that he would live—and now he hauled himself along the branch, hand over hand, sucking breath through his clenched teeth, hauled himself until he felt the murderous drag of the water lessen—and knew, at last knew, that he was safe.

When Rennie arrived at Port Royal, dropped anchor off the Dockyard, and went ashore, it was to discover that the Port Admiral had died. A burial service had been conducted two days ago, and at the admiral's request—expressed by him in writing in his last will and testament, dictated on his deathbed to his clerk—his corpse had been sewn up in a shroud, weighted with shot, and buried at sea; the ceremony had taken place aboard the ship sloop *Ventura*, standing off the admiral's favourite point to the south. There had been a salute of guns.

Preparations for the Reverend Laycock's departure had been a little delayed, Rennie was informed by a message from the King's House, brought in a boat from Port Henderson; he must await further instruction, and say nothing to anyone—other than that he had returned to Port Royal to take in stores.

There was still no word of his first lieutenant. The impression was—the general impression—that Lieutenant Hayter was very likely dead. The boat taken from Port Royal on the night of his disappearance had been found, but in all likelihood he had fallen overboard and drowned.

Rennie fretted, and worried, and was wholly dissatisfied with his position. He decided that he would go to Spanish Town himself, and was preparing to go in his launch when a second message arrived. Under no circumstances should

Captain Rennie come to Spanish Town. He must remain in his ship at Port Royal, allowing only those vessels necessary to revictual her to come alongside. There was to be no shore leave.

He obeyed. What else could he do? He obeyed, and found himself obliged—when the Dockyard Commissioner and the Master Shipwright paid *Expedient* a courtesy visit, to inquire as to whether he had everything that he needed—Rennie found himself obliged to explain the loss of his carronades.

'It don't matter to us, Captain Rennie,' said the Commissioner, glancing at the Master Shipwright. 'It ain't a matter for us, at Port Royal. You was preserving the safety of your ship.'

'Well well—I was.'

'No, it don't matter to us—unless you was expecting to *replace* your carronades.'

'Well, as a matter in fact——'

'There cannot be any hope of that.' Another glance at his companion, a shake of the head. 'We are happy to revictual you, as a matter of course, and we were happy to help you in the matter of copper sheeting, but there can be no question of new guns, Captain Rennie. We are put to great trouble in keeping sufficient powder and shot for our own squadron, leave alone armament.' An afterthought, kindly meant: 'I was very sorry to hear of the loss of your first lieutenant. He was—he was gentlemanlike.'

'I do not know that he is lost, entire. I do not yet accept that he is lost.' Stiffly.

Rennie did not find Port Royal a very congenial place. The ship took in her water and stores, her officers and people were disgruntled, and Rennie fretted. In his troubled condition he took little notice of the merchant ships lying at anchor in Kingston Harbour, until one of these ships did catch his eye, as he came on deck. He sent a midshipman below to fetch his glass.

'I have seen her before, I think.' Focusing the glass.

'Sir?'

'Aye,' still peering through his glass, 'it is the same ship, I would swear to it.'

'Shall we send a boat, sir?'

'Eh? No no, Mr Abey, thank you. I will like merely to keep my eye on her, or in least keep her in my mind.'

'Very good, sir.'

PART THREE: THE CHASE

James came at night to Spanish Town, battered, limping, exhausted, hungry and in tattered rags, into the smell of convolvulus and foetid habitation—having begged a lift on a provision cart a mile or two on the road coming out of the mountains, and walked the rest of the way after dusk. Contrary to his strong belief in his navigational skills, he had become lost after surviving the flood. The cloud, mist and rain had prevented him from seeing the stars at night, and the heat of the day had slowed him down. Unused to rough country, and alone—he had not again met up with Archimedes—he had found nothing but berries, which he was afraid to eat in case of poisoning. Had he been stronger, and more in possession of his senses, he might have made his way to an estate, but he was weak, and disorientated, and unable.

He came to the great square of official buildings—the House of Assembly, the Memorial, the Guardhouse—and recognised in the pale, cloud-emerging moon the colonnade of the King's House. He crossed the square, pulled down the ragged sleeves of his shirt, and in a daze of determined intent went up to the entrance—and knocked. Knocked, and was about to knock a second time when a firm hand gripped his shoulder, and a second pushed the point of a bayonet in his ribs. He twisted round and saw two soldiers. They seized him, and pushed him out into the square, and against one of the stone columns.

'Fuckinell, what we got 'ere, then?'

'A mumper, corp'l. A fuckin' beggar.' Poking James with his bayonet.

'I am not—I am not a beggar . . .' Panting, trying to free himself. The corporal held him firmer, and jerked his arm.

'Then who is you, eh? King of Spain, izzit? King of fuckin' France?'

James was tremulous with fatigue, and now furious anger. 'You bloody fools! Cannot you understand! I must see the Governor!' Twisting and struggling, his voice hoarse.

'Ho, yes. See the Governor. Yes. Break in, and steal. Break in, and thieve. Shall I tell you what it is, mump? Which you will kindly do? Fuck off out of it, right quick.'

'Fuckin' trull.' The other, pricking James again with the bayonet.

'Or should we take 'im down the alley, Bill? Hey? And kick the shite out of 'is carcase!'

Another prick of the bayonet. Foul breath, the stink of sweat.

James closed his eyes, summoned up all his remaining strength, all his remaining dignity of purpose, made his back straight, and said in pure quarterdeck:

'Stand away, now! Listen to me! I am Lieutenant James Hayter, of His Majesty's *Expedient* frigate. I am come on a mission of vital importance to the Governor, whose enemies have held me captive. You will assist me, if you please—or by God know the consequence!'

This was sufficient—just sufficient—to alter the direction of the wind, and presently James found himself in the Guardhouse, in the presence of Lieutenant McFadden—summoned from his bed.

'Good Lord, it is you, Hayter!' Astonished in his nightshirt, his britches and boots hastily pulled on. 'We had given you up, you know. We all thought you was dead. Corporal Flint!'

'Sir?'

'Fetch the surgeon from his bed, with my compliments.'

'I do not need a doctor, you know. I need to see the Governor, at once.'

'Your need is to sit down, my dear fellow. You are all in.' Kindly, firmly, taking his arm.

James made to protest further, staggered a little, and was guided to a chair and given brandy from a flask. The spirit burned going down his throat, parched as he was—and revived him a little.

'What o'clock is it?'

'It is two o'clock in the morning. Too late—or too early—to wake the Governor, or anyone in the household. You had better rest here, we will find you a cot. The surgeon——'

'For Christ's sake, now, Mr McFadden. This cannot wait!' He told as much of the facts as he thought would convince the lieutenant, and at last the lieutenant was persuaded to go to the King's House, and there insist that Colonel Hepple should be wakened and informed of James's arrival. At three o'clock James was in the Governor's private quarters, with more brandy, and Colonel Hepple, whose supercilious manner had vanished.

'You are certain it was Darder took you to the mountains?' In shirt and breeches, a cheroot clenched in his teeth.

'Either Darder or his accomplices. I had discovered him for who he was, had found his false keys, and his only protection was to murder me.'

Colonel Hepple straightened from his leaning position, and paced the room. Paused, and looked at James.

'I believe I owe you an apology, Mr Hayter. I confess that before this I did not believe anything you said to me.'

'That is why I went to his shop, at night, and broke in—I knew that you would regard the business of the disguise . . . well, I feared that you would not believe that, neither.'

'We must go to Port Henderson, and from there to Port Royal.' Buckling on his sword.

'Port Henderson?' Bewildered. 'But—should not the Governor be informed? Do not you——'

'I shall inform him, but for now there is no time to lose. Laycock has gone in the carriage to Port Henderson, at midnight.'

'The Reverend Laycock?'

'To be transported to your ship, at Port Royal. In course, you do not know the whole thing. I will explain as we ride. That is—if you are strong enough to ride?'

'Oh yes—yes, I am.' A direct contradiction of facts, but brandy had lifted him, and Colonel Hepple's urgency.

'I will lend you some clothes. Joseph!' And to the steward when he appeared, sleepy and barefoot in his page's coat: 'A basin of water for Lieutenant Hayter, and a towel. And bring something from the kitchen to eat as we go, and a flask. Hurry!'

'Hurry hurry—too damn late, all this, too damn early.'

As they rode, Colonel Hepple revealed to James the Reverend Laycock's true importance, and the role *Expedient* was to play in getting him safe to England with his all-encompassing plan of defence, covering all of the Caribbean islands.

'We must make certain that Laycock has gone aboard your ship and is safe, tonight. We sent him away under cover of darkness to be sure of absolute secrecy in getting him aboard—but in view of all you have told me Darder may have had the King's House watched.'

James, having washed, dressed in clean clothes, and eaten something, was now sharp and fresh, and ready to aid Colonel Hepple in anything. He knew that exhaustion might very probably soon overwhelm him, after his ordeal, but for the moment he was fresh.

'You think Darder knows who Laycock is? Knows his entire purpose?'

'We must assume it.' Urging his horse with his heels. The sound of hooves thudded on the night air as they hacked towards Port Henderson. 'He was behind the two attempts at burglary of the Governor's quarters, I make no doubt.'

'You think that he struck Reverend Laycock? On the night Laycock shot Monsieur Lange?'

'It is likely, don't you think so?' A pause. 'Something has come out, about Monsieur Lange.'

'Yes?'

'I must ask you to keep this to yourself, Hayter.'

'Very well, Colonel, certainly.'

'Lady Merrick had been—at an earlier time, when she and His Excellency first came here—she had been ill, and acquired a liking for tincture to relieve her distress.'

'Tincture of opium?'

'Indeed. She took more and more, incessantly sip-sip-sip, and His Excellency grew concerned. Dr Stroud was consulted. He too was concerned, and insisted that she must cease. If she did not she would grow mortally sick, he said. She agreed, and the pharmaceutical in Kingston was instructed to end all delivery of tincture to the King's House. However—however, Monsieur Lange began to obtain the drug for himself, saying that he suffered crippling headache, and he passed all he obtained to Lady Merrick, in secrecy. She was thus again incessantly sipping, when His Excellency thought she was cured of her attachment to the drug. When Monsieur Lange was killed she became quite hysterical—not from grief at his passing, but at the loss of the damned poison.'

'Ah, that would explain——'

'What? What d'y'say?' Glancing at James's shadowy figure in the darkness.

'Nay, nothing . . .'

'She did fall ill, very ill, with convulsions and fainting fits—Dr Stroud nearly despaired of her—and thus at last the whole truth came out. Even now she is not wholly recovered, poor woman.'

James, after a further moment: 'You do not think, do you, Colonel—you do not think Laycock may probably have shot Monsieur Lange on purpose?'

'Hm. I will admit the notion crossed my mind, afterward.

That he knew what Lange was doing, and shot him to save Lady Merrick, hey?'

'Possibly, possibly. But do not you think he might perhaps have been—I am half inside my head—do not you think he might have had another motive?'

'Another motive? What motive?' Reining in abruptly. James pulled up a little ahead, and turned his horse.

'Is not there a possibility that Monsieur Lange was working in harness with Darder? He was French, he had come into the household and attached himself to Lady Merrick, and made himself indispensable to her, he was living there almost as a member of the family, and had the freedom of the private quarters; he had their trust, entire. The perfect situation for a spy.'

'The thing is fantastic, good God, it is utterly fantastic.' Digging in his heels, riding on.

'Aye, so it may be.' James, clicking his tongue and following in the darkness. 'It may be pure fanciful speculation on my part, and nothing more. However . . .' catching the colonel up, '. . . however, allow me to make this supposition: Reverend Laycock discovered that Lange was giving opium to Lady Merrick, and decided to keep his eye closely on everything that Lange did thereafter. He distrusted him now in all particulars. He thought him a very devious, underhand, deceitful and reckless fellow, in risking the health of Lady Merrick—and at last he discovered something that led him to believe Lange was a spy. Perhaps to believe that *he* was Lascelles.'

'You have left me far to your rear, sir. Why did not he say anything to His Excellency, if he thought that? What did he discover, anyway? A letter? A document? If so, why did not he speak up?'

'I do not know that, Colonel. I am putting to you an hypothesis, a supposition. Reverend Laycock is employed by the same institution as employs his brother clergyman Jepp, and Sir Robert Greer—the Secret Service Fund. All of these men have a certain cast of mind, I think.'

'Inventive, Mr Hayter? Hm?' A returning hint of mockery.

'Concealing. They have the lifelong habit of concealing everything they discover.'

'I find it very difficult to believe that Laycock——'

'Colonel, you and I are serving officers. The Governor is a serving officer. We are plain-spoke men, that must do our duty according to regulation. That is not the world the Reverend Laycock inhabits. His world is underneath, in darkness—whispers and echoes of whispers.'

Ahead, a clatter of movement. The colonel reined in, and now out of the shadows cast by the cloud-breaking moon came wandering horses, trailing tackle. A carriage stood behind, athwart the road.

'We need not whisper this—that is the carriage Laycock was in.'

When James came aboard *Expedient* at dawn, it was with a mixture of relief, regret, and euphoric fatigue. Relief that he was at last back in his familiar wooden world, where order was certain; regret that he came with deplorable intelligence; fatigue because he had not slept in four-and-twenty hours. Rennie—when he came to the door of the great cabin—was unreservedly glad to see his lieutenant safe and well.

'By God, James.' Gripping both of his hands in his own, pumping them up and down. 'By God, you are alive.' He shook his head in wondering joy, and tears started in his eyes.

'I fear I am not properly dressed, sir, for a sea officer.' Plucking at the lapel of his borrowed military coat.

'Never think of that, my dear James. It is what lives inside the coat that matters—your dear good self. Well well, hey? Well well.' He blew his nose forcefully. 'Come in, come in. Cutton!'

Rennie was eager to hear all that had happened to James since his disappearance, but James first told him about the disappearance of Laycock from the carriage on the road to Port Henderson. Rennie's smile faded, and his face assumed its customary natural solemnity. He took out the communication he had received from the Governor, tapped it with his fingers, showed it to James, and:

'They will see this as our failure, you know, James.'

'Sir, forgive me, but that is nonsense. It ain't our fault he was kidnapped——'

'Aye, no, it ain't—but they will see it as such.' He dropped the letter on the table, sighed, then his eyes widened. 'Christ's blood, James. The merchant ship.'

'I am a little slow, today . . .'

'The merchant ship! We will go on deck! Come on!' He snatched his glass from the rack, and bounded up the companion ladder. James followed him, beginning to be bleary.

On deck Rennie swept the harbour with his glass, cursed, and faced the stern. 'She is gone. The American merchantman has gone.'

'You think . . .?'

'I am certain of it, James! The Reverend Laycock, and his damned plan, is in that ship—and she has sailed away in the night!'

'Then—then we had better pursue her, sir, at once.' Mildly. 'Don't you think so?'

Captain Rennie wished to chase, was ready to do so without consulting the Governor, or anyone ashore, but as he was preparing to weigh a boat had come to *Expedient*, a boat carrying Colonel Hepple, who briskly climbed the side-ladder into the ship. Darder had vanished from his shop, he said, which premises had been stripped of all his effects, and the clocks he had taken in for repair left in the middle of the floor under a loose canvas covering. There could now be no doubt that Darder was Lascelles, had kidnapped Laycock, and spirited him away. His Excellency the Governor wished to see both Captain Rennie and Lieutenant Hayter at once.

'My dear Colonel Hepple, we cannot go to Spanish Town *now*,' protested Rennie. 'We are engaged in a chase, a sea chase.'

'Chase?'

'The Reverend Laycock is in a ship, an American-flagged merchant ship, which has escaped in the night. She is already many hours ahead of us, and unless I am much mistook will rendezvous with a frigate on the open sea. I believe that rendezvous will take place somewhere in the region of the Windward Passage.'

'You saw Laycock taken into this ship? You saw her depart?'

'No no, in course he was smuggled aboard. Then they escaped under cover of darkness, as I told you.' Impatiently.

'With respect, how do you know that Laycock was aboard—if you did not see him, nor see the ship sail away? Gentlemen, we are wasting time. His Excellency believes that Darder—Lascelles—has accomplices in the island, who will help him conceal the Reverend Laycock and hold him until they have extracted from him the cryptographic key to his plan.'

'His plan is all in cryptographic?'

'In course it is, Captain Rennie. Reverend Laycock is not a fool. Neither does he lack courage. However, he is not very hardy, not very strong in his person. When they torture and beat him, which is certain, he may probably at last tell them the key. We must find him before. His Excellency will like to hear a direct account of Lieutenant Hayter's experiences in the mountains, so that armed search parties may be assembled at once, including the ablest men of your crew——'

Impatiently, heatedly, Rennie interrupted the colonel and gave him an account of *Expedient*'s encounter with the merchantman and frigate weeks ago, his subsequent sighting of the merchant ship at Kingston, her recent reappearance, and disappearance. Colonel Hepple's face said that he was sceptical. His shoulders said so in an impatient shrug. Before he could speak:

'Cannot you grasp the explanation, Colonel? Lascelles came here in that ship, and he has gone away in that ship, taking the Reverend Laycock with him!'

Colonel Hepple held up a hand, shook his head, and: 'I am correct in saying, I think, that you are now under the direct command of His Excellency?'

'Yes.' Curtly.

'Then perhaps you will be kind enough to return with me to Spanish Town, as His Excellency wishes—as he commands.'

Rennie gave a little hop of indignation, and stamped his foot on the deck. 'How *can* I do what you ask, for Christ's sake, without I let Lascelles escape!'

'That is conjecture, Captain Rennie, conjecture entire.'

'It is nothing of the *kind*! It is *nothing* of the kind! Mr Hayter supports me. He knows everything I have just said to you to be the truth. James, be so good as to iterate that to the colonel, so that we may weigh and proceed.' Rennie gave a sharp sniff, and stood legs braced apart with his hands clasped behind his back. James nodded, and drew breath, but the colonel:

'Mr Hayter's opinion is neither here nor there!' Equally sharp. 'It is facts we need! I do not think you will disobey a direct order, will you, Captain Rennie?'

'Good God, man! Are you really so obtuse!'

'Well, sir—will you?'

Rennie turned away a moment, his face very dark, and came to his decision.

'Mr Duggan! Lieutenant Duggan, there!'

'Sir?' Lieutenant Duggan appeared at the waist ladder, and came up on to the quarterdeck, his hat off and on.

'Mr Duggan, you and two of your marines will escort Colonel Hepple into his boat.'

'Very good, sir.'

'Never mind, Lieutenant, you will not escort me anywhere, thank you. I will go into the boat of my own accord. It may be, I fear, that your next escorting duty will be to your own commanding officer, whose foolhardy actions have made it certain that he will face a court martial. Good morning, gentlemen.'

As the colonel descended into the boat, and sat stiffly in the stern as he was rowed away, Captain Rennie was silent. Presently he ceased staring angrily at the receding boat, sniffed again, looked aloft, and:

'We will weigh immediate, if y'please, Mr Hayter. We must be on the open sea, all-a-taunt, in half a glass. We are left behind—far behind—and I mean to chase, and chase, until we are not far behind any more. And then, by God, we will teach those damned blackguards the meaning of fear.'

At 16 degrees 54 minutes north, 76 degrees 32 minutes west, and four bells of the forenoon watch, *Expedient* beating towards Santo Domingo on the larboard tack, under a heavy press of canvas. Larboard watch on deck, and aloft, and part of the starboard watch at musket practice. The armourer standing by. The *crack crack crack* of muskets in the maintop. James watched from the break of the quarterdeck, not with approval entire, since musket practice in the tops, his first commission, had led to a topsail taking fire from powder flashes, and great alarum. But they were in a chase, a chase that could end in fierce action, and the carronade crews, without their smashers, should not be left idle.

Now the boatswain's mate, Roper Saggert, appeared in the waist with a corporal of marines, the pair of them manhandling a defiant, struggling figure. James heard the commotion, and as he stepped to the breast rail there was an outburst of language:

'Let me alone, let me go, I am free! Y'got everyt'ing mix up, now! I am free, damn and curse you!'

'Christ's blood.' James stared down, astonished. At the same moment, the struggling man looked up.

'I see you, James! Tell them f'Christ's sake let me go, will you!'

'Archimedes, where have you come from?'

The boatswain's mate and the corporal of marines inadvertently loosened their grip when they saw recognition on the lieutenant's face, and Archimedes broke free. As they attempted again to seize him, he called loudly:

'I am comin' wit' you in your ship, to England, James! Tell them to leave me alone, will you? Say I am your friend!'

'All right, Saggert. All right, corporal. You may let him go.'

'We found him hiding in the breadroom, sir. He don't belong in the ship.'

'Yes, thank you. Let him go, now. Archimedes, climb the ladder.'

'You will allow him on the quarterdeck, sir?' The corporal of marines was shocked. 'A breadroom skulking villain?' Reluctantly he released Archimedes's arm, and Saggert let him go on the other side, and Archimedes came running up the ladder and shook James's hand vigorously.

'I am so happy t'see you, my good friend. I said so all along, that I would come along wit' you to England, and now it will happen, as we agreed.'

'Did we? How—how in God's name was you able to get aboard?'

'Swimmin', y'know. I am a damn fine exponent of swimmin', and I climbed up the side in the night, when all these fellows was asleep.' Waving vaguely at the larboard afterguard.

'At Port Royal?'

'Yes, at Port Royal. I went hidin' downstair, in a store down there, underneat'.'

'Ah. Did you? I am glad to see you, Archimedes—but this

puts me in a damned awkward position.' Taking his arm, guiding him away on the sloping deck to the lee rail. 'You are not here official, and——'

'Mr Hayter!' Behind him, from the companion.

'Sir?' Turning to face his captain, and endeavouring to shield Archimedes from the captain's inquiring gaze.

'Who is that man, Mr Hayter?'

'Well, sir, he—that is, he——'

'Stand away from the rail, if y'please, and let me see him.'

James did as he was told, and Archimedes—in his shirt and breeches and battered tricorne—was revealed. Rennie looked at him without favour.

'And who the devil are you, sir? There is no passenger in my ship this commission, that I knew about. Are you a seaman, sir? Or a damned idling miscreant supernum'ry landman? Hey!'

'No, your honour, I am a free man.' Stepping towards Rennie with a broad smile. 'Wit' your help.'

'Are you acquainted with this fellow, Mr Hayter?' Turning to James.

'Yes, sir, I am. May I introduce Archimedes, that saved my life in the Jamaica mountains.'

'Saved ye, did he? And for that service you made payment by smuggling him into the ship.'

'I did not, sir.'

Rennie turned back to Archimedes, whose smile now faltered: 'You are an escaped slave, sir, I'll wager an hundred guineas on it! At any rate, you have broke the law by coming into my ship!'

'Sir, allow me to say——'

'Be quiet, Mr Hayter. Well—are you an escaped slave, Mr Archipelago?'

'My name is Archimedes, sir. And I am a free man, a free man, a *free man* . . .' Tears formed in his eyes, and he stood staring at Rennie, breathing through his nose as the tears dripped on his cheeks.

Rennie was not insensible of the passion of this assertion—this plea. He averted his eyes a moment, and cleared his throat. 'Well well, I have no means of knowing the exact circumstance of your escape, and we have sunk Jamaica astern.' Facing him again. 'Can you work, sir? Can you make y'self useful in the ship, and earn your rations?'

'I can work at anyt'ing y'like. I ain't afraid to work—as a free man.'

'With your permission, sir, I should like to take Archimedes as my steward.' James, politely.

'Your steward, Mr Hayter? Your steward, particular to you, as a gunroom officer?'

'I know it ain't usual, sir, but I wish to take him under my care, so to say, and——'

'You may take him as your personal servant, Mr Hayter. Make it so, and enter him in the books rated landman idler. When you have done it, I will like to see you, and Mr Peak, and Mr Loftus in the great cabin.'

'Very good, sir, thank you.' His hat off and on, and he ushered Archimedes forrard to the ladder.

Rennie stood at the table in the great cabin, a pair of chart dividers in his hand, and a corner-weighted chart spread before him.

'Santo Domingo,' he said. 'And our position, gentlemen—is here, fifty mile west of Cape Tiburon, an hundred and thirty mile sou'west of Gonaves Isle.' Measuring with the dividers. 'I believe the frigate has laid in wait south of that island, at the port of Leogane—here.'

'All that time, sir?' Bernard Loftus peered at the chart. 'Why there?'

'It is where I would lie quiet—was I in his ship as captain, waiting under orders to make rendezvous. Our merchant ship will sail along the coast, and attempt to make that rendezvous—here.'

'You say "our" merchant ship, sir. In what sense—"ours"?'

'Well well, not ours quite yet. But she will be ours before very long—if we stalk our prey very careful, and run up close astern before we are seen. Mind you, we must not be over-careful. We must risk yards and parrals and canvas to bring her in sight, and *then* be careful.'

'Aye, sir—but surely . . . we cannot take prizes, in the peace?'

'Bernard does make a good point, don't you think so, sir?' James asked politely. 'Whether to attack such a ship when we are not at war is a most difficult, fine-judged——'

'Difficult? Fine-judged? Pish pish, gentlemen. They have stole military secrets, they have kidnapped a servant of His Majesty the King, and contrived to make bloody fools of us all. To attack such blackguards is our plain duty. That is what I mean by "ours", Mr Loftus. Our prey, our target, our duty!' A sniff, the dividers poised. He glanced at each face in turn. 'That is, that is—if I am not mistook in the whole damned enterprise, hey?' A grim smile.

'Mistook, sir?'

'That I have not led you all upon a wild-goose chase . . . I see that y'do think that, Mr Loftus.' Straightening up, putting down the dividers.

'Sir, I would not wish to contradict you——'

'But you are doubtful, very doubtful—I am correct?'

'I beg your pardon, sir, for interrupting you.'

Rennie bent forward again over the table, with a flicker of a glance at Mr Loftus, who saw that he had certainly better not interrupt again, nor reflect in his face any thought that was not entirely concordant with those of his captain. Rennie took up the dividers.

'She will, I think, bear east—here—and run close in along the coast—here. And we, in course, must find her before she does.'

'When do we expect to sight the ship, sir?' Young Peak.

'At any moment, Mr Peak, at any moment. We have look-outs at the masthead, and certainly she cannot outrun us. She is there ahead, and we shall find her. Very good, very good.' Straightening again. 'And now, gentlemen, we will exercise the great guns.'

'While we are chasing, sir?' blurted Bernard Loftus, and at once bit his tongue.

'Indeed, while we are chasing, Mr Loftus. *Expedient* is a ship of war, a fighting ship. Soon she must engage, and fight, and the gun-crews lack practice. Between now and the moment we sight the American ship, we will exercise the great guns as often-times as I shall think fitting. You have me?'

'Aye, sir, very good. Perhaps the American captain will prefer not to resist, and we shall not then need to fire on him.'

'That will be his wisest course, but I do not intend to be found asleep if he don't take it. Hey, Mr Loftus?'

'I think you will never be guilty of that, sir.' And he made his obedience in a bow.

'Mr Tangible! We will beat to quarters!'

The roll of the drum, and running feet; quarter bills, posted in the waist, hastily consulted by anxious midshipmen; officers to their sections; Rennie on his quarterdeck, legs braced, pocket watch in hand. Frantic activity along the gun deck—and:

'Starboard battery loosed and run out, sir!'

'Very well, thank you, Mr Hayter. But it will not do. We are slow, slow—too damned slow.' He held up his watch, high, and turned it in his hand so that it caught the glint of the sun. '*D'y'hear me, all of you! We are too damned slow!*'

'De-e-e-ck! Sail of ship!'

'Where away?'

'Three points on the starboard bow! Hull down!'

Expedient soon began to overhaul the sighted ship; her hull came up, and her colours could be made out.

'She is a British ship, sir.' James, from the mizzen shrouds, one arm hooked through as he focused his glass.

'British? No no, that is a ruse.' Rennie raised his speaking trumpet. 'Lookout, there! What size of ship is she?'

'Three masts, sir—and she flies the St George, and the red ensign!'

Rennie lowered the speaking trumpet, and shook his head. 'Nay, nay - that is his damned trick. That is not a British ship. She is American, and she carries the Reverend Laycock confined in her orlop. Mr Loftus!'

'Sir?'

'I want more speed.'

'We cannot risk more speed close-hauled, sir . . . I will try, sir. Mr Tangible!'

The chased ship was soon in plain sight, and Rennie cleared for action. As *Expedient* drew closer, the merchant ship put her maintopsail aback, and hove to on the swell. It had become clear that she was not the American vessel after all. Her lines were different. She was stouter, bluffer, and an hundred ton heavier. Rennie saw all this, sighed, and paced away to the rail; he stood alone there, his glass held tight under his arm, his hands clasped behind his back.

Her master came to *Expedient* in his boat, and Rennie felt himself obliged to receive him. She was the *Gentoo*, 550 tons, out of Bristol, carrying sugar on the homeward leg. Her master, Captain Danks, had not sighted an American merchant ship, nor any ship. He was to have sailed from Manchioneal Harbour with three other ships through the Florida Straits. There had been delays in the loading of these ships, he explained, and his owners being impatient men he had risked sailing alone via the Windward Passage, to lessen the risk of attack by pirates. However:

'If you will be kind enough, Captain Rennie, to escort me through the Windward Passage, I shall be very grate——'

'Escort you, Captain Danks? I cannot, sir.'

'It is only a matter of an hundred mile, an hundred and fifty——'

'It is out of the question. I am under orders.' He did not elaborate.

'Ah. Then I must not hinder you. Is there anything I can do for you? May I carry your letters?'

'No no, no thank you.' Aware that his manner verged on rudeness, he added: 'You are very kind, Captain Danks, but——'

'I should like to send a letter, sir, if I may be permitted to scribble a few lines,' said James now. 'It will take me only a minute or two, and——'

'We have no time at all for writing letters!' snapped Rennie. 'Captain Danks, will you go into your boat, sir? I must get under way.'

'Very well, very well.' Captain Danks was very put out, but he contrived to keep his temper, and his manners. 'If that is your wish. I had hoped to be able to persuade you to dine with us . . .'

Rennie saw that he had offended him, and endeavoured to make brief amends: 'Yes, I do not wish to seem unduly brisk, and in the ordinary way, you know, it is I that should invite you to dine. However, I am in a very great hurry, and I must now bid you good day. You see?' With what he hoped was a pleasant smile, but was more an impatient menacing grimace.

'Very well, Captain Rennie, thank you.' And he went down stony-faced into his boat.

'He is angry with me,' muttered Rennie. 'He thinks I was hasty, and ungentlemanlike. Well well, I cannot help it. He has held me up, and slowed me down, the fellow.' Raising his voice: 'We will get under way, Mr Loftus! Lively now, if y'please!'

As darkness fell, *Expedient* had not seen another sail, and Rennie was obliged to shake out reefs and bear away, to avoid falling on the rocky western coast of Santo Domingo at night.

'He has outwitted us, the villain.' To his first lieutenant, on the quarterdeck. 'He has flitted away and hid himself, whilst we was buggered about by that damned lubberly fool of a sugarman.'

James thought, but did not say, that *Expedient* could have sailed straight past the Bristol ship, gaining what little intelligence she had to give by hailing back and forth. He was aggrieved that Rennie had not allowed him to scribble a few lines to Catherine, and hand the note down into the boat to Captain Danks. It would have taken a few moments; it could easily have been done; Rennie had snappishly refused him permission. And now the chase must be abandoned overnight, anyway.

'I have changed my mind.' Rennie paced to the rail, and back. 'I have changed my mind. We will go about, and continue east, under Gonaves Isle. We might probably be able to overhaul him before dawn, and prevent the rendezvous. We must at all cost try to prevent that meeting, James. The frigate would take Laycock and his plan, and outsail us into the Atlantick. And then we would never find them.'

'Conditions is very hazardous along that coast, at night.'

'I must take the risk. I must risk my ship—or fail.'

'Very good, sir.' Striding abreast the binnacle. '*Prepare to go about! Hands to tack ship!*'

Rennie had eaten his dinner hurriedly, alone, and was rapidly writing up his journal—intending to return straightway thereafter to his quarterdeck—when Thomas Wing came to the great cabin. He hesitated at the door, and steadied himself against the heeling of the ship.

'Yes, Doctor?' Looking at him in the light of the deckhead lantern, seeing that hesitation. 'You have something to tell me? Come in—I must just complete this line—damn this quill—now.' Laying down his pen, scattering chalk, closing the book.

Wing took a breath, a grave breath. 'I fear I must inform you, Captain—there is fever in the ship.'

'You are certain? Damnation, I thought we had escaped unscathed. You are quite certain?'

'I am, sir. It is the yellow fever—yellowjack.'

A long, sniffing sigh, and: 'How many?'

'Eight men, so far. I think that there will be many others.'

'Did I do the wrong thing, in allowing Mr Hayter's escaped slave into the ship?' Half to himself. Then, addressing Wing again: 'I should have consulted you about him, and required you to examine him.'

'I did examine him, sir, at the first lieutenant's request, before he was entered on the books. I am strongly of the view he did not bring fever into the ship. He was on the contrary exceeding healthy, and remains so.'

'But he had been hiding in the deep forest, had he not? In heaven knows what squalor of mud and filth, and disease-laden air.'

'He was very clean in his person, sir. Cleaner than most seamen. Any wise, we was at sea before he was discovered. You did not allow him to come aboard, in truth. He was already here.' A pause. 'Surely—surely the question that must occupy us now, Captain, is not *how* the fever came into the ship, but how we are to fight it?'

'Yes, yes, you are right, in course. You have it exact, Doctor. How am I to fight the disease, and fight my ship?' Rising, turning away a moment.

'You are not alone in neither struggle, sir.' Gently. 'We are all with you—we are all Expedients.'

They did not find the American merchant ship. At first light *Expedient* was beating east towards Gonaves Isle, into a blustery wind, the coast of Santo Domingo to the south. These were not comfortable waters for Captain Rennie. Ahead, south-east of the island, lay Leogane and Port au Prince, and the frigate was somewhere there, he was sure of it. If his surmise was correct, and she was French, lying there in a French port, and all of the actions of the merchantman and the frigate were part of a French scheme, a French plot—he had better be careful. England was not at war with France. Carefully contrived accommodations had been established between England and France throughout the Caribbean. Were he to sight the frigate on her own—what could he do? He might chase her, if she was pleased to run, as she had run before. He might venture to chase, but he could not risk firing on her unless she fired first. It was one thing to suspect and assume that there was a plot, and quite another to act aggressively upon that assumption. However—pacing on his quarterdeck, hatless, wigless, head bent—however, he was surely justified in pursuing the merchantman, pursuing and finding her, and firing a warning shot across her, to force her to heave to and submit to a boarding party, and inspection. He nodded in agreement with himself. There was perfectly cogent justification for such action. A British subject, employed in the King's service, was held prisoner in that ship, by God, and he meant to rescue him. As to Mr Loftus's quibbling, vexing questions about the taking of prizes, well . . . he could not take her as a prize. What to do if she was to run? Run away defiant? He would be obliged to fire on her then, would he not? Rake her stern, and smash her rudder?

'On what grounds, though?' Aloud, but to himself. The men of the afterguard kept their faces neutral, the quartermaster and the helmsman the same, as their commanding officer paced, and muttered, and shook his head in frowning self-absorption.

'On what grounds may I fire on the merchant vessel of another nation, on the open sea, in the peace?' He paused, peered over the taffrail, shook his head again, turned:

'Mr Cross!' To the master's mate—no longer Acting Lieutenant Cross—taking the watch.

'Sir?'

'Mr Cross, my compliments to the doctor, and beg his pardon and so forth for waking him at this early hour, and will he kindly attend on me in the great cabin, at his earliest convenience.'

'Very good, sir.' Departing.

Rennie stepped to the wheel. 'Daley Wragg, you will conn the ship until Mr Cross returns.'

'Aye, sir.'

Rennie glanced aloft, and forrard, and sniffed the wind. 'She points up well. We have a fine, weatherly ship under our legs, hey?' An involuntary breath-snatching yawn made his eyes water.

'She is, sir. She may not be flying fast, but she is right weatherly.'

'Eh? Not fast?' Rubbing his eyes.

'I never meant she was *slow*, sir——'

'Never mind, never mind. I am going below a short while. Hold her so, just so.'

'Aye, sir. Just so.'

Thomas Wing came to the great cabin, bleary from his cot, endeavouring to be attentive.

'Is it about the fever cases, sir?'

'No no. In least, I will like your report presently, but just now—just now I need something to keep me awake, Doctor.'

'Forgive me—are not you awake now, sir?'

'Yes yes, in course I am awake, good God. I wish to *remain* awake, Doctor. I wish to *be* awake all the day and all the night following, if need be. You see?'

'Oh yes, yes, I do see. I do not know quite what I should recommend . . .' A hand to his chin.

'Recommend? For Christ's sake, man, I wish you to *give* me something, not recommend it. Hm? Hm?'

'Very well, sir, very well. I shall give you some shred leaf of *Erythroxylon coca*.'

'Erotical what?' Alarmed.

'It is a stimulant.'

'Yes, but stimulating what? What part of my—my person does it stimulate? Hey?'

'Chiefly the brain, sir. You will be made alert.' A straight face.

'Good, very good, then that is what I wish for, exact. An alerted mind.'

'Yes, sir.'

'An alerted mind—and nothing else.'

'Indeed, nothing else. Will I bring it to you at once, or later in——'

'Yes, at once, thank you. And then I will like to hear an account of the fever cases. I am sorry to have woke you so inconvenient early—but I cannot allow myself to fall into a slumber.' Another sudden yawn. 'I must be awake, awake, awake. And alert.'

As noon was officially declared, the ship was running south of Gonaves Isle, in the channel between the island and the coast of Santo Domingo, at 18 degrees 26 minutes north by 72 degrees 52 minutes west. Fishing boats had appeared, and small trading vessels, but there was no sign of the American merchant ship, nor of the frigate. There were now twenty cases of fever in the lower deck, and there was a feeling in the ship that every man in her might soon fall victim. There was no room for twenty sick men in the small area set aside as a sickbay forrard on the starboard side of the lower deck. Thomas Wing was obliged to suggest to the captain that a part of the forrard upper deck, below the forecastle, should be made over into sick-berthing.

'That is the manger, the animal pen. We cannot have men, sick men, cheek by arse with grunting beasts, good heaven.'

'Then the grunting beasts must be killed.' Firmly. 'Killed, and ate, and the place they have lived washed and smoked and made fit. There is no choice in the matter, Captain. If these poor men are to be given any chance at all of life they must be proper housed, in sweetened air.'

'Very well, Doctor, you make an unassailable case. It shall be so. Mr Peak!'

*

By the evening, as hammocks were piped down, there were twelve new cases of fever known to Thomas Wing, and he began to be seriously anxious and alarmed.

'The whole of the upper deck, forrard of the galley stove, must be made into a sick berth,' he declared to the captain.

'Out of the question, Doctor, wholly out of the question.' Holding up a hand.

'No, sir, it must not be "out of the question", in the least. I must have——'

'Listen to me, now. At any moment we may be required to fight our guns. I cannot have sick men swinging in their hammocks over and about gun-crews that is attempting to load and run out.'

'Well, I cannot have sick men left to——'

'The hammock numbers of the lower deck must be so arranged that all sick men is confined to one section, and all the other men kept separate from them.'

'I cannot have the animal pen?'

'It will not do. There is too many.'

'Captain, you gave me your word that I might have the manger!' Standing fierce to his full height, which was not much above the captain's midriff.

'Well well, I have changed my mind. I require the upper deck to be left free of all encumbrance.'

'Sir, I must protest, in the strongest poss——'

'You will be quiet, Mr Wing.' A breath, to calm his rising anger. 'Doctor—Thomas—we have lost our carronades, and have only our long gun batteries left to us to fight. They may only be fought where they lie in the tackles, on the upper deck—the gun deck, that gives us our purpose and meaning as a ship of war. You see?'

'Then what am I to do if the hale men refuse to sling their hammocks near to the sick men in the lower deck? What must I do, then?'

'You will refer them to me, by God.' Grimly. And now he sent for his first lieutenant, who was in the gunroom.

'Sir?' Attending.

'I will like you to go with the doctor, James, and arrange lower-deck hammock numbers so that hale men do not lie proximate to sick men. You may take Mr Duggan with you.'

'Mr Duggan, sir?'

'Aye, Mr Duggan, and two marines. It must be made plain to the people that the new arrangements is for the good of the ship, and not for their private convenience. You have me?'

'Sir.'

'Doctor, when you have done this, I will like you to alert me to all new cases of fever you detect, glass by glass. I am to be informed at once, d'y'hear?'

'I do hear, thank you, sir. I am not yet a deaf man.'

Rennie nodded, relenting a little, and asked in a kinder tone: 'You have physic enough to treat all of the sick?'

'I have got physic in my chest, but it will not answer, I fear. The yellowjack is very pernicious when it has once took hold in a man. It will grip him and sweat him to delirium however liberal I may be with physic.'

'Then may God be merciful on us all.' Quietly. A moment, then: 'By the by, I must keep awake at all cost, and I will like to have some more of that plant of yours, Doctor.'

On the lower deck the new arrangements caused consternation and resentment, and James was obliged to say to Rennie afterward that although the men had accepted them, if others fell sick the new arrangements would likely be blamed.

'I will address the people on the morrow.' His face very white and waxy, his eye over-bright.

Rennie turned north-west and sailed up Gonaves Bay, with the island to larboard in the darkness, Santo Domingo to starboard; he relied on the stars and his seamanship to see them through. His conviction was that *Expedient* could not have missed both ships in these confining waters, and that the rendezvous would now be effected nearer the Windward

Passage. He would listen to no doubt, no hazarded question on the matter. James retired to his cabin.

When he came on deck again to take the morning watch, at four o'clock, he found Rennie absent. The duty quartermaster informed him that Rennie had not been seen through the night.

'He has at last allowed himself to sleep,' James said to himself. To the duty quartermaster: 'How does she lie, Jarrett? What is our speed?' &c., &c.

At eight bells of the watch, with hammocks piped up and the ship at its breakfast, James was relieved by Mr Peak, and he went below to give Rennie an account of the last glass of the watch. The lookouts had quartered the horizon and found nothing. The ship was now in the open waters of the bay, well to the north of Gonaves Isle, making west-by-north-west and a point west for the Windward Passage. He found Rennie sitting at his desk in the great cabin, unshaven and ghastly ill, in his nightshirt, sucking at a can of tea.

'I have ordered sail shortened, sir, as there is a squall approaching us from the south——'

'Shortened sail!' His hand trembled as he put down the can on the desk. 'We are in a chase, and you have shortened *sail*?' A stale smell came off him, floated off him—stale sweat, stale breath, hints of stale urine, and a general sourness. The trembling, James now observed, was not confined to his hand, but was there through his frame entire.

'You are ill, sir, I think.'

'I am not in the least ill, not at all. I have merely overslept . . . ohhh!' He raised his hand clutching to his head, and knocked over the can of tea on the desk, where it spilled through papers. James moved quickly to his side, righted the can and removed it.

'Jesu Christ,' little above a whisper, 'my head pains me, and I am d-deathly cold . . .'

'You are ill, sir. I must help you to your cot. You must lie down and rest. Sentry!'

'I cannot lie down, damn you.' Without conviction, shivering violently. He allowed himself to be half-supported, half-carried to his sleeping cabin, and helped into his hanging cot. James ordered the marine on duty to pass the word for the doctor. Soon Thomas Wing came to the great cabin, his own face grey with exhaustion. He examined Rennie, and emerged to surprise James:

'It is not the fever, thank God. It is rather I think an adverse bodily response to coca. I gave him *Erythroxylon coca* leaf, at his earnest request, so that he might stay awake. He has eaten too freely of it, and now he suffers.'

The squall when it rushed over *Expedient* was nearly too much for her. As first lieutenant, with his captain indisposed, James had returned to the quarterdeck to aid young Peak. James had ordered the guns double-bowsed, and all hatches battened down and secured, but the wind came whirling with such violent force that the ship heeled far over, only righting herself because of an equally sudden lull, followed by deluging rain. The wind returned in tearing gusts, formidable in strength, unpredictable in duration. The sea grew chopped, and troubled, and the ship pitched heavy—a flaw in frigates—thudding into troughs and heeling on the lift, running blind. With dozens of men sick, many of them rated ordinary and able, the topmen were short-handed and James fretted on the quarterdeck, bellowed through his speaking trumpet, was drenched, half-drowned, clinging to a backstay, turning his head to leeward in the savage blasts of the wind so that he could breathe.

'If we don't drown in the sea, we shall drown in the rain.'

The wheel was double-manned on the weather, double-manned on the lee, each man struggling to hold the ship to her course. A clewline block tore loose on the mizzen topsail yard, tumbled, dangled, whipped crazily over their heads in a swooping arc, flung out to larboard, smashed like a roundshot into the lift of a wave, and was lost.

'Secure that line, there!' bellowed James, but his voice was entirely lost in the hissing scythe of the wind, and he turned his attention to the men at the wheel. The ship heeled and plunged, and a huge sea rode up over the lee, drowning the chains and lower shrouds, seething aft and surging over the hances.

'Hold her steady! Hold her steady!'

The four men at the helm struggled to stay on their legs, with the sea sucking at their ankles; they clung to the spokes, fighting the wheel, straining against the deep shivers of the rudder—and felt the wheel go slack in their hands. The ship shuddered, at once became uneasy, and began to wallow and drift.

'The weather rope has parted, sir!' The leading helmsman.

'Put your helm over!' bellowed James.

The ship rode up in a brief lull—and helm over was managed.

'Hook up the relieving tackles! Jump, there!'

Again managed, and the wind struck once more, with renewed and vengeful violence. The main hatch cover tore away, the battens dislodged. The boats on the skids over the waist began to bounce and jostle in their fastenings, another huge sea rode over the lee, and James lost his footing, clung for his life, saw his speaking trumpet slither away and submerge, and then his mouth and nose filled with water and he began to choke.

'If I did not die in that damned flood, I will not die here.' A thought, a defiant thought, and he gained a purchase with his right foot, kicked, lifted himself, and coughed, spluttered and gasped his way to breath. 'Mr Peak!'

No response. Water sliding over the deck in frothing fans, and sluicing over the side. The wind roaring aloft. '*Mr Peak!*'

'Sir . . . ?' A bedraggled figure.

'Hands to man the pumps! Hands to secure the main hatch! Jump now! Jump!'

Being told to jump like a midshipman did not sit well with

the junior lieutenant, but he was too miserable, too buffeted by the storm to take umbrage, and did as he was told.

In half a glass more the squall had blown itself out, and the ship was again secure. The tiller ropes were repaired, under the stern eye of the boatswain, the main hatch newly secured, and running repairs carried out to the rigging. The launch had been damaged. There was too much water in the well, and the pumps would have to be manned the next watch through. Aside from these minor difficulties *Expedient* had weathered the storm well, and she was safe. James shook out his canvas and sailed on, with the wind on the starboard quarter. At two bells the captain came on deck. He had made an attempt to shave, and had cut his chin. There was blood on his shirt. His face was still ghastly pale, and his hands shook.

'Well well, Mr Hayter, we have had a brisk little blow.' Sniffing deep, and attempting to appear hale, and alert, and altogether in possession of himself. He clasped his hands behind his back, stepped forward, lost his balance, staggered—and was supported upright by Mr Peak.

'What the bloody hell d'y'mean by grasping my arm, Mr Peak!' Furiously shaking himself free. 'D'ye seek to restrain me, sir?'

'No, sir! No indeed! I wished only—only to come to your aid, sir.'

'Aid! Aid! Am I in need of aid on deck, like a bloody drunken landman idler, damn you!'

'No, sir. I am very sorry.'

'You may go below!'

'Very good, sir.' His hat off and on, his very wet hat.

'Who is that midshipman aft?' To James, then twisting his head to peer. 'I have never seen him before today. Who is he?'

'Mr Delingpole, sir.'

'Eh? Delingpole?' Another sniff. 'Ah, yes, you are quite right. Mr Delingpole!'

'Sir?' Hurrying.

'Kindly go below and ask my steward to send up a can of tea. I will like it hot, say to him, and not his wretched tepid half-stewed slovenly excuse for hot. You have me?'

'Yes, sir.'

'Jump, then.' And as Delingpole hurried away: 'Uncommon thin, that boy, and ungainly tall. Now then—how does she lie?'

James told him, and began giving him a report of damage and repairs, &c., but Rennie waved this impatiently aside, and 'Lookouts? How many men is posted at the masthead?' Shading his eye, looking aloft.

'I relieved the men that was aloft in the storm, and have only now sent replacements——'

'Only now? That is very bad, Mr Hayter. That ship is there. That ship is out there, somewhere ahead of us, and we must find her.'

'And so we shall.'

'What? What d'y'mean by that?'

'I mean—that we shall find the ship,' shaking his head briefly, 'if it is there.'

'Do not shake your head at me, sir! Am I surrounded by insolence, and wretched——'

'Sir, here is your tea.'

Rennie drank his tea, glanced aloft at the mizzen topsail, rubbed his cheek, worried at his cut chin, looked at his fingers, glanced aloft again, and presently:

'Mr Hayter.'

James said something to the quartermaster, and moved aft to the captain's side. 'Sir?'

'Yes, James, I was perhaps a little hasty just now, you know, and I—well, I hope that you did not take it ill.'

'I did not, sir.'

'Very good.' A sideways glance, and he noticed a stain on James's shirt. 'Are you hurt? There is blood at your shoulder.'

James peered down at his shoulder, felt there at the back,

and winced. 'It must have happened when I fell in the squall. It is an old injury opened.'

'I should ask Wing to look at it, if I was you. Such things cannot be neglected in this climate. I will keep the deck.'

'Very good, thank you, sir.'

'And whilst you are there, I will like you to make an assessment of the sick men. How many is genuinely sick with fever, and so forth. Perhaps we can think of relieving distress by slinging hammocks on deck at night, if that will answer. We must do what we can for them.'

'Will you not go below yourself, sir, and say a word to the sick? It would cheer——'

'No no, I do not wish to see Wing at present.' Lowering his voice: 'I don't mind saying this to you, James—the fellow has poisoned me. I asked him for something to keep me alert, and he gave me a noxious weedish mouth-numbing poisonous root, or leaf, or plant, good God. I cannot quite forgive him, when we are in a chase. No no, James, you go below and make your judgement, and then report to me, will you? We must know to a man how short-handed we are.'

'Very good, sir.'

The conditions he found now on the lower deck were very shocking to James. Used as he was to the foetid atmosphere of many men confined in a dark, poorly ventilated place, the added stench of illness—of faeces, urine, sour sweat, of saturated hammocks and befouled clothing—repelled and disgusted him after the clean saline air of the quarterdeck, and he had to pinch shut his nose. Added to the smell were the shivering moans and mutterings of delirium, and the sounds of retching. The sailmaker's mate was sewing shrouds.

'How many dead?' James asked the doctor.

Thomas Wing sighed, wiped his filth-slathered hands on a piece of cotton waste, and said: 'Three have died in the night, and a fourth died in the storm. Many more will die this day, I fear. Cannot we open the hatches, and allow in air? We are very wretched indeed down here.'

'I will see that is done, Doctor. How many men is confined with fever?'

'Forty-seven, the last count. It cannot fail to rise.'

'Thank you, Doctor.' A grim nod.

'And now let me look at your injury, Lieutenant.'

'I will not trouble you with such a trivial thing, at present.' Quickly, glancing down at the doctor's hands. 'I must report to the captain.'

'He is out of his cot? Up and about?'

'Oh yes,' a half-smile, 'and complaining that you have poisoned him, Thomas.'

The relief as he came up the ladder into the sunlight of the open waist—into fresh sea air and the sounds of the world, of wind in rigging and the rinsing smack of waves—was like the lifting of a sentence of death. He had glimpsed the pit of hell, and was set free. He did not feel free long. Rennie paced the quarterdeck, vexedly paced, his glass under his arm.

'Your servant is in great trouble, James. He was caught pilfering, and then attacked the master-at-arms.'

'Archimedes? I am sure there is some mistake, sir——'

'There is no mistake, but I cannot attend to it now. Tell me the number of fever cases.'

'Forty-seven, and four dead.'

'Christ, half an hundred men. How in God's name are we to handle her, and bring her to action, if this should continue?'

'I fear that it will continue. Thomas Wing says so, and I have seen for myself the condition of the stricken men. I will like to open the fore hatch and rig a windsail, with your permission, sir.'

'It is willingly given, James.' And he nodded and went below, leaving his lieutenant to ponder the difficult matter of Archimedes and pilfering. Presently James sent for the master-at-arms, John Painter, and learned the substance of the accusation. Archimedes, who had concealed himself in the breadroom aft when he first came into the ship, had apparently continued to go down there and avail himself of its contents. When the master-at-arms, learning of it, upbraided him——

'Forcefully, master-at-arms?'

'Aye, forceful enough, sir. And he——'

'You did not strike him?'

'I did not, sir. I hupbraided him, only. He thereupon drew a pistol from under his shirt, and presented it at my head—cocked, at my head.'

'He did that?' Surprised.

'He most cert'ly did, sir. Whencefore, he was at once placed under arrest by the ship's corporal, sir, and the marine guard summoned.'

'Very well, thank you, Painter. Where is he now?'

'Confined in the orlop, sir. Shackled in irons.'

'Yes, I see, thank you.'

James now sent for the sailmaker and arranged to have the windsail rigged at the fore hatch, then went below to the orlop, and saw Archimedes. He was indignant and miserable in the stinking darkness, and blinked in the glow of the lantern James carried with him.

'James, James, f'God's sake now, tell them to let me go. I am a free man. Look, you could let me go, by takin' off these iron t'ings. Why have they put me down heer in chains?'

James crouched beside him. 'You cannot attempt to pistol the master-at-arms, Archimedes, when he is simply doing his duty.'

'But I was only takin' a biscuit or two. Why not? There is plenty, and I am workin' my passage in the ship, as a free man. Why did he try to seize me?'

'It is the duty of the master-at-arms to keep order among the people, and prevent pilfering. I am very sorry, but I cannot release you. The captain must decide what punishment you will suffer.'

'Punishment?' Hurt and surprised.

'I am very sorry. I cannot prevent it, I fear. I did not know you was still armed, else I should have took your pistol away for safe keeping, until we reached England.'

'But it is *my* pistol. Why should I not have a pistol to proteck m'self? Alls I took was a biscuit, and he tried to seize me.'

A sigh. 'Theft in one of His Majesty's ships—any sort of theft, of anything—is looked on with great disfavour, Archimedes. I will do what I can to plead your case—in least you did not *fire* the pistol—but I fear I must warn you that the captain may be very severe.'

'You mean—he will beat me?' Tears of anger and bewilderment stood in his eyes in the dim light. 'You will allow him to beat me, James?'

Another sigh, and sadly: 'It ain't a question of my *allowing* anything, you see. I am not in command. The captain is in command, and it is the captain will decide.'

'Oh, but why will y'not proteck me, James? If you would just hide me in your cabin, then these fellows could not reach me, or beat me.'

'I will do what I can for you, Archimedes, but it may probably be very little—too little.' And he rose and left him there in the darkness. He climbed the ladder and went straightway to see the captain. Rennie refused to discuss the matter, beyond:

'There is a great many more important things to occupy me, James,' with a hint of exasperation, 'and to occupy you, and all of us.' Holding up a hand before James could speak again. 'In due course he will be dealt with on the list of defaulters, at divisions. And now that will do, if y'please.'

'Very good, sir. I will only say that I would not now be here, in this ship, alive——'

'Did not you hear me, Mr Hayter? There is more important things! As an instance, our chase is slipping away. If we do not find her soon she will meet that damned frigate, deliver up Laycock, and we shall lose everything. I shall face a court martial, and in all probability be cashiered. With how much favour d'y'think your own position in the service will then be looked upon, hm? You will likely remain a lieutenant, on the beach, on miserable half-pay, the rest of your life. Only consider: a lieutenant still, at fifty; you and your wife living like paupers, in two cramping rooms, at let us say Deal; old age and bitterness—bitterness and deep regret—your whole reward.'

'You forget, sir, my father has given me a house. It is in Dorset, very far from Deal.'

'You will never keep it, on a lieutenant's half-pay. You will be forced to sell, to pay your debts, and then to sit on the outside of the coach, in the cold and rain, in your threadbare blue coat, all the bitter way to Deal.'

'It sounds as if you will like me to die of the consumption, sir, in the bargain.'

'You wish to make jokes, at such a moment! When we both face ruin! You are a bloody——'

'De-e-e-e-ck! Two sail of ships, fine on the larboard bow, hull down!' Ringing down from aloft.

The two officers stared at each other a moment, their mouths open, then both jumped together for the companion ladder, petulant dispute forgotten.

The island of Cuba fifty mile to the north-west, the Windward Passage half that distance, and the two ships ahead —now coming hull up—sailing into that passage together. *Expedient* gaining on them, the wind on her beam and quarter.

'Why do they continue together?' mused Rennie. 'Why?'

James, descended from the main crosstrees—where he had gone to look for himself through his long glass from the best point of observation in the ship—came to the quarterdeck and asked:

'We cannot be quite sure of them as the ships we seek, can we, sir? They are both three-masted, certainly, and one might possibly be a frigate, but——'

Rennie, who did not like very often to go aloft himself—an

aversion to heights had persisted from his earliest days at sea—interrupted dismissively:

'That is our chase, and the frigate, I will stake my warrant of commission.'

'Very good, sir.' Glass under arm, very correct.

'You do not agree with me?' Rennie turned his head at an angle.

'I will not presume to disagree with you, sir.'

'However . . . ?' Raising his own glass.

'Well, sir—with respect, I think you was of the opinion that if the ships we seek made rendezvous, they would soon after part company, and——'

'Yes yes, well well, they have not parted.' Impatiently, lowering his glass, then, pointing: '*That weather stunsail is not properly sheeted home! How are we to overhaul these buggering villains without we bend our canvas to harness the wind, for Christ's sake!*'

'We are short-handed in the tops, sir.' James found and raised his speaking trumpet, then lowered it unused as he watched the offence quickly put right by a seaman who hauled home the sheet, securing the clew of the sail to the boom so that the leech curved full and clean. James turned to Rennie and was surprised to find him chuckling.

'He felt my foot in his arse, that topman, by God, ha-ha-ha. We will pipe the hands to dinner early, Mr Hayter. I do not want men handling the ship, nor fighting the guns, without meat in their bellies.'

'Very good, sir.'

'Straightway after we will beat to quarters, and exercise the great guns in a continuum until we engage.'

'Aye, sir, very good. Mr Tangible!'

When the orders had been given, and acted upon, James said to Rennie: 'May I have your permission to release my servant, sir?'

'Eh?' Peering through his glass, lowering it, distracted. 'Mr Dobie!'

Alan Dobie, peremptorily summoned, came on deck. 'Sir?'

'I will like you to stand by with your pen, or a pencil will do, to make a rough drawing of my plan of tactics in the coming action.'

'Drawing, sir?' Puzzled. 'I am certainly able to make accurate notations, but I——'

'I do not require you t'make dainty drawing-room sketches, with cherubs puffing wind, Mr Dobie. A rough rendering of the plan will do very well.'

'Yes, sir.'

James again pressed the captain. 'My servant, sir. May I release him?'

'What?' Half-turning, glancing aloft.

'I think he will be of much greater use to us released, than kept in irons——'

'No no no, he has attacked a warranted man. I cannot countenance that in my ship.'

'He is strong, a good shot, a good fighter. We are short-handed——'

'No, I am not inclined to change my mind. Mr Loftus! Where is the master when I want him? You there!' Singling out a boy. 'Find Mr Loftus and tell him—— No no, belay that. Ask him, with my compliments, to come and see me as soon as he is able. Jump now.'

A slight haze falling over the sea, and the wind lessening a little, as the men ate their early dinner, the noon formalities were dispensed with quickly, and Rennie remained on his quarterdeck. Presently he said:

'Before we beat to quarters, I will address the people. Muster them in the waist, if y'please.'

The calls, and all able-bodied men—seamen, marines, idlers—assembled to hear the captain's address. Rennie stood at the breast rail, as James reported to him that all hands were on deck and lifted his hat. Rennie removed his hat, was silent a moment, and swept their faces with a purposeful gaze.

'Soon, today or on the morrow, *Expedient* may come to

fight an action. I will not conceal from you that this action may be very hard. We are not at war, but a great deal is at stake. In one of the ships ahead an Englishman in the employ of the King is held prisoner. His captors will not give him up without a bitter struggle. We must rescue him. That is our task. We are short-handed, with fever in the ship—fever is an enemy in any ship—but our real enemy lies ahead. We must defeat that enemy, in the King's name, in England's name—in *Expedient*'s name. I will expect from you, as you will expect from me, courage—real fighting courage, no matter how fierce our foe. Together we will out-sail, out-gun, out-fight him—and we shall win! And now, Expedients all, we will give three cheers for King George, for England, and for our ship!'

'HUZZAY! HUZZAY! HUZZAY!'

Not for the first time all James's doubts about Rennie—his judgement, his sometimes vacillating belief in the commission and his duty, his resolution—were washed away by the simple and direct way in which he appealed to his men. Irascible as he was from time to time, absurd even, in some of his pronouncements, he knew and understood seamen, and could make them believe in him.

'What has he offered them?' James asked himself. 'Not prize money, not glory neither; nothing but a hard and bitter fight, and yet they cheered him to the echo—and meant it, too.'

Rennie replaced his hat. 'Mr Tangible!'

'Sir?'

'We will clear for action!'

Early in the afternoon a brief ceremony—under sail—to bury the dead. *Expedient* sailed on, the wind steady, and the great guns were exercised—run out in the tackles, but not fired—a dozen times and more. A lone seabird joined the ship, hovering at the level of the main topsail yard, and kept pace, with delicate balancing flutters and dips of its wings, high there alongside, until the lookout in the cross-trees bellowed:

'De-e-e-ck! The two ships turn to the north-east, and beat to windward!'

The bird wheeled up and away in alarm, fled down to the wavetops and skimmed away to the west over the wide sea. On the quarterdeck Rennie nodded, his mouth turning down a little, nodded and sniffed, and said: 'Aye, they are making for the Caicos Passage, and away into the Atlantick. Hm. Have they not seen us? They must have seen us, and yet they have not attempted to part company one from t'other, nor have they attempted to outrun us. Mr Lamarr!'

'Sir?' The midshipman ran and stood, and made his back straight.

'Look out my Colours Confused, will you?'

'C-colours—confused, sir?'

'Aye, you heard me right. Ask the sailmaker, he knows what to give me.'

'Yes, sir.' Dashing away.

Ten minutes and the Colours Confused—red, white and blue ensign, jack and pennant, of eccentric design, blocks and stripes of colour representing no particular nation, in fact no nation at all—were run up to flutter in the wind, replacing the British colours, and Rennie ordered: 'Port your helm!' *Expedient* came about into the wind, and began to track north-east-by-north towards the other ships. By late afternoon, with the sun a red glare in the west, he had to concede that:

'We have gained, but we cannot overhaul them before nightfall. We must assume that they will sail on together, since they have done so all today. We must assume also that they will keep to their present heading.' A sigh, and he flexed his stiffened shoulders. 'Very good, very good—we will stand down, Mr Hayter, and the men may go to their supper. It is late, but there was need to exercise the great guns, which they have done tolerable well today—they have benefited from it—and now they must not be deprived of their food and grog any longer.'

'Very good, sir.'

'I will like you to take supper with me. Mr Loftus and Mr Peak will join us, and Mr Dobie.'

In the great cabin Rennie laid out his proposed tactics, aided by Alan Dobie's neatly executed drawings of ship movements, wind direction, speed close-hauled, &c.

'We must take and keep the weather gage, that is the key.' Rennie leaned over the table, with Mr Loftus, James, young Peak and Mr Dobie grouped about. 'When we have overhauled them tomorrow morning, I mean to rake the merchantman's stern, rake and smash his rudder, and disable him. That will leave him helpless, and we can then engage the frigate—that is to say, if the frigate wishes to engage.'

'May I put a question, sir?'

'Yes, Mr Loftus, by all means.' Waiting, an eyebrow lifted.

'Well, sir, with respect, I feel that I must raise a particular matter again: should not we—well, should not we in least make an attempt to speak to the merchant ship? You have surmised that the Reverend Laycock is in that ship, but——'

'It is more than surmise, I think. It is assumption based on high probability.' Evenly.

'Very well, sir, assumption . . . but if the reverend gentleman ain't in her, then we really have not got any reasonable grounds to attack—have we?'

'Hm, hm, hm.' A musing nod or two. 'If he ain't in the merchant ship, then he is certainly in the frigate, instead. The question to concern us, therefore, is what to do if the two ships should decide to part company in the night, and each run away in a separate direction. What are we to do then, gentlemen? *That* is a question to ask, hey?'

'May I ask another, sir?' James, politely, and when Rennie turned to him: 'Why do they sail on in line together—at all?'

'Hm . . . hm . . .' Rennie tapped the drawings. 'Anybody else? Do you wish to put a question, Mr Peak?'

'I—I have never yet fought in an action, sir. May I ask: is it thought usual for an officer to assist at a gun if some of the crew is killed? Assist in hauling on tackles, or in handing cartridge, or worming?'

'That is the best question I have heard today, Mr Peak.' Approvingly. 'The answer is yes, certainly. You are a sea officer in a fighting ship. When we fight our guns, and men suffer injury or death, others must take their places, including officers if the numbers hurt or killed is very great. The purpose of an action at sea is a very simple one—to prevail. We prevail by doing our duty, every last man.'

'Thank you, sir.'

'You are easier in your mind, now?'

'Not easier, sir, exact. I am clearer in my mind.'

'Very good. I will like men placed at the gangways to make certain that tacks and sheets is clear in going about, if they can be spared——'

A commotion on deck, far forrard, shouts and running feet, then a boy came breathless to the door, with a message:

'What is it? Speak up, now.' Rennie, turning.

'Captain, sir—a man——'

'Man overboard, sir!' Mr Delingpole, appearing behind him.

It was Archimedes. He had insisted on being brought in chains from the orlop to the heads, in the prow of the ship, to relieve himself on the seat of ease. He would not suffer the indignities of emptying his bowels in a bucket in darkness, below. Reluctantly his marine guard had brought him to the heads, and allowed him to make his way to the head stool. Archimedes had then contrived by rapid hopping to leap over the netting, skid off the starboard boomkin, and plunge straight down into the sea. He had made no sound, but had stared fiercely at the marine as he made his leap.

Rennie would not lose way and go about, at James's earnest and urgent request, nor would he heave to and lower a boat. As they stood looking aft on the quarterdeck, at the rail:

'He was in irons James, shackled in irons. He could not swim, he could only sink. He was lost the moment he stepped off the bow.'

'What in the name of heaven made him do it?' James, quietly, turning from the rail.

'I do not know that. That damned marine should have known better than to grant him his wish.'

'No, it ain't the marine's fault, sir. He was merely doing his duty, and escorting his prisoner. No, I think that if anyone is to blame, it is myself——'

'You!' Looking at him. 'Good heaven, you are not to blame.'

'He was my servant. He was the man that had saved my life. I should have protected him.'

'How? How?'

'By releasing him from his chains when he asked me to do so.'

'Now then, now then.' Severely. 'I had forbade it. He was in irons for his offence, and you could not have released him without my direct consent. For good reason I did not give it.'

'No, sir,' very subdued, 'but had I wished to preserve his life, as I should have wished—I would have done it all the same.'

'You astonish me. An escaped slave? That attacked the master-at-arms with a pistol?'

'He thought I was his *friend*. And as his friend I failed him, failed him . . .'

Rennie, seeing his lieutenant's great distress, was silent a moment. He hesitated, then placed a hand on James's shoulder. 'You must put it from your mind.' No longer severe. 'What is done is done—and we are in a chase. Mr Abey!'

'Sir?'

'You may take my night glass, and jump up to the

mainmast cross-trees. Relieve the lookout, and make a thorough search ahead for stern lights. The moment you see anything, you are to call down to the deck.'

'I will go with Mr Abey, with your permission, sir.'

'As you like, James, as you wish—only take care not to fall in the sea, hey? I cannot afford to lose you.'

Rennie had been prepared to press on during the night—if he could see lights ahead. However, rain now obscured the view from the cross-trees, and all hope of observing the stern lights of the chases was lost. Soon that rain swept over *Expedient*, and James descended to the deck, bringing Mr Abey with him.

Rennie was obliged now to be careful. To the north-west lay Great Inagua, to the north-east lay the innumerable treacherous cays of the Caicos Bank—and alternative passages: the Caicos Passage, and the Turks Passage. He reduced sail, and placed men in the chains, reduced sail further, when the weather closed in, and at last decided to drop anchor and ride out the night.

'They cannot but do the same. No seaman but a lunatic would attempt to make headway in these waters, in these conditions. We must await the morrow, and daylight.'

Daylight, first light, and further curtaining rain, which cleared by hammocks up—revealing ahead a clear and open sea, with no sign of their quarry. At 21 degrees 34 minutes north, and 72 degrees 29 minutes west, *Expedient* now under way, Rennie grey-faced and fretful on his quarterdeck.

'I cannot believe they sailed on, in weather-blind darkness. They must certainly have sought refuge somewhere, in a bay, or an anchorage among the cays.' He went fretfully below to consult his charts, and emerged fretfully to harry his look-outs, demand soundings from the men in the chains, and pace about like a guard dog chained—that knows a pair of villains is concealed nearby. At three bells of the forenoon watch, three glasses during which no one had dared to approach his stalking, hunched figure, at three bells he paused at the rail, glass under arm, shrugged, and:

'They have escaped. We will head north-east-by-east, and a point east, for the Turk Isles Passage into the Atlantick, and pray to God they have done the same thing before us. Damnation!'

James did not attempt to point out, either facetiously or otherwise, that the contradiction of entreaty and hellfire combined would not likely aid them. He was in sombre mood still, made the more sombre by Thomas Wing's report:

'Nine further cases of fever, including Mr Duggan, and the master-at-arms. And five men have died in the night, including, I regret to——'

'There! I said it was that damned escaped slave of yours brought fever into the ship! He did well to throw himself over the side, by God, only it was too late!' Rennie, savagely to James, wishing to vent his frustration upon someone living. This unjust and intemperate snarl James let pass. His concern now, as first lieutenant, his chief concern was the depletion of able men to handle the ship and to fight her guns, should *Expedient* come to action after all.

'We must bury the dead, sir. May I arrange that, at once?' Crisply efficient.

'What? Yes yes. Mr Cross!'

The doctor began: 'Mr Cross has——'

'Are you still here, Doctor? Have not you duties below? Mr Cross! Where is the master's mate?'

Raising his voice to a firm carrying tone: 'Sir, Mr Cross has died in the night.'

'Young Cross?' Turning.

'Yes, sir. He——'

'Why was I not told? I required you to inform me glass by glass of all such events, Doctor!'

'Will you be calm, a moment?'

'What did y'say! What!' Tearing off his hat.

Thomas Wing, tired as he was, saddened and worn and tired, was unable to prevent a rise of near fury: 'I required you to be calm, and to listen to me! Mr Cross sickened late yesterday, and died in the midnight watch. I did my utmost to save so young and pleasant a fellow, as I make attempt to save every poor fellow that comes under my care, good God, what else would you expect of me?' A breath. 'I administered willow bark, but alas he was unable to keep it inside him.'

Rennie, taken aback, and finding himself abashed: 'Ah. Ah. That is a remedy?'

'A remedy, no. A relieving agent, sometimes. It failed to relieve him, and I lost him. Fever is a virulent affliction, once it has took hold. Smallpox may be inoculated against, but we have no cure, no remedy, for the fever.'

'No, just so.' A pause. 'Thank you, Doctor.'

'I—I must beg your pardon, for losing my temper.'

'No no, you was merely making your report.' A nod, a sniff. 'I may perhaps have been hasty myself.' And he put on his hat, and went to the rail. 'In the chains, there!'

Mr Storey came on deck, just as the doctor went below. Rennie saw him, and beckoned to him.

'I would wish, after all this damp weather, to worm and reload all of our guns, with your permission, sir.'

'Very well, Mr Storey, you may do so, by section, with your own crew.' An afterthought. 'Was not the lead aprons placed over the locks?'

'Yes, they was, but it is the atmosphere entire that is damp, and we need dry powder in our cartridge, from the filling-room.'

'Aye, very well. Save what powder you can, will you, Mr Storey, that is not spoiled?'

A day, and a night, and another morning dawned, and *Expedient* was now passed through the Turks Isle Passage, all the treacherous cays and reefs far astern, the Caicos to larboard, Grand Turk away to starboard—all far astern, and the ship in the Atlantick, 22 degrees and 10 minutes north, 71 degrees and 30 minutes west.

The lower deck half-filled with sick men, trembling, sweating, jaundiced men, with hope faded in their dazing eyes. Rennie all but despairing now, though he endeavoured not to show anything of his emotions on deck. James knew that he must support his captain, even if—as now looked very probable—their chase should end in emptiness, in the overcast, rolling, empty sea, stretching away to rain squalls and sun shafts in the half-lost distance.

Rennie had ceased to drink wine, and drank only tea, by the quart. He ate next to nothing. His steward brought him snacks unbidden, and received nothing but irascible complaint for his trouble:

'D'ye attempt to stodge up my guts with this biscuit? I have no need of sustenance at all, at present, d'y'hear? My mind must be clear and alert. The chase is my sustenance.'

And: 'Why d'ye bring me this heavy, bloating pie, and wedges of cheese? Hey?'

And: 'Is this wine you have brought to me, you damn' fool?'

Until Cutton, not a man in usual given to depressive thoughts, or low self-opinion, was driven below to his kennel like a whipped cur.

'Why does he take it out of me, when alls I'm atrying to do is feed the bugger?' he asked the ship's boy assigned to assist him.

'Perhaps you never smiled at 'im, Colley, when you give 'im the dish.'

'Oo give you permission to address me as Colley, you impudent dwarf?'

'Ouch! I ain't a dwarf!'

'D-e-e-e-e-ck! Two sail of ship, hull down!'

'Where away?'

'Fine on the larboard bow!'

And presently: 'Cutton! *Cutton!* Where is my damned slothful steward when I want him?'

Colley Cutton hurried on deck. 'Sir?'

'Ah, there you are at last. Have you nothing for me to eat, man?'

'I—I had only jus' brought the pie below, sir, that you did not wish——'

'Have you no notion yet of my pattern of life, good God! Something to eat, and a flask. Cheerly, Cutton, cheerly! I am famished!' Striding to the wheel. 'Luff and touch her—and hold her so. Lookout, there! What ships are they?'

More rain, and the ships ahead obscured. Rennie, with Bernard Loftus's anxious assistance, crowded on sail, and *Expedient*—pitching and groaning with complaint—beat towards those ships, smashing waves into fans of spray, as rain streamed down on her decks. A glass, two glasses, the squall passed, the sun lit everything with a sudden bright clarity, and there much closer were the two ships. The first lieutenant now on the quarterdeck, in his working clothes.

'D-e-e-e-e-ck! They are hove to, together! Three leagues distant, fine on the bow!'

'Hove to?' puzzled Rennie. 'Hove to? Then it cannot be our quarry . . . that must still be running.'

'Unless they are not aware of us, sir.'

'Eh?'

'Is it not possible, even probable, that they do not *know* they are chased?'

'No no, I do not think that probable, at all. This is two quite separate ships, quite different, other ships. Else they would not likely have hove to, and——'

'One ship is a frigate!' The lookout.

'Frigate! You are certain!' Calling up.

'Three masts, and one deck of guns, sir!' Calling down.

'James, I will take it very kind if you will jump up to the masthead, and see for yourself. Take my glass.'

'I have my own long glass, thank you, sir. It is the work of a moment.' He went forrard to the weather main chains, swung easily into the shrouds, and went quickly aloft, pulling himself hand over hand, his glass slung safe inside his piratical jerkin. Rennie watched him anxiously. His aversion to going aloft himself was very strong. He could push himself to do so if the occasion absolutely demanded it, but the experience was always severely taxing to him, and unpleasant. He watched James swing into the futtock shrouds of the main top, hang upside down a moment, then haul himself up into the top. A moment later he was running up to the cross-trees by the topmast shrouds, and then he stood beside the lookout, unshipped his glass, focused, and studied the ships far ahead.

Rennie peered up, shading his eyes. James remained there a minute or two, put his glass away inside his jerkin, waited for the roll, then stepped off—apparently—into thin air and certain death. Instead he had wound his leg round a backstay, and now slid effortlessly to the deck. When he stepped away from the backstay his jerkin and britches were stained with long streaks of tar.

'It ain't a thing to do in a dress coat,' lightly, wiping his tarry hands, 'but it saves a modicum of time in other rig.'

'Hm, just so. Well?'

'It is the frigate, sir, and the merchant vessel. I am nearly certain they have not seen us. My sense is . . .'

'Yes yes, go on.'

'Well, I cannot swear to it, in course, when we are still an hour and more distant—but I think they may be suffering difficulty of some kind.'

'They are damaged?'

'I don't say that, sir. I could just make out boats, between, but . . .' A breath. 'No, it is the way the ships lie, almost as if they was not managed or handled with any care. I cannot be more specific than that, sir, I fear. It is just a—a sense.'

'Well well, it is to our advantage, if they are in trouble. That makes them easier prey, hm?'

'Aye, indeed.'

'Very good, James, thank you. Mr Tangible! We will beat to quarters, and clear the ship for action!'

Expedient managed, with the assistance of frequent masking showers of rain, to approach to within half a league of the two stationary ships before she was seen, confirming the first lieutenant's opinion that they had not been aware of being chased, until now. And now the confused activity between the ships—boats round and crossing between—became frantic, even hectic activity. Yards were braced round, sails unbrailed, and boats either clumsily hauled in by tackles—one dangled and swung at a steep angle—or allowed to drift astern to be towed. Neither ship was worked with seamanlike efficiency; neither came to the wind swiftly. Both were:

'Handled very poor, James.' Lowering his glass. 'Did y'see how the frigate braced her main and mizzen yards? Christ's blood, that was wretched badly done.' Cheerfully. 'If that is how they handle their ships in the French navy we shall have no trouble from that quarter. Mr Lamarr!'

'Sir?'

'We will hoist our own true colours. There is no longer need for *confusion*, ha-ha.' Bracing his legs, sniffing deep. 'I smell an easier triumph than I had anticipated, James. We shall have the Reverend Laycock safe in the ship, eating his dinner among English friends, in no time at all.'

'I hope you are right, sir.'

'Well well, I have been right thus far, hey?' Jerking his head confidently. 'We have chased them—aye, and caught them too—just as I have always said we would.'

'And, now?'

'What?'

'Which ship should we attack, sir?'

'Why, good heaven, James—the American, in course, as we agreed in our tactical plan.'

'Sir, might not we give them a recognised signal, first? A gun?'

'I hope that between you, you and Mr Loftus, you do not attempt to thwart me in this, James? I hope that you have not allowed your feet to freeze, and your testicles to shrivel up?'

'Indeed no, sir. However, when you come to record today's events in your journal, officially and precisely record them, will not you wish to describe a proceeding that was entirely justifiable, and honourable, in all particulars?'

'In other words—you wish to save me from myself, from my own folly?'

'My only wish, sir, as I am sure it is yours—is to prevent bloody loss of life, if that were possible.'

'Very well, very well, we will do everything nice and polite, and try to save lives. We will give them a gun.'

'Thank you, sir.'

'And then when they ignore it—as they most certainly will—we will do our duty, and rescue Mr Laycock.'

The gun was fired. Neither ship responded, except to continue to make sail, the frigate now a little ahead of the merchantman.

'Very well. We are on the larboard tack, to windward. We will come about through the wind and cut across the American's stern on the starboard tack, and smash his rudder as our guns bear.'

'Very good, sir.'

'I will then like to go about on the larboard tack, and engage the frigate, while we still have the wind gage.'

'Very good, sir. *Hands to tack ship!*' Striding to the binnacle, speaking trumpet raised. 'Cheerly, now! Weather braces, stretch along! Lee tacks, weather sheets, lee bowlines—haul through!'

Ropes clapped on to, legs, arms, backs braced, the strain taken and weight pulled.

'Down with your helm!'

The ship to the wind, still making way, but beginning to lose speed.

'Helm's a-lee! Fore sheet, foretop bowline, jib and staysail sheets—let go!'

The foresails pushing her head round, now. The world of water slowly turning about the world of wood and rope and canvas.

'Off maincourse tacks and sheets! Stand ready to clear on the gangway, there!'

The ship in the eye, still with momentum, turning, sails shivering a-flap. The sea heaving and rolling, smacking up under her hollowed lines forrard, and shattering over the bow.

'Mainsail haul!'

Main and mizzen yards braced round, mainsail and mizzensail bringing her stern through the pivoting turn.

'Let go and haul!'

Fore yards braced round, the ship now finding her feet and beginning to pick up speed on the new heading.

'Trim braces and sheets! Weather helm, bring her north-west-by-west, with the wind on your quarter!' Looking aloft, then: 'How does she lie?'

'North-west-by-west, six point large, sir, and flying free!'

'Very good. Let us make all possible speed!'

'Very handsome done, James.' Rennie, approvingly, bracing his legs as the ship heeled with the wind. 'We will need to come about just as smart on t'other tack, directly, when we have fired our broadside of guns. Boy!'

'Yes, sir?' The ship's boy, poised on his bare feet, was eager as a whippet.

'Pass the word to Mr Peak that I want our starboard battery reloaded in two minutes—*two minutes*—from the moment of firing. Jump!' Staring aloft, his eye critical. 'Lee braces, the afterguard, there!' Pacing to the breast rail, pacing back, raising his glass.

'The American follows the frigate, sir, beating to windward north-by-east.'

'He cannot turn full before we cross his stern, James. We have him, by God.'

As *Expedient* ran in to within a cable of the merchantman's stern, crossing nearly at right angles, James lifted his speaking trumpet:

'*Starboard battery—stand by to fire!*' A long, sliding moment, and on the lift: '*FIRE!*'

Flintlock lanyards jerked, the length of the tilted, sand-strewn deck, and:

BANG BANG BANG BANG BANG BANG

A fury of fire belched from the ports. Thirteen roundshot, with a total weight of 234 pounds, hissed across the sea at a thousand feet per second, and smashed the stern gallery of the merchantman into matchwood. The rudder, torn from its pintles, hung splintered and useless. Smoke drifted in boiling, hanging clouds. The stricken ship began to drift, came beam on, and now Rennie gaped in total astonishment.

Facing *Expedient* as she prepared to go about was a line of ten open gunports, with the black gaping muzzles of ten twenty-four-pounder carronades. Almost as one, in a ballooning blast of flame:

THUD THUD THUD THUD THUD THUD

Expedient's breast rail exploded in scything splinters, buckets spraying water and sand flew whirling, the binnacle disappeared in a fractured *crack* and the weather helmsman's corpse slumped headless, the neck frothing bright red blood across the quarterdeck timbers. The quartermaster lay sprawled at an angle on his back, staring up, his body unmarked.

Midshipman Lamarr stood open-mouthed and motionless,

his face spattered with blood and bloody brains, his eyes staring in terror. Rennie stumbled to his feet, felt himself for missing limbs, found all intact, and bellowed:

'*Stand by to go about! Starboard battery reload!*'

But *Expedient* had suffered more than damage to her upper works. The short-range smashing power of ten carronades had disabled four of her long guns, blasting them off the carriages and scattering gun-crew. Ten men had been killed outright, and another dozen were severely injured and disabled. Mr Delingpole, at his section under the forecastle, had lost a leg.

'We must handle the ship with even fewer men, sir. Else we cannot fight our guns.' James, his britches covered in blood splatters, splintered wood clinging in his hair.

'Mr Lamarr, you will stand to the wheel, and steer! *Stand by to go about!*'

Expedient now came about and beat to windward, the manoeuvre slow and hesitant, the ship as if in pain. And as she lay close-hauled Rennie found that the French frigate was not so clumsily handled, after all, and now had the wind advantage. An advantage great enough to have allowed her captain to swing in a long loop and run back with the wind across *Expedient* to starboard, and bring her guns to bear. *Expedient*'s starboard battery slow to reload, the crews hampered by damage and shortage of men, the decks slippery with blood, the guns reduced from thirteen to nine. The French frigate at near point-blank range.

'*Why don't the starboard battery fire?*' shouted Rennie, and at the same moment the ports of the French ship burst into flame, and *Expedient* was raked across the length of her upperworks with lethal scatterings of shot, cutting shrouds, halyards, jeers, smashing rails, fife rails, bitts. Rigging slumped and tangled. Men attempting to mount swivels at the quarterdeck rail were cut down, seamen aft hauling on falls, men on the forecastle. Shrieks, moans, chilling screams. Midshipman Lamarr, gripped the spokes of the wheel, desperate to do his duty as ordered, closed his eyes and held on, shutting out sights he could not bear.

'The bloody murderous blackguards!' Rennie, outraged. 'They are firing grape! *Why don't our guns fire, for the love of Chr——*'

BANG BANG BANG BANG BANG

Smoke, and splinters on the French frigate, but low on her strakes, with little serious damage. A crackle of small arms now, from her tops. Musket balls fizzed and cracked across *Expedient*'s deck. Rennie heard a hornet's wing and felt a blow to his head. He lifted his hand and felt a long wet stripe across his scalp. Looked at his hand distractedly, saw blood.

'Mr Hayter! Mr Hayter!'

'Aye, sir, I am here. Are you hurt?'

'No no, I am——' From the corner of his eye he saw flame explode from the French frigate's stern ports as she retreated. Then the spanker boom shook itself in half overhead, crashed over the rail in a tangle of vangs and blocks, and the sail tore wild on the gaff. At the same moment the twin **BOOM-BOOM** of long brass guns.

'We must stand away from this, James, and gather our strength, or we shall be bested.'

Perhaps it was Rennie's silent prayer, as he stumbled to the break of the quarterdeck, pulling aside ropes, blocks, canvas, perhaps it was his unmouthed prayer—or merely that share of luck that is any fighting ship's due—but a further shower of rain now moved in a billowing curtain across the sea, and in a few moments *Expedient* was alone.

Expedient repaired as best she was able—with such heavy damage, and so many injured, killed, or ill of the fever. The spanker boom was replaced, in slightly shortened form, so that now the sail could not be bent to the boom, but must be worked loose-footed. The breast rail was dismantled, and rope and cable rigged in place of the smashed timbers, for hanging buckets. Mr Adgett and his crew worked long, and shored up, plugged, tore away and repaired, and patched. A makeshift binnacle, with spare compasses brought from Bernard Loftus's stores, was rigged. The sailmaker worked without respite, aided by assigned men who could manage fid and twine. Mr Tangible's crew was likewise increased to repair *Expedient*'s shredded rigging. Mr Storey examined her smashed guns. He found that three were beyond saving, and these were heaved over the side. The fourth had suffered only shattered trucks on one side, and a broken flintlock, and these were replaced, the gun fitted with new breeching rope and tackles, and reloaded. The ship now had as her main armament twenty-two guns, and Rennie ordered the numbers evenly divided, eleven to a side. Even with fewer guns, crews would have to be reduced, but he was determined to fight his ship.

The dead were sewn in their shrouds, and put over the side without ceremony of any kind. When Alan Dobie, a little shocked by this, asked a question, his captain replied:

'We will say a prayer for them at another time, Mr Dobie, when we are not so hard pressed.'

'They deserve something more than to be thrown away like slops out of a pail, do they not, sir?'

'Yes yes, I have said so. They are not forgot, by no means. Now then, where is Adgett's lists?'

'Here, and the boatswain's also. I have made a note where the repair is incomplete as yet.'

'So you have, yes,' glancing through the lists, 'and I am grateful, thank you.—Mr Dobie.'

'Sir?' Turning at the door.

'Never think that I am an unfeeling man. We are all Expedients, every one of us, and I bitterly regret the loss of any man's life.'

Midshipman Delingpole, who had lost a leg in the action, his left leg, was in a very low condition when Rennie looked in on him—after he had looked at the other sick and wounded men. Mr Delingpole had refused tincture, he was grey-faced and sweating, and involuntary groans escaped his lips as he lay in his cramped berth. There was no room for him in a more comfortable place, owing to the great numbers of incapacitated seamen who were being treated forrard, and in the orlop. His leg had been smashed at the knee, and Thomas Wing had amputated just above. The stump had been sealed with hot Swedes tar, and heavily bandaged.

'He has been most exceeding brave,' said the doctor now, in an aside to Rennie. 'He would not take tincture before, and he will not take it now. He has been very courageous, but I fear the pain will overwhelm him.'

'You mean, he would swallow none even before you took off the leg?'

'He would not. He bit clean through a strap of stitched leather that I put between his teeth, and fainted, but he would take no comfort.'

Rennie sent a boy for his steward and a bottle of wine and glasses. To the doctor: 'And now I will speak to him.' Turning to the berth: 'Mr Delingpole. Now then, the doctor has had to deprive you of your leg, but we will not like to be deprived of you altogether, in the ship. You are of great value to us, Mr Delingpole, hey?' Taking his hand, and gripping it a moment.

'Thank you, sir.' A breath, tight-drawn.

'Indeed you are. I will accordingly take it as a great kindness to me, personal, if you will allow me to honour your bravery by drinking a glass of wine—Cutton!'

'Sir?' Attending.

'Pour me two glasses of claret, will you?'

As Cutton handed him the first glass, Rennie surreptitiously tipped into it the generous dose of alcoholic tincture of opium given him at the side by Thomas Wing. With a grave show of kindness he handed the glass to Mr Delingpole, who took it and endeavoured to raise himself, painfully attempted it, and Rennie helped him, lending an arm. And now Rennie took the second glass, reaching behind for it, bringing it round and raising it to the sweating young man. In the semi-formal tones of a great-cabin dinner:

'A glass of wine with you, Mr Delingpole—the bravest man in *Expedient*.'

'Thank you, sir.' And supported further by the doctor, he raised his own glass, and drank it off. Gently the doctor lowered him in the berth, and let him lie down, taking the glass from his hand.

In the tropicks the evening is not long, and as night fell Rennie sat in the great cabin studying the lists of wounded, sick and killed, the lists of repairs not yet completed, and making calculations for a rejigged plan of action for the morrow. The boy came to his door:

'The doctor sends his compliments, sir, and begs to inform you that Mr Delingpole——' The boy faltered.

'He is dead?'

'Aye, sir. It was very peaceful, the doctor says. He never felt nothing again, sir.'

'Thank you.' A moment. 'You may say to the doctor—nay, I will say it myself.'

He went below, and saw Thomas Wing, and then he went on deck. Rain was again falling.

'Mr Hayter.'

'Sir?' Moving to his side. Rennie took his elbow, and they walked to the taffrail. 'I have formed a new plan of action, James, a new and I think bold stratagem, and I will like your opinion.'

'Very good, sir.' Wiping his face with his kerchief, and retying it on his head.

'If we find—when we find the two ships again, we *must* be bold, it is our only chance to prevail. We are limping, we are short-handed, we are out-gunned. We must seize the initiative.'

'With respect, sir, do not we already have it? Don't forget, we damaged the American ship very severe. If she is to be protected by the frigate, then the frigate must wait for her as she repairs. This long period of poor weather has further aided us.'

'I have not forgot, James—but we thought to have the advantage our first fire, did we not? And was very nearly defeated. This occasion—tomorrow—we must find them, and attack at once. Here is what I propose . . .'

At first light, having carried out repairs sufficient to make her at least workable as a fighting ship, *Expedient* recommenced her search for the enemy, and to Rennie's surprise found the enemy astern. Astern and slow. The frigate was with the limping merchantman—not only with her but towing her.

Rennie, on his quarterdeck, ordered his ship to go about, and:

'We will bear down on them, Mr Hayter, and run between them, just as we planned, and cut that damned towing cable.'

Expedient ran with the wind on her larboard quarter, closed the gap quickly, and ran between the two ships, severing the cable, and at the same moment Rennie bellowed:

'*Fire as they bear!*'

A fury of flame and smoke, near-simultaneous broadsides from *Expedient*'s undermanned guns, blasting both enemy ships:

BOOM-BANG BOOM-BANG-BANG-BANG BOOM BOOM-BOOM

The starboard battery, double-shotted, smashed the frigate's stern gallery and scythed away part of her rudder. Glass, splinters of wood, a writhing length of rudder chain, and the sea pocked white in a hail of fragments.

The larboard battery, loaded with Rennie's one locker of eighteen-pound bar, near two hundred pound of lethal tumbling bar, tore through the American's bowsprit, cut the forestay, smashed through the waist and splintered the quarters aft. Screams. Her foremast, gravely injured, leaned, teetered, and went by the board, dragging yards, sails, ropes and blocks in a great tangle over the side, and the ship was hopelessly crippled. But she was not killed. Her carronades—notwithstanding the frightful damage to the ship—were brought to bear on *Expedient*, and fired:

THUD THUD-THUD THUD THUD THUD

Six twenty-four-pound roundshot went wide of *Expedient*, sending up great plumes of spray beyond her. Four shots went home, in a splitting eruption of smashed timbers. Sauve-tete netting had been rigged over the waist, but the carronade broadside tore it away, allowing lethal splinters to devastate the gun-crews beneath. And now there were screams in *Expedient*. Men fell horribly injured and dying, sliced, cut, dismembered. A powder boy took a foot-long splinter full in the forehead. This sight caught James's eye for a long split second, one of those moments of dreamlike clarity that seem suspended in time. As the boy slumped on his back on the deck, all shocking sound, all else of agony, of flying debris and roiling smoke—was quite shut out.

'*Reload! Reload! Full allowance cartridge, and double-shot your guns!*' bellowed a voice. His own voice.

The French frigate was very badly damaged, but unlike the merchantman was not yet disabled. She came about, with dismaying purpose came about, and attacked.

BANG BANG BANG BANG BANG BANG BANG

A deadly mixture, in alternate guns, of canister and chain, and of star and grape, came in a storm of metal into *Expedient*'s rigging, masts and sails. Men in the tops, and on her forecastle and quarterdeck, working the ship, handling her, were rent, torn, cut bloodily asunder.

James stumbled down the ladder to assist one of the gun captains in the larboard waist section, who had lost all but two of his crew. James snatched up a handspike, dropped it, and took hold of a tackle rope. He began to haul on it with all his weight and strength, but the trucks of the gun were damaged and would not turn.

''Vast there! Leave it, now!' He herded the captain and his remaining men to the next gun forrard, and they joined the few men left there, joined them and ran the gun out, and James crouched at the flintlock, aimed, and fired. And saw twin roundshot strike home and smash the frigate's wheel through the boiling smoke as *Expedient* ran past her.

James ran half-deafened along the line of remaining guns, and: '*Fire! Fire! Fire! They cannot steer her, now! Fire at her rudder and finish her, as your guns bear!*'

BANG BANG BANG-BANG

And now he ran aft, jumped up the ladder to the quarter-deck, and was at once struck by a musket ball in the left shoulder. He was spun round by the punching force of the ball, and fell in a sprawl on the deck. Got to his knees, and felt that his left arm was useless to him. Stood up, steadied himself against the heeling of the ship, and peered at the French frigate. Her stern gallery gaped open and shattered, her rudder had been blown off entire, but a long brass gun was being run out of her one undamaged stern port—run out, and now was fired. An orange flash and *BOOM*. And James, in a rooted moment, saw the nine-pound roundshot as it rocketed straight towards him, a black expanding sphere, and felt it hurtle past his head in a buffeting whack of wind.

'Mr Hayter! James!'

'Aye, sir. I am here.' His voice sounding oddly in his ears, inside his head—that was intact.

'His rudder is smashed! We will run alongside, and board!'

'Aye, sir. Very good.' His head echoing and ringing.

'By God, James. You are hurt.'

'It is only my arm, I think. I am all right.'

'You had better go below, and let Wing look at you.' Anxiously peering at James's shoulder, from which blood welled, through the torn cloth of his tunic, and trickled down the length of his hanging arm to splash on the deck.

'I am all right, sir, you know. It is a slight wound only, a flesh wound. I am not in pain.' He strode to the makeshift breast rail, and shouted: 'Mr Peak! Mr Peak! We will muster a boarding party! Sergeant of marines! Muster your men on the forecastle! All able-bodied men, any man that has the use of his legs, and can hold a cutlass, or a pistol! Mr Tangible! We shall need grappling irons!'

Rennie flew straight at the frigate, with the wind now behind him, flew at the French ship, and at the last possible moment spun the wheel himself, bawled for topsails aback, and ran his ship in alongside with a nudging, scraping rasp and a spiking clash of yards. As he did so, the French fired their last broadside, gunport to gunport with *Expedient*, and roundshot thudded and slammed into her timbers, so that she shuddered like a wounded animal. Smoke, reeking and heady, boiled across the deck, and made a thick mist, through which the few dozen men that *Expedient* could muster howled and bellowed and clambered—brandishing pikes, cutlasses, muskets with bayonets fixed, and pistols—clambered over the rail, stepped out and over the French ship's rail, and on to her forecastle.

The hand-to-hand fighting on the French frigate was at first very fierce. A one-pound swivel was turned upon the boarding party, and a round of canister fired straight into the leading five men, killing three outright, and felling the other two. James Hayter led the second wave, and nearly fell between the two ships. He saved himself by treading on a grappling line, and jumped on to the forecastle, sword in hand. When the French crew saw that the deadly canister shot had had no effect upon the English morale, their own morale began to slip. They continued to resist, with cutlass and pistol and belaying pin, but when they saw the determination with which the boarding party advanced, firing pistols, throwing them aside, then hacking with blades, and bellowing like the hounds of hell, they fell back. Soon it became clear that they were not properly led, and had no stomach for a prolonged fight. The forecastle fell to the boarders, then the waist. As the Expedients forayed aft to the quarterdeck, and James ran up the ladder, his sword held high and glinting in his hand, the reason for the French collapse became even clearer. Their captain and first lieutenant had been killed, the second lay mortally wounded, and the third, a boy of twenty who looked seventeen, was effectively—or ineffectively—in command of the ship, and her now demoralised people. The young lieutenant advised James at once, in English, that he proposed to surrender.

'Then strike, monsieur, if you please.'

'Strike? You wish for my sword?'

'No, thank you. Just haul down your colours, will you?'

'Ah, yes, the flag, I see.' And he hauled down the plain white ensign himself.

'Thank you, monsieur. Will you give me your word, now, that all resistance has ceased?'

'Certainly.' He removed his hat, and bowed.

James had the frigate quickly searched. Her papers, in the extensively damaged—indeed wrecked—great cabin, revealed that she was the frigate *La Verité*, thirty-eight, commanded by Capitaine Loup. Her shot-smashed transom had been overpainted with the name 'Bernadette'. Below James found that there were a great many men ill of the fever, just as there were in *Expedient*. The conditions in the lower deck were squalid in the extreme. There appeared to be no surgeon in the ship. Wounded men lay suffering unattended, alongside the fevered men. The stench was appalling. The Reverend Laycock was either not in the ship, or was perhaps very well hidden. James returned to the quarterdeck. The young lieutenant, guarded by a marine, now said to James, with what James saw as an arrogant frown:

'Of course, you know, we are not at war. You have made an unprovoked attack upon a French ship, an act of piracy. You have killed the captain. This will have grave consequences for you, when the news reaches my country.' Looking James in the eye.

'Yes, thank you. Where is Mr Laycock?'

'Laycock?' Shaking his head, his boy's face innocently puzzled.

'Is he aboard your frigate, or is he in the American ship?'

'Yes, you have also attacked an American ship, and you will be made to pay for it, I think so.'

'Lieutenant, you gave me your word just now that all resistance had ceased. I will not take it kindly if you persist in this damned foolishness. Where is the Reverend Laycock?'

The lieutenant again shook his head, shrugged, and: 'I do not know this Laycock. He is not in this ship, and I think you——'

'Mr Peak!'

Mr Peak came aft, and climbed the ladder from the waist.

'Mr Peak, I am leaving you in command of this ship. The corporal of marines and three of his men to assist you. You may choose four other men from the boarding party, all of them to be armed. You will put Lieutenant . . .' Turning to the Frenchman: 'What is your name, monsieur?'

'Lampard, Georges Lampard.'

'Thank you.' To Peak, continuing: 'You will put Lieutenant

Lampard under close arrest, and confine him below. I do not trust him.'

'I protest! I protest most strongly!' The Frenchman's unwhiskered cheeks flushing.

'You will be *quiet*, monsieur, and behave yourself, or Mr Peak will run you through.' To Peak: 'I will try to send our surgeon aboard, if he can be spared. Conditions below are very bad. If they are as bad in the American ship, I wonder if the Reverend Laycock can still be alive.'

James went to the rail, climbed over it with difficulty, his left arm stiffening now, and becoming painful. He nearly tripped in the hammock cranes, steadied himself with an effort, and jumped over on to *Expedient*. He found Rennie sitting in a daze by the wheel, leaning against it. He had suffered a further injury to his head, and the new blow had opened the scar left by the musket ball, and had bled freely, leaving a great congealing smear. But the sight of his lieutenant now revived the captain.

'I assume Laycock is not aboard her?'

'He is not, sir.'

'We are drifting, grappled together.' Pulling himself to his feet. 'We must ungrapple and stand away, James, and board the other ship. Laycock is in that ship, as I have always thought.'

'You are badly hurt, sir——'

'Pish pish, we are both of us hurt, but we are alive, hey? And our task ain't near completed.'

'Conditions in the French frigate—she is called *La Verité*, by the by—conditions in her are infinitely worse than in *Expedient*, sir. Her captain and most of her officers are dead. There is no surgeon, and her people are very wretched. With your permission, I will ask Thomas Wing to——'

'I do not give my permission, James. Wing is busy here in *Expedient*, more than busy, and he cannot be spared.'

'Very good, sir. Here are the frigate's papers.' And he handed to Rennie the scorched and tattered documents he had discovered in *La Verité*'s great cabin, and gave him the numbers of Expedients killed and wounded.

Expedient ungrappled, untangled herself, and stood away from the crippled French frigate. Her own condition was poor, but not nearly so poor as the ship she had defeated. *Expedient* could be handled, steered, and if necessary fought. Lieutenant Peak, in command of *La Verité*, had been ordered to deploy sea anchors, maintain strict order and discipline, and wait.

Expedient approached the American ship, drifting now about half a mile distant, and as they came nearer Rennie and James could see that something like panic had begun to prevail in her. Fire had broken out in the forecastle, and black smoke, tinged with fiery red, poured up round the splintered stump of her foremast. A makeshift rudder had been fitted overnight, but the chains had not been properly linked, or had broken in the action. Those gun-crews that had manned her carronades to such pounding effect had left their posts, and were now either fighting the flames or attempting to hoist out her one undamaged boat. James hailed the ship:

'*We are going to board you! Strike your colours, and we will not kill any man!*'

At first this instruction was ignored, then when it was repeated, and a gun fired, the American merchant ensign of red, white and blue bars was jerkily lowered.

Expedient's launch, towed during the action, was now manned by an armed boarding party. James insisted on leading this party. Thomas Wing had looked at his wound, and found that the ball had torn through the top of his left shoulder, damaging the trapezius, so that his shoulder was lowered and his left arm hung useless. He found turning his head to the left difficult; his whole left side was increasing stiff; he was now in considerable pain. Wing had strapped up his arm in a sling, and forbidden him to undertake any further duty. James had nodded, and smiled, and ignored his advice. He drank a double ration of unwatered rum, took up his sword, and went into the boat.

The American ship was the *Valley Wraith*, a hired vessel out of Boston. Her master, Captain Brewster, had been killed, her first mate could not be found. The devastation in her was general, the fire forrard now out of control. She could not live long. James went quickly aft and below, having sent his boarding party to aid those seamen, under the second mate, attempting to hoist out the boat. He found *La Verité*'s surgeon, Dr Gascogne, tending to a man who was clearly doomed, in his foetid little cabin, like the ship in which he lay. His face was bluish white, his eyes sunken, his lips crimson and sticky. There was dried blood in his ears, and in his hair.

'Reverend Laycock, sir?'

Dr Gascogne answered, in his native tongue, his voice indignant and sad: 'He is indeed Monsieur Laycock. He has been barbarously treated, he has been tortured. Had I not been occupied all the time with fever cases in both of our ships, all these last days, I should have tended to him sooner, and tried to prevent what was happening. But I am only a medical man, moved from ship to ship each day, under orders. He should have been removed from this infamous vessel, and into our frigate, where he would not have been so ill-used. It was Monsieur Lascelles . . .'

James nodded, and in French: 'May I speak to him? Is he strong enough to understand me?'

'He is dying, monsieur. It cannot do him any harm, I think.'

'Thank you.' In English, moving to the hanging cot: 'Reverend Laycock? Can you hear me, sir?'

Laycock turned his sunken eyes on James, and gave a nearly imperceptible nod.

'I am Lieutenant Hayter, of His Majesty's *Expedient* frigate. We have come to rescue you, sir.'

Painfully, opening his half-glued lips with the tip of his tongue, Laycock began to speak, his voice very hoarse and low. 'Thank God you have come—you are too late—to rescue me—I am going to die.'

'We will try to prevent that, sir——'

'No, no, no—there is no time for pretence.' A huffing breath, an effortful swallow. 'The cryptographical cypher—is concealed—in my back passage—you understand? My persecutor—my most diligent torturer— Monsieur Lascelles —I am near certain is dead—killed when the ship—was fired upon. He did not—succeed—in discovering the hiding place—perhaps he was—too fastidious a fellow.' Another breath. 'You must not—blame Colonel Hepple—for my abduction. I did not—fully trust him, or anyone—at Spanish Town—as I should have. It was—hhh—my own fault.'

'Yes, sir, very good . . . and the plan, sir?'

'Lascelles took it—into his own quarters. You must—must retrieve it—and take it to England.'

'Thank you, sir.' Urgently now, in French, to Dr Gascogne: 'Where is Monsieur Lascelles's cabin? Quickly. The ship is afire.'

'Why, it is the next cabin, monsieur.'

'We must get Reverend Laycock into a boat.'

Dr Gascogne shook his head. 'Please not to move him. Let him be peaceful in his last moments, monsieur.'

'The ship is afire, Doctor! You will excuse me, I must find something at once. Then I will return for Monsieur Laycock. It is imperative that I get him into the boat.'

James stepped past Dr Gascogne, into the space that served as a wardroom, and saw the next cabin, its slatted wooden door closed and locked. Without waiting he kicked the door off its hinges, the stink of fire in his nostrils, and burst into the small cabin. Shelves, a hanging cot, a small desk and chair. He upended the hanging cot, sprawling the bedding on the deck.

He kicked away the chair, and began to rifle the desk, pulling out drawers and tipping them upside down. He found nothing in the desk. The stench of fire was now very strong, and wisps of smoke were beginning to drift through the quarters.

'Where in God's name has the fellow hidden it?'

He poked in every corner of the little cabin, thrusting the point of his sword into the woodwork to test for hollow spaces, secret drawers. There was nothing. He returned to Laycock's cabin.

'Doctor, you must help me get the Reverend Laycock on deck, and into the boat.'

'Monsieur, he is dying, cannot you see? Please to have some compassion for him . . .'

'You would leave him here to burn?'

'Oh, very well. If you insist.'

'I'm afraid that I do.'

With great difficulty—for James had only one arm—Reverend Laycock was carried in his hanging cot forrard into the waist, and from there he was handed down into *Expedient*'s boat. As this was done James saw that the merchantman's boat had now been hoisted clear, and lowered, and was rapidly filling with the remaining men of her crew. A figure now darted out of the smoke, and hovered on the gangway, waiting his turn to go down the side-ladder. Behind him came two seamen, effortfully carrying a small heavy chest. The face was almost hidden by a large tricorne, pulled low over the eyes. There was something about that figure . . .

'By God, that is Lascelles,' muttered James, pausing on the gangway a little aft. At the same moment, Lascelles lifted his head and the scar on his face was exposed. There could be no doubt. And now as if by instinct he flicked his eyes in James's direction—and saw that he was recognised. James drew his sword.

'You there! Yes, you, sir! Stand away from the rail, now!' Advancing.

Lascelles seized the chest from the grasp of the seamen, shouted something into the boat, then with wiry strength heaved the chest through the gangway port and down into the boat, where it was received by several seamen, one of whom was knocked down on the thwarts by the weight of the chest, and broke his arm. Lascelles did not climb down the ladder, but leapt straight down after the chest, scrabbled to his feet, stepping over thwarts, and drew a pistol from his coat. He shouted an order, and the seamen at the oars began to give way. Lascelles held his pistol at the coxswain's head, and pointed towards *La Verité*, half a mile distant, riding the swell.

A blast of fiery wind, crackling with sparks, blew over James and the remaining American crew on the gangway. James sheathed his sword, ran quickly down the cleats into *Expedient*'s boat, and beckoned for the seamen above to come down and save themselves.

'Follow that damned boat!' shouted James to Randall South, the coxswain at the tiller. 'Give way, give way! Cheerly, now!'

Expedient's boat was pushed clear by a seaman standing in the bow, and began to pursue the American ship's boat, whose crew were pulling with a will.

Dr Gascogne, amidships, tending to the prostrated figure of the Reverend Laycock, caught James's attention with repeated gestures.

'Yes, Doctor, what is it?' Impatiently, in French, peering at the boat ahead.

'He is dead, monsieur.'

'You are sure.'

'I am a doctor, monsieur. I am sure.'

'Very well, thank you.'

Randall South, at the tiller: 'Mr Hayter, sir.'

'Yes.'

'Has the sick man perished, sir? Can we put him over the side? He is only extra weight in the boat, when we are chasing, and already considerable heavier with the rescued hands.'

'No, certainly not! I *must* get him into *Expedient*—that is, that is, he must have an honourable burial, from the ship.'

'Aye, sir—the boat ahead is pulling away, sir, I fear.'

'Yes, I can see it is.' A moment, standing in the stern sheets, then: 'Very well, we will steer for *Expedient*, Randall.' To the crew: 'Pull with a will, now! We must make all possible speed!'

As the launch reached *Expedient* the American ship's boat was already alongside *La Verité*. James had no glass with him, and could not see what kind of welcome the boat had received, except that men were going out of her, and into the frigate. He ran up *Expedient*'s side-ladder, and went aft to report to his captain. As he did so there was a great flash across the sea, followed by a rush of wind, and a moment later a rumbling roar and boom, as the American ship blew up. James turned to look, and saw a dense cloud of black smoke, with spearing plumes of white smoke arcing up from its heart. A further explosion lit the cloud from within, then another, and another; and all round the death ship ripples and splashes as fragments fell into the sea.

'God help the poor devils lying wounded in her,' muttered James, and hurried aft.

'Well? Well?' Rennie, anxious on the quarterdeck. 'She has blown up, James. Is Laycock with you, in the boat? What is that other boat? Why have you allowed it to go to the French ship?'

'Reverend Laycock is dead, sir. Lascelles is in the other boat. I am certain he has the plan——'

'Lascelles! And you allowed him to escape, good God! He will——'

'If you please, sir.' Forcefully. 'He held a pistol to the coxswain's head, and I had no means of preventing his flight.' A stab of pain in his shoulder, and he now gripped it with his right hand.

'Yes yes, I can see that you are all in, James.' The bandage round his own head was stained with leaking blood. 'No doubt Mr Peak will deal with Lascelles, and place him under arrest. The villain cannot escape us in a captured ship.'

'No, sir. But Lascelles is a very wily and ingenious fellow. May I suggest we again close with *La Verité*, and make certain that Mr Peak has not been outwitted.'

'You think . . .?' Looking at him. 'Yes, yes, we are of one mind, James. Mr Peak is not an ingenious fellow. Mr Tangible! Hands to make sail!'

When *Expedient*—still cleared for action as a precaution, and her starboard battery manned—reached *La Verité*, and lost way to run in alongside, all appeared to be well aboard the French ship. Men were carrying out repairs to her rigging, marines in their red coats stood guard, and Mr Peak stood on the quarterdeck. Rennie hailed his junior lieutenant:

'Mr Peak! Mr Peak, there!'

James, at his side, drew a sharp breath. 'That is not Mr Peak, sir. It is a man in his coat——'

A fusillade of small arms fire, and swivel guns. Musket shot and canister whipped and cracked across *Expedient*'s upper works. The red-coated marines fired from *La Verité*'s deck. Men in the tops fired down. Both Rennie and James ducked down, and were unscathed behind the hammock cranes. After the first rattling burst of fire, a steady crack-crack-crack of individual shots.

'Has Lascelles done this, James?' Rennie, peering over the hammock netting. A ball pocked the hammock immediately by his head.

'You had better keep down, sir.'

'The bloody lunatic wretch!' Standing to his full height. '*Stand by your guns!*'

'No, sir! No! We dare not fire on her!'

'God damn them, I will not be shot at by a ship that has struck and surrendered! *Stand by to fire!*'

Another shot sang past Rennie, and a further ball dug a splinter out of the deck at his feet.

'Sir, Lascelles has the plan! We cannot risk its destruction by a fire aboard, or an explosion. The American ship is already destroyed by fire.'

'Don't talk womanish, James. *By section, now . . .*'

But the French ship's broadside was first, and her guns were double-shotted. A tremendous blasting weight of metal smashed into *Expedient*'s already damaged side, as *Expedient* by pure good fortune rode up a little on the lift of the sea, and took the full force of the broadside beneath her chains, along the wales. Rennie was thrown off his feet, and pulled in under the barricade by James, dragging desperately with his right arm.

'Are you hurt, sir? Are you hurt?'

'No, only deafened, thankee. The buggering treacherous villains, they have outwitted——'

His words cut off by *Expedient*'s reply—in grapeshot. Rennie had ordered grape, as a further precaution, and now her guns, fired as *La Verité*'s dipped on the fall, and *Expedient* was on the rise, let fly a murderous scything hail of iron. Small iron spheres that cut down her mainmast, cut down the man in Mr Peak's coat, the marines, the crews at their guns. Cut them down, and ended the action, in one fierce lethal stroke.

James obtained from Thomas Wing a dose of tincture, sufficient to dull the pain in his shoulder, and had a brief conversation with the doctor.

'The Reverend Laycock is not to be sewn straightway into his shroud, Thomas. A discreet procedure must first be undertaken.' And he explained about the need to retrieve a certain hidden document.

Then, in a tincture-induced euphoria, he boarded *La Verité* once more. His euphoria evaporated. All of the party he had left on board with Mr Peak were dead, including the junior lieutenant—their throats cut and their bodies dumped into the ballast. A great many men, including most of the American crew that had gone in the boat with Lascelles, had been killed by *Expedient*'s broadside of grape. Lieutenant Lampard had been killed. *La Verité*'s decks were slippery with blood, and dead and dying men lay everywhere, sprawled in leaking clumps in a tangle of yards, parrals, ropes and blocks. James searched the ship, in the light of lanterns, with a small party of marines, and found the dead men in the hold. But Henri Lascelles, Comte d'Argenton, was nowhere to be found.

Expedient again under way, sailing slowly north, her shot-pounded side now plugged and repaired, and now with the crippled *La Verité* in tow. James gave his full report to Rennie, with lists compiled by Alan Dobie—lists of damages, of losses, of major and minor repairs, and long lists of casualties. In a condition of returning daze, born of fatigue, James accepted a glass of wine. Rennie himself, a fresh bandage on his head, was equally in a daze. Without saying so, both of them knew they were lucky to be alive.

Rennie sat at his desk, his table not yet brought up from the hold, where it had been struck. He glanced through the lists, sipped wine, sniffed, looked over at James in the chair opposite:

'Lascelles was likely killed, James, and fell into the sea when the mainmast went by the board. The plan has gone with him, I fear.'

'That is possible, yes. But I think he is too canny a fellow to have allowed himself to be killed by a broadside of guns. The truth is, we cannot be quite certain——'

'Surely you don't think that he has survived? You searched the ship.'

'Aye, sir, and found nothing.'

'Hm. Hm.' A further perusal of the lists, then he pushed

them aside, and sighed. After a moment: 'Will I tell you my own view of the thing?'

'Lascelles?'

'No no, of the whole bloody business. *My* view is . . . that I no longer care. Do I shock you? No, I think I do not. The whole bloody business—and it has been very bloody, horrible and destructive and bloody—has been a waste, James. Waste of time, waste of ships, waste—above all else—of men's lives. I think it is only fitting, with Laycock dead, and Lascelles too, almost certainly dead, and the plan lost—I think we must allow ourselves to say that the commission entire has been a damned miserable waste, and a failure. I have lost all sense of my duty. I do not know what it is, any more. It does not seem to matter.'

'Our duty—is that we must go home to England, sir.'

'Aye . . .' A sigh. 'Aye, we must, I expect, and face things there.' Both hands on the desk, and fingers tapped twice. 'But what am I to do with the French frigate, and her crew, hey?'

'Well, sir, well—I had thought . . .'

'You have a suggestion? I am more than willing to hear it, James.'

'We cannot take her as a prize, since we are not at war. As it is, we shall have very great difficulty in explaining the damage and loss of life we have sustained in this action—an action which the Admiralty, and His Majesty's government, would find it nearly impossible to justify, was we to appear at Spithead with the evidence in tow. These difficulties would be greatly reduced, sir, should we choose to relieve ourselves of our burden.'

'Relieve ourselves . . .?'

'*La Verité* is crippled almost beyond repair. She is a burden to us, towing, an impediment. Why do not we scuttle her, sir, and put her crew, and the remaining Americans, into her boats?'

'Let them go?'

'They would have their chance, if they are navigators

enough. We could allow them a compass, and sufficient food and water to reach one of the islands, or even the American coast. They deserve that chance, in least, don't you think so?'

'They deserve to be hanged, every last man of them.' A sniff, a musing glance. 'But I see the wisdom of your suggestion, James. It would resolve at least one of our difficulties.' Another tap, and a breath. 'Very well, we will sink the frigate, and put her people into the boats.'

'I will go aboard her myself, sir, a last time, and see that it is done.'

James stood alone in the cable tier of the French frigate. The carpenter's mate had already bored the requisite holes and been sent away, and water was beginning to flood into the bilges. All of her crew, able-bodied, wounded, sick, were going into her boats, with the remaining Americans, and Dr Gascogne. A party of *Expedient*'s marines was supervising their exit from the ship. All that remained for James to do was remove himself into *Expedient* without delay. He glanced aft, in the reeking air of the hold, and thought of poor Archimedes, hiding in *Expedient*'s breadroom . . .

'By God . . . the breadroom!' under his breath. 'We did not search the breadroom, the first time we came below, because the door was jammed shut by a fallen cask.'

Lascelles had jammed that door, he was certain of it, and was hiding there now, waiting until the last possible moment to make his escape into one of the boats.

'He will not escape me, however.' Grimly, muttering to himself. But when he reached the breadroom the door stood gaping open. James cursed, and jumped for the ladder. He must go on deck at once, and prevent the boats from——

A footfall, behind him. James whirled, lantern held high. A figure ran at him, shadowy, from the depths of darkness. Almost too late James saw the blade of the sword.

He had no time to reach for his own sword, only to hurl the lantern in a swinging arc at the blade's tip, deflecting it, and to lurch aside, before the figure was on him. The lantern was whipped away and smashed into blackness, and James felt himself carried bodily against the frame of the breadroom door. His breath was knocked out of him, and he half-fell, gasping, and heard feet clattering up the ladder. Blindly, still gasping, he stumbled towards the ladder, hauled himself on to it with his one good arm, and began to run up in a clumsy stagger.

'Lascelles, damn you . . .' Breathlessly.

Above, a single lantern had been left burning in the lower deck, and James came up into this gloomy space, a-swing with a line of empty hammocks and stinking of excrement and putrefaction. Heaved himself up, and heard feet on the next ladder, the ladder leading to the upper deck. There were marines on deck, and their presence would likely dissuade Lascelles from venturing forrard, thought James. No, he would attempt to conceal himself in the captain's quarters, then try to jump into one of the boats and commandeer it as before, by presenting a pistol at the coxswain's head and defying all opposition.

'Well, he will never get into a boat while I am on my legs, and can run my blade in his guts.' Savagely, moving to the second ladder.

In the wrecked great cabin there was no hope of concealment, but in the coach a drape of number six canvas lay dangling down in a mass of tangled clewlines and blocks, from the breached quarterdeck above. James advanced, his breath restored, and filled his lungs:

'*Lascelles, damn your blood, I am come to kill you!*' His sword in his hand. The sword his father had given him upon the occasion of his first commission, a thirty-inch blade by Cullum of London, well balanced, light-wielding, ideal for his deadly purpose now.

A movement behind the canvas, a little bulge, and *crack!* a pistol ball sang past James's head, and embedded itself in the timber behind with a splintering thud. James did not duck, or flinch. He ran with his sword an extension of his arm straight at the burnt hole, and thrust deep. Felt the blade strike metal, and heard the clatter of a pistol butt on the decking. Another movement, and James slashed with his blade, and tore the canvas aside.

Lascelles, his eyes staring, the scar livid on his cheek, leapt straight at him, a second pistol aimed full at James's breast, and fired. The snap of the flint, a spark—and nothing else.

'*Haaaagh!*' bellowed James, and thrust. Lascelles side-stepped neatly, and when he faced James again his own sword was in his hand. James thrust again, was parried, and off balance felt steel run through his shirt and into his flesh. A searing pain.

'*God damn your soul, you bloody wretch! You will not pink me again!*'

Lascelles said nothing, his eyes alert, his expression formed round that declaring scar: I am a man that is used to killing, that will kill you. He walked in a light-footed half-circle, and back, his blade poised. A single nod. You may try again.

And James thrust again, and was again parried. With a curse he pretended to thrust yet again, and at the last instant feinted. The answering parry was lost in the air as his blade went under, and in, and pierced the shirtfront. Pierced bone. James pushed with all his anger and strength, his avenging strength—and ran Lascelles through. At last, a sound:

'*Dieu . . .*' A little sob of breath.

The dark fire went from his eyes, and his legs buckled under him. James jerked his blade, and it came free with a sucking rasp. Blood drooled on the decking, and welled spreading through the pierced shirt. Lascelles fell dying on his back, a bubble of blood at his mouth, that broke as he grew still.

James too was very still, his sword in his hand, and at last he heard the sounds behind him of the marines shouting instructions into the boats, felt the ship settling, and came to himself.

'The documents . . .' he said. 'I must find the documents—and I must have that chest.'

He knelt awkwardly, in pain, and searched Lascelles's corpse, and found himself surprised at how slight was the dead man's frame. In the pocket of the coat he found a sealed packet. He stared at it a moment, contemplated breaking it open, then pushed it away inside the flap of his breeches for safe keeping. Rose, and hurried aft to the waist.

He was too late. All three boats had stepped their masts, and set sail, and were already bearing away to the west.

'We must stop them!' he shouted to the marines.

'Stop them, sir? We has only just let them go . . .'

'Come on!' Running down the ladder into *Expedient*'s boat. 'They have something I want!'

He found it in the second boat, the launch, stowed under a sail amidships, beneath the thwarts. The chest he had seen Lascelles take out of the American ship. He pointed impatiently at the chest, and said to two of the American seamen:

'You there, pass that out now, will you.'

Resenting scowls, and they did not move. James, in pain, lost patience.

'Light it along now, else I will drown the bloody lot of you, d'you *hear me*!'

The chest was reluctantly passed over, nearly dropped into the sea between, then safely stowed in the bottom of James's boat, and he returned to *Expedient*.

Behind him *La Verité* settled in the water, bow down. The sea ran eager over her decks, she heeled a little at the end—and disappeared in a great boiling of released air, taking Henri Lascelles, Comte d'Argenton, to his last reward.

*

James first visited the grey-faced and exhausted Thomas Wing, and had his sword cut attended to. Then, newly bandaged:

'Thankee, Thomas. By the by, d'y'have that item, that I asked you to take from Mr Laycock?'

Thomas Wing drew back his blood-smeared sleeve, and found a small cylinder of waxed paper tucked there. 'I have, in course, wiped it down.' A faint smile, through his weariness.

James nodded, returning the smile, and repaired to the great cabin, where the chest had already been delivered, and now stood on Rennie's desk. It was double-locked. Rennie was peering at those locks as James came in.

'I have tried three or four of my own keys, James,' beckoning him to the desk, 'but they do not answer. I must send for the armourer. Boy!'

The armourer came, and James sat down on a locker at the side to ease the pain of his wounds. The locks were duly broken with mallet and chisel, the armourer dismissed, and James again joined Rennie at his desk. Together they prised open the lid.

'What's this . . .?'

The trunk was lined, and it was filled with squat leather bags tied at their gathered tops with silk. Rennie took one up, untied the silk, and tipped the bag on the desk. From the opened mouth fell dozens of gold coins, which rolled heavily across the desk and fell flat, gleaming in the light from the stern gallery window.

'These are gold louis, James.' Holding a coin between finger and thumb.

'I see that they are, sir. Are all the bags the same, d'y'think?'

Rennie untied another bag, with the same result—then another, and another.

'Good God, there is a fortune here. Thousands of pounds.'

'Ten thousand, perhaps more. Certainly not less, sir.'

'Well, well . . .' Softly, straightening up. 'What are we to do, hey? With all this specie?'

'Do, sir? Surely, we must turn it over to Their Lordships? It is clearly Lascelles's ill-gotten gains, for kidnapping Laycock and stealing his plan—that is in this packet.' Putting the packet on the desk.

'Yes, yes, you are right—I am in no doubt you are right. We had better just make sure of the plan, hm?' Looking at James, and feeling suddenly ashamed. 'My dear James, I have not thanked you for what you have so bravely done—in disposing of Lascelles, the villain, and getting back the plan, and the chest. Did he give you great trouble?'

James, touching at the bandage under his shirt: 'Not very great trouble, sir, no. When I was avenging the death of a friend.'

'Ah, yes—yes, your friend Dorrell, that he killed in a duel.' A nod.

'Torrance, sir.'

'Just so. Now, then . . .' Taking up the packet.

'You will need this, sir.' Handing him the little cylinder of waxed paper. 'Reverend Laycock's cryptographical key, without which the plan is undecipherable, I think.'

Rennie took the waxed paper, peered at it with a puzzled frown, then tentatively sniffed at it. 'It has a most curious odour. Did Laycock give this to you himself?'

'In a way, he did. To the doctor.'

'Ah, to the doctor. Was not Laycock dead, when he was carried aboard?'

'He was, sir. Thomas Wing has—has removed it from his person.'

'Ah. I see. Hm.' And he put down the item on the desk, and wiped his hand. Without further comment Rennie took up the sealed packet from Lascelles, and cut it open with his penknife. He drew out the documents folded within, opened them, and smoothed them out before him on the desk. He riffled through several sheets.

'Aye, it is gibberish. You was quite right about the need for the—the key.' A sniffing breath. 'So this is the wretched thing, at last, for which so many poor fellows have died. I have almost a mind to throw it over the side, and this damned cryptical key with it, too.'

'I should be happy to take charge of it, sir,' said James, 'and to attempt a translation, if you wish it.'

'Eh? Translate it? No no, James, it is secrets, and so forth. We are merely sea officers, that must do our duty, and leave such things as these to higher men.' He smiled ferociously as he said 'higher'.

'Very good, sir.' He stood straight, as straight as his wounds would allow, and: 'If you do not need me for anything else, sir, I must take my watch.'

'Take your watch, good God? James, you will do nothing of the kind, when you are wounded. I will send word to the quartermaster to take your watch. Stay here, and drink a glass of wine with me, and then retire to your rest, hey?'

'Thank you, sir, but I fear if I take even a drop of wine I shall fall insensible.'

'Then we will not drink. I wish to have the benefit of your opinion, James, your considered opinion.'

'I am here, sir.'

'Hm. Hm.' Glancing at him. 'There is no need for you to give your answer immediate. Sleep on it, if you like, and give me your answer in the morning.'

'I will be glad to consider anything you wish to ask me, sir.' Weary, puzzled, suppressing a sudden yawn.

'Yes, very good, thank you.' He paced to the stern gallery window, stood a moment, turned. 'You and I are the only two persons in the ship that know what is in that chest, are we not?'

He spoke in a quiet tone, a confidential tone, only just loud enough for James to hear him.

'Nobody else has seen the coins, certainly.' James answered, instinctively adopting the same tone.

'Just so.' Returning to his desk. 'What I am going to say to you must not go beyond the door of this cabin. Have I your word on that, whatever you may think, or decide?'

'You have it, sir.'

'Good, very good. Now then, James—I propose that you and I should share out the specie between us, say nothing to Their Lordships, nor to anyone else, and give it out in the ship that the chest held only the personal effects of the dead man.'

James—astonished and bemused—remained mute.

'You say nothing, James . . .'

'Well, sir, well—you did say that I might give you my answer tomorrow, did you not?'

'Just so, I did.' Peering at him, narrowly peering.

'Well, sir—I should prefer to do so—to give you my answer tomorrow.'

'Ah. Hm. In little, you do not approve of the proposal.'

Again James was silent. Soon after, he went on deck, exchanged a few words with the duty quartermaster, who had the deck, made certain that all was well, and then he went below, effortfully removed his clothes, and swung into his hanging cot. He slept through two watches without stirring, and woke refreshed in the darkness. He dressed, and went on deck for a breath of air. To his surprise he found Rennie standing by the binnacle.

'I took you at your word, sir. I did not stand my watch, after all, sir—I was all in.'

Rennie shook his head, took James by the elbow and drew him aft to the taffrail. 'A question has occurred to me, James, a puzzling question. Why did not Laycock send his plan by the regular packet-boat? And then travel separate with the key, or indeed send the key by a different packet-boat? Had both the documents been sent amongst a welter of other despatches, plain-covered, unremarked—would the whole thing not have been safer? Would not everything have gone to England safely, beyond the reach of Lascelles and his associates?'

'With your permission, sir—that is why I should like to attempt to translate the plan, using the key.'

'You think the answer may lie in the plan itself? Perhaps you are right, perhaps you are right. Very well, you may attempt a translation.' A pause, his hand still grasping James's elbow. 'Had you—had you thought more on that other matter, I wonder?'

'Sir, if you please, I should like to make the translation before I give you my final decision.'

'Hm. Well well, as you like. The documents are in the great cabin, in the desk. Here is the key. You may take them into the coach and study them there, where you will not be disturbed.'

As the first rays of dawn crept over the eastern horizon, pinkening the clouds, and staring red across the long ocean swell, James rose from the cramped little table in the coach—Alan Dobie's usual place of work—and went on deck. He stretched, yawned, stepped by force of habit to the binnacle, noted the direction of the ship, the glass-by-glass notations of her speed, and then he stepped away and glanced aloft, into the canvas towers. He sniffed deep, and smelled the sea, the sharp saline tang, and reflected that for what he knew now, for what was in his head, certain very high people in France would pay a very large sum—the kind of sum that lay below in the chest in the great cabin at this moment. Presently, as eight bells sounded for the changing of the watch, James went below and knocked on Rennie's door. He found the captain in his nightshirt and cap, sitting at his desk drinking tea.

'Ah, James, good morning to you. Tea?'

'Thank you, sir.' And as Rennie poured tea: 'May I tell you the content of the plan?'

'You have made the cryptical translation? Excellent, excellent.' Handing James his tea. 'Well?'

'The plan—is not for the defence of Jamaica, sir, exact.'

'No? It is not? Go on, James.'

'It is for the concerted attack upon, the invasion, and the taking by British forces of all French possessions in the Windward Isles: Guadaloupe, Marie Galante, Les Saintes, Martinique, St Lucia—thereby to effect domination of the Caribbean entire, and thus to ensure the complete safety of Jamaica and of all her riches.'

'Good God.' Putting down his cup. 'So it is *our* plan to invade . . .'

'Exactly so.'

'When?'

'Whenever war may again occur between England and France—or threaten to occur. The document makes much of the number of such wars during the past century.'

'Indeed, nearly numberless, hey?' A pause, taking up his cup, and: 'As a matter in fact then, Lascelles could be said to have had every good reason to abduct Laycock and steal his plan—from the French point of view, you know. Which brings me again, James, to the question: why did not Laycock *send* his plan, hidden among all the other despatches, in the packet-boat, where it would likely never be discovered by any of His Majesty's enemies?'

'I think because he trusted no one but himself, sir. He did not trust Colonel Hepple, he told me——'

'Ah, well, I can understand him in that, certainly.' Nodding. 'Hepple is a fool, a palpable dolt.'

'There were spies at the heart of the Governor's household. Laycock's background experience in the Secret Service Fund had taught him exemplary caution and distrust—therefore, he took all responsibility for the plan upon himself alone, since he had devised and written it. Written it, by long custom, in cypher—to a key that he alone possessed.'

'Indeed, James, you argue the case excellent well. He trusted no one.'

'I expect, sir, I expect that we must keep our mouths shut

about this . . .' He drank a mouthful of tea, looking at Rennie over the rim of the cup.

'Yes, in course you are right, James. We must.'

'We must deliver the plan and the key to Sir Robert Greer, and Their Lordships—and say nothing of our having discovered the content.'

'Indeed, no—we had better say nothing at all of that.'

'Indeed, no.' Another mouthful of tea. 'For which service—saying nothing, you know—I am inclined to think we should be rewarded. That we should reward ourselves. Accordingly, I am happy to agree to your suggestion, sir.'

'You are! Excellent James, excellent! You make me excellent happy and glad!' Sucking down the last of his tea, and banging the cup down on the desk. 'By God, they have led us a dance among them, a not very merry dance, neither—the whole deceiving, scheming, condescending, damned collection of them. Their Lordships, the Secret Service Fund, Greer, Jepp—all of them together. Aye, very well then . . . two may play at the same game! We shall have our reward, James, and shall say nothing more. They shall have their plan, and the well-sourced key to that plan, out of a dead man's arse—and shall *know* nothing more!'

'However, sir . . .'

Looking at him. 'However, James . . .?'

'However—we surely cannot keep *all* of the gold for ourselves, when the people have suffered so grievous in aiding us to get it. Everyone in the ship. Hey?'

Rennie frowned, and tapped the table with his fingertips. 'That is a risk, James. What you propose is a very great risk. If we share out this gold, there will be loose talk. Seamen cannot hold their tongues above half a glass when they are ashore, with money in their pockets and drink flowing. Cannot hold their tongues no more than they can tie down their pricks.' Shaking his head.

'Then, if I may suggest?' and when Rennie nodded: 'I suggest we take the money to a bank in London, my brother's bankers—Lambles'—and there change the louis into sterling money. Lambles' are the souls of discretion, by long practice. When we have changed the money, we could then distribute a just share among the people, saying that it is reward money for all they have endured—but must not be spoke of. We will not name any source. Even if some few of them *do* speak of it, after that, who will notice? They will not be spending gold louis, but English money, in English inns. Seamen in drink. An ubiquitous circumstance, in any seaport, nothing to be remarked at all.'

A silence. The ship creaked, and rode the sea. At last, with a nod and a decisive sniff, Rennie lifted his head and:

'You are right. They must have their reward, and it shall be managed in just the way you suggest. I have asked them to risk their lives, and they have responded with all their hearts. They have placed their confidence and trust in me to bring them through, and have fought for their King like lions. They must have their reward, as we must have ours. And I will like to do something for the next of kin of those killed, in course, James. Cutton!—Colley Cutton, where are you! Open a bottle of wine, and bring it in!'

And so it was that Lieutenant James Hayter RN, in the winter of 1788, came home to Dorset, to his beloved wife Catherine, in good time for the birth of their firstborn child, and brought with him in his dunnage a sum above three thousand pound sterling of money, in gold. The child, their child, delivered the month following, was to the very great joy of both parents—a son.

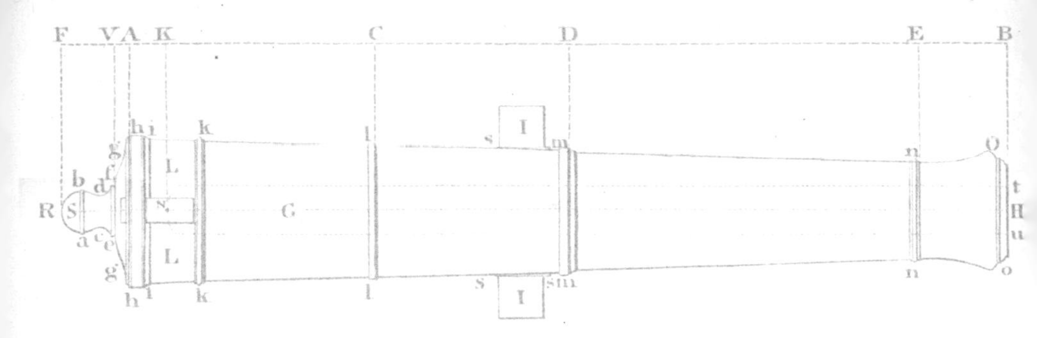

NAMES OF THE SEVERAL PARTS OF A GUN.

AB	*Length of the Gun*	L	*Vent Field*	h	*Base Ring*
AC	*First Reinforce*	N	*Vent*	i	*Base Ring Ogee*
CD	*Second Reinforce*	O	*Swell of the Muzzle*	k	*Vent Field Astragal & Fillets*
DE	*Chase*	VAK	*Breech*	l	*First Reinforce Ring*
EB	*Muzzle*	S	*Button*	m	*Second Reinforce Ring & Ogee*
FA	*Cascable*	a b	*Button Astragal*	n	*Muzzle Astragal & Fillets*
GH	*Bore*	c d	*Neck*	o	*Muzzle Mouldings*
RH	*Axis of the Piece*	e f	*Neck Fillet*	s	*Shoulder of the Trunnion*
I	*Trunnions*	g	*Breech Ogee*	t u	*Diameter of the Bore or Calibr*

Before Loading.

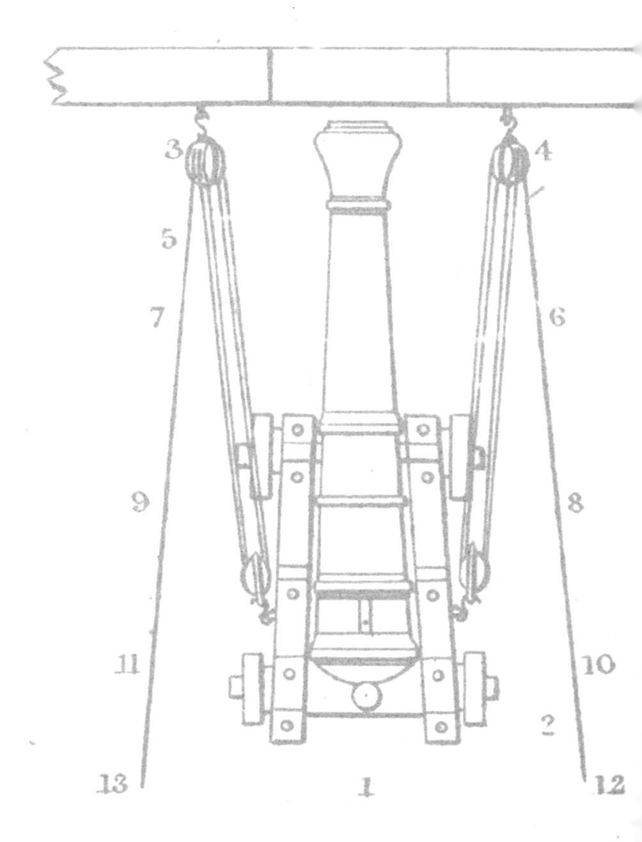